HAVENWOOD FALLS HIGH BOOKS

Predestined by Valia Lind

Rediscovered by Morgan Wylie

Ashes of Fate by Apryl Baker

Stay up to date at www.HavenwoodFalls.com

ABOUT THIS BOOK

Three novellas (books 20-22) in the young adult paranormal fantasy series Havenwood Falls High, Home of the Dragons – and vampires, wolves, fae, and much more.

Promise the Moon by Kallie Ross - Sequel to *Written in the Stars*
    Seventeen-year-old Elle has been snubbed by her dad's bloodline-obsessed vampire family while her mom's dryad side has already determined her future—to return to New York City and protect Central Park. Held to promises her family made, Elle dreads leaving her friends as well as breaking things off with her wolf-shifter boyfriend, Kase Kasun. Intent on savoring every last minute together, Elle, Kase, and their friends plan an epic Spring Break camping trip. But when one of so-called friend turns out to be an enemy, her life may come to an untimely end. Promises are made to be broken, and only the moon has the power to save her now.

Blurred Lines by Daniele Lanzarotta - Sequel to *Avenoir*
    Heidi Bennett's destiny was changed forever on the night of the Cold Moon Ball two winters ago. Months later, she was given a second chance in life—one that was supposed to restore her back to normal. Unfortunately for Heidi, things are not that simple. Being able to read people's memories and learn secrets of many residents in Havenwood Falls is just one of the consequences. As time passes, Heidi distances herself more and more from the human she used to be, testing the boundaries of her new abilities. But when she's manipulated by a mysterious entity that controls her dreams, her behavior goes from reckless to downright dangerous.

Ascending Darkness by J.L. Weil - Sequel to *Falling Deep*
    Mallory Dorian only wanted a normal, boring life, but life has a

way of interfering with her carefully laid out plans. Insert Torent Stark, the drool-worthy demon who makes her want to throw away all her dreams. But before Mallory can open her heart, a dark shadow of death looms inside. Mallory must face the past before she can think about the future, and her family's history has a few dark spots. It is up to her to break the blood curse looming over her family or risk all that she has grown to love.

HAVENWOOD FALLS HIGH
VOLUME SEVEN

A HAVENWOOD FALLS HIGH COLLECTION

J.L. WEIL   KALLIE ROSS   DANIELE LANZAROTTA

PROMISE THE MOON

KALLIE ROSS

HAVENWOOD FALLS HIGH

Promise the Moon

KALLIE ROSS

~ A Havenwood Falls Young Adult Novella ~

ALSO BY KALLIE ROSS

Defying Gravity: A Havenwood Falls Novella

Written in the Stars: A Havenwood Falls High Novella

A Pack of Lies: A Legends of Havenwood Falls Novella

Descent: A Lost Tribe (Book 1)

Defend: A Lost Tribe (Book 2)

Evelyn: A Cupid Chronicles Novella

Unbreakable: The Cupid Chronicles

Dedicated to Morgan.
The accountability and encouragement you've given me over the years
has meant the world. Thank you!

CHAPTER 1

ELLE

The Havenwood Falls High bell rang sharply, alerting me to the end of the school day. Finally, spring break. Lifting my head from the pages of my assigned reading, *A Tale of Two Cities,* I watched the rest of the class hustle toward the hallway. Normally, I loved losing myself in a good book, but even with two years of French, I had a hard time keeping up with Darnay and the Defarges.

The thick novel didn't fit in my backpack, so I secured the tattered paperback in my coat pocket, shouldered my bag, and made my way to my locker. There was no need to carry thirty pounds of books, since I'd only need one of them to complete my homework. The weight didn't bother me, because I had super strength. Being a vampire half-breed had perks; for example, I didn't have to deal with bloodlust like my father did. Dryad blood pumped through my veins, powerful enough to subdue any unbecoming urges a young vampire would have. Only problem was each half-breed benefit came with inconveniences, like being able to hear every thought from every mind in the building. Over the last year, with the help of my parents, friends, and night classes at the Academy, I'd mostly learned to control each of my abilities, including the ones I hadn't expected.

The school's hallways always buzzed with the latest gossip and hormones. Tuning out self-conscious teenagers had become second nature. Disregarding arrogant and even lustful thoughts took a little more concentration. And the weirdest part of mind reading wasn't all the jumbled thoughts, but it was seeing them in my mind's eye. My ability was similar to reading a book and visualizing the story like a movie.

So when I heard Ana Novak's thoughts about Kase Kasun, I not only caught a few details about what a good kisser he was, but I envisioned Kase's lips so close I could feel his warm breath brush over my cheek.

I pressed my palm to my forehead to clear my thoughts.

When I looked up, the two were at the end of the corridor across from my locker. Ana was leaning against the old blue-painted metal facing Kase, and she grinned up at him and giggled. Then, as if she sensed I was watching, she nudged his shoulder playfully. Her touch lingered a second too long. He glanced down at the spot she'd touched and shook his head. Her bottom lip pouted out flirtatiously, and he ignored her attempt to win him back and turned to walk in my direction without a word.

As his eyes met mine, he frowned. We'd both been trying to ignore the spectacle Ana made of herself on a daily basis, but somehow she'd found out I called things off romantically with Kase during the holiday break. Ever since, I'd been trying to avoid both of them. Kase had known from the beginning, since his split with Ana, that I wasn't staying. My family had always expected me to move back to New York after graduation. Not to mention, I'd die if I didn't bond with a tree in Central Park by my next birthday. After I'd gained control of my strange powers, and the rumors about the mysterious death of my ex-boyfriend were replaced by who wore what at the latest gala, I'd had to beg my parents to allow me to stay in Havenwood Falls to graduate. Neither of my parents were biological, but they'd been looking after me since the night they found me. I'd been no more than a few months old, and I'd been laid at the foot of my mother's tree in the park.

Kase and I had agreed to stay friends after the holidays, but seeing him through Ana's thoughts made me want to vomit. Every day, the love I felt for Kase grew heavier in my chest. For the last few months, when I knew he had a class in one hallway, I'd go down another so I wouldn't have to face him. Lugging love around, instead of giving it to Kase, made me realize sadness isn't a void. True sorrow is a weight.

Behind him, Ana gave me a death glare. I shrugged and turned toward the exit. Avoiding Ana had become essential for both of us. She had a way of making me crazy, and I couldn't risk losing control in a school filled with humans who didn't know about our supernatural world.

Thirty pounds wasn't that heavy anyway.

Kase walked faster to catch up with me, and I could feel him getting closer. Eluding him had been impossible. The warmth he radiated had to be because he was a wolf shifter; at least, that's what I'd convinced myself. It couldn't be anything more. We couldn't be anything more than friends. It would be easier the next time I saw him. The truth was I'd be seeing him more this next week than I'd allowed myself for months.

Kase cleared his throat, and when I looked over at him, one corner of his mouth pulled up, revealing a dimple.

"You have mean girl cooties," I teased, and wrinkled my nose when he tried to hold my hand—again. It was partially my fault he kept trying. The few times we found ourselves alone, usually because I'd been hanging out with his sister, I felt drawn to him. He had to feel it, too.

When Kase frowned, disappointed at my rejection, my heart ached.

Kase Kasun was everything I'd wanted in a guy when I was wishing for the perfect boyfriend in middle school. Back then, I was just a normal girl, my powers hadn't been triggered, and I'd attended an all-girls prep school in New York City. There was something dreamy about ending up with the All-American athletic good guy. Only, this good guy had gotten himself caught in the claws of an evil, power-hungry she-wolf before I'd arrived.

Kase's steps synced with mine, the rhythm echoing slightly in the emptying hall, and he reached in front of me to open the door leading to the parking lot. My backpack brushed against his forearm. In an effort to avoid knocking him over, I shifted the weight and nearly tipped myself over from being so top heavy. Kase used his wolf-like reflexes to catch me.

I stiffened in his arms.

"Come on, Elle," Kase whispered, and I melted. His olive skin was smooth and his dark eyes warm and inviting. Kase had been the star quarterback of our high school's football team the last two years, and there was no mistaking the muscular build under his letterman's jacket.

He brushed some of my long blond hair over my shoulder to get a better look at my face. He'd discovered all of my tells while we dated, and I could feel him analyzing me. Forcing myself to remain indifferent, I relaxed my jaw, released the inside of my cheek from between my teeth, and loosened my grip on the straps of my backpack.

"How about I take you out for coffee?" he asked. The simplicity of his invitation didn't imply anything more.

I gave him a tight smile, determined to stay strong and let him down easy. "I could use one, but you know I have training."

"Will you stay with me? Please. Even if it's only for a few minutes." Kase's voice croaked, and he gently pulled me a little closer. "We can just talk out here. I miss being with you."

My body betrayed me and leaned into him. Why couldn't we sit at Coffee Haven all afternoon and hang out with our friends? I thought after pushing Kase away for so long, it would be easier to turn him down. Last month, on Valentine's Day, I'd stayed home and claimed to be sick, all in an effort to keep Kase out of sight and out of mind.

My wall was crumbling.

"How about we get that coffee," I agreed with some hesitation, and quickly scrambled to rebuild my façade. "But as friends."

Kase slowly released me, careful to make sure I had my balance.

"I'll take what I can get." His mouth formed a tight smile, and he waved a hand in front of himself, allowing me to lead the way.

Our cars were parked side by side at the back of the lot. His blue truck made my black smart car look like a toy. He and his twin sister, Willa, shared the truck, but Willa always had archery practice after school. Her boyfriend, Tarron, also on the team, always gave her a ride home.

"Wanna ride together?" Kase asked and chuckled as he looked from his truck to the car. "I'll even try to squeeze into your car if you want to drive. Maybe you can open the sunroof so I can sit up straight."

Before I could stop myself, my hand flung out and backhanded his chest. Kase was over six feet tall, and while I was considered average height, he still towered over me. He'd always teased me about my car, and it almost felt normal to joke about it. Only, our normal had been being *together*, and we would have to figure out a new normal. My goal the past few months had been to avoid running into him altogether. Since his sister was one of my best friends, it proved more difficult than I'd anticipated.

"Haha." My fake laughter was filled with a good dose of sarcasm, and I rolled my eyes as I rummaged through the front pocket of my backpack for my keys. Kase moved around my car to open the driver's side door, and I pushed one of the buttons on my key fob as he rounded the front.

A loud honk blared, making him jump, and I couldn't contain my real laughter. The surprise on his face morphed into a genuine grin.

"That's what you get." My chest filled with warmth, even though it was freezing outside. Being with Kase made me happy, so why couldn't we ride to Coffee Haven together without it being *together*? My lips twisted as I thought, and I made my decision.

"Let's just take your truck," I said and reached for the handle of the passenger door. Kase beat me to it, and opened the door for me. Always the gentleman, he took my backpack and tossed it into the back. Pulling *A Tale of Two Cities* out of my coat pocket, I set it in the middle of the bench seat. Kase climbed into the driver seat and looked down at the novel, with its dog-eared pages and worn cover.

"Is that one for class or for fun?" he asked as he started the truck.

The novel was not what I'd call fun, but Kase was really trying. His friendship would be the one I'd miss most when I moved back to New York.

"Definitely class," I answered. "It's been too long since I've read a book for fun."

Kase put his truck into reverse and backed out of the space. He'd started to put his arm along the back of the seat when he looked behind to check for other cars, but stopped himself. He sounded easygoing, but his posture was rigid, and he almost seemed nervous. After maneuvering out of the parking lot, he relaxed a little.

"So what have you been doing for fun?" he asked softly, keeping his eyes on the road.

When I shifted to face him, the seatbelt threatened to decapitate me. Wrapping my hand around the stiff fabric, I pulled it under my arm and answered, "Mostly training and hanging out with Scarlet and your sister. My parents are still back and forth to New York on business. I almost think they feel bad about being gone so much. Last week, my dad brought a telescope home and said I needed a hobby."

"Soon you'll have track and field season to keep you busy," Kase said, and he shrugged sheepishly. "But until then, astronomy sounds cool."

"Yeah, I guess," I agreed half-heartedly.

"No, really, the sky can tell you so much, especially at night. Knowing the phases of the moon and the different constellations can help you navigate by the stars. You can even tell time by connecting Polaris to the Big Dipper."

Squinting at Kase, I wondered who the imposter was, and asked, "Who are you, and what have you done with Kase?"

He smiled and rubbed at the back of his neck with one hand. "It's me, I promise. There's a lot more that goes into patrolling the town borders than racing against Joe from one ridge to the other. And, in the state he's in, we haven't done much racing. It's not like I have to worry about the phases of the moon because I can control when I shift, but I've had to use the constellations a time or two to stay on course. And I've used the moon to help tell time. Did you know the moon has no light of its own? It's how the sun shines on it that makes it useful."

"That's cool," I said and placed a finger on my chin thoughtfully. "Maybe I'll actually tilt the telescope up and take a look."

"Tilt it up, huh?" he asked with a mischievous grin.

"You may patrol the borders, but somebody has to keep an eye out for the people in town." A giggle escaped me.

Kase slowed the truck down as we approached the four-way stop at Main and Eighth Streets. He looked over at me and asked, "And who exactly do you feel like you need to keep an eye out for?"

"Oh, no one in particular. Think of it as a neighborhood watch," I said with a smirk.

"Sounds more like stalking to me," he mumbled with a chuckle. The truck moved through the intersection, and Kase was on the lookout for a parking space.

"I don't like your tone." So I decided to flip the script. "What have you been doing for fun?"

Kase pulled into a space across the street from Coffee Haven. He kept the truck running, with the heat on, and unbuckled his seatbelt. "Hanging out with Joe mostly. He's missing Infiniti. It's kind of making him crazy. I know you're going to find this cheesy, but kind of like the moon needs the sun to be useful, I've discovered I don't have much fun without you in my life."

Shifting in my seat, I faced forward. He'd gone there. My head pressed back into the seat, and I sighed.

"I can't—no, I won't let you talk me into *this*." I waved my pointer finger between us back and forth a few times. Pausing to gauge where his mind was at, I heard nothing. Kase had blocked me. He'd learned to veil his thoughts from me by the end of our second date.

"I know you're trying to protect me—" he started.

"Don't think I'm some saint. I'm also trying to protecting me." My hand covered my heart.

"I promise to never hurt you." Kase scooted closer, and the paperback between us pressed against my thigh. He lifted his hand and cupped my jawline.

Leaning into him, I closed my eyes and whispered, "That's like promising me the moon, Kase. It kills me to see you every day in those hallways, and a few weeks ago I even stayed away, thinking it might be a little easier. But not seeing you was worse. I thought a half vampire, half dryad dating a wolf shifter was trite, but the fact that I don't know how I'm going to live in New York without you feels pathetic."

"You are anything but pathetic," Kase muttered, his warm breath caressing my cheek. "Elliot Martin, the only I question I have for you is are you doing all of this—keeping me in the friend zone, moving back to New York—for you or for your parents?"

Pulling away, I felt weak. He was the only person in town I'd ever explained my past to, and he was partially right. I wanted to press my lips against his more than anything. Even though I'd been training for over a year to build my strength, to learn to control my power, I was completely vulnerable when it came to Kase.

So I reached for the handle and opened my door. The ice-cold air flooded the cab of the truck. When Kase pulled back in shock, I turned and retreated across the street and into Coffee Haven.

CHAPTER 2

ELLE

SCOOBY GANG

Willa: Where are you E?

Elle: I'll be a few minutes late

Willa: Are you with the boy version?

Kase: I heard that, and I'm parking

Scarlet: I'm caffeinated and ready to hit the slopes

Bale: I plan to eat black diamonds for lunch

Willa: It won't officially be spring break until we're all together E! What's the hold up?

Elle: The parents are calling, give me 10

Kase: I'll order you a cinnamon latte

Bale: Awwww . . . Bro, I think you have something brown on your nose

Kase: Shut it

Elle: Uh, thanks! B4N

. . .

A snowboard would have been easier to fit in my smart car. Last spring break, the gang had so much fun on the slopes, we'd agreed to start the upcoming two weeks off with a friendly race. As much as Kase, Willa, Tarron, and Bale tried to convince me snowboarding was better, I wouldn't budge. Scarlet must have taken my side just to get on Bale's nerves. Skiing made me feel alive.

Skis are faster.

As I turned my car on, my cell started buzzing. Impatient as always, I figured it was my friends, so I checked it. Considering the measures my parents had gone to to protect me from texting and driving, I replied before shifting the car into drive. Then my phone started ringing. When I saw the picture of my mom and dad flash across the screen, I wondered if they had some sort of camera watching me. Pressing the green button on my steering wheel, I answered the call.

"Hey, Mom," I greeted with excitement, guessing she was calling from the airport. She and my dad had been in New York for three days and promised to be back tonight, so we could spend some of the break as a family.

"Good morning, sweetie," she said cheerily. "What are you up to today?"

"I'm going skiing with Willa and Scarlet," I said, but quickly added, "and the guys. But I'll totally be home in time to have dinner with you and Dad."

"Oh, honey, I hope it's getting easier to be around Kase." My mom sounded sympathetic, but she was over two thousand miles away. Yesterday, I'd needed her after awkwardly sipping a latte across from Kase at Coffee Haven. She'd never signed up to raise a child. Typically, a dryad was born with their tree, but I'd been abandoned at hers. I immediately felt guilty.

"It's actually gotten a lot better," I assured her, but I meant it got better when Scarlet showed up. She'd walked over from her family's herbal store to pick up a coffee for her mom. Making an excuse to leave with her, I'd told Kase I needed to buy some candles.

My mother paused, probably unsure of what to say, and I didn't hear the typical background noise I would have if she and my dad were waiting at their gate. There wasn't anything she could say to make me feel better. I just wanted her to be home, but I had a bad feeling.

"I'm glad it's better, sweetie—"

"You're not coming home, are you?" It felt like an anvil had landed on my chest.

"Well, there's a party we're expected to attend tomorrow, and your father has a meeting Monday morning," she explained. "And it won't be long until you're here with us. We're working hard to make sure things are ready for you."

"What do you mean, *ready*? I still have a month here before graduation."

My mom sighed, and I could picture her pinching the bridge of her nose. She'd done that for as long as I could remember. She and my dad filled my memories, and they assured me it was for the best. Before I'd been left in their care, a vampire killed my dryad parents. Someone from my father's clan stopped the rogue vampire before he killed me, and I have no recollection of any of it. I'd been raised balancing on a tightrope between two supernatural worlds—dryad and vampire.

"I don't know if I want that life anymore, Mom." My voice croaked. "I don't miss New York. I miss you."

"You don't mean that," my mom reasoned with an angry edge to her voice. "I mean, I miss you too, and when you get back here, you'll remember how much you love it. We have to hold up our end of the agreement with the Court in Havenwood Falls, and that includes us leaving after graduation. It will be a shock at first when you return, but maybe we can soften the blow. Your father asked me to tell you he's sending a surprise, and it should arrive later today."

My nose scrunched up in frustration. "Whatever."

I couldn't imagine what he had in mind, but maybe it included a box full of shoes. That's the only thing I could think of that could make me feel marginally better. At no point had anyone inquired about what I wanted. My father wanted to assume his duties in his family's business. My mother ached to stay close to the oak tree she was bonded with in Central Park. The Court of the Sun and the Moon had only agreed for us to stay in Havenwood Falls until I turned eighteen.

When I said goodbye, I tried to not to sound too let down, but I wasn't even sure my mom was paying attention. She'd been distracted for the duration of our conversation, even though she'd been the one to call me. Repeating the conversation in my mind over and over, I drove to Coffee Haven on autopilot. Colorado was waking from a deep winter slumber, and I could almost feel energy emanating from the earth. I was electric with anticipation, like waking up on my birthday, and even the trees seemed to stand taller, alert and ready for anything.

When I parked, I wondered how I'd arrived without driving straight through the gazebo in town square. Colorado would be in mud season soon, but the green pine trees, snowcapped mountains, and blue skies had a way of keeping one's eyes on the beauty around them instead of the mess they might trudge through. It was only last month that store owners were shoveling record-breaking amounts of snow off the sidewalks so tourists could enter their shops.

The entire Scooby Gang waited out in front of the quaint coffee shop. Willa had coined the name of our little band of nonconformists. Each of us was distinctly different, supernaturally and in appearance, but we accepted each other for who we were, and that kind of friendship was scarce in high school.

Kase jogged up to my car, the jock. He opened my door and handed me a cup of hot cinnamon goodness. "Glad you could join us," he said, with a smile that would make any girl swoon. "Want me to take your skis out of the back?"

"Please." Keeping my reply short made me feel like I had more control of my emotions. And I'd need to feel in control all week, since we'd made these plans to spend spring break together last year.

"Did I hear that right? You haven't gotten a board yet?" Bale complained in his native tongue, sarcasm. He'd been the hardest of my friends to get to know. The wall I'd built to keep Kase's and my relationship in the friend zone looked like a beaver's dam compared to the Great Wall of China he'd constructed around himself. "This would have been a great year to learn how to ski on a board. The powder this season was ridiculous. And I mean that in a good way, not in the same way I'd mean it when referring to you looking ridiculous on those skis."

"Stop giving her a hard time," Scarlet scolded, and tugged on the metal chain hanging from his belt loop and connected to his wallet. She wore her long red hair in two Dutch braids, and instead of a ski bib, she'd layered sweaters over sweaters.

Willa moved around my car to help her twin brother. They'd grown closer since she shifted last year. It also helped that Kase stopped dating her arch nemesis. It was hard to picture the cute ex-cheerleader as the leader of the Kasun Wolf Pack. But determination and loyalty ran in Willa and Kase's blood.

Tarron, Willa's boyfriend, rearranged a few of the items in the back of the Kasun twins' truck to make room for my gear. He looked up, and I could hear his thoughts as he watched Willa walk over with my skis. Tarron adored Willa, and I quickly pressed my palm to my forehead to focus.

"Are you okay?" Kase asked, and he walked over to me.

There was no danger of falling over, but I could feel his anxiety. Shaking my head clear, I answered, "I'll be fine. My parents called to tell me they aren't coming home tonight, and I think I'm just a little bummed."

"I'm sorry, Elle," he said, and slid his hand around mine. I didn't pull away. Of all my friends, he understood how much it bothered me that my parents were away so often. They'd been a couple in New York before finding me, and children hadn't been on their radar, seeing as they couldn't naturally have any of their own.

Luckily, I had wonderful friends in my life.

I glanced around us and realized something was off.

"Where's Joe?" My voice was low, trying not to draw attention to my inquiry.

Kase and Joe had always been best friends, but if Joe's lack of attendance had something to do with his search for Infiniti, I knew he wouldn't want the others to know. Kase had confided in me that Joe had a wild notion he could find his girlfriend, but Kase had been quick to shut it down.

"He's not doing great," Kase said with a frown. "All he wants to do is patrol, and I'm not sure if it's because he's looking for Infiniti or if he's trying to keep himself busy so he doesn't think about her. He's not sleeping well, and honestly, I think it'd be hard for him to see you, well, you with me."

"Me? But why?" My mouth fell open in disbelief.

Kase tugged on my hand, and as I looked up, his eyes met mine. "You didn't do anything, but he'd do anything to find Infiniti. You broke things off with me a few days after Infiniti left, and while I missed you, I got to see you almost every day. He's also been dealing with some shifter repercussions, since he recognized her as his mate. My dad tried to explain that we need to be supportive, but it was still different for him. My mom died, but Infiniti is still out there somewhere—or somewhen."

"That sounds horrible."

"It sounds like you had a pretty horrible conversation with your parents earlier."

"Thanks, but I'd rather not talk about it." Squeezing Kase's hand before letting go, I moved to help put my gear in the back of the truck. "I think I'll channel my frustration into winning this race." Glancing at Bale, I challenged, "You're going down."

He snarled at me and said, "Whether I win big or I win ugly, I'm still winning." He tucked some of his chin-length black hair behind his ear.

"You got big and ugly right," Kase said with a chuckle and nudged Bale with his elbow.

Bale shook his head and made his way around to the passenger side of the truck. "Let's just get to it, Kase," Bale said as he opened the door. "You guys are wearing me out with all your wit, and I need to save some energy for the race."

CHAPTER 3

KASE

*B*ale, Scarlet, and Elle piled into my truck. Willa would argue it was ours, but she rarely drove the old blue Chevy. Tarron and Willa opted to take Tarron's car, and I was relieved. Since Elle left me in the friend zone, Willa had been a helicopter sibling. She hovered whenever Elle was around and checked in with me constantly. Her heart was in the right place, but her nose needed to butt out.

Bale climbed into the back seat with Scarlet, surprising me. He typically called shotgun, but swore he never got carsick. I wasn't about to complain, because it meant Elle would sit next to me. Immediately, I decided to omit any conversation that would include Joe or her parents. When I looked over my shoulder, Bale gave me a knowing grin. He probably planned to make Elle as uncomfortable as possible as payback for all her trash talk.

Our drive wasn't long, but when we arrived, the slopes were busy. The next day would be the last day of ski season. Everyone grabbed their gear from the back of the truck and started suiting up. We pulled out boots, hats, gloves, boards or skis, and even a pair of snowshoes.

"I'll be the referee," Scarlet said as she stood. It looked like she'd strapped two flat canoes to her boots. Then she pulled a backpack onto her shoulders. "I brought some homework to finish."

"You won't have enough time to finish homework, babe," Bale said to her, then addressed Elle, who stood next to me. "Right, Elle? Since you'll be skiing down the mountain so fast?" He smirked.

"That's the plan," she replied and bent over to buckle her boots. As she mounted her skis, she warned, "Just stay out of my way riding that boat."

"Looks like there'll be a fleet of boats for you to have to navigate." Bale nodded to everyone else buckling into their boots and grabbing their snowboards. Then he reached for Scarlet's backpack, secured it over his shoulder, and said, "At least walk with me to the lift, babe."

"Fine." She took his hand, and they made their way.

The rest of us followed, two by two. Willa and Tarron were less affectionate, but they silently considered each other as they moved. Elle walked next to me and remained quiet. She'd keep her distance until I could break down the emotional wall she'd built. My attempts to spend time with her, without everyone else, had failed until yesterday.

Maybe Elle was having a change of heart.

Shutting her out of my thoughts was probably for the best. While I wanted her to know how much I loved her, I knew she'd believe it more if she saw my love through actions. Anyone could think they loved someone. She'd probably heard ten guys think they loved different girls in our school hallways on a daily basis.

"I wish we'd gotten some fresh powder for the race today," Elle said loud enough for everyone to hear.

"No excuses," Bale blurted over his shoulder. "But it is hard to believe we had over twenty-two feet of snow this season."

A chuckle escaped me, and Elle looked over at me with her mouth hanging open.

"I wouldn't dream of making excuses," she mocked. "But I think a wager might be in order." A dramatic pause followed as we approached the lift in silence.

Those of us riding a board had to stop and strap our front boot on, and then we glided into line. It was late enough in the morning that we'd missed the early rush, but we still had to wait a few minutes. The sun was shining, and the brisk air had already begun to freeze the tip of my nose.

"What are you thinking, Elle?" Willa wondered out loud. "Please tell me it involves the losers carrying the winner's camping gear Wednesday."

"That's a good one," Scarlet agreed, "but I'm not racing. Dang it!"

Bale laughed and wrapped an arm around her. "I'll carry your gear even if you're not racing, because Elle will be carrying mine."

"You're dreaming," Elle countered with confidence, "and you're on."

Bale nodded his acceptance of the bet and silently waved a goodbye to Scarlet as he slid up to the lift. The rest of us rode two at a time up to the mountain top. Willa and Tarron, in front of us, were enjoying each other's company as we drifted in the air. Tarron leaned in and whispered something to Willa, but Bale scanned the mountainside, probably looking for Scarlet.

Elle and I sat in awkward silence all the way up. Zoning out, I hoped to keep my mind empty, staring out over the trees. Everything Elle had done the past four months had been to keep us from hurting each other, but sitting next to my best friend, unsure of what to say, was torment. We used to be able to talk about anything.

I missed her.

"Board up," Elle warned, but her voice sounded muffled and far away. "Kase?" she asked, and the next thing I knew her arms were around me, and we were catapulted off the lift chair. "Kase!"

We slid ten feet before I realized what had happened. Instinctively, I shifted my weight to try to slow down, but my snowboard collided with one of Elle's skis. To avoid taking her down with me, I swerved into a snowbank.

"Crap! Are you okay? I'm so sorry." She glided over to me quickly, and extended her hand to help me up.

One side of her mouth pulled up in a half smile, easing my concern that she might have been injured. When she took my hand, I remembered the first time I accidentally held her hand. We were competing in the tug-of-war, and my hand slipped over hers in the middle of the game.

In that moment I knew she was special, and she'd always be special to me.

Elle let out a gasp, ripping me from the memory, and fell next to me in the snow. I looked at her and saw she'd covered her mouth, trying to hide her smile.

"What just happened?" I wasn't sure if her reaction was from losing her footing or reading my thoughts.

"I felt like making snow angels," she teased, and began to spread her limbs out as best as she could. Both her skis had come off and her poles lay haphazardly at her sides. I joined in and shoved snow in Elle's direction with one arm. She started laughing and rolled over to her stomach.

Her face was inches from mine. Everyone around us faded away, and I spoke softly, "You read my mind." My hand brushed over her knuckles, pushing aside the snow.

Could being with Elle again be as easy as this moment? Threading my fingers with hers, I took a chance. Her eyes widened, and she flinched.

"Let me help you up," I said, securing my grip.

She looked at our hands, then back at me.

"Thanks," she murmured under her breath.

"Are you two done?" Bale blurted with impatience.

Elle and I sat up to find the others waiting a few feet away. Willa wore a knowing grin, but when our eyes met, she quickly bent over to strap her back boot to her board. Everyone followed her lead.

"I was thinking we'd head somewhere a little more secluded,"

Tarron suggested and tilted his head to a yellow sign warning tourists away with bold black letters.

Our season passes were used as often as we could all get away from school or work or family. We each had our favorite routes, mostly black diamonds, but as supernaturals they weren't always challenging. Once in a while, we'd choose to go off the map for a more unpredictable run.

"I'm in," Bale blurted, and he jumped, pulling his knees and board into the air, and twisted to glide in the direction of the prohibited area.

"Wait up," Elle called, and scrambled to stand. She rushed to bind her boots to her skis, and used her poles to propel herself after them.

Willa held out a hand for me to take and pulled me up. Once I found my balance, we glided past the treeline together. The farther we skied off the path, the quieter it grew.

A fluttering sound behind me caught my attention. I turned to see what it could be, but there was nothing. Frozen in place, I hoped whatever I'd heard would reveal itself. As I inhaled, a familiar feeling grew in my chest. My wolf senses were on alert.

The presence hadn't felt bad or good, but mysterious. Someone or something was watching us.

"Hey," Willa said and grabbed my shoulder.

She'd startled me. I jumped, both my hands flying into a defensive pose between us.

"Willa," I growled, "I almost took a swing at you."

"Where'd you go just then?" She stepped back to give me some room.

Inspecting the area around us, I whispered, "I thought I heard —no, felt—something following us."

Willa just stood there and examined me. As wolf shifters from the same pack, we had a connection. Not only did we have a weird twin way of knowing where the other was, but Willa was one of my best friends, and she was also my alpha. If we were going to catch up with the others, I'd need to convince her everything was okay—in the forest and with Elle.

"It was probably nothing." I dismissed the feeling and waved my hand in front of me.

Willa opened her mouth and closed it. She searched the trees around us with her heightened senses. Whatever she was thinking, she wasn't saying, and that wasn't like her. Usually, she'd give me an earful on any given topic, whether I wanted to hear it or not.

"Yeah, probably nothing," she assured with her brows furrowed. Willa set her jaw and continued, "Let's go win this race."

CHAPTER 4

ELLE

J'd never felt more connected to the mountain's terrain. After I won our race, Bale wanted to double down. He figured two out of three wins would provide more sound bragging rights. His confidence didn't wane when I explained that I'd be happy to win all three races if he couldn't hear the victory in my voice. So I won them all. Bale's head hung low until I offered to make things square if he bought us all Coffee Haven. So to end the first official day of spring break, we each ordered our favorite drink and bakery item and let Bale foot the bill.

My hot mug of chai tea warmed my hands. Tarron and Scarlet also sipped on hot tea, but Willa, Bale, and Kase opted for espresso. The manager had come out from behind the counter and began to sweep under the tables. His shaggy brown hair fell over his brow while he pushed crumbs into a dustpan. Most of the tables were topped with overturned chairs, and we decided to stay until Davis kicked us out.

Davis had made a life in Havenwood Falls for his human family. He managed the coffee shop, and I frequented enough each week that I probably paid his salary. The fae owner, Willow, employed Davis, as well as supernaturals, but he didn't have a clue our magical world existed. It was safer that way.

"Hey, Davis, how are you doing?"

He looked up from his work and smiled. "Um, I'm doing pretty good, thanks for asking."

The place was typically buzzing with coffee addicts, and I realized I'd never taken the time to stop and have a conversation with the man. Sometimes I wondered if I had what it took to work as a barista. My parents would never allow it, of course. Father would have argued I didn't need the money or the temptation of fresh warm blood pulsing through customer's veins. Mother, on the other hand, would've said I was born for a greater purpose. Last year, when I'd first arrived in the little mountain town, a girl named Paisley worked behind the counter.

"Have you heard from Paisley lately?"

He looked down at the pile of debris at his feet, then back at me, and answered, "You know, she comes back to town about once a month. She'll come in for her favorite, a blueberry scone, and go on about how much she misses it here. But I know she has to be having a blast at college."

"That's great she comes back to visit." Deep down I knew that if she didn't return every month, she'd forget Havenwood Falls and everyone in it even existed. The wards that protected our town would wipe her memories, something most humans didn't know.

"Yeah," he agreed. His brows pulled together with curiosity, and he asked, "You doing okay?"

"Yeah," I said with a shrug. "I'm hanging in there. With graduation coming up, I'm just trying to figure it all out."

"Let me know if you do figure it out," he said with a laugh, and went back to work sweeping the hardwood floors. "You guys have about ten minutes before I have to lock the doors."

"Okay, thanks." Nodding, I tuned back into the enthusiastic debate Tarron and Scarlet were having about which book-to-movie adaptation was better, Harry Potter or Lord of the Rings.

"Have you seen the extended edition?" Scarlet asked, with her hands waving in the air. "I have a hard time believing you've read the novel. If you had, you'd appreciate the extra scenes and agree with me."

"Well, have you read all of the Harry Potter books?" Tarron asked, mocking her with his nose in the air.

"Yeah," Scarlet scoffed, "in third grade."

"Oh." Tarron's shoulders sunk.

Willa chuckled and took his hand. "Just tell her why you want to watch the Harry Potter movie marathon tomorrow. She'll understand, I promise."

Tarron sighed and looked from Willa to Scarlet. He closed his eyes tight and blurted, "I just finished reading the series for the first time."

He opened one eye to check for scoffing, and when he saw it was safe, he opened the other eye.

"Really?" Scarlet asked with wide eyes. "Then we have to watch Harry Potter." Her lips spread into a wide smile. "I'll even buy the makings for butterbeer!"

"I totally thought you guys were going to make fun of me," Tarron admitted.

Bale gripped the arms of his chair and said, "She may not, but I totally will."

He pushed himself up to his feet and held out a hand for Scarlet.

"Leave him alone," she warned, and handed him her empty coffee mug. "Now, let's help Davis out and take our stuff over to the counter."

After we set our dishes and mugs on the bar, Davis said, "Thanks, guys." We said our goodbyes, and as we exited, he called out, "My vote would've been for Frodo!"

Everyone laughed as we moseyed out to the parking lot behind the Main Street businesses, drawing out the inevitable. My friends were the best. When we were together, it felt like the world around us, along with the worries and responsibilities that came with it, faded away. As I grew closer to each member of our Scooby Gang, I questioned whether my feelings for Kase were real or a result of everyone coupling up.

In New York, I'd had similar feelings for someone, but they'd proven to be unreliable. Once I'd learned to trust Kase and my growing love for him, I realized it hadn't been my feelings that were uncertain. The guy I'd had feelings for was deceitful.

The girls moved toward my tiny car, and I realized my skis would make it impossible for us all to fit. I'd have to ask one of the guys to help transport us to my house. Bale's motorcycle was out of the question, and Tarron's sports car wouldn't be much help either.

"Hey, Kase, can I talk to you?" My heart skipped a beat.

My eyes met Willa's, and she took Tarron's hand and pulled him toward his car. Maybe she knew something I didn't, or maybe she was just up to no good. Willa had never once made me feel bad about breaking up with her brother, but I could tell she hadn't given up on the idea of us getting back together. Scarlet's reaction wasn't as quick, but when she realized what Willa was up to, she yanked Bale in the opposite direction from where Kase and I stood in the parking lot.

"Sure." Kase kept walking, getting off the road, and turned to face me when I stepped up on the sidewalk next to him.

The lights mounted on the old brick building and the streetlights standing at a nearby intersection made the area appear cozy, but it was frigid. I kept walking to stay warm, and he met my pace.

"Today was fun."

Kase's hands were shoved in his pockets, and suddenly I wanted him to try to hold my hand again. Not because my resolve had weakened, but because I was stronger with him at my side.

"Yeah, it was," he agreed, but he felt distant. And I'd been the one to push him away earlier when he'd asked about my parents.

Stopping short of the wooden gazebo steps, I turned to face Kase. "What are you thinking?"

Kase bit the inside of his cheek and wouldn't meet my eyes. After a few seconds of silence, he said, "Don't get me wrong. I want to tell you everything I'm thinking. But I'm curious what you're thinking?"

There was no train of thought I was following, or plan. In fact, my intention had only been to ask Kase to drive my skis to my house so the girls could ride with me. But when Kase asked me what I thought, I realized I'd been thinking too much.

So I went with my gut and slid my hand out of my pocket to reach for his. Kase's attention was drawn to the movement, and his hand hesitated. He looked up at me, and one of his eyebrows was slightly raised.

"I'm thinking, I'm sorry." My hand slid into his. "And I'm thinking I need to stop thinking so much and listen to my heart."

Kase squeezed my hand and smiled at me.

"I'm thinking it's freezing out here, and you guys can sort this all out tomorrow over butterbeer!" Willa yelled from the driver's seat of the blue Chevy. Obviously, she'd been listening with her heightened sense of hearing. "Tarron's going to give you a ride home, Kase. I'm taking the truck tonight."

The old Chevy engine roared to life, and I giggled at the sight of Willa behind the wheel. My giddiness could have also been attributed to the kiss Kase placed on the top of my hand before he walked me back to my car. Willa waited for Scarlet to jump into the truck, then pulled out onto the quiet street. With most of the shops having closed hours earlier, there weren't many people roaming around town square.

My friends wouldn't be able to get into my house without me, so I placed a quick kiss on Kase's cheek before getting into my car and leaving. Glancing in my rearview mirror, I found Kase already in Tarron's car. They turned and headed to the Kasuns' cabin, and I drove toward my neighborhood, Creekwood.

The girls' sleepover at my house had been planned as a preview to the movie marathon the following day. We'd spend the night painting nails, filling our prom Pinterest boards with potential dresses, and choreographing epic lip sync numbers. As I pulled into my driveway, I found Willa and Scarlet arguing with a man on my front porch.

"Get out of here, creep," Willa warned, waving her phone in the air, "or I'll call the sheriff." Little did the guy know, the sheriff was Willa's dad.

The man turned to see who'd pulled up, and I gasped, recognizing his profile. It couldn't be. The man standing on my porch died two years ago in New York City. My body froze in horror.

"Just hear me out," he reasoned. "You can call the cops if you want, but I arrived a couple hours ago to surprise an old friend, Elliot Martin. Do you know her? I could have sworn I had the correct address."

He looked down at his phone, and the light from the screen illuminated his face. It wasn't the man I'd feared after all, but his not-so-little brother. Marcel Cushing looked different, older, but that was impossible. Being a vampire, he hadn't grown up physically like me. I'd been a dryad before being bitten, but my parents discovered my dryad blood was stronger than the vampire who'd tried to sire me. Still, Marcel bore an uncanny resemblance to his older, sired brother. The only reason they called each other brother was because they'd been bitten by the same vampire and raised to control their urges by him. Marcel's dark hair was shaggy, but perfectly mussed to appear casual, though the Cushings were the most formal family I'd ever encountered. Marcel had deep-set brown eyes, and his fair skin could be attributed to his lack of exposure to the sun.

"Elle, do you know this guy?" Scarlet asked from behind Willa. She looked over Willa's shoulder at me and frowned.

Slowly walking around my car, I knew in the back of my mind that he couldn't hurt me, but I was still cautious. My mind thought through a couple different ways to convince Willa and Scarlet to move away from him, but Willa had probably already deduced what Marcel was, a vampire. The Cushings were one of the oldest vampire families in New York, and I understood firsthand how much power he wielded.

"Yeah, I know him." With each step closer, I attempted to read his thoughts. "But I don't know why or how he's here."

The reason my family moved to Havenwood Falls was for the protection it offered from the outside world, from my past. If Marcel wasn't supposed to be in town, there's no way he would've been able to drive past the town border, let alone up to my house and wait on the front porch, without a slew of supernaturals being magically alerted.

"Your parents flew me out," Marcel said as he stepped down from the porch toward me.

Willa let a low growl rumble in her chest.

Marcel glanced back at her with wide eyes, then he explained, "Since the Martins' return was delayed, they thought it would be a good idea for me to visit. Special permission from the Court and everything. Think of it as reintroducing Elle's old life in bite-sized pieces." He sounded kind and charming.

Whether he meant to be punny or not, his wording wasn't lost on Willa. She smiled in response with a menacing, overly toothy grin. What she didn't know was Marcel had always been bad at telling jokes. While his older brother had been suave and charismatic, Marcel hadn't cared about the bloodlines and politics. He'd been called unrefined and annoying in the socialite company our families kept.

"I'm not sure my parents thought this through." My eyes rolled, remembering the earlier conversation with my mother. "You must be the surprise package she mentioned this morning."

"Too bad you can't stamp him *return to sender* and let him be on his way," Scarlet clipped curtly, and propped a hand on her hip.

My fingers pinched the bridge of my nose, trying to come up with a way to deal with Marcel and our current predicament. My parents couldn't have expected him to stay in our home. Marcel had been my friend growing up, but after what happened to his brother, I'd expected him to blame me and never want to see me again.

"I need some time to process, Marcel." Trying to hide the unease in my voice, I explained, "It's only, we have this sleepover planned, and a movie marathon, and camping—"

Saying it out loud helped me stay grounded. Marcel wasn't a part of my plans or my life in Havenwood Falls, and I didn't know if I wanted him to have any part in my life. But I couldn't be rude.

"What she's trying to say is, we'll call you tomorrow," Willa cut in and walked over to stand next to me. "Do you have a place to stay tonight? I can call my dad to help set you up at the inn, or somewhere more secluded without windows."

Scarlet giggled at Willa's humor, and I felt the corners of my mouth pull up a little. He *was* a vampire. He didn't need a daylight ring, but bloodlust was an issue for most vampires so young. The only reason I could control my appetite was because of my hybrid blood.

"The Court of your quaint town has already made arrangements for me, but thank you," Marcel said with a tight smile. "I can understand your surprise at seeing me after two years, but before I go, I need you to understand that I've come to apologize. I'm sorry it took so long to find out where your parents brought you. I'm sorry I didn't fight for our friendship. What happened to Armand was tragic—" He sounded heartbroken.

"I don't want to talk about him." My words cut him off, and I squeezed my hands into fists, nearly breaking the skin of my palms with my fingernails. "Please."

Willa and Scarlet had never pressed for details about why my family moved to Havenwood Falls, and I didn't want them finding out from a stranger.

Willa stepped in front of me protectively. "It's getting late." Her nostrils flared, and her lips tightened.

"Tomorrow, then." Marcel nodded reluctantly and walked straight to a silver sedan with a familiar car rental logo stuck to the bumper. Before he ducked his tall lean frame into the driver's seat, he glanced at us. His eyes were wet.

None of us moved a muscle until his red taillights disappeared beyond the Creekwood Country Club sign. Scarlet made for the truck first and started unloading. Her determination to only make the trip once broke our silence and probably woke the neighbors. A pair of snowshoes clattered to the ground when Scarlet tripped over herself trying to beat Willa to the front door.

"So what's on the schedule?" Scarlet asked, and she dropped all of her possessions in the middle of the living room floor.

My teeth bit at the inside of my lip, worrying about what Scarlet and Willa would think of me when they found out why I really ended up in Havenwood Falls. Would they want to leave when they found out I was involved in a murder? Could they understand I had no other choice if I'd wanted to survive Armand's attack?

"I think we'll tell ghost stories first." My body collapsed onto the couch. "I have a really good one." My voice lowered and sounded grim.

My friends joined me, and I started to tell a story about a girl who wanted to be loved. She'd thought she'd found the love she desired, but it was only a manipulation to gain access to her hybrid blood.

"In a moment of weakness, I'd agreed to allow Armand a taste. My sweet dryad blood proved too tempting, and Armand got carried away. I begged him to stop, and pushed him away, but he continued to pursue me. Marcel overheard our scuffle and came to my rescue, only Armand didn't see it that way. My blood had made him crazy. When Marcel entered my room, Armand thought his younger brother was trying to steal me for himself."

"What happened next?" Willa asked, sounding worried, and leaned forward.

"Armand lunged for Marcel, and the two wrestled across the floor, breaking my antique wooden rolltop desk. The legs had been snapped in half, and Marcel grabbed one of the splintered ends in defense. So when Armand charged Marcel again, the makeshift stake pierced his heart."

"Oh, man, Elle," Willa soothed and laid a hand on my knee.

"I'm so sorry you were attacked, and had to witness what happened between Armand and Marcel."

"Me too." It had been horrible. "Until tonight, my parents and Kase were the only people I ever told." Sharing with my friends had only made me feel freer.

Fear hadn't kept me from telling Willa and Scarlet, but it was the darkest part of my past. Kase hadn't been any different, and because of his support, he deserved to know about Marcel's visit.

"Do you guys mind if I make a call?"

Willa and Scarlet nodded their consent. Reaching for my cell, I pulled it out of my back pocket and pressed my finger to the screen.

CHAPTER 5

KASE

*I*t had taken everything in me not to shift and guard Elle's house that night. She assured me Marcel didn't mean any harm. The memories were hard for her, but Elle was strong. And when she needed a distraction, I knew Willa and Scarlet would be there for her.

"Hey, man," Tarron said, and nudged me with his elbow. "You okay?"

"Yeah." My eyes felt dry, and I blinked a few times to wet them.

Tarron's classic car was more comfortable than Elle's smart car, but not much bigger. Driving through the heart of Havenwood Falls, I'd been in a daze. We passed the high school, and the next right would usher us to Creekwood Estates. The neighborhood had been built over a couple decades and the homes were at least twice the size of our family's cabin in the woods.

"I know we're headed to Elle's to talk about this guy, Marcel," Tarron started as we turned, "but I'm curious what your take is?"

Shrugging, I said, half serious, "I want to hurt him."

Tarron chuckled, and when I didn't laugh he glanced at me and grimaced. "Okay."

"Honestly, I don't know. He's an old friend of Elle's, and he saved her life back when she lived in New York. There's more to the story, but it's not mine to tell."

"I get that, but from what Willa texted last night, it's not a happy reunion," Tarron revealed, encouraging me.

"I'm not sure Elle even knows how to process Marcel showing up. He arrived without any warning, and I think Elle wants our help to find out if he's really in town for the reasons he explained last night." I said, trying to sound neutral.

The last thing Elle needed was for us to speculate crazy conspiracies about why Marcel was visiting. I'd come up with at least three ideas since we'd turned onto Blackstone Road. As we pulled into Elle's driveway, I compartmentalized my cynicism. If Elle read my mind and I hinted at thoughts of Marcel sweeping her off her feet or him making grand gestures, she'd think I was jealous and immature.

I might have been both, but she didn't need to know it.

As we approached the front door, I noticed the T-shirt Tarron wore under his coat. It read, *I solemnly swear I'm up to no good.* He'd really been looking forward to the movie marathon.

I'd really been looking forward to holding Elle's hand during said movies. Last night, I thought we were finally back on the same path. Baby steps. The last thing I wanted to do was scare Elle off, and I didn't mind taking my time. If I had my way, we'd have the rest of our lives together.

Holding my hand out in front of Tarron, I asked, "Can I tell you something?"

"Sure, anything," he replied, and with concern, he crossed his arms over his chest and met my eyes.

"The problem is, you can't tell Willa." My eyebrow raised skeptically.

Tarron pressed his lips together in a straight line and fell silent.

"If it makes a difference, she wouldn't even know to ask you about it."

He raised his chin slightly and consented. "If that's the case, shoot."

My words rushed out uncontrollably. "I applied to NYU just before the holidays, and I'm waiting for an email to find out if I got in. What if I don't get in? Then Elle will leave in June, and I'll be stuck here. Or, what if I do get in? My—"

"Your sister will freak, and I'll be stuck here with her. You can never tell her I knew about this," he begged, sounding anxious.

"I won't tell her." Avoiding eye contact, I looked down at my feet and said bleakly, "I may not have to say anything at all if I'm not accepted."

"One thing at a time, my man," Tarron encouraged me, and patted my arm. "Let's figure out this Marcel character, then we can tackle the possibility of you moving several states away."

My lips spread into a grin. "Maybe *tackle* isn't the best word to use. Knowing Willa, she may decide to tackle me when she finds out."

Tarron nodded and asked, "We good?"

"Yeah."

He lifted a fist to the wooden door, and knocked three times. From inside, we heard the three girls holler to come in. The door was unlocked, and as it swung open, the scent of bacon and cinnamon filled my nostrils. Someone was cooking breakfast.

Anytime I'd been invited to the Martins' house for dinner, I felt the need to wear a suit. The modern art, sleek furniture, and minimal approach to decorating made the place feel less like a home and more like a museum.

"We're back here," Elle called from the kitchen.

Elle's house in New York probably looked similar, and I wondered if her father did the decorating. Mr. Martin had the suave charm and riches of a character like Jay Gatsby, as well as the mystery. The difference was Mr. Martin could live forever.

"Did you guys get any sleep last night?" Tarron asked as we walked into the open living area.

Willa sat on a stool at the island that separated the space into three parts—living, dining, and kitchen. She looked up with puffy pink eyes and said, "Sleep? Who can sleep with unpainted nails?"

She wiggled her violet fingernails in the air at us.

"So what you're saying is you'll need a nap later?" Tarron asked and looked over at the entertainment system longingly.

A flat screen as wide as the wall was mounted at one end of the room in front of a large sectional, brushed silver appliances nestled between white cabinets at the opposite end, and the back wall was made up of windows.

"I promise to stay awake through *Goblet*. Just don't hate me if I rest my eyes during *Order*," Willa pleaded, then she glanced at Elle, who looked annoyed. "That is, if we have time to watch all the movies. You do realize we'll be up all night watching them."

"If we have time?" Tarron whined. "I got up before nine during spring break for this. And I'll stay up as long as it takes."

"I know, but Elle needs our help." Willa tried to console both her boyfriend and her best friend. Her patience had not only put out a few fires between our friends, but it was preparing her for becoming alpha of our pack.

Elle used tongs to carefully turn a piece of bacon. Scarlet opened the oven door, and the fresh smell of warm bread and cinnamon filled the space. She moved the hot baked goods to the island and started icing them.

"Where's Bale?"

Scarlet's eyes darted from Tarron to Willa, then to me, before she answered with a frown, "Sleeping in."

"Is there anything I can help with?" To be nice, I'd asked in the general direction of the kitchen. Cooking hadn't ever been a talent of mine, but I could hold my own. It was another thing for Willa not to help. She'd never been good at cooking anything that didn't involve a microwave.

"No, I'm almost done," Scarlet answered.

Elle looked at me, then down at her frying pan. With a grin she said, "I don't trust you with the bacon."

"Fair enough." With a smile, I asked, "You mind if I go outside until it's ready?"

"Not at all," Elle said casually.

My favorite part of the Martins' property was their backyard. Elle's mom was a dryad, and even though the tree she was bonded to stood in Central Park, she made their yard feel like home. The patio was lined with potted plants, and a few spruce and pine trees provided privacy. A pair of oak trees were located at the center of the space, and a hammock hung between them.

A shot of cold air hit me as I slid the back door open. Quickly closing it, I glanced through the glass behind me. The thought of us all disbanding after graduation made my chest feel tight. Walking to the hammock, I wondered if any of us would leave Havenwood Falls and forget. The town had wards protecting it, but there were also magical precautions taken so that anyone who left without returning for more than a few weeks would lose every memory of the place and its inhabitants.

With less coordination than I'd hoped, I leaned back into the green hammock. It rocked back and forth, and the sunlight above appeared to be moving as it shone through the bare branches. The same sun would shine in New York if I was accepted to NYU, but returning to Havenwood Falls before the end of every moon cycle would be crucial to my plan working.

Elle didn't want to leave, and I could feel it. Her sense of loyalty and obligation to her parents wouldn't allow her to stay.

And I didn't want her to leave, so I'd study law at NYU and come back to Havenwood Falls in order to stay connected with my family. My gut told me her parents weren't telling her everything, or maybe they didn't know everything. Like other hybrids in town, the mixed bloodlines had a way of changing supernatural rules and traditions. Celeste Long came to mind. She'd only just learned she's part fae, and to go through it all without her mom to guide her had to be difficult and scary.

"Hey," Elle called from the deck, "breakfast is ready!"

Behind me, I heard the door slide shut and carefully sat up. As my weight shifted, the hammock swung, and I jumped with super agility to my feet. Being a shifter had perks.

"Nice move," Elle said with a giggle. "If only you'd been that quick on your feet the last time we were back here."

She meant when we lay back here enjoying the last day of summer. When we both attempted to stand at the same time, we'd both ended up on our butts in the grass. It would have been a dream come true if we could've stayed like that, laughing without a care in the world.

"Being a klutz is part of my charm," I said with a smile. "But it only seems to happen when I'm around you."

"I wanted to let you know, without everyone else listening in —" Elle started.

"And by everyone you mean my sister," I interrupted, amused.

"Yeah," she said with a raised eyebrow. "Well, I wanted to tell you that last night was—"

"Not a mistake." Interrupting her, I was not amused, but more worried about where she was going with this conversation. "Following your heart—"

"Kase, stop interrupting me," Elle said through gritted teeth. "It's annoying, and not what I was going to say."

"I'm sorry." Looking down at my brown boots, I waited for the inevitable.

Elle placed a hand on my chest, and my heart pounded underneath it. The scent of balsam with notes of berries grew stronger the closer she stood. Elle didn't smell like fake, sugary, mass-produced lotions; her scent was one of a kind.

"You don't need to apologize. I've given you plenty of reasons to react that way. I'm the one who's sorry, and last night was a step back in the right direction. Marcel being here doesn't change the way I feel about you. That's what I was trying to say." Her words had been spoken earnestly.

Elle's hand lingered on my chest, and I was tempted to lean forward and kiss her full lips. Behind her, I heard the back door slide open. Our friends had the worst timing. Glaring over Elle's head, I found Bale gnawing on a slice of bacon.

"Dude, I'm not promising there will be anything left once I head in for seconds," he warned with a lopsided grin.

"I'm so glad you could join us," I said sarcastically, and took Elle's hand in mine. We walked toward the deck. "But if you eat more than your share of the bacon, I'll have Tate and Conall make your life miserable."

"Whatever," Bale said, unimpressed, waving his bacon in the air.

But I understood how Bale dealt with threats that hit too close to home. My reactions were similar. The dragon shifter knew I couldn't take him in a supernatural fight, but I could convince my two oldest brothers to torture him. And if it that didn't carry enough weight, I always had our dad to use as a last resort. No one wanted to be on Sheriff Ric Kasun's bad side.

Elle and I entered the kitchen, and I watched as Bale bypassed the food and plopped onto the couch next to Scarlet. Everyone else had made a plate and found a spot to eat. Elle topped her plate with a reasonable three strips of bacon and cinnamon roll. I, on the other hand, piled three cinnamon rolls and a handful of bacon onto mine. A glass of milk and a mug of hot tea sat at the end of the island.

Elle nodded for me to take the milk after she'd picked up her mug. Following her to the sectional, I made myself comfortable beside her. My stomach rumbled, and I couldn't wait to dig in.

"I'll get the movie started," Tarron said with excitement as he reached for the remote. The large screen lit up on the wall, and Tarron clicked through to sign into an app. "I bought digital copies yesterday."

Elle sat her plate down on the coffee table in front of us, cleared her throat, and said, "Do you guys mind if we discuss my friend, Marcel, before it starts? I was hoping we could go to the inn around lunchtime so I can introduce everyone."

"I'd be happy to meet him." My voice sounded a little too eager. The truth was I'd be happier to see him leave.

Bale chuckled, and asked, "Is he staying? I was under the impression we were meeting him so we could run him out of town."

"I'm not sure how I want to handle Marcel being here," Elle said with furrowed brows. "If he's in Havenwood Falls to apologize, I feel like I should give him a chance."

"Why else would he be here?" Willa asked.

"I'm not sure. I just have a weird feeling about it," Elle admitted hesitantly.

"You know, we should attempt the whole *keep your enemies closer* thing," Tarron suggested, his eyes still glued to the television. "If only we had an invisibility cloak."

"How would an invisibility cloak help?" Willa tilted her head in confusion.

"Oh, I just want one," Tarron admitted nonchalantly. "Since Marcel's a vampire, it would take some serious magic to get the truth out of him. And while we have the resources here in town, there's no way the Court would approve it."

"Tarron's right. If the Court gave him permission to be here, it would take incriminating evidence to convince them to help us," I agreed.

"Then we keep him close," Elle said with a hint of inflection in her voice, making it sound more like a question. "I don't want to jump to any conclusions, but better safe than sorry."

"He may be here to see you, but to be safe, we won't leave you alone with him for a moment," Scarlet offered, and laid a hand on Elle's knee supportively.

"Thanks," Elle said and gave her a tight smile. "But I'm sure this whole visit will turn out harmless."

"Well, if that's settled, let's get started," Tarron said, and waved the remote in the air. "Revelio!"

CHAPTER 6

KASE

*W*e'd only tackled two of the movies, but promised Tarron we'd finish the rest after lunch in town. Piling into my truck, the six of us drove to the town square. Bale, Scarlet, and Tarron sat in the backseat, and Willa and Elle shared the front seat with me. Searching for a parking space, I spotted one near the police station. With it being spring break and lunchtime, the area was busy.

"I hate when we have to park this far," Bale complained as he stepped out of the truck. We'd have to walk across the town square to reach Whisper Falls Inn.

Willa glanced at me, as if asking permission to explain to him, and I shrugged my consent. It was a twin thing. Most of the time we followed each other's thought process, but over the years, puberty had mangled a few of our attempts at working our dad over. As wolves, our pack could communicate telepathically, but in our human form we went with our guts.

"Bale, it's crowded downtown," Willa began, "and we're here to find out Marcel's motives. If for some reason our new friend reacts badly, we'll want some backup." She nodded at the police station.

"What do you think he's going to do? Attack us? Go on a bloodsucking rampage in broad daylight?" Bale scoffed.

"Of course not," Willa said, agitated.

"Chill. Have you considered what this conversation will lead to if we really want to know what this guy's up to?" I said, knowing we'd have to act like we wanted him around, and coax him into revealing the truth.

Bale pressed his lips together in a flat line and shook his head.

I added, "Let's just say, we can't come right out and ask him why he's here, and I hope Marcel likes butterbeer." My hand took Elle's as we walked.

She laced her fingers between mine, and said, "Oh, we don't need—"

"No, he's right," Tarron interjected. "We've got to get to the bottom of this. Did you talk to your parents again?"

"No, my dad's in some meeting, and my mom is convening with the other dryads in Central Park," Elle answered with a hint of agitation.

"Maybe they don't even know he's here. He definitely gave me a Malfoy vibe last night," Scarlet added, and wrapped her sweater tighter around herself.

"I bet he's a Slytherin," Tarron said with a mischievous grin.

"As much as I dislike this idea, the point I was trying to make is that we'll need to invite Marcel to spend time with us this week." I knew if I tried to hide how I felt, Elle would probably be able to read my mind anyway. "If there's something up with Marcel, he'll probably want to avoid being anywhere near the police station or City Hall. So we'll invite him to ride back to Elle's with us."

"Um, that won't work," Bale said with a hint of arrogance. "Your cab is already full with all of us in it."

"It is," Willa chimed in. "I guess I'll have to drag all of you into the station to borrow the keys to Dad's truck."

"Nice," Tarron said with a nod. "If anyone can scare the truth out of Marcel, it would be Sheriff Kasun, especially when he's carrying his gun."

We all laughed, and I almost felt bad for Tarron when I looked over at him and realized he hadn't meant it as a joke. Beyond him, in the distance, I saw Brice Blackstone, with his brown floppy hair, skate by, probably headed to his family's wine-tasting storefront, Soothing Sips. The guy was a year younger than us, but we'd grown up with the same familial obligations. In addition to my dad being sheriff, my family's outdoor supply store, Backwoods Sport & Ski, was located across the street.

Inspecting the block across from us, I started with the display of skis on the sidewalk in front of Backwoods. A few other faces were familiar, and I was surprised to see Joe exiting Howe's Herbal Shoppe, a stranger following him. Joe looked up and recognized us, but darted off in the opposite direction.

The stranger behind him wore a nice black pea coat and carried at least four shopping bags. Initially, I figured he was a tourist visiting for spring break. Then he glanced up, and I felt him recognize Elle.

Elle stiffened beside me.

"He's just walked out of the Howe's shop," I grumbled, and glanced at Scarlet.

She conducted her own inspection of the situation, and blurted, "Why on earth would he want a scented candle or souvenir mug?"

"Do you think you could ask your mom what he bought?" He didn't look like the type of guy who collected souvenir coffee mugs.

"Sure," Scarlet answered, "but how will you guys keep him occupied?"

"Are you sure we have to invite him to join us?" Elle bit her bottom lip, then suggested, "What if we just have coffee with him?"

Willa tucked a piece of hair behind her ear and said, "We need to tell him about our plans this week, and see if he wants to tag along."

"This week? I thought we might invite him over today, but I don't want him intruding on our camping trip," Elle complained disapprovingly.

The group had changed course, and we walked to meet Marcel in front of the herbal shop. Marcel didn't exactly blend in with the natives. Most of the town's male inhabitants wore jeans, layers of flannel, and scuffed boots. Marcel waited patiently until we stepped up to greet him. Elle shared everyone else's names, and when she introduced me, Marcel's eyes widened in surprise.

"Kase, it's nice to meet you." Marcel offered his hand to shake, and I realized I'd have to release Elle's hand to shake his.

"The pleasure is all mine." My hand gripped his and gave a sturdy shake.

As my hand fell back to my side, Elle quickly took hold of it and made a point of stepping closer to me. The gesture didn't go unnoticed by Marcel. He shifted his weight from one foot to the other.

"Nice boots," Willa said and pointed at his feet.

Marcel's brows furrowed, then he looked down and said, "Thanks, I just bought them. That store, Backwoods, sells everything, even sweatshirts that say *Take a hike, because people suck!*" He sounded amused.

Bale laughed and said, "That's one of my favorites. I'm not sure where Tate gets all of his quips, but I resemble most of them."

"Don't you mean relate to?" Marcel asked, confused.

Bale shoved his hands in his pockets and answered, "Nope."

"Well," Scarlet interrupted, "I'm going to run in and say hi to my mom real quick. I'll be right back."

She stepped toward Howe's Herbal Shoppe, where a tourist could find the perfect Havenwood Falls postcard or essential oils, and a local supernatural could purchase a magical talisman or potion. Marcel watched as Scarlet walked into her family's store, and a set of bells hanging inside rang. A cloud of herbal scents filled the air around us. Then Marcel turned back to the rest of us, composed. He pulled his bags up and started buttoning his coat.

"Can I hold something for you?" Elle asked.

"I think I've got it all," Marcel assured. "So, have you guys eaten lunch?"

"Not yet," Willa answered. "Do you want to go with us to Burger Bar?"

"Sure, if it means I get to hang out with Elle, I'm in." Marcel smiled at Elle, but his smile faltered as he took each of us in.

His enthusiasm came across as fake to me, but Elle smiled back at him like she didn't catch his excessively flattering tone. Her hand still secure in mine, I squeezed it softly. She looked up at me and gave me a quick wink. Could she read his mind?

"You can ride with us," Willa offered, and pointed over her shoulder toward the police station. "We're just parked over there."

"Actually, I should probably go put this stuff back in my room at the inn." Marcel shrugged, lifting the bags hanging from his arms.

The sound of bells chimed, and Scarlet joined us on the sidewalk, smelling of cloves and orange. Her lips were twisted as tightly as her braided red hair. She rocked onto her toes and back to her heels, and finally asked, "So what's the plan?"

"Burgers," Bale informed, "but Marcel here says he needs to take his souvenirs back to his room first."

"Cool," Scarlet said with a smile. "You probably saw Burger Bar on your way into town. You can meet us there."

"But," Willa started with a frown, "we could all ride together. It would be fun."

She attempted to sound casual, but was as successful as Marcel at blending in. Willa wanted to see her plan play out, but I could tell Scarlet was up to something too. It made sense to keep Marcel close and find out how he'd react to authority. My dad wasn't an official member of the Court of the Sun and the Moon, but until Willa was ready to take over as alpha of the Kasun pack, our dad served in the role. He would have been made aware of any and all supernatural visitors.

"I appreciate the offer, Willa," Marcel said with a tight smile. "But I don't want to be a burden, and don't say I wouldn't be. I'll just meet you guys at Burger Bar."

"If you insist," Scarlet approved. "We'll go get a table and order some shakes. What kind is your favorite?"

"Uh, vanilla," Marcel answered, looking perplexed with

furrowed brows. "So I'll meet you there as soon as I put these away."

"Perfect." Elle beamed. "Then we'll head that way."

Elle squeezed my hand and tugged me to turn around and follow her. The group of us made our way back across the square, and as we passed the fountain at its center, I glanced back to find Marcel watching us. He hadn't moved. At the end of the block behind him, Joe stood, observing the scene with a blank face. Weird.

"Vanilla?" Scarlet marveled.

"I can't believe you're surprised," scoffed Willa.

"I can't believe you two are still talking about milkshakes." Tarron grimaced, trying to hide his disappointment from Willa by turning to Scarlet. "What did he buy from your mom?"

"Well, I have good news and bad news. My mom wasn't in the shop. My grandmother said she had a few errands to run before lunch," Scarlet informed, then paused.

We'd reached the truck, and all piled inside. I started the engine once everyone had buckled in, and pulled into the flow of traffic. In the distance, Marcel was walking into the inn. With a hint of impatience, I asked, "Was that the good news or the bad news?"

"Neither, I was trying to decide which to tell you first," she answered.

"The good," Elle requested. "Give us the good news first."

"Okay, my grandmother remembered selling some valerian. It's an herb that helps people rest," Scarlet explained.

"That makes sense." Elle sounded relieved. "Vampires don't really sleep regularly. You know, they tend to rest during the day. So if Marcel is trying to fit in, he'd need to take the valerian to help him shift to our sleep cycle."

"Yeah, but it might have been Joe who bought the Valerian. He's been having a hard time sleeping the last few months." My intel didn't help. Everyone sat in silence for a few seconds before I asked, "What's the bad news?"

"He also bought something from our back room," Scarlet said with wide eyes. "Something to give the herbs a supernatural kick—"

"Still makes sense," Elle interrupted. "Valerian on its own wouldn't do the trick for a vampire."

"Or a troubled shifter," I added.

"But you guys know my grandmother can get a little spacey sometimes. My mom and I think she picks and chooses who she's coherent with, but there's no way to really tell," Scarlet worried.

We all waited for Scarlet to continue, because we understood her worry wasn't limited to this one instance. Ruby Howe was a legend in the supernatural community, but as she aged, her mind wandered more and more. From a human's perspective, she came across as extremely quirky and forgetful. Scarlet and her mother, Rose, had to keep tabs on Ruby constantly to make sure she didn't accidentally misuse her powers.

"She said something about a disillusioned, charming man coming by, so I went to check the books. Gram is supposed to write everything down, but when I looked at the latest entry, it had been jumbled," Scarlet said as she rubbed her temples.

"Jumbled?" asked Bale, confused.

Looking at him in my rearview mirror, I could see he was focused on Scarlet. He reached his hand over and placed it on her knee consolingly. We waited for her to answer, while the sound of the truck's heater let out a low whistle. As we approached Burger Bar, it was funny to see the high school's parking lot deserted, and the best burger joint in town buzzing.

"It looked like Gram tried to write something down in the ledger, but she must have been confused because she wrote one of her mysterious incantations. Her chicken scratch is already hard to read, but when it's a jumbled mix of rhyming words, it's impossible to make sense of." Scarlet shook her head and added, "It was gibberish. All I could make out was, *seener unseen, fader evade.*"

After I parked, everyone exited the truck, and I repeated the words in my head. Tarron headed inside to get us a table, Bale pulled Scarlet in his arms and whispered to her, and Willa gave me the *eye*. It was never good when she made that face at me. All of her features appeared to shrink, but her right eye seemed to double in size. There was no way I would be able to talk to her alone. It was like every car that parked at the school on a daily basis had decided to park at Burger Bar.

"Hey," Elle said, smiling as she walked around the front of the truck to me. "I need to run to the ladies' room. Willa," she called back over her shoulder, "wanna come with?"

It wasn't a good idea to wonder why girls always traveled to the bathroom together, but the thought escaped its compartment. Elle turned back to face me and playfully shoved my shoulder. Stepping back, I held my hands up in surrender.

"It's one of the greatest mysteries of all time."

"What are you two talking about?" Willa asked.

"Oh, nothing," Elle answered. "I'll be right back. Unless you want to go with?"

"Nah, I'm good for now," Willa said and waved her away. "I'll stay with the boy version and make sure he doesn't get into any trouble."

Elle giggled and weaved between the cars parked in the drive-in stalls. I inspected the area, wanting to make sure we could speak freely. Willa hooked her arm around mine and pulled me with her.

"I have a really bad feeling about Marcel," she cautioned with a frown.

"I do too, but it's mainly because I think he came here to win Elle over," I admitted. "I can't think it around her, but her parents were glad to see us break up, and I wouldn't be surprised if her father already married her off to some vampire family to solidify his position on their council."

The life she'd lived in New York hadn't all been miserable, but the way her father's vampire clan orchestrated bloodlines and revered supernatural species was creepy. At first when she'd described it, I thought her life in the city had been filled with formal galas, private school, and French tutors. Underneath, the clans weren't all bad, but some valued power more than anything else.

"That's horrible to think, and I can't imagine Mr. Martin doing that," Willa scolded, and she was right. Elle's dad may not have liked the idea of me in her life, but he wouldn't force her to marry someone. "But Marcel strikes me as someone who cares more about how he's perceived than who he really is. He's fake, and I'm not sure we'll get the truth out of him."

"You may be right, but we have to try."

And, as if he'd heard us saying his name, Marcel Cushing turned into the Burger Bar parking lot and waved at the two of us, sporting a wide, duplicitous smile.

CHAPTER 7

ELLE

*B*efore I left the bathroom, I closed my eyes and took a few deep breaths. Controlling my mind and the thoughts I allowed in was more difficult with Marcel around. Because of my desire to want to know why he was in town, my guard hadn't been up. As vampires, we couldn't read each other's minds unless we fed from each other. So it didn't make sense for my mind to reach out to his; it was merely habit.

Walking over to the table Tarron had saved, I recognized a few classmates enjoying spring break too. Joseph Greg, Kase's best friend, stepped away from the diner's counter with a paper bag. He glanced in my direction and frowned. Joe's blond hair fell over his brow, longer than normal, unkempt. A pallid complexion and sunken features made me question whether he was really eating the food he carried or just keeping up appearances.

"Joe," I called out as he reached the exit, but he either didn't hear me over the crowd of enthusiastic teens or ignored me. When we'd noticed Joe leaving the Howes' store before Marcel, I'd thought I picked up some anxiety from Kase. At the time, I figured it was from meeting Marcel, but it made more sense for Kase to be anxious about Joe and how he looked.

My eyes surveyed Burger Bar's dining room. The three walls of windows revealed cars parked in every drive-in stall, and the booths and tables weren't any different. The place was crawling with teenagers. I avoided looking too long at one booth in particular, because Ana Novak sat with her bestie, Marie, and a few of the Kasun pack guys from the football team. The group laughed hysterically at one of the boys suffering from brain freeze after chugging his milkshake.

Bale and Scarlet were sitting with Tarron, and four empty chairs were tucked under the table. The scent of fresh fried food pulled me to the basket in front of Tarron like a waft of air in a cartoon. I sat in one of the red-and-white-cushioned chairs across from him and found a few tater tots left at the bottom. When I reached for one, Tarron flinched.

"What? I can't have one?"

"Sure, but they were here when I sat down." He shrugged and tilted the basket toward me. Looking at Bale, who sat next to him, he warned, "I'm sure you don't care."

Bale shunned the greasy goodness, lifted his chin in the air, and folded his arms over his chest.

Maggie Hopkins, one of the owners, skated by and circled the table. "What can I get started for you guys?"

She pulled out a pad of paper from her apron and reached for a pencil tucked behind her ear. She took each of our orders. Bale and Scarlet recited their usuals, and Tarron ordered for himself and Willa. Kase's order was easy, and I guessed for Marcel. Then I ordered my favorite—the steak finger basket with tots instead of fries and a chocolate shake. Maggie grabbed the red basket of old tots before she skated away and clipped our ticket to a wheel hanging between the soda bar and the kitchen.

The front door squeaked as it opened, and roller skates clattered on the black and white checkered linoleum repeatedly. It wasn't until we heard a collision—specifically a tray toppling to the floor —that we all turned to find Marcel covered in milkshake and french fries. Kase and Willa stood behind him untouched, and one of the carhops looked mortified by the accident.

"I'm so sorry," she said, and began wiping the front of Marcel's coat.

Everyone in the diner clapped like we were back in elementary school. Marcel's jaw clenched, and his body stiffened. Willa wedged herself between Marcel and the carhop and encouraged her to stop.

"How about you go get a mop," she suggested, "and I'll help with this." Willa held her hand out in front of Marcel and waved it in a circular motion.

The carhop skated away, making room for Willa, Marcel, and Kase to move around the mess. Marcel worked on unfastening the buttons on his coat and hung it over the back of a chair at the end of the table. Kase made his way to sit next to me, and Willa took the seat next to Tarron.

After a few moments of awkward silence, Tarron blurted, "So, Marcel, have you read the Harry Potter books?"

Lunch was delicious as usual. Whenever an awkward topic came up, someone just shoved a burger in their mouth, or in my case, a steak finger. Marcel went from complimenting Tarron's taste in literature to agreeing with Bale about snowboards being faster than skis.

When the topic shifted to life after high school, Bale became quiet. Out of all of us, he was having the hardest time with the idea of all of us growing up. Scarlet would have talked about his aversion to adulting, but I wasn't sure she even knew what bothered him so much about graduating and going to college.

We all leaned back in our seats, waiting for our check. Everyone was getting along like it was an episode of a Disney Channel sitcom. Kase propped his arm on the back of my chair around me and leaned in close to ask me a question.

"Do you have a request for the jukebox?"

"Mr. Moonlight."

Before Kase dismissed himself, I kissed his cheek. Then he

walked over to the old-fashioned record player and dropped a couple quarters in the slot.

Marcel cleared his throat and asked, "Is that your nickname for him? Or am I missing something?"

"It's the name of an old Beatles song. I guess you could say it's our song."

"From what your father told my mother, he's under the impression that it *was* your song," Marcel said with a hint of accusation. He'd remained perfectly casual, but I could tell he didn't like being out of the loop.

In fact, everyone had frozen in place, and I wasn't sure if it was because of Marcel's observation or because they were all wondering too. Kase and I had barely discussed getting back together, and I felt the need in that moment to defend my love for him. Because I knew it was love, and not the silly infatuation I'd felt for Marcel's brother, Armand.

My mouth started to open, and Kase's hand squeezed my shoulder. His touch calmed me. When I first met him, I thought he was a jerk, like his girlfriend at the time, Ana. He'd used the rest of our junior year to prove me wrong.

"If you came here because of something my father said, you've come a long way for nothing." My mind raced trying to think of another reason he'd be here.

Marcel crossed one leg over the other, toward me, and retorted, "My visit was orchestrated by our parents, but I came for my own reasons. I think it's nice you have someone in your life."

He sounded genuine, but I couldn't help notice Willa's eyes narrow suspiciously. As she watched him, I could tell she was holding her tongue. So far, Marcel had been a little awkward, funny, and kind. He'd been the same Marcel I remembered from before I'd started dating his brother.

We all knew if we went on the defensive, we'd never figure out why Marcel was in Havenwood Falls, but I was starting to think he'd really come to apologize. As a group, we'd come up with a game plan earlier that morning, and we had to follow through.

"Hey, kiddos, I've got your check here," Maggie said as she skated to our table. She placed the ticket at the center of the table, and grabbed a few of the empty baskets. "You can square up with me whenever you're ready."

We all pulled out cash. My ten-dollar bill was crisp. Kase revealed a twenty and tossed it on the table.

"I've got yours," he offered.

Marcel started to pull his wallet out of his back pocket, and I held my hand up to stop him. "I'll pay for yours."

"You don't ha—" Marcel started to refuse.

"Don't argue, it's the least I can do."

He resigned and leaned back, watching the people around us.

"So, Marcel, if you've got reasons for being here, please share," Bale said flippantly, as he set a few fives in front of him. "But I should warn you, if skiing is on your list, you're out of luck. The season ended today."

Sometimes the dragon shifter amazed me; other times, I wanted to smack him in the back of the head. Most of the teenage guys I knew elicited those feelings, but Bale had a way of coming across as more sullen than all the rest.

"You can check *best burgers in town* off your list," Scarlet added with a smile and a shrug. She set some money on the table too.

"Relaxing, some hiking, and spending time catching up with Elle," Marcel listed out loud.

"We can take care of relaxing today. How about you come over and finish the movie marathon with us?" I invited hesitantly, but couldn't imagine Marcel's mother allowing him to read or watch anything Harry Potter. Her idea of raising children included piano lessons, a French tutor, and fencing practice.

"And we're going hiking Wednesday," Tarron said. Watching his face, I could tell he hadn't thought the remark through.

My head shook slightly, and I forced a smile. "Oh, Marcel won't enjoy the type of hiking we have planned. Three days is a long time, and I don't think he's ever been camping before."

Marcel's brows furrowed, and his eyes shifted from Tarron to me. His shoulders hunched forward enough that I could tell he was disappointed. I couldn't bring myself to ask him to join us, since the trip was for the Scooby Gang. They would argue it would be the best opportunity to get Marcel out of his comfort zone and talking.

Kase slipped his hand in mine and pulled me up to stand with him. With a gentle squeeze, he looked from me to Marcel and said, "If you've never been camping before, then we need to fix that. Mount Alexa is the most beautiful hike, and everyone should be able to say they've slept under the moon and stars at least once."

"When do we leave?" Marcel asked with a giddy grin as he stood.

"Wednesday." My heart sank as I confirmed the day. Getting down to the bottom of why he was in Havenwood Falls was one thing, but allowing him to intrude on our last trip together before graduating felt wrong. It was like Scooby and the gang taking a joy ride with Nate Archibald from *Gossip Girl*.

Willa made her way around the table and chimed in, "Kase, I forgot to ask, who'd you get to cover your shift Wednesday?"

Kase's mouth turned down for a split second, and he answered, "Joe."

"Is he doing any better?" Scarlet asked, and worry lines creased her forehead.

"Not that I can tell, but I figured work would keep his mind off things. And he'll be with Tate, so they might even have some fun." Kase's frown lightened.

Their older brother, Tate, was adventurous to say the least. The Kasun family had an interesting dynamic, since Willa would be alpha of their pack someday. Their oldest brother, Conall, was a clone of their father. And Kase was the perfect mix of all of them, fun and cautious. The weight of the family name and the expectations that came with it were a burden, but Kase never failed to be himself.

As we made our way to the exit, Marcel paused to carefully fold his milkshake-stained coat over his arm. Behind him, I noticed Ana and her crew getting up from their table. The compact blonde had a way of making herself seen, and today was no different. She saw Marcel and elbowed her partner in crime, Marie. When Marie's eyes widened at the sight of fresh meat, Ana quickly elbowed her in the side and let out a low growl.

"You must be new in town," she started, and turned her nose up. "I'm Ana Novak, and you are—"

Marcel, with impeccable manners, held out his hand and said, "Marcel. It's a pleasure to meet you, Ana."

The varsity mean girl glanced over at the rest of us, her top lip curled up when she looked back at Marcel. "You are definitely not from around here, but that doesn't change the fact that you're not my type." Ana pressed her finger to Marcel's chest, and added, "It's too bad for you my dating policy only includes guys with a beating heart."

One corner of Marcel's mouth twitched upward, giving him away. He liked the attention from Ana, and maybe the challenge, but it made me want to barf. There wasn't a jealous bone in my body when it came to Marcel. Since I'd learned that Ana had been behind a plot to steal Willa's position as alpha last year, I'd wanted to teach her a lesson. But Willa and Scarlet assured me she'd get what she deserved one day.

"Hey," Bale called over to Marcel, "we're headed to Elle's house. I promised Tarron we'd finish these movies. You coming?"

Marcel looked from us to Ana and winked at her teasingly. She looked over at me in disgust and flipped her hair over her shoulder before walking away.

Marcel said, "I'll be right behind you guys."

CHAPTER 8

KASE

ednesday morning was cold. I woke up early and loaded my truck with three days of supplies. The night before, the girls had insisted on including the makings for hot dogs and s'mores, but I'd refused to pack air mattresses. The weather promised to be clear, and if everything went according to plan, I'd have a surprise for everyone when we reached the top of our climb.

Before leaving the cabin, my dad warned Willa and me there was to be no funny business. He sternly requested we stick to the hike we'd discussed. We both nodded, and he winked at me. Willa wasn't in on the scheme, but I'd enlisted my dad's and Tate's help.

As my sister and I pulled up to Elle's house, the others were gathering their packs into a pile at the end of the driveway. While parking, I rolled my window down and called, "Good morning!"

Bale glared at me in disgust and asked, "How are you a morning person and a night person?"

"I'm just excited. This camping trip is going to be epic."

After the movie marathon Monday—and into early Tuesday morning—we'd all gone home late—or early. Tuesday meant work for most of us. Willa and I manned Backwoods, Scarlet had a shift at Howe's Herbal Shoppe, Bale was working on his motorcycle, and Elle spent the morning trying to get ahold of her parents. On my lunch break, she and I met at Coffee Haven, and she told me she was only able to get in touch with her mother.

Mrs. Martin promised she and her husband would be back in Havenwood Falls by the time we returned from camping on Friday, but she hadn't been included in the plans for Marcel's visit. Because Elle hadn't talked to her father, Mrs. Martin reasoned he must have set it up. Supposedly, Elle's parents had important jobs in New York City, and it sounded like their jobs took precedence. They hadn't seen each other much on their trip. If I moved there for college, I hoped Elle and I would still make it a priority to spend time together.

"Kase, please don't be mad," Elle said, tearing me away from my thoughts. Her bottom lip pouted out. "But I packed one more teeny, tiny bag with some extra food."

She made it impossible to be upset with her, and curiosity got the best of me. "What all did you add?"

She walked up to my door, pushed up onto her toes, and kissed my cheek. Then she said, "Popcorn, apple juice, cinnamon sticks, and icing."

"Icing?" I asked with my head tilted.

"Whipped milk chocolate, if I'm not mistaken," Marcel confidently predicted.

"No, I know which kind she likes. I'm just surprised she needs it for camping."

"You never know what you'll need," she countered and kissed me on the cheek again.

I grinned from ear to ear.

"Marcel helped me shop yesterday," she said softly, and winked at me. I glanced over at Marcel, and his eyes were on me. He wore a smirk, but I couldn't tell what he meant by it. He quickly took his phone out of his coat pocket and proceeded to type something out.

Yesterday afternoon, while we each worked a second shift, Elle gave Marcel a tour of the town. My skepticism was difficult to hide when he'd called during our lunch date, but Elle mistook it for being worried about my friend, Joe. And I was concerned, because he'd shown up at Coffee Haven and appeared distraught. When I tried approaching him to settle our differences, he wouldn't stay to hear me out. Joe almost came across as angry at Elle when she added that she missed seeing him. The encounter led me to text my dad about Joe. And while we were camping, my dad promised to confront Joe.

Before I left Elle to go back to work, she revealed she had some reservations about being alone with Marcel that afternoon. We came up with a few ways she could make sure they stayed in the public eye. And last night, after we listed out everything we each needed to pack, Elle told me and the others that Marcel was a gentleman all afternoon.

"Don't forget, whatever we take, we're carrying up the mountain." Opening my door, I stepped down from the driver's seat. Patting the side of the truck, I added, "We should be able to fit everything back here."

Willa walked around from the passenger side and assured, "Tate should be here in a few minutes."

"Oh, is someone else joining us?" Marcel asked, and loaded his backpack into the bed of the truck.

"Our older brother is just helping with transportation," Willa informed. "He knows these forests better than anyone, and his Jeep can handle the muddy terrain better than Tarron's or Elle's cars."

Marcel nodded his understanding and stepped out of the way as Bale lifted Scarlet's bag. Once everything was loaded, Tate arrived. He steered with a hand full of pastry, and after he shifted his vehicle into park, he took a swig from a Coffee Haven cup.

Not long after Elle and I started dating last summer, my brother settled into a relationship of his own. Tate and Alex were perfect for each other. They were both adventurous, and where Tate lacked organizational skills and focus, Alex made up for it. They complemented each other. The difference between my feelings for Elle and Tate's for Alex was Tate had experienced a magical connection to Alex. He'd found his mate.

"Who's riding with me?" Tate asked from inside his Jeep, unwilling to expose himself or his coffee to the cold.

Elle surveyed the group as they moved around each other to load the truck. As I shoved Tarron's bedroll into a corner, I noticed Marcel scrolling through his phone again. There was no way he'd get service while we were in the forest, so I didn't blame him for wanting to send a text or two. Anyone I would have wanted to check in with, other than Joe, was right here.

"Let's see," Elle reluctantly started. "How about Tarron, Willa, and Marcel? The drive won't be long, since we're hiking up the mountain."

No one argued with the arrangement, and just as we were piling into the truck, Tate stopped Elle. "Do you want to leave a house key with me? I'd be happy to keep an eye on the place since your parents are out of town."

"Oh, I think it'll be—" Elle started, looking confused.

Nodding, I offered my opinion, "That's a good idea."

Getting keys to Elle's place was crucial to my plan, and Tate and I had agreed asking for them at the last minute and taking her off guard would be the best way to keep the surprise a secret.

"Okay." She shrugged and handed her keys to him through his window.

Elle and I walked over to my truck, where Bale and Scarlet were already strapped in, and we took off on our adventure.

Hiking up Mount Alexa was a test of endurance and patience. Being a group of supernaturals, conquering the physical challenge came naturally. The first couple hours went smoothly, but then we had to make multiple stops for food and bathroom breaks. We took our time, to keep everyone happy, and finally reached the peak of the ridge we'd planned to set up camp late in the afternoon.

"Where do you guys want to set up the tents?" Marcel asked with eagerness. He slid his pack off his back and onto the ground.

"It'll be more important to find some dry wood and get a fire started," Willa informed, and crossed her arms over her chest.

Taking Elle's pack, I set it next to mine, and offered, "We'll look for the wood."

She smiled at me, and it was all the thanks I needed.

"Okay." Willa tapped her chin with a finger, then pointed at Marcel. "How about you find some rocks? We'll need to create a rock circle around the campfire."

Marcel fidgeted with his bag and offered a tight smile. "Since I'm new at all this, and don't know my way around the forest, how about I go with Elle?"

Willa glanced at me, and I gave her a lopsided grin, and said, "Feel free to join us."

The guy hadn't left Elle's side during our hike, and I could tell Willa noticed too. But I was determined not to let Marcel Cushing ruin our trip. It was his first time camping, and the concrete jungle he came from was very different from our forest. Willa assigned the stone-gathering to Scarlet and Bale, while she and Tarron went to fill our water bottles. There were several streams and creeks that threaded through the area.

Marcel talked nonstop about all the places he wanted to take Elle when she moved back to New York. He wouldn't let me get a word in. Marcel knew the trip was about all of us spending time together before we graduated, but he seemed determined to make sure no one else could get close to Elle.

"I'll even go with you to Central Park, so you can scout out which tree you would want to bond with," he rambled.

"*Want* to bond with?" Elle asked, and froze under an aspen tree. "You make it sound like I get to pick the tree."

"You know what I mean, Elle," he backtracked in a soft tone. "You'll find the tree you're meant to bond with, and you'll want to protect it."

"I guess you're right," she conceded. "My mother has always said something similar. I just wish I could talk to another dryad, and ask them about how they handled 'choosing.'" Elle held up her hands and made air quotes.

"I think that's a great idea." My eyebrows rose in approval. Seeing Elle among the towering trees, I knew it was where she belonged. She'd become as strong as the oldest pine trees in the forest, and her power rivaled the currents of the Colorado River.

Marcel frowned and said gruffly, "Mrs. Martin has been a dryad for hundreds of years. I'm sure she's told you all you need to know."

Picking up another dry branch, I avoided an argument. Ever since I'd known Elle, her parents had filled her head with their expectations of her. Some of their ideas for Elle's future even conflicted with each other. Because Elle was a hybrid, I believed she was capable of so much more than they knew.

My arms were full, and it was time we headed back to camp. Inspecting the area around us, I noticed Elle carrying a few twigs, but Marcel's hands were empty. We were surrounded by spruce and fir trees, all covered in green needles. It would be easy for anyone to get turned around out here. Luckily, I'd been running the perimeter of Havenwood Falls for years on patrol.

I asked, "Elle, do you know which way it is back to camp?"

We'd been wandering, and I was curious if she'd been paying attention.

Marcel took a step to the right, pointed, and answered, "This way, right?"

Ugh. He wouldn't even let Elle answer my question, so I'd have to find a way to ditch him. The key would be to play to his own lack of desire to lift a finger to do manual labor.

"You're right, so do you want to take this load back or collect some more branches?"

Marcel looked from me to Elle like he was searching for the correct answer, but there wasn't one. I was too smart for that.

"I think I'll take your load back," he said with a smug smile. "Elle and I can get the fire started, and you can pick up some extra wood."

"Actually, this doesn't weigh that much," I countered. "I bet you're strong enough to handle my load and the pieces Elle has."

"O-oh," he stuttered, and his nose wrinkled in confusion. "Of course I can handle it, but—"

"Great," Elle cut him off, catching on to my motives. "Then I can grab a few more branches too. You never know if we'll need them, and it's better to be safe than sorry."

Marcel didn't attempt to argue with Elle, and we piled the wood in his open arms. He started walking back to camp and disappeared from view about twenty feet away. Finally, Elle and I had some time alone.

Approaching her with a knowing smile, I slipped my hand into hers and pulled her toward a stream I knew flowed nearby. The warmth I felt in my heart knowing Elle wanted to be with me made me forget the cold air that left the tip of my nose numb. Our steps were in unison, and with it being late afternoon, we couldn't be away for long. It would be getting dark soon, and my surprise would be arriving soon.

As we moved out to a clearing near the stream, I turned to face Elle. Behind her, I thought I spotted a wolf. A striking white wolf from the Kasun pack—Joe. If I'd been in wolf form, I could have communicated with him. But he bound off farther into the forest before I had time to alert Elle.

"Do you want to go after him?" she asked softly, with a concerned frown.

"Nah, I'll check in on him when we get back Friday. I think he's missing Infiniti, and only time is going to mend his broken heart." I walked backwards and asked, "Are you doing okay?"

"I'm better now that we have a little time alone," she admitted with a relieved smile. "Being with you always makes me feel better."

Elle moved closer to me. I wrapped my arms around her waist and whispered, "You make me better."

We leaned into each other, and my lips met hers. As I kissed her, I allowed my heart and mind to open to her. Thoughts of a life with her and the love overflowing from me made her pause. Elle's lips brushed against mine as she murmured, "I love you, too."

~

The time away from the group was just what we needed before returning to the chaos Elle and I walked up on. Bale faced Marcel with a stone in each hand, and Marcel held a tree branch like a baseball bat. Bale was breathing smoke, but not because it was cold outside. Marcel's top lip curled up over his fangs.

"The stones first," Bale growled.

Marcel hissed, "Stacking the wood goes first."

"Dude, chill," Tarron said softly with his two arms outstretched between them. Tarron had the power to persuade if he wanted, but I knew it was a power he didn't like to use. From what I understood, persuasion on a supernatural level could have crazy side effects.

Dropping my load of branches, I distracted Marcel. He saw Elle at my side and immediately shuffled back from his confrontation with Bale, then said, "Whatever, dragon. I'm going to work on putting up my tent."

Marcel dropped his branch and walked away. When Willa asked if he needed any help, he ignored her. The guy had been fine with Elle around, but without her nearby, his attitude had the potential to ruin my plans tonight. So I'd have to stroke some egos.

"Bale, do you mind finishing while I go check on him?" He was the best candidate to get the fire started. He could breathe fire.

"Nah, go on," he said coolly and waved me away.

Marcel sighed when I reached him, and said, "I don't need you to come over here and tell me what an idiot I am."

"I wasn't going to. I wanted to let you know that Bale can come across strong sometimes. And that you don't need to set up your tent yet."

Marcel tilted his head to the side.

"Thing is, we're not staying here for long." Marcel didn't say anything, so I added, "After we eat, I have a surprise for everyone."

"But I'll need my tent eventually, and I'd rather assemble it now, before it's dark," he reasoned thoughtfully. "It's my first time camping, and I don't want to look—"

"How about I promise to set it up for you later? That way you can come back over to the campfire and cook hot dogs with the rest of us." My proposition didn't make a ton of sense, but I could see Marcel's wheels were turning.

"Okay, but I still think it would be best if I kept my distance. At least from Bale," Marcel said cautiously.

It probably was a good idea for Marcel not to assert himself, but his ability to have an opinion about everything made that impossible. I patted his shoulder, my goal to form some semblance of friendship. He flinched, and any connection I thought I'd made snapped.

Marcel pouted while roasting his hot dog, then glowered at Elle when we made s'mores. His attention had become focused, like he'd made the decision to disregard the rest of us. His behavior felt familiar, like how Joe had started obsessing over finding Infiniti. Joe hadn't intended to hurt anyone, but pushing others away hurt everyone. I tried not to make a big deal about it, because there were too many things for me to remember tonight.

First, I had to make sure it didn't seem odd when I suggested everyone go on a night hike. Second, timing was everything. If we left too early, it wouldn't give Tate enough time to set everything up. Lastly, the night needed to be perfect for Elle.

So when the girls started to complain about having sticky marshmallow fingers, I mentioned taking a walk to a nearby stream to rinse them off. Of course, the guys couldn't let them go alone, so I condensed a few things into one pack in case of an accident. We strapped headlamps to our foreheads. And then everyone hiking at night without any suspicion.

Once we were approaching the spot Tate and I had agreed on, I knew Willa would get suspicious. She hadn't patrolled as many years as I had, but she'd been raised in these forests just the same. Tate waited to drive us out to the town border. He pulled up in the pickup and didn't say a word. We all piled into the back, and as we approached the enchanted border, Willa's mental warning bells went off. I could tell when her eyes grew wide. She understood I was leading my friends to come close to crossing it, but the area we were headed provided the best views. All my life, we'd been taught to keep the good in and drive the bad out.

I leaned over to Willa, and whispered, "Trust me."

She did.

As we cleared the thickest part of the forest, I spotted the lights Tate left behind in an open field. A campfire had been started several yards away in the distance. Two large tents were set up, one for the girls and the other for the boys. Lanterns were lit inside them, and they glowed green and orange. Between the tents, Elle's telescope stood, pointed at the sky. A few blankets were folded and stacked at its base.

"What is all this?" Elle asked from beside me.

"I thought stargazing would be fun, and I figured I could teach you the proper angle to use when looking through your telescope." A chuckle escaped me.

Elle laughed, then said, "This is perfect."

Tate had really outdone himself. He stopped the truck, and we all jumped out. With a wave and a honk, Tate headed back to town. He'd return the next morning.

Near the campfire we found the kit for making hot chocolate and tea that I'd arranged. The tin cups reminded me of the ones we had in our cabinets at home. Willa and Tarron were the first to grab a blanket and lay it over the ground.

As they stretched out, Willa asked, "How'd you make this happen?"

"Let's just say I'll be covering patrols for Tate for the unforeseeable future. Dad pulled a few strings with the Court since we're so close to the border. And if anyone asks, it's all for a science project." My laughter became uncontrollable at the thought of any of the Court members falling for the story.

Bale and Scarlet followed Willa and Tarron's example. Like me, Willa knew all the constellations and pointed them out to Tarron. Bale was doing something similar with Scarlet, but the stories he told about the stars were filled with more dragon history. Being dragon shifters, his ancestors had their own stories about how the sky became filled with fire and lights.

Past Elle, I watched as Marcel prepared to boil water in the kettle. At least he'd made himself busy. It was a beautiful night, even if it was cold. We were all bundled up, but a hot cup of tea would help warm us from the inside.

Elle and I made our way to the telescope, and she looked through the lens first. If Tate had followed my instructions to the letter, Elle would be looking at the moon. As she pulled away, her eyes widened with wonder.

I definitely owed Tate big time.

"Thank you," Elle said sweetly, and she pulled me to her and gave me a soft kiss.

Looking into her eyes, I said, "I promised you the moon, and I'll always keep my promises."

CHAPTER 9

ELLE

*J*ostled out of a deep sleep, I had no control of my body. Someone was carrying me over their shoulder and running. Everything was black, and I couldn't tell if my eyes were still closed or if it was the darkness of night. The sound of boots hitting the ground and the scent of sweet apricot surrounded us.

"To have seen her now unseen, to fade her now evade," a deep voice whispered, then repeated over and over, "To have seen her now unseen, to fade her now evade."

The words felt familiar, but I couldn't place them. My brain was foggy, and my breath tasted awful. The urge to check my surroundings nearly outweighed my desire to know who carried me. It had to be a man, because his shoulder was broad enough to throw me over it, and the steps he took made me feel like I was dangling high up from the ground.

The smell of herbs and my muddled mind made it difficult to place the man.

"To have seen her now unseen, to fade her now evade," he continued to chant. His movement was fluid, supernatural, and he moved around the forest swiftly, like someone who knew the area.

Could it be Joe carrying me? Was he in so much pain over Infiniti's leaving that he'd try to keep me from Kase? I couldn't believe it.

My predicament was bad, but I wouldn't panic. The longer the guy, whoever it was, thought I was still asleep, the longer I had to come up with a plan. The vampire side of me wanted to attack, but I needed to keep myself in check. I'd never bitten anyone before, and being a dryad hybrid had allowed me to live a life sustained by food any human would eat. Even so, I'd choose steak over vegetables or fruit any day. Most vamps in New York succumbed to the temptation of bloodlust, but used their desire for power as an excuse to take advantage of humans. I wouldn't allow myself to lose control like them.

My father was different. He'd risen to power because of his ability to control his bloodlust. He'd been the only vampire to ever love a nymph or fae without losing control. He and my mother were great leaders because of their determination to live life following their hearts instead of the social expectations.

"To have seen her now unseen, to fade her now evade," the man said a little louder.

Pushing my supernatural senses outward, I took in a slow deep breath and listened for a heartbeat. A metallic scent filled my nose first, then my tastebuds tingled. The blood smelled old and rotten, like someone was dead. The sound of pounding feet filled my ears, matching my own racing heart, but there was no echo of another heartbeat.

That's when I knew: Marcel Cushing had kidnapped me.

The longer he ran, the clearer my thoughts became, and the farther we would be from the others. I had no way of knowing what time he'd grabbed me or how long we'd been gone, so I waited.

The terrain was uneven and with my powers extended around me, I could tell we were still surrounded by trees. Every now and then, tree limbs brushed over the fabric of my pants and coat. Being under the cover of trees made it seem darker, and if Marcel gave me and the others something to knock us out, there would have been no way to tell how late or early it was. Unless I could look up at the sky.

Kase had taught me a little about how to tell time using the stars and the moon while we admired the view from my telescope. It was difficult to imagine Marcel could take me from my friends without them hearing something. We were all supernaturals. Willa and Kase had super hearing, Bale's strength was impressive, Tarron had the ability to persuade, and Scarlet could cast spells and charms.

What if one of them heard a commotion? Or what if Marcel had made sure none of my friends could follow us? Impossible. Marcel may have been attention-hungry, but he hadn't said or done anything that made me think he was capable of violence.

My stomach turned, and my body seized, betraying me. We all suspected something was off about Marcel, and by inviting him to join us, I might have gotten them all killed.

Gasping, I pictured my friends—and my boyfriend—dead.

Marcel jerked to a stop. "Elle, I'm going to set you down, but don't try anything," he warned in a calm voice, like he was trying to talk me down from a ledge.

The forest's noises became deafening when I didn't respond. A breeze filled the air with the scent of pine and a rustling sound of needles brushing against each other. Creatures stirred in the trees, scurrying up and down branches. I could even hear the sound of water flowing in the distance.

"W-where are we?" My voice wavered, but I tried not to sound panicked.

"All you need to know is that we aren't in Havenwood Falls anymore," he answered and gently slid me off his shoulder and set me on the ground.

He wore a satisfied sneer.

My legs felt wobbly and weak, but I fought the urge to grab hold of something. The last thing I wanted was to come across as weak. I reached with my power, through my legs, into the ground for support. While the earth braced me and replenished my strength, I knew I needed to keep him talking.

I asked, "How?"

"Your adorable boyfriend and his family worked it all out for me," Marcel said arrogantly. "I'd prepared to put up a bigger fight, but when he surprised us all with front-row seats to the town's border, I knew the Court wouldn't give any notice to a blip on the supernatural radar."

Marcel Cushing wasn't the same little brother eager to please I remembered. We'd both changed, but I was afraid of who he'd become. Kase had set up an unforgettable night, and if someone in town felt a disturbance in the wards protecting Havenwood Falls, they might have dismissed it. No one would suspect anything until Friday. Our families expected us to be back Friday afternoon, but none of us would show up.

"Are the others—" My mouth wouldn't form the word *dead*.

Marcel's eyebrows pulled together, and his eyes narrowed. His lips pressed together, then he said, "You think I could do something like that?"

"I don't know." My voice came out raspy, and I was sure I'd struck a nerve. "I didn't think you could do *this*." My hand waved in front of me, motioning at where we stood.

"I did *this* for us," he said, sounding surprised that I didn't understand.

"F-for us, Marcel? What all did you do? How did you find me?" Something clicked for me in that moment, and the thought of my father sending Marcel to Havenwood Falls suddenly seemed absurd.

Marcel gritted his teeth together and took a deep breath through his nose, then he said, "Your stupid friends aren't dead, unless one of them is allergic to valerian."

My relief came out in a sigh. We'd all been drugged with a powerful sleeping herb. They would sleep through the night, so I had to think of a way to leave them clues. My pause sparked more anger from Marcel.

"There's no way they'll find us," he promised. "At least not before we get to New York. Then you won't want to come back here."

What Marcel said didn't make sense. Asking more questions would only make him angrier, so I decided to take a different approach. Marcel's family had become accustomed to other vampire clans stroking their ego over the years. The thirst for power burned as strongly as the thirst for blood in my father's world.

"You know, if you'd waited a few more months, you wouldn't have had to go to all this trouble." My mouth pulled into a tight smile.

Marcel's mouth spread into a wide smile, and he said, "Waited? I've never waited for you. Since the night I killed my brother, I've been searching for—no, hunting—you. When I killed Armand that night, I got a taste for what he was after. He was only pretending to join our bloodlines, but where he was weak, I'll be strong. I won't lose control like he did."

What he referred to was my deepest fear. My blood had the power to make vampires go mad, and it wasn't until I'd gotten too close to Marcel's brother that I found out the lengths a vampire would go to to get it. Armand hadn't even kissed me, and I knew something was terribly wrong. In my struggle to keep him from biting me, I was scratched. His thirst took over, and he was stronger than anyone I'd ever known. If it hadn't been for Marcel, I would have died that night.

"You saved me two years ago," I whispered. "But you're not saving me now."

Marcel may have thought he was strong enough to withstand the temptation of my blood, but after he killed his brother, I was swept away to Colorado. Because he'd been exposed to the scent of my blood, I wondered if it had been torturing him since then. If so, Marcel wouldn't be able to accept that I didn't want to be with him, or any vampire.

"That's where you're wrong," he growled. "Your parents have kept you from the best our world has to offer. I could give you everything you ever wanted. Your middle-class mutt can't offer you an eternity like I can. I'm saving you and me."

"What do you mean saving you?"

"Our family was shunned after word got out about Armand losing control. Your father exposed my mother as the mastermind, and I've been on the run since. With you at my side, I can restore the Cushing name and lead the New York clans to a new way of regulating the supernaturals in the area. Discovering Havenwood Falls was an accident, and the Court is on to something, but they aren't seeing the full potential. You're lucky I love you."

"If you really loved me, wouldn't you let me decide my own future?" Marcel's train of thought confused me. He only understood obsession.

"Love is making the hard choices," Marcel said flatly. "And let's be honest, the decisions you've made for yourself here are questionable. With Kase, you're weak, but with me you'd be the strongest you've ever been. The hybrid blood flowing in your veins needs to feed off a superior bloodline."

My mouth fell open.

Heat rose in my chest, up my neck, and into my cheeks. Something carnal inside me wanted to be released and let loose on Marcel. Squeezing my hands into fists, I was determined to stay in control. Channeling my physical strength into the ground under my feet, I released power instead of pulling it, and the earth vibrated. The sensation shocked and scared me, as well as Marcel.

Even though the power that left me felt chaotic and vengeful, it rippled back toward me and gave me a sense of peace. I knew the comfort I received came from someone else in the forest. But who?

"What did you just do?" Marcel asked in rage.

"I don't know. It was a first."

Marcel reached into his pocket, pulled out his fist, and said, "Well, I can't risk that happening again."

He opened his hand and blew a cloud of silvery dust into my face. It was the last thing I saw until sunrise.

~

Slowly, I regained consciousness, but I was hanging over Marcel's shoulder again. Careful not to move any other part of my body, I opened my eyes to survey the ground. It didn't look any different from any other forest floor.

Extending my supernatural powers outside of myself, I could hear rushing water, but there weren't any minds nearby I could read. My sense of smell picked up on a few rodents in the vicinity, maybe squirrels. But the sound of the stream was consistent, and eventually made me thirsty.

"Marcel?" My voice feigned grogginess.

It was light out, but until I saw the sun's position in the sky, I wouldn't be able to approximate the time. There was no way to know if the others would wake up with the new day or if the valerian would keep them sleeping through noon. Since Marcel bought it from Howe's Herbal Shoppe, I figured Ruby added a charm or spell to increase its power. Until I woke up slung over Marcel's shoulder, I had thought there'd been a possibility Joe bought it.

"Marcel," I said louder, when he hadn't slowed down. "I'm thirsty."

He kept walking at a steady pace, unfazed, and asked, "Thirsty for what?"

"Water."

Marcel turned right and took about twenty paces before letting me down next to the stream I'd heard. Kneeling down at its edge, I scooped water to my mouth with my hands. It was cold and refreshing. To help wake myself up, I splashed one handful of water on my face. Then, dipping my hands in the water, I tried to replicate the power I'd sent into the ground by mistake. The force I emitted fizzled in comparison.

"Okay, let's get moving," Marcel ordered impatiently.

"Can't we rest a few more minutes? You have to be tired, and I would love a snack, if you have one."

"If you'd drink from me, you could not only be sustained, but your powers would be strengthened by my bloodline. You'd be unstoppable, and I'd never leave your side," Marcel said as he knelt down beside me.

"That's not what I want. It's what you want. You're not fooling anyone. I know you want to feed on me," I spat, and in my peripheral vision, I caught a flash of white fur in the distance. Before I could call out, I felt something collide with my chin.

This time, it wasn't a powder or spell that knocked me unconscious, but Marcel's fist.

CHAPTER 10

KASE

Thursday morning I woke up in a haze. The amount of light shining through the tents' orange walls made them appear neon. My dreams had been filled with scenes of Elle and me in New York together. Closing my eyes, I attempted to fall back into my dreamland, but a shadow caught my attention as it moved quickly across the far wall.

"Kase?" Willa called softly, from outside the tent.

Unzipping my sleeping bag and then the front flap of the tent, I crawled out. "Hey, are you okay?"

"I'm fine, but when I woke up, Elle wasn't in our tent. I thought I'd check to see if you were with her," she explained.

Surveying the area around camp, I didn't see anyone, but I told myself it didn't mean she wasn't out exploring. My mind felt like it was full and empty at the same time, so I shook my head. With one hand, I lifted our tent's flap and counted sleeping bags. We were missing one. I looked back at Willa, and her eyes were wide with worry.

"I have a really bad feeling," she said ominously.

"Go wake Scarlet up, and I'll get the guys."

We all met back at the center of camp in less than three minutes. Tarron yawned into his elbow, probably hiding his morning breath. Scarlet scowled at everyone, but she'd never been much of a morning person. Bale rubbed his forehead like he had a headache.

We'd stayed up late the night before, but other than seeing Joe in the distance again, nothing had felt off. There weren't any more weird vibes coming from Marcel. I didn't think he would hurt Elle, and I naively kept telling myself they could be scouting the area.

"Elle never really sleeps through the night," Willa reasoned with a forced smile.

"You're right," Scarlet agreed in a monotone voice. "But we're *never really* drugged, either."

"Is that why my head feels like a snow globe a kid's shaken too much?" Bale asked and pressed his hands to his ears.

"Yeah," she answered and smacked her lips. "The aftertaste makes me think it was valerian, and the effects it's having leads me to believe it's the same charmed order I saw in my grandmother's ledger."

"He must have put it in the drinks last night," Bale guessed while picking up his backpack.

"The hot chocolate would have hidden the scent and flavor of the valerian, and if Marcel wanted to get as far as possible, he would have left right after we all fell asleep," Scarlet explained.

"He would have drugged her too. There's no way she'd go with him alone," I said through gritted teeth, and began to pace. "At this rate on foot, they could be ten to twenty miles away. And I gave Marcel the perfect opportunity to get a head start."

"You can't blame yourself," Willa consoled. "But you can go find her."

"You're right. Without a cell signal, you'll have to shift and run back to town to tell Dad. You're the fastest."

Bale cleared his throat, and Willa added, "I'm the fastest who won't scare the crap out of tourists if they see me running through the forest."

"Accurate," he said with a nod.

In wolf form, Willa could get to town and risk being seen by the public. As a dragon running down Main Street, Bale would put the supernatural community in jeopardy. There have been some wild stories told by humans in town, but they'd been diluted into rumors and legends.

Willa didn't excuse herself and take the time to undress, but shifted out in the open. Her clothes ripped to shreds as her body supernaturally morphed into a black wolf with golden eyes. Before the shimmering magic disappeared, she'd taken off at full speed, back the way we'd come the night before.

"So we'll need to split up if we want to cover more area. Scarlet, will you go with Bale?" I asked.

Scarlet scoffed at me, and said, "I can search by myself if we need to cover more area. I'm not scared of anything in this forest."

"I don't doubt that, but I need someone to calm Bale down in case he's the one who finds Marcel. I want to wring Marcel's neck, and Tarron will go with me to keep me calm."

"Which way do you want us to head?" Bale asked, and strapped his backpack on.

Peering into the forest, I had a gut feeling, so I told him, "Northwest. Anywhere south of us will be deeper within the town's borders. Fanning out northward will be our best bet of picking up their scent."

"Got it." Bale nodded, then met my eyes. "If we find them, there's a 99% chance we won't have cell reception. How do you want me to—"

"I want you to save Elle, period," I gritted out, and my chest pounded anxiously. "If you have to shift and airlift her and Scarlet, do it. It's less likely someone will see a dragon out there, and if they do, we'll take care of them after Elle is safe."

"My mom has cast memory charms on a few of the citizens of Havenwood Falls," Scarlet pointed out. "All Court-approved, of course."

"Okay, if you don't find them or pick up their scent in two to three hours, start heading back here. If one of us doesn't show up, then we can assume the other is tailing Elle and Marcel." Grabbing my own backpack, I slipped it on.

We started walking toward the forest at the far edge of the field. The closer we got to the tree line, the farther away we veered from each other in an effort to cover more ground. The spring day would be shorter than a summer day, so we'd need to move fast. Once Tarron and I reached the cover of a towering pine tree, he stopped.

"Give me the pack," Tarron ordered with a somber tone. "I'll only hold you back, and if you're in your wolf form, you can use all of your powers to find her. I promise to keep moving, and I won't be too far behind."

"Are you sure?"

But he was right. If anything happened to Elle because I'd been a second too slow, I'd blame myself, and maybe everyone else, too.

"Go," he insisted.

Shifting mid-stride into a black wolf, I ran faster than I'd ever run before.

CHAPTER 11

ELLE

The taste of coppery, tangy blood was the first thing I noticed when I woke. Licking along my bottom lip, I found one side swelled, as if I'd tucked a gumball behind it. The second thing I noticed was rocky ground underneath me, but I wasn't outside. Darkness loomed around me. It was as if the sun, moon, and stars had blinked out of existence. My ability to see in the dark didn't come in handy, because there wasn't anything or anyone that I could see. Stone walls surrounded me.

"Hello?" I whispered, and my voice echoed, like I was in a cave. "M-M-Marcel," I called a little louder, pushing past my fear. Had I been buried alive?

The idea of Marcel entering the room scared me, but the thought of being left in a tomb of sorts without a way out terrified me more. There was no way to tell how long I'd been unconscious until I made it outside.

When I pushed myself up from the ground, my muscles groaned in protest. My neck especially felt sore, and when I rubbed from my hairline to my throat I understood why. Two small scars, one next to the other, marked where someone had punctured my carotid artery. In a moment, I went from being thankful I hadn't been killed to being angry Marcel had taken my blood without consent. Searching the cavern for an exit, I noticed an overlap of rock along one of the walls.

"Stay there," a raspy voice ordered. It had to be Marcel, but I couldn't see him.

Vampires had a reputation on television for not caring about where they acquired their life source. In movies, bloodsuckers were charming murderers or glittering celebrity crushes. But in the social circles my father had been raised in, it was crucial to maintain a pure bloodline. A vampire only sired a human worthy of their name, unless they didn't have control of their bloodlust. Then, once turned, they fed on supernaturals.

My father's influence in New York came from being remarkably disciplined. Most vampires survived by more base desires. His clan had elected him leader because he earned the love and consent of a dryad. With my mother as his life source, my father did gain a vitality other vampires longed for, but he saw it as a gift. Feeding on a supernatural against their will had serious consequences, physically and emotionally.

"Why?" My voice croaked as tears streamed down my cheeks, not in fear, but in shame. Why hadn't I fought him earlier? Maybe I could have escaped.

"I don't have to answer to you," he snapped in anger, and began chanting, "To have seen her now unseen, to fade her now evade."

The sweet scent of herbs filled the cavern, and the sound of his voice bounced off the walls differently than mine. While he was distracted, my hands reached for the wall closest to me, and I made my way around the room slowly until I came to an opening.

"Don't," he snarled. "If you try to leave, I won't be able to control myself. I'll hunt you until one of us is dead."

And there it was—the consequence.

The same way a human's taste grew into an addiction without boundaries, a vampire's taste ended in death without a mutual consent. When Marcel struck me, he'd probably tried to resist the scent of blood emanating from my lip, but eventually lost control.

Unsure if I even had the energy to fight back, I knelt down and tried to reach out magically through the stone floor. What power I had built up in my fingertips searched for life under the rock. Sensing a conduit, my power surged into the earth. The cave rumbled, and dust fell from the ceiling, except at the center of the room.

When the dust settled I looked up. Marcel clung to the ceiling with his hands unnaturally and skittered across the stone like an insect. He stopped above me and began to hum to himself. Spiderman movies would never be the same.

I ignored his tune and focused on the sound of my heartbeat until it filled my ears. Closing my eyes, I tried to center myself. I thought of Kase and the others. Like Kase was in the next room, I heard his thoughts call my name. *Elle.*

In that moment, I'd known my physical and mental strength were waning. I had to be hallucinating. If I stayed in the cave much longer, I would never be able to escape. Making a move soon would be the only chance I had. Once outside, I had a feeling I could find safety, but I'd have to outrun Marcel. With my supernatural blood flowing in his veins, Marcel's reactions and powers would be unpredictable.

"I know what you're thinking," Marcel's voice gritted in anger.

I shuddered.

He'd been able to read my mind since he'd tasted my blood. How could I have forgotten that? I'd never be able to get away from him.

"That's right," he hissed. "And now that you're conscious, we'll climb over this mountain and meet up with the transportation I've arranged."

"I can barely move around this room. How do you expect me to climb a mountain?" I argued, irritated.

Marcel let go of the wall and landed a few feet away from me. As he inhaled, his nostrils flared, his chest expanded, and a maniacal smile spread across his lips. His tongue swept over his fanged teeth.

"I would offer to carry you, but I'm afraid you'd prove too enticing at such a close distance. It was all I could do to stop myself before," he said with a laugh. "I don't want you dead. Eventually, I know I'll convince you to feed, but until then, I'll settle for you to be in a weakened state at my side. I can be patient."

Marcel's brother died trying to get a taste of my blood. I found myself curious, like someone drawn to look in the direction of a car crash, and asked, "How did you stop yourself?"

"Oh, I've been practicing for two years," he said as he crossed his arms over his chest and leaned against the cave wall. "That night you left, when my brother lost control, I fought to have you for myself. Your parents dragged you away, and I can't blame you for leaving with them, but you left a part of yourself with me."

"You did save me from Armand, and I'm thankful for that, but I never gave you the impression that we were anything more than friends. Why would you hold on to the idea that we were anything more?" My voice softened, trying to keep either of us from getting angry.

"No, you're not listening." His smile faded into a frown. "You are a chalice among coffee mugs. I've had a part of you with me every day we've been apart. Your injuries from two years ago left traces of blood at our home. Mother insisted on a deep cleaning, but I managed to steal away a piece of fabric with just enough of your blood to help me learn to control my bloodlust. During my search for you, I conditioned myself, making me stronger than my brother ever was. And I will drink from my chalice while the vampires who shunned me slurp from their mugs."

The pieces were slowly fitting together, but I didn't have the picture of the puzzle to refer to. Marcel must have been going mad trying to build up a tolerance to the scent of my blood since I moved to Havenwood Falls. He'd driven himself to this point. His search for me started as a crusade. He wanted me to choose him, but in the last two years, he'd become homicidal.

"So the only way out of here is with you."

"You're catching on." Marcel nodded, and his hand reached out to touch my face. I flinched, and he forced the issue and tucked my hair behind my ear. "The charm I'm using should hide us from your annoying friends. I'd hate to have to kill them, but I'm sure you'll cooperate so I don't have to resort to such violence."

And I would. I'd go wherever Marcel wanted to keep the others safe, but when he mentioned remembering my friends I suddenly realized we hadn't crossed the town's border. If we'd passed the wards, Marcel wouldn't have been able to recall Havenwood Falls or anyone he met while visiting. If he'd gotten turned around in the forest, maybe there was still hope the others would find me.

Marcel took my hand and led me out of the cave. Surprised by the sight of stars in the sky, I focused on searching for the North Star. There was no way to tell exactly where we were, but I could figure out which direction we were headed. Unlike Kase, I hadn't grown up wandering these forests. The names of the different peaks and rock formations were lost on me.

"You must not let go," Marcel ordered. "The climb is steep, but as you've witnessed, I have enough strength from your blood to cling to anything. I won't let you fall."

His eyes gazed at me longingly, and I shivered. His bloodlust would never be satiated by me, or anyone for that matter. He'd given in to the darkest part of being a vampire. There was no way to tell if he'd be able to control himself the next time he decided to drink from me.

Marcel clenched his jaw in anger at hearing my thoughts.

"Let me make myself clear. If you do let go or make a run for it, I won't bother going after you. I'll find Kase and drink him until there's no life left in him."

After I nodded my understanding, he yanked me forward.

We were already a third of the way up the mountain when we passed a beautiful formation of aspen trees. Their bare branches waved at me as if saying goodbye. My heart ached at the thought of leaving these mountains. Then a feeling of calm came over me. The sadness wasn't gone, but something outside myself shared their confidence, their peace. I supernaturally knew everything would work out.

My eyes darted to Marcel, expecting him to respond to my

thoughts, but he didn't. The thoughts and feelings being shared with me were from someone else out in the forest, and they were somehow protected. We were definitely still in Havenwood Falls.

Reach within and distract him.

The words were clear, but I had no clue who they were coming from. Like my doubt had been heard, the voice responded.

Trust me and flee.

So I started rambling. "How do you think my family will react to what you've done? You have to know my father will not be happy. And even if your mom put you up to this, like she did Armand, you can't explain away feeding on me without my consent."

Marcel stilled, and his grip on my hand tightened. It hurt. He turned to face me, and gave me a devilish grin. "Oh, my mother didn't have anything to do with this. She's grown complacent over the last year, alone. With you at my side, we'll take over leading a nest of our own, and eventually you'll convince your family to join us. Your parents don't need to know about our little mishap. It was your fault anyway. If you hadn't fallen for my brother, none of this would have happened. I had to kill him to protect you. I'll kill anyone who threatens to separate us."

His last words were a promise. Understanding he meant my friends, I took a step up the mountain in his direction.

Suddenly, a ball of light revealed itself ahead of us. It was bigger than a firefly, but smaller than a flashlight. Power emanated from the glowing source, and I instinctively knew it was the entity trying to help me. The problem was I didn't know if it wanted me to follow it or flee in the opposite direction.

Remembering Marcel's last words to me, I considered the direction we were headed. If he'd been telling the truth, he'd pursue whatever or whoever flickered in the distance. Before my thoughts could betray me, I bolted away from the light and Marcel.

My hand jerked out of his, and the magic hiding us shattered.

"Elle," he howled.

My legs struggled to stay under me. Running down the

mountain, my upper body wanted to tumble forward as loose stones and rocks skittered underfoot. The sound of Marcel running faded behind me, and I pushed my worry for whoever saved me to the back of my mind. Marcel was jacked on my blood, and after he ripped whatever that light was to shreds, he'd come after me.

My best chance of escaping Marcel would be to get back to the Havenwood Falls border. Hopefully, the wards would trip and the Court would send reinforcements. The stars told me I was headed south when I glanced up, and the moon had almost rotated out of view. It was around midnight. The next thing I needed to listen for was water. It would be easier to follow the current to the town's waterfall, and the noise would muffle the sound of my boots pounding the ground.

It felt like I'd been running for hours when I finally found the babbling water. My heart, mind, and body raced.

The stream grew wider the farther I ran toward Havenwood Falls. Something supernatural called from ahead. Whether it was the town itself or the people in it, the desire to be home overwhelmed me. All the while, the thought of Marcel following me made my stomach turn. All I could do was push forward.

Rock formations and trees along the water's edge helped keep me hidden, but the sound of a twig breaking sent me scrambling for cover. I noticed a white wolf in the distance running on the other side of the water. Joe. He was too far away to have produced the noise. On my side of the river, two large bristlecone pines had a narrow opening where their twisted trunks entwined. Sliding into the crevasse, I pressed my hand against my mouth, trying to silence my breathing.

Oh my dear, do not fear. A singsong voice invaded my thoughts.

The thought was followed by a warm sense of peace. In the arms of the trees, I felt protected. I knew, because of my mother's dryad blood, I had a connection with the earth. Eventually, I'd bond with a tree and be connected more permanently.

We are of one kind, and of one mind. I want to help you, because we are so few. There is a place for you here, there is no reason for tears.

"Where are you?" Whispering, I dared to peek out of my hiding place.

A small light, the size of a luna moth, floated in the air around the tree.

"You are beautiful. Are you the one who helped me earlier?"

Your need called out to me.

"Thank you, but I don't understand how we are of one kind. There's no one like me."

We may be different in body, but our purpose is to protect all trees. Your heart is pure, but your mind unsure. The place of your true intention will also be your destination. Do not fret in this hiding place. You are safe.

And she had made me feel safe. Her calm, steady emotions flooded me. "Who are you?"

Cyllene, the oldest of our kind in this forest growth. Fading with my true love, soon rest will claim us both. Until then, I protect the worthy, both man and tree.

"Before, you mentioned my destination. Do you sense where I belong? I thought I had to go back to New York, but after tonight I'm not sure I'll ever want to. I don't know if we'll even survive. What would happen if I chose to stay in Havenwood Falls?"

Cyllene was constantly moving. She, and her light, were warm and inviting. Her grace and wisdom reminded me of my own mother, but Cyllene's presence felt ancient.

Born of blood and born of earth, your path has varied since your birth. Home is heart and heart is home. Roots will grow deep, there's no cause to roam. Follow your heart. Protect and guard, the trees are not your whole but part.

Her rhyming helped me remember her words, but they didn't help me interpret them. My life always felt like I was balancing on a tightrope, but I'd looked forward to bonding with a tree so I could feel rooted. Maybe the reason I'd been struggling to leave Havenwood Falls was because I shouldn't leave. My heart belonged to Kase, my friends, and this mountain.

"Elle!" Marcel's voice thundered from a distance, making me jump. My head bumped the underside of one of the trees.

"Can you feel how far away he is?" Panicked, I pulled myself out into the open and hoped Cyllene could tell me how much time I had before Marcel reached me.

You've reached the earth your heart longs for. No need to run, merely open the door.

"Thank you." My appreciation fell flat, because my fight-or-flight response was to run into the forest, away from Marcel.

Cyllene had told me I didn't have to run, but if he caught up with me, I feared I might not survive his wrath. My eyes searched the mountain for the door Cyllene mentioned, but there were only trees and boulders in sight. The river's current grew stronger, and a light mist filled the air. The spray was shockingly cold against my skin and coated my jacket with beads of water. The cool moisture made me feel alive, and I increased my pace.

The wet stone underfoot made it difficult to get traction, and I slipped. Falling face forward, my chin hit rock. My hands flung forward too late and scraped against the rock. The impact took my breath away.

When I shook my head, my jaw ached. Pushing up to get my feet underneath me, I glanced at the bank of the river and recognized the door Cyllene had referenced. It wasn't a plank of wood with a knob or a metal gate with a latch. A few feet in front of me, a majestic pine tree stood with its roots exposed. Some of the roots reached into the river, and it looked like the tree was dipping its toe in the water. The other roots spread over a boulder the size of Kase's truck. They reached through cracks in the rock for earth. One space between the roots appeared to be large enough for me to walk through, and the trunk above reached over fifty feet high with a canopy of limbs stretched over the river.

"Where do you think you're going?" Marcel spat from somewhere behind me.

"Leave me alone!" What I'd intended to shout came out as more of a cry. Looking down at myself, I saw I was covered in mud. "I will never be yours. Can't you see I belong here?"

A laugh mixed with a sob escaped me.

Still terrified, I knew I was meant to be at the bank of the river. The tree in front of me, the water flowing beside me, and the earth beneath me were my home.

Elle, I'm here. Kase's thoughts reached me. My head turned, not sure where I'd find him. He had to be close.

The surprise on my face alerted Marcel to my thoughts. I'd given Kase away. Marcel crouched down and surveyed the area.

On the other side of the tree. Kase couldn't read my mind, but it felt like he knew exactly what I was thinking.

My feet shuffled back a few steps, until Marcel spotted my movement. He hissed at me, and I froze. The doorway between the roots was only a few feet away. I wasn't sure what would happen once I passed through, but my heart longed to find out. It was enough knowing Kase would be there waiting for me.

The sound of rock colliding with the mountainside echoed from above us. Marcel looked up, and I darted for the tree's protection. A white wolf, Joe, moved in on the scene, distracting Marcel while Kase stepped under the roots from the other side. Having Kase, my black wolf, at my side sent relief through me. It wasn't until Kase growled and flashed his canines that I realized we weren't out of danger.

"I hear they eat dog in other countries. I've never been curious what it tastes like until now." Anger oozed from Marcel's words when he glanced back at me to find Kase.

Marcel would have a fight on his hands with Kase and Joe, but I wouldn't underestimate his power. I had power of my own. Broadening my stance, I pressed my boots into the earth and spread my arms out. My fingertips touched the roots of the tree, and I reached outward for a source to connect with. Still weak, I hoped to meet the life source the roots were joined to, but something greater latched onto me.

Marcel's heightened abilities would eventually end in Kase's and Joe's deaths, and maybe my own. I had to protect us all. My heart longed for Kase and Joe to live, but it also yearned to protect this place from supernaturals who would abuse their power, or the power of the falls.

Unaware of how deep the tree's roots went or how far they reached, I called out with everything inside of me. I pleaded for help, not for myself, but for the mountain, my friends, and the falls. Magic tingled in my toes first, as if testing me. Power slowly made its way up my frame, and the surge filled me until it couldn't be held inside any longer. Flowing from beyond the tree's roots up into and through me, I accepted all of the magic and allowed it to use me as a vessel.

The strength of the stones making up the mountain made me feel indestructible. The speed of the water flowing in the river energized me. The awareness of the trees and the depth of the earth made me aware of everything and everyone around me.

I realized the amount of power made available to me could protect us all and that I hadn't merely bonded with the tree above me.

I'd bonded with the entire mountain.

Marcel lunged forward, rage etched on his face. A roar erupted from his lungs. Connecting to the mountain must have severed my blood bond to Marcel, or he would have been more careful before attacking me. Instinctively, I reached out with my power to a boulder. The giant rock lurched forward, groaning as it rolled in Marcel's direction. He leapt into the air over the boulder, avoiding what would have been a crushing weight. The near miss didn't rattle me, but Marcel's escape put him in closer proximity to Kase, who'd protectively bounded in front of me.

Marcel's eyes looked from me to the black wolf, and I didn't need to read his mind to know he had a new target. A low growl rumbled from Kase. The two stood facing off under a canopy of branches. I reached down, searching to communicate with the roots under me. The mountainside answered. One of the branches over Marcel popped and creaked, then broke loose. Marcel didn't have time to evade the attack, and the chunk of lumber struck him across his shoulders and knocked him to the ground.

An angry war cry erupted from Marcel as he pushed the branch to the side and laid eyes on me. He lunged with super speed, and I reacted by lifting one arm, summoning the waters to rise from the river. As I moved my hand in the air toward Marcel, a wave of water crashed into him.

Being swatted to the ground like a fly, Marcel had been knocked prostrate and soaked. He shook his head, and drops of water were flung in every direction. As he gathered his senses, his grimace slowly twisted into gaping awe. His eyebrows pulled together in fear. Marcel resembled a drowned rat, and when he twitched, I sensed he was about to run away.

My will communed with the mountainside, both reaching the same conclusion—Marcel must be stopped. The earth beneath me shook, and power vibrated in my chest. Both of my hands jutted forward, reaching out in front of me. The roots underground untangled and stretched up through the dirt to chase after and bind Marcel to the forest floor.

Thin leathery brown vines broke through the soil and wrapped themselves around Marcel's wrists and ankles. He bellowed in discomfort, laid out on his back, a wet, muddy mess. The trees around me waited for further instructions, and it blew my mind that I'd been entrusted with so much power. Kneeling down, I pressed my hands into the soil and said, "Thank you."

A bark sounded from behind me, and Kase nodded in the direction of the river. We had company. Joe was being followed by Willa, Scarlet, Tarron, Bale, Sheriff Kasun, and my parents. They all stood on the other side of the river, with a front-row view of what had just happened, each with their mouths hanging open.

CHAPTER 12

KASE

The Havenwood Falls High bell rang, signaling the end of the first school day back after spring break. My plan was to meet Elle after school and distract her long enough to carry out my epic promposal. She'd probably want to lose herself in a good book, but I needed to play to her adventurous side.

"Elle!" Calling out to her in public was usually something she hated, but today she turned to face me and smiled.

Over the last few days, with the help of her parents and friends, Elle had mostly figured out her new abilities, including a couple we hadn't expected. Her demonstration when releasing Marcel into my dad's custody was impressive. At one point, Marcel, roots still holding him, dangled ten feet in the air. I'd witnessed her power in the past, but we hadn't anticipated her control of water and rocks, or how she could sense things in the soil.

"What are you up to?" Her eyes narrowed suspiciously.

Focusing on anything but my plans, I answered, "I'm hoping to find out what you're up to. Want to hang out this afternoon?"

A few people looked our way when I took her hand. Students hustled around us in the hallway, and the latest gossip caught everyone's ears. Of course, Elle's kidnapping had remained a secret.

The Court didn't like the idea of the supernatural community finding out a vampire made his way into town under false pretenses. They were under the impression Marcel arrived to vacation for the week. He left town with an official escort, and it was clear he'd never be welcome in Havenwood Falls again.

We discovered Mr. and Mrs. Martin boarded a flight on Thursday, after Mr. Martin explained to his wife that Marcel Cushing had been missing for two years. He hadn't told his wife or Elle about the Cushing family being excommunicated two years ago, because he thought Elle would blame herself.

"I'd love to do something. What are you thinking?" she asked me with furrowed brows. After I opened the door for her, Elle stepped outside. She waited for me to follow, then slid her hand up to my elbow and wrapped her arm around mine.

My chest filled with warmth. Giving up on Elle was never an option. I'd never stop loving her.

Elle Martin was everything I wanted in a girl. I just hadn't figured it out until she walked into my life. She was strong, confident, thoughtful, protective, and the most gorgeous woman I'd ever met. She paused mid-step and looked up at me with a smirk.

She caught me.

"Come on, Elle." My lips pulled together in embarrassment. "How about I take you out for coffee? I'll even throw in a scone."

The simplicity of my invitation was key. It couldn't imply anything more or she'd become suspicious.

Elle winked at me and said, "Why not? I'll take what I can get."

We walked to our cars, parked side by side at the back of the lot.

"Wanna ride together?" Driving my truck would be more comfortable.

"Are you offering to drive or ride?" she asked.

"Drive."

"Okay," she agreed with a shrug. So I reached for the handle of the passenger door. My dad and brothers had taught me to be a gentleman. I held a hand out for her backpack, and when she gave it to me, I tossed it into the back.

I started the truck and pulled out into the flow of traffic. A ton of the cars crossed Main Street and parked at Burger Bar for an "after school special." They thought they were pulling a fast one on us by calling the basket of fried food that, but Tate had filled me in on the teen dramas that used to be televised before I was born.

After maneuvering out of the parking lot, I relaxed a little. Getting to our destination after our friends was crucial. So I'd have to take the scenic route to Coffee Haven. I turned left on Fourth Street and waited for Elle to say something. Not one word came out of her mouth.

Taking a right on Blackstone Road, I could feel the curiosity bubbling inside her. She peered out the window, not looking my direction. When I turned right on Eleventh Street, Elle relaxed. We were headed toward the coffee shop again. The town square wasn't too busy, but I noticed my brother Conall in his patrol car in front of Backwoods. He was probably radioing Tate to warn them we were close.

Pulling into a space across the street from Coffee Haven, I kept the truck running, with the heat on, and unbuckled my seatbelt. "I know you're going to think I'm cheesy, but I'm thankful to have you in my life. I love you."

Shifting in her seat, Elle faced me and said, "I love you too."

"Remember when I promised to never hurt you?" I leaned closer to her and lifted my hand to her neck.

She nodded.

"I meant it, Elle." Reaching back behind my seat, I pulled out a white box—smaller than a shoe box and bigger than a jewelry box.

Elle's eyes widened, and her lips parted as she accepted it. "Do you want me to open it now?"

"Sure." My smile felt like it was going to split my cheeks.

She pulled the tape off and opened the lid. Beneath the tissue paper, a soft glow illuminated the inside of the box. Elle folded the thin paper back to reveal a white globe the size of my fist.

The moon had become a symbol of something more for us, and the night-light would always remind her of my promise. Capturing the moon was impossible, but I'd never give up on making Elle's dreams come true. She'd decided to stay in Havenwood Falls and take college courses online. While her parents were going to miss her, they supported her decision. Her mother understood on a personal level, and her father conceded after setting a few ground rules. Elle promised to finish college and pursue a career. She also agreed to visit New York once a quarter.

Elle pulled the globe out of the packaging, revealing a folded letter underneath. "What's this?"

"Read it." Even after everything that had happened in the last week, I knew she needed to read it.

She carefully unraveled the paper. It was plain printer paper, clearly printed from home, and Elle's head tilted when she recognized the logo, a purple square with a white torch at its center, at the bottom of the email. Elle's eyes swept over the first few lines, then she looked up at me.

"You've been accepted to NYU," she said, but her voice grew higher at the end like it was a question.

"Yeah."

She looked back at the paper, and wouldn't meet my eyes. "Are you leaving?"

Sliding my fingers to her chin, I lifted it. "Not unless you are. I wanted you to know that I'd planned to follow you to New York. I'd go anywhere with you."

Elle leaned forward and kissed me. Her lips searched mine, and I was tempted to forget the elaborate scheme I'd set in motion. Bale and Tarron had asked Scarlet and Willa to prom before spring break, so when I told them I wanted to ask Elle, they all insisted on helping.

Gently pulling away from Elle, I cleared my throat and said, "How about I start by following you into Coffee Haven?"

"Sounds like a plan, but what about this?" She smiled and waved the acceptance letter.

"I'll be taking classes online, and staying here to help with the store and patrolling."

Elle gave me a peck on the cheek, affirming my decision, and jumped out of the truck.

As we approached the coffee shop, I held my breath. Willa convinced me to let them handle most of the details because she was sure Elle would read my mind and figure everything out. This year's prom had a Wonderland theme, and I told Willa I wanted to ask Elle to prom during a tea party.

Before I could open the shop's door, Tarron bound out of it in a green top hat and jacket. He waved us inside, to one of the larger tables in the corner. Each of our friends wore some sort of costume. Willa sported a vest and pocket watch, Scarlet's cardigan was pink and purple stripes, and Bale had a yellow T-shirt on with a blue bowtie.

"Are you Tweedle Dum?" Elle asked Bale with a snicker.

"Don't push it," he warned. "I'm Tweedle Dee. I have an identical outfit for your boyfriend. He can be Tweedle Dum."

As hard as I tried to stay straight-faced, I couldn't, and neither could anyone else. We all started laughing. The teacup in front of Elle almost toppled over when she hit the table top with her hand. A teapot, with a card hanging from the handle, rattled. Willa had written *Open Me* on the card, and made similar decorative cards for the food and drink on the table.

We finally settled down, and Scarlet poured everyone tea while Tarron passed a plate of pastries. Elle reached for the lid of the teapot in front of her, and a string had been attached to the inside. She lifted and lifted, until the end of the string revealed two prom tickets. That was my cue.

Pulling a poster board out from under the table, I held it up for her to read. It said, *I wonder if you'll go to prom with me? Please, don't drive me mad, say yes!*

"Of course, yes," Elle said, so elated she hugged my neck.

It helped having a sister who could convince your buddies to dress up, but it was Tate who'd worked his magic with the markers. He'd always been the most creative of us all. And Conall probably worked out all the food and drinks. Then there was Elle. She lit up the room, and I was lucky to be close enough for her light to shine on me.

EPILOGUE

ELLE

Wonderland

*P*rom night had finally come. I'd been anticipating the
dance for months, and the Havenwood Falls High
School gymnasium had been transformed into Wonderland. Kase
and I walked through a curtain of moss to find the gym
transformed. Willa and Tarron walked in front of us, determined to
find a table for the group. Folding chair surrounded life-sized
mushrooms, for students to sit and eat at. The centerpieces were
made up of toppling teapots. A chessboard had been set up at the
center of the court for a dance floor, and an area beside the DJ
booth was covered with green turf to play flamingo croquet.

Bale whistled from behind us, calling attention to the buffet
tables. He and Scarlet went to grab snacks. Giant playing cards
blocked off the bleachers, and the walls were covered in greenery
and white roses sloppily painted red.

My own dress had been inspired by the roses. I wore a strapless
white gown with a black floral print. The silver, glittering heels I
wore had been a gift from my father—the actual surprise he had
sent during spring break, not Marcel. They'd been delivered after
my friends and I left for our camping trip. I'd thought about

throwing them away, but they were too gorgeous to waste and went perfectly with my dress.

Kase had given me a wrist corsage made up of red roses. His tux was traditional black, and I'd pinned a red rose to his lapel. He looked more handsome in formal attire than I remembered.

Tarron and Willa waved us over to a table. Once we were all settled, and Bale had come back with thirds, Willa asked everyone about their favorite high school moments. We laughed about the time Tarron messed up Valentine's Day by persuading Ana Novak to be loving. Kase stayed quiet, but he didn't hold back his thoughts from me about missing Joe. His best friend had tracked me and Marcel and led Kase to us. Kase wanted to make it up to Joe and help him find Infiniti, if he could. Bale had us rolling when he started to try to explain who was who in our Scooby Gang. And then I asked everyone where they wanted to be in ten years.

The whole table fell silent. The beat of the music could be felt in the air, and the crowd's chatter had become white noise. I'd hoped the question would spark hope and maybe bring us closer together, but instead it created some unexpected space.

"Fine, I'll go first," I started, planting my elbows on the table. "In ten years, I still want to be friends with all of you."

I knew Willa was staying close to home for college, and Tarron was taking a gap year. Scarlet would be working at her family's store. When I glanced at Bale, he met my eyes and clenched his jaw.

"I want to be a mechanic," he blurted.

Everyone looked back and forth at each other, not sure how to respond. Scarlet even looked surprised. Kase was the first to find words.

"That's great, man. I'd trust my truck in your capable hands any day."

"Our truck," Willa corrected.

We all laughed, and before I could catch my breath, Kase scooted his chair back.

"Do you want to dance?" he asked and held his hand out.

"You know it." I took his hand and dragged him behind me to the checkered dance floor.

When we reached the center, Kase wrapped his arms around me. Above us, the Cheshire Cat sat on top of a spinning disco ball. Soon, Tarron and Willa, and Bale and Scarlet were dancing around us. The teen anthem faded into a classic, Mr. Moonlight. I looked up at Kase, and he smiled.

"How did you—"

Kase cut me off with a soft, lingering kiss, and it brought a smile to my face.

"I will always promise you the moon, Elle Martin."

ABOUT THE AUTHOR

Writing unique adventures with heart.

Kallie Ross has a passion for writing that has become an adventure in itself. She desires to create unique young adult fiction that incorporates legend, conjecture, fantasy, and conviction.

In addition to loving her life as a writer, Kallie adores being a wife, mother, friend, and teacher. She began her creative journey with books, a blog, a podcast, and lots of caffeine. Ross never imagined her own adventure would be filled with so many wonderful people or words!

KallieRoss.com

@KallieRoss {Instagram & Twitter}

Kallie Ross Books {Facebook}

ACKNOWLEDGMENTS

Thank you, Kristie Cook, for trusting me with the Kasuns. Kase and Elle are a story I've been thinking about since writing *Written in the Stars*. These two deserved to find love. I couldn't have finished this story without Morgan Wylie pushing me to write and holding me accountable. She is a wonderful friend and great writer. Go read her books!

Thank you, Rose Garcia, for letting me borrow Joe. Your patience with me, and love for Joe's story, made it possible for Kase and Elle to work out their story. All the Havenwood Falls authors are so supportive, and their input is always appreciated. Thanks to all of you.

Jessica Gibson was also a huge encouragement. I couldn't keep all my thoughts together without Jessi's help. She's my brainstorming buddy, as well as the one who keeps me calm when a deadline is looming.

My family is always supportive of my writing, and I am truly grateful for that blessing. Whether I'm hashing out an outline over breakfast or talking through a scene in the car line, my husband and kids always speak into my storytelling.

Lastly, I want to thank the Havenwood Falls readers. Your enthusiasm for this world keeps me dreaming up stories and writing them down. Thank you!

BLURRED LINES

DANIELE LANZAROTTA

HAVENWOOD FALLS HIGH

Blurred Lines

DANIELE LANZAROTTA

~ A Havenwood Falls Young Adult Novella ~

ALSO BY DANIELE LANZAROTTA

Academy of the Fallen Series – YA

Wide Awake

Nephilim

Sins of the Fallen

Forsaken

Sudden Hope Novels – YA

Sudden Hope

Catch Me If I Fall

Imprinted Souls Series – YA

Imprinted Souls

Bloodlust

Divine Ashes

Blood Bound

Shattered Souls

Reawakening Series – YA

Venom

Blood Ties (Coming 2019)

A Mermaid's Curse Trilogy – Adult

Insatiable

Fated

Unbreakable

Individual Titles

The Right Kind of Wrong – Adult

Lost Souls – YA

The Sinners – Adult

To the readers who fell in love with Heidi and Zane.

CHAPTER 1

ZANE

I sit on the roof at the house across the street from Heidi's and stare at her window from a distance. I've been sitting here for hours, and the open window has become this cruel joke. I can't stand knowing that she's right there, yet that I must stay away. Her lights are out, and the music is blasting. As much as I hate to admit it, I miss the pop songs she used to listen to. At least those had lyrics that could be understood. These new songs that she seems to like now sound like someone is screaming incoherently at you.

"Well, well." I hear a female's voice from behind me. I turn around to find Gabriella wearing a blue dress and high-heeled boots. She annoyingly taps her foot on the roof. Her arms are crossed, but she smiles when my eyes meet hers. "It's about time you decided to listen to me and check in on your girl. And thank you for clearing the snow off the roof this time."

I glare at Gabriella, the angel who has been keeping an eye on Heidi while I serve my punishment for bringing her back to life.

"She is not my girl," I say in a cold tone, to hide the fact that I wish more than anything that she could be.

Gabriella gives me a dramatic eye roll, then extends her hand.

"I need your jacket," she says. I take off my leather jacket and hand it to her. She lays it down and sits on top of it.

"Seriously?" I ask.

She shrugs. "It's not like you really need it. And I'd hate for my dress to get dirty."

"Yeah, because that seems like something you should be worried about," I say.

"Watch your tone, angel," she says jokingly. "I'm over here helping you out of the goodness of my heart, when I really shouldn't. You asked for help, and I volunteered to be her guardian angel, but I should be reporting all the stupid little things she has been pulling. Yet I'm keeping them a secret."

I look away and sigh.

"How is she?" I ask.

She chuckles. "Do you mean since the last update I gave you just a few days ago? When I begged you to come?"

Growing impatient, I just shake my head. "It's not exactly easy for me to leave without them knowing. They think I'm watching over someone else right now." I pause. "Now can you please just stop torturing me and answer the question?" I beg.

"Such a funny request coming from someone who is known to be incapable of giving straight answers," she says in a sarcastic tone.

I glare at her.

Gabriella puts her hands up. "Fine . . . fine. She's not doing any better. She's not herself. She's lonely. She skips school. She wanders around in the woods. The list goes on and on . . . and there is not much I can do without breaking rules to intervene with her life."

I sigh. I used to hate watching Heidi and Jace together. Since they have broken up, I hate the fact that she's alone even more. At least he was good for her. He was helping her heal in ways I cannot.

"I'm sure she's just acting out," I say. "She and Jace aren't together. I'm certain she's just sad, depressed—whatever human reaction is normal in those cases. She'll come around."

"Argh." Gabriella lets out a frustrated growl. "And that is exactly why I begged you to come back—so you can see it for yourself."

I open my mouth to argue with her, but she cuts me off.

"And yes, she is lonely. She barely talks to anyone, but that and her other behaviors can't possibly be for breaking up with someone she fell out of love with."

I lean my head down. "How do you know she fell out of love with him?"

Gabriella pauses, but I keep my head down. I'm afraid to hear her answer out loud.

"You know," she says, "for someone who has been around for so many decades, you sure are dense." Her tone grows frustrated.

I look up and stare at Heidi's window again.

"She's not home, by the way," she finally says.

"Where is she? Why aren't you watching her?" I growl.

She chuckles. "Let's say she has become an expert at escaping." She nods toward the window. "The lights out and music thing seems mostly to fool her parents. They think she's sleeping. I followed her all the way to her dad's market on Miller's Plaza. She probably knew I was near. She left through the back door without me noticing. We both know we lost the ability to track her, so I decided to just come straight here and wait."

I stand up, agitated, and start to pace back and forth on the roof. "Any idea where we should look? Where has she been going lately?"

She shrugs. "You could go to the library and look for her. I know she liked spending time there. Or you can sit and wait. She'll come back home eventually. She always does."

CHAPTER 2

HEIDI

I sit at the dinner table, staring at my plate as Mom lectures me about missing school. This is our new routine. As Mom goes on and on about being disappointed, Dad gets lost in a memory of us eating a peaceful dinner together just a little over a year ago. I was excitedly telling them about my day at school and then about my dance recital's costume. He misses how things used to be. I know that, logically, I should too. But I feel nothing.

That was before I was killed. December 2, 2018, was the night I disappeared. Hurt by some screwed up angel, I ended up in a coma and died months later. Another angel, Zane, brought me back to life, and somehow, I came back with a special ability to read people's memories. If Mom and Dad only knew . . . Like most, they believe I have no recollection of what really happened to me. They just know that I went missing and eventually found my way back. I wonder if things would be less awful for them if they knew that this curse to pick up on people's memories is what destroyed so many things I used to love. I can see every single detail of a memory with such clarity, it is as if I were there at the moment when it happened. Some days—well, most days—I just need a break.

"I'm going to bed," I tell Mom in the middle of her sentence.

She just sighs and throws her napkin down on the table. I can tell she's on the verge of giving up on me. I can't believe she hasn't already.

Without looking back, I rush upstairs and slam my door shut. I turn the music on and pace back and forth. This music tends to numb my thoughts in a way, but tonight, nothing seems to be helping. I feel like I'm all over the place. I feel irritable about . . . well, everything.

"I need to get out of here," I say out loud.

I put on a dark hoodie and coat and walk out of my room, locking the door from the inside and putting a hair clip in my pocket so I can get back in later. If Mom and Dad come to check on me, they'll think I'm doing homework or that I fell asleep. I quietly make my way downstairs. I hear them talking in the kitchen, so I go the other way, grabbing Dad's store keys on the way out.

I curse myself for not waiting until later to leave. I have come to love nighttime, when there is barely anyone out. Right now, the streets have more people than I care to see. I avoid going anywhere near Town Square to get to Miller's Plaza, but even the back roads have a few tourists walking around and admiring the small-town charm and stunning mountain views. I roll my eyes at the sound of that. You'd think after a day of skiing, they would be tired and want to lock themselves in their rooms.

I freeze in place when I see a family of four walking around. The parents carry the two little boys. Based on their memories, I can tell they are visiting from Italy. *If they only knew they're putting their kids in danger just by walking around at night*, I think to myself. Anger consumes me as I start to wonder how many of these tourists will actually make it back home after vising here.

I decide to approach the couple.

"Excuse me," I say. The young couple stops walking and looks at me with smiles on their faces, even though they look tired. There is no telling how long they've been walking around carrying their kids in the snow.

"Hello," they say.

I smile back. There is no easy way to tell them this. I look at my watch. "Are you heading back to where you are staying? It's not too safe to be out at this time of night."

Well, that didn't sound creepy at all.

"But you are out," the man says in a heavy accent.

I take a deep breath and try not to sound rude. "Well, yes, but I live right here," I tell them. "And I know what I am talking about. It's not safe."

Yep. They think I'm crazy. I can tell by the nonchalant look in their eyes.

"Thank you," they say and start to walk again.

I sigh. It's not like they would have believed me if I told them there are vampires roaming around—among other things.

I keep walking west, and once I get to Miller's Plaza, I absentmindedly stop in front of the dance studio I used to love. I zone out for a while. It's the feeling of my fingernails digging into my skin that brings me back to the here and now. I turn around and keep walking toward my dad's market.

Once in the market, I welcome the quiet of being here after hours—when the store is free of people walking around. Thankful for Dad being in the midst of switching security systems, I take my time walking down every aisle, even though I know what I'm here for. When I get to the aisle with hair products, I stop and stare at the variety of options. I grab the darkest one I can find. *Perfect.* I need a change, and this is fitting. I make my way to the back of the store. Dad bought a machine to make T-shirt designs shortly after he bought the store, so he can make some extra cash during the many town events and fundraisers. From that day, I started to design my own collection of shirts. I grin at the thought of people's reactions when I start wearing them.

As the first one is printing, I grab a bag of chips and a can of soda from the office. I sit down and reach for the can first.

"Ouch." I feel the small piece of metal piercing through my skin as I open the can. It's a small scratch, but enough to cut through my skin. I watch it as it quickly heals right before my eyes. This happened once before with a paper cut, and it healed just as fast. I stare at my finger for long after it is healed. *Maybe I should be happy about this.* I chuckle. *Happy—I can't even remember what that feels like.* Either way, this just opens up a whole new set of questions— like what the hell am I? I see my parents' memories. They miss the cheerful, sweet, nice daughter I once was. Not the distant, alone, cold version of her that they have today.

"Ugh. Snap out of it, Heidi," I tell myself. I open the bag of chips and start eating it.

I spend the next half hour or so enjoying my peace and quiet, until I get a text from Ani Rukska, the witch who made it possible that I no longer pick up on Jace's memories, and the only person whom I've told the truth about my abilities.

Ani: I'm by the back door of the store. We need to talk.

I roll my eyes and contemplate just ignoring her message, but unfortunately, that doesn't mean she will go away.

I hop off the office chair and let her in.

She closes the door behind her, and I cross my arms over my chest.

"How did you know I was here after hours?" I ask.

She grins. "Location spell," she says proudly. She pauses. "By the way, someone followed you here."

Of course, I think to myself. That is the angel Zane has following me around. I can't pick up on her memories to know when she's around, but luckily, she doesn't care to hide the fact that I'm being watched.

"I'm aware," I say. "Female, long hair, dark skin, extremely well dressed?" I ask in an annoyed tone.

"Yep. That would be the one."

"So . . . Do you want to go somewhere else and talk?" I ask.

She nods. "That would be best. Let's go to my house."

"Just give me a few minutes," I say. I turn off the machine and grab the first few shirts and the bag with hair dye. I throw the drink and bag of chips out, but leave the lights on so the angel thinks I'm still here. Dad will probably just think that he forgot to turn it off anyway. We get out through the back door, and I follow Ani to her house.

When we are some distance away from the store, she chuckles.

"What?" I ask.

"I'm guessing you escaped from her before?" she asks.

I shrug. "Wouldn't you have? I don't particularly like being followed." I pause. "Or found through location spells," I snap.

She smirks. "Something is different about you. Sneaking out, being out this late, snappy comments," she says. "I like it."

I roll my eyes at her. "I'm sure you do."

We continue the walk in silence. At some point, I hear howling in the distance, but those sounds don't even faze me anymore. I find it amusing that Ani watches me to see if I react at all. She doesn't say anything when she realizes that I don't. When we get to her house, I walk in after her.

A part of me expected to walk in and find potions and such all over the place, but her house is actually normal. No one would even be able to tell that she is what she is.

"So, what is it that you wanted to talk about?" I ask.

"Have a seat," she says. "Do you want something to drink?"

"I'm good. Thanks," I say in a cold tone. *Who in their right mind would accept a drink from a witch?*

"Okay, then," she says as she sits down. I remain standing. "I'll get right to it so you can get home. I'd like to collect on the favor you owe me."

"Go on," I tell her.

She hands me a piece of paper with five names. I read over them: Michaela Petran, Mathilde Augustine, Lilith Blackstone, Lawrence Mills, and Roman Bishop. I chuckle at the last name, as I already know a few of his secrets. I fold the list and look at Ani.

"I'd like to know everything you can get on their memories," she says.

I grin at her.

"Why would I do that?" I ask as I tilt my head to the side.

"Because you owe me," she says in an awkward tone.

I sigh. "Now, see . . . we have a difference in opinions about that. I came to you and asked you to keep me from reading memories in general and to forget a certain someone. All you did was block Jace's memories for me."

She stands up and closes the distance between us. She tries to look collected, but I can tell she's in shock. My grin widens.

"You're playing with fire, child."

"Am I?" I ask her.

She nods. Once. "I can just as easily undo that spell."

I shrug. "We have broken up since then. What's one more person's memories to pick up on?" I smile at her.

"I could tell your secret," she says.

I laugh. "You could. But then again, I have this list you just gave me. I'm sure you wouldn't want these people knowing of your interest in their memories—or that you knew about me and have been hiding my secret for your own selfish reasons."

She gapes.

I chuckle. "I guess I should let myself out," I say, turning around to leave.

"You don't know who you are messing with, little girl," she warns as I open the door.

"Uh huh," I say before heading home.

CHAPTER 3

ZANE

"She wasn't at the library. Or at Jace's house," I tell Gabriella when I get back. She is calmly sitting on the roof, reading a fashion magazine. She slowly puts the magazine down on her lap, which drives me insane.

"Why would she be at Jace's?" she asks, confused.

I throw my hands up in the air. "I don't know! I didn't know where else to look! And why are you so calm?" I ask.

She smiles. "She got home not long ago. Listen." She pauses. "No music," she says. "I honestly don't think I could take another second of that."

I look toward the window, tempted to go in there and see her.

I try to make conversation with Gabriella to keep my mind off Heidi.

"What are you looking at?" I ask, sitting next to her.

"Just looking at dresses. The Sweetheart Dance is coming up. I was thinking about stopping by. You know . . . just to make sure Heidi stays on track."

"Why would she go to the dance?" I ask.

She shrugs, and I watch her as she flips through the pages. This is more than just about Heidi. Gabriella dresses up more than any angel I know.

"Any news on Bryson?" she asks, referring to the angel responsible for Heidi's death. I shake my head. "Nothing. Not that I've had much time to look, but as far as I know, no one has had any leads in a long time. It's like he vanished."

"Maybe you should give up on trying to find him. Spend any extra time you can get away here. Heidi needs you. I told you before —her behavior tends to improve slightly when you are around. I bet it would improve even more if you could actually stay a while."

I shake my head. "He could always try to come back and hurt her again. And your theory is nonsense," I tell her. "She's probably just acting out because she misses having someone. She misses Jace." I pause. "Is this your way of telling me you're getting tired of helping?" I ask.

She smiles. "On the contrary. Heidi keeps things interesting. Especially when she knows she's being followed. It has become a challenging game really. I haven't had this much action in decades."

"Keeping her safe is not a game," I growl.

Gabriella rolls her eyes at me.

"Do you actually think she will go?" I ask. "To the dance," I say when she gives me a puzzled look.

She nods. But something doesn't add up. She mentioned that Heidi likes to be alone. Why would she go to a dance? I don't bother asking or even trying to understand.

Gabriella goes back to looking through the magazine, while I sit here, looking toward Heidi's window.

When morning finally comes, Heidi doesn't come out when I expect her to.

"She should be at school by now," I tell Gabriella. "Did she look okay when she came back last night?"

She shrugs. "As far as I could see. I told you—skipping class seems to be her thing lately."

About thirty minutes go by before the front door starts to open.

"Hide," says Gabriella. We both go to the side of one of the two-story houses on her street and stand where she can't see us, since making myself invisible to humans no longer works with her.

The moment I see her, I'm stunned. Her hair is shorter and pitch black, contrasting with her light skin in a way that takes my breath away.

"Well, that is new," says Gabriella. "Edgy. I love it."

Gabriella goes on and on, but I stop listening at some point as Heidi consumes my full attention. I stand here and watch her walk away, heading toward the school, and I have to fight the urge I feel to go toward her.

Once she turns the corner, Gabriella pulls me back to reality. "Come on," she says. "I have things to show you."

I follow Gabriella to Heidi's room.

Her room looks the same as always, leading me to believe that Gabriella is exaggerating. At least that is what I think at first.

Gabriella grabs Heidi's laptop and opens it. "Here."

She hands it to me.

"It needs a password," I say.

She grins from ear to ear.

"Try your name." She laughs.

I look at her like she has gone mad.

"Do it," she orders. I do, and it works. I glare at her, warning her not to say a word about this.

On the screen, there is a story about a guy who is in love with two friends—dating one, dreaming about the other. I don't think much of it until I see their names . . . and last names.

"What's this?" I ask Gabriella.

"That, my friend, is a private blog where your girl writes every single memory she sees during the day."

I look down. "This is the only entry."

She smirks. "You're welcome," she says proudly. "Every day, I come here. I spend some time reading the material, and then I delete them."

"And she keeps writing them?"

She nods.

"Always in private?" I ask.

"Yes."

"Have you tried to delete the blog?"

"Once," she says. "She just started another. I figured I'd let her get it out of her system and then delete it." She pauses. "Besides," she continues, "it's quite amusing. The girl has a great future writing gossip columns if that is something she wants to pursue."

"Only, this is not gossip," I say. "If someone finds out . . ."

I shake my head, frustrated at how careless she has been. I decide to leave her a message on the computer. PLEASE STOP. I start to type my name under it but decide not to.

"What else has she been doing?" I ask, almost afraid of the answer.

"She's curious about things, Zane. I've seen her looking at certain people differently. Approaching people she didn't hang out with before, almost as if she is trying to pick up on their memories on purpose."

"Any idea on how we can fix this?" I ask.

She smiles. "There is a certain angel I know who is a great influence on her."

I lower my head. "I can't, Gabriella."

"Why not?" she asks. I don't answer her. As an angel, Gabriella has responsibilities of her own. I could never admit to her that I can't be near Heidi without wanting to be with her.

"I have my reasons," I tell her. "Just keep an eye on her for me, okay? I need to think, and I can't think straight here. I'll be back later." I say, and I leave, getting as far away from her room as possible—trying to escape from her scent—from every reminder of her.

CHAPTER 4

HEIDI

*W*alking to school, I can't help but to replay my talk with that witch. The look on her face . . . Standing up for myself like that felt great, and it was nice feeling something good for a change.

I take my time walking to school, knowing that I'm already going to be in trouble with Mom and Dad for being late anyway.

I stop at Coffee Haven on the way. I've been coming in here for years, but for the first time, I stop to look at the paintings and drawings by local artists displayed on the walls. I heard once that you can tell a lot by people's artwork—that sometimes, that is how they tell the world things they could never say out loud. So I stand here and analyze them, searching for anything supernatural. And I don't see anything out of the ordinary. Anger consumes me as I think about how the humans in town, including my parents and Jace, live every day under a threat they don't even know exists. I clench my fists. *I need to find a way to put an end to this,* I say to myself.

Feeling like I'm being watched, I turn toward the counter and fake a smile when I see Harlow Augustine looking at me curiously. She takes my order. I know she's wondering why I'm not in school, but I also pick up on memories of her telling someone how she feels bad for me going through so much—gone missing and then not remembering what happened, which is what everyone thinks. Like Ani, she is also a witch, but she doesn't rub me the wrong way. I also know I could never ask her for any favors or put her in a position where she needs to keep my secret, because she likely wouldn't. I knew that Ani lacked morals—Harlow, not so much. *Augustine.*

My mind goes back to the list, and curiosity piques again at why Ani would want information about them in particular. As I stand here waiting for my hot chocolate, I hope to pick up on any useful memories that Harlow may have of her grandmother, which was one of the names on the list.

Not getting anywhere, I finally ask her, "How is your grandma?" hoping that will at least trigger some thoughts.

Harlow just gives me a puzzled look. "She's good," she says, then turns around and hands me two hot chocolates with a smile on her face. I give her a confused look. She shrugs. "Give that to your teacher. Maybe he—or she—won't be too hard on you for being late."

I thank her and head to school, getting there during second period, in the middle of an English Lit pop quiz.

Mr. Zander looks up at me, and before he can say anything, I apologize for being late and hand him the drink.

"It's hot chocolate," I say in an apologetic tone.

"Take your seat, Ms. Bennett. Thank you for the drink, but you won't be getting any extra time to complete the quiz." I nod, turn around, and walk to my seat. I immediately curse myself for giving him the hot chocolate when I catch the curious look that Celeste and a few others give me. I have no doubt I'm being judged, and I wouldn't be surprised if someone starts spreading rumors that I hit on Mr. Zander. I know he is a popular bachelor and all, but . . . ew.

When lunch comes around, I don't go for my usual table, but I do sit alone. I usually grab a book from my bag and pretend to read, knowing that people are a lot less likely to bother me. But not today. Today, I sit next to a table with a few vampires and a shifter, among others. I put my lunch down on the table, then I pull my sweater over my head, showing off my black T-shirt that has the design of fangs. The writing on it says, *Vampires suck.* I can't even hide my grin as I sit here, even though I'm careful not to make direct eye contact with anyone in particular.

Soon, Miranda, who is one of them, sits at my table. I like Miranda, though. She's always been nice, and there is something about her cheerful personality that draws people in—even me. She laughs. "Nice shirt. Where did you get it?"

I tell her I ordered it online. The last thing I want is to get my dad in trouble, or put him in danger. After I say that, the conversation goes dead, which is not normal when Miranda is around. She's now tense.

"Heidi," she finally says, her tone completely changing. "I need to tell you something but that is just because I don't want you to be surprised, and—" Before she can even finish that sentence, I'm already lost in her memories, her voice becoming muffled. She saw Jace with Elsie earlier. They were holding hands as they walked into school, talking about the upcoming Sweetheart Dance, and then kissing. My mind gets flooded with memories of my own, knowing that Elsie is the reason why everything changed. I remember seeing her room when I possessed her and finding out about her obsession with Jace. His pictures were all over her walls. Her brother, an angel, caused my death because he wanted his sister to have what she wanted, and now, she does.

I don't realize that I've clenched my fists out of anger until I feel Miranda's cold touch on my hand. I quickly relax my hands and pull away.

"Are you going to be okay?" she asks.

I nod, feeling even more numb than usual. I expected to at least feel jealous, or hurt, but I don't. All I can think about is that I need to find a way to get Jace to see who Elsie really is. Whatever they have going on won't last, and I decide to make the Sweetheart Dance my deadline. Elsie ruined my life, and I'm determined to do the same to her.

As they sit down on the other side of the cafeteria, I feel like all eyes are on me, and sadly, not because of my stupid shirt.

Jace quickly glances at me, and Elsie puts her arms around him as she glares in my direction. I give him a half smile and look at Miranda.

"I need to get out of here," I tell her.

"No way," she says. "Don't give them the satisfaction of knowing that this bothers you."

But that is the thing. It doesn't bother me. I just want revenge. And yes, protecting Jace is a bonus. But Miranda is right. I don't want to give Elsie the satisfaction. I smile at Miranda, and almost wish I could apologize for wearing this shirt.

CHAPTER 5

HEIDI

*T*he rest of the school day is uneventful. I'm grateful for not having any classes with Jace or Elsie, but seeing them together during lunch was enough to put me in a bad mood. Not needing a conversation starter, I ended up putting my hoodie back on to cover my T-shirt and kept to myself for the rest of the day, staring at the piece of paper with those five names as if that were enough to give me answers. Michaela Petran—vampire; Mathilde Augustine—witch; Roman Bishop—mage. I'm not quite clear on what the other two are, but so far, I see no connection between these names at all. I fold the paper and put it away for now.

When I get home, I go straight to my room with every intention to crawl into bed and watch TV for the rest of the day. Out of habit, I check my computer first and decide to do what I do every day—type the memories I find useful; duplicate it into another blog, knowing that this one will be deleted; and erase the history so it can't be found. But today, when I open the laptop, I find a note on the screen.

PLEASE STOP.

"Zane," I say under my breath.

I quickly put the laptop down and stand up. I open the window and look around. There is no one. There are few things that make me feel any type of good emotion. A few weeks ago, I realized that Zane was one of them—but this time, I feel angry. Angry that I miss him. Angry that I want him around. Angry that he left me again. Angry that he is what he is. I stare at my laptop screen. As my fingers graze the keyboard, I close my eyes and see him here, typing this warning. I sigh and open my blog to see everything gone once again. I find myself writing something else instead, hoping that he will come back and read it. It starts out as a way to manipulate him into showing up and facing me, until anger gets in the way.

I didn't ask for any of this. In two years, I was planning to go away with Jace. I was going to go to dance school. I was going to teach dance classes. Have a family. Maybe follow Jace as he tours around with his music. I had dreams. I had goals. I had a soul mate. I had everything.

Now, everything is gone.

Everything—except for this curse of knowing what I do.

So no, I won't quit. Did you ever stop to wonder if I was meant to still be here? That I was given this ability for a reason? That my purpose is to reveal secrets when they need to be revealed?

I stop typing and look outside before looking back at my computer. My hands start to tremble out of anger. Maybe if I hadn't picked up on his memories on the day I returned, I wouldn't have known just how he feels about me. I wouldn't have started to entertain the idea that maybe I was starting to feel something too— enough that I allowed it to create this void between Jace and me. I clench my fists, debating whether I should just delete it all, but instead, I keep going. I glare at my finger where I should have a cut or at least a scratch.

I don't even understand things that are happening to me.

I think back to the nightmares I have. At least that is what I think they are—I close my eyes at night, and all I remember when I wake up is darkness and fear.

I don't even know what the point of this letter is. Even if you had answers, it's not like you'd share them. I'm not looking for you to fix things. I'm obviously broken beyond repair. And I'm guessing you can't fix what you don't understand. I mean, I know you don't go around bringing people back from the dead.

And you—the only being who knows what happened to me . . . well, the only one I could talk to—you keep leaving, and I keep wondering . . . was bringing me back such a horrible mistake? Is that why you are so afraid to come near me?

I leave it open on that screen, facing the window, and I lay down. I'm determined not to fall asleep. I watch the window, just hoping he will show up.

After a while, my eyes start to feel heavy. I fall asleep, and for the first time since I came back, I dream. I find myself at a beach on a warm sunny day.

"Hello, Heidi." I hear a male voice I don't recognize. I look around, but there is no one.

"Hello?" I say back, but no one answers. I walk toward the ocean, feeling the warm sand against my feet.

The voice goes silent for a moment. Then it starts to cut in and out, before darkness takes over.

When I open my eyes in the morning, my computer is facing me.

Mad at myself for falling asleep, I slowly walk toward my laptop, almost afraid of what I will find.

I put in my password and find that most of what I wrote is

gone. There is only one question still on the screen and then the answer.

Was bringing me back such a horrible mistake?

Yes.

I stare at the screen for what feels like an eternity before I slam the laptop shut. I get dressed, and instead of going to school, I run toward Havenwood Heights, the wealthy side of Havenwood Falls, and I find myself hiking into the woods, to the area where I disappeared from. Out of breath, I crouch down against a tree and just sit here, wishing I wasn't brought back.

CHAPTER 6

HEIDI

*P*ain.

A stabbing headache hits me, and I put my hands over my temples, massaging my head. I haven't felt pain since that night. Right now, the pain doesn't last long, but it is excruciating.

"You should be in school." I hear his raspy voice. I close my eyes and stay where I am in an attempt to avoid facing him.

I want to tell him to leave me alone. That he shouldn't have brought me back. That he shouldn't feel like he needs to be around because he did this. But what I read on the computer screen keeps replaying in my head over and over again, and he is right. Me being here is a mistake. I shouldn't be here, and maybe that is why I feel so wrong.

"Heidi?" he says.

I force a smile before I turn around, and when my eyes meet his, I can see fear in his gaze. I try to pick up on any memories he may have. Any signs that he truly believes that I am a mistake, but I don't get anything. At all.

I close the distance between us.

He tenses. The last time we were this close, we kissed. That was right before he took off in a hurry.

I take another step closer. He tenses even more. I grin at the thought that he is so nervous right now; that I have this impact on him. I stop. *This should feel wrong*, I think to myself. *I shouldn't have these feelings toward him. I should be in love with Jace. I should steer clear of Zane, knowing that he can be punished for having feelings for me, and probably even more so for kissing me like he has in the past.* Still, my gaze goes to his lips. Confusion clouds my thoughts. I look down, realizing that my fists are clenched and my nails are digging into my skin. I relax my hands and look up into his eyes.

"Do you think it was a mistake to save me?" I blurt out, curious to see if he will say it to my face.

"I don't regret it," he says in a cold tone.

"That is not what I asked you, Zane. Can you ever just answer a question?"

I cross my arms over my chest and wait.

He stands here and stares at me, watching my every movement. As I look into his eyes, my anger is replaced with fear. *I'm a mistake. Or he wouldn't take this long to answer.*

"Your hair is different," he says.

I roll my eyes at him for his inability to answer my questions.

"Answer me," I demand.

He hesitates. Then sighs.

"I feel that letting you go would've been a bigger mistake," he says as he continues to stare at me.

I chuckle. "And where was your kind when I needed protection?" I snap. "Or was I not important enough to rank a guardian angel of my own?"

He lowers his head. "I'm sorry I failed you," he says.

I rub my hand against my forehead. *Why did I even say that?*

I take a few deep breaths to calm myself down. "You didn't fail me. I wasn't your responsibility."

He ignores my attempt at an apology. "I'm worried about you," he finally says.

I scoff. *Obviously not enough, or he would stick around.*

He tilts his head to the side.

"I don't understand why you are trying to draw attention to yourself," he says. "Is this about Jace?"

I raise an eyebrow at him.

"About you not being together anymore," he continues. "That seems to have an odd effect on you. That is why you kissed me back at the library that night, wasn't it? I thought you were just confused at first, but you were hurt because you had just broken up with him. I understand that now."

"Is that what you convinced yourself of?" I shake my head.

I close my eyes and take a deep breath, then another. And another. It doesn't do a damn thing to calm me down.

I open my eyes and glare at him. I don't tell him it's because somewhere along my screwed up existence, I developed feelings for him. After all, he should already know that, and what difference did that make?

"I'm going home, Zane. This is goodbye," I tell him.

He doesn't answer. He just stares at me. I turn around and walk away.

CHAPTER 7

ZANE

"*D*reaming awake once again, angel?"

I lean my head down and stare at my boots. I spent the rest of the day trying to figure out what I should do, how I can help her move on with her life, and I have nothing.

"What do you want, Gabriella?" I ask without looking back.

"Did you think about whatever it is that you needed to think about?" she asks.

I scoff and look at her. "I tried to talk to her," I say.

"I'm aware," she says. "I was around."

I sigh, and look toward Heidi's window. "She's all over the place, Gabriella. Her body language felt all wrong."

She looks like she's deep in thought.

"What?" I ask.

"Nothing." She pauses. "Well, there was a shift in her when you were around. I think that is why she was confused. I've told you before—something in her changes when you are around. Maybe you should consider getting close to her."

"Only, I can't get close without being able to be with her in a way that I was never meant to be," I blurt out.

I freeze. I should never have said that. I reluctantly look at Gabriella, but she doesn't even look surprised.

"Maybe that's part of your punishment," she says under her breath. "Sorry. I just don't think you have much of an option, Zane. She is getting worse. She is a time bomb. She may wake up one day and decide to say everything she knows. Can you imagine the consequences? She will have half the town wanting her head, and the other half wanting to use her for their own benefit."

I look down, knowing she's right, and this is my fault.

A noise from across the street sends me into full alert mode.

Gabriella follows my gaze to Heidi's front door. Heidi walks out, wearing black pants and a black coat, with a hoodie covering her head.

"I can't say this enough—she does keep things interesting," Gabriella says. "Am I going alone tonight or are you coming with me?"

"You go," I tell her. "I need to get back before they realize I'm missing." I pause. "Please take care of her," I beg, before I'm forced to go back to the last place I want to be, but not before Gabriella stops me.

"Zane?" she says.

"Yes?"

"There are other things I haven't told you."

I freeze and watch her.

"She has made a deal with a witch in town, among other minor things. I had to report some of those. I had no option. There are theories that part of her soul was lost when you brought her back. Our kind is planning to intervene if she doesn't improve."

"Intervene? What does that even mean?" I growl.

She shrugs. "It could be making her and her family move out of Havenwood Falls, and forget everything they've ever known. Although there are theories that it wouldn't work on Heidi, considering she's immune to our abilities. And let's face it—the Court goes to great lengths to make sure things run smoothly. Can you imagine the consequences if they knew one of the residents is immune to the town's memory ward, and that she knows what she does and has no desire to keep their secrets?"

"What is the alternative?" I ask.

Gabriella looks toward Heidi's house. "That would be to correct her fate and undo what you have done."

I shake my head and sit back down, knowing I have no option but to stay.

HEIDI

I rush out of the house as soon as Mom and Dad aren't paying attention. I feel like I'm suffocating. Dinner tonight was awful again. With the memories, the lectures about school attendance, my lack of friends, and my lack of interest in anything I used to love, I just had to leave and clear my head.

When I walk by Burger Bar, I see Jace's car. I can see from a distance that Elsie is with him. I decide to focus my energy on saving Jace from Elsie instead of feeling sorry for myself. At the moment, it no longer feels like revenge. It's for Jace's own sake. I just need to grab proof of how much of a stalker she is.

I make my way to her house and go in through her back door after grabbing the hidden key from under a frog statue—a perk of picking up on memories when I possessed her. I walk into her room, hoping it's still the same. Sure enough, on her walls, there are tons of pictures of Jace. Some of the pictures were of Jace and me; only, she replaced my face with hers. *Creep.* It concerns me even more that she still has all of this up, even after they started dating. I grab my phone and take several pictures of the wall. I contemplate saving them to release anonymously on the night of the Sweetheart Dance.

When I turn around to leave, I find the angel Zane has following me around, standing there, waiting for me.

"What?" I ask.

She moves her hand up and holds it there, palm facing up. "Phone," she says. "Hand it over."

I laugh. "Why should I?"

She looks at the wall, then back at me. "I can't say the girl doesn't have issues," she says.

"Well, obviously," I say.

She sighs, then continues, "She means no harm, Heidi. And as much as you blame her for what happened to you, that wasn't her fault. She had no control over or awareness of her brother's actions."

I swallow the lump in my throat.

"She just loves Jace." She pauses and glances at the wall with disgust. "Maybe a bit too much," she says. "Just let them be. Who knows? Maybe she will help him move on. Unless you're doing this because you want him back," she says as she raises an eyebrow at me.

I shake my head. Jace was my everything. The perfect guy. But that wouldn't be fair to him. Not when . . .

"Has he left?" I ask her, referring to Zane.

She tilts her head to the side. "Does it make a difference?" she asks.

I roll my eyes at her. "I guess he's rubbing off on you," I say when she doesn't answer my question.

"Get home, Heidi. Delete those pictures. Try to . . . I don't know . . . make a friend. Try to move on before you get Zane in even more trouble."

And just like that, she vanishes.

CHAPTER 8

HEIDI

*a*t night, I lie in bed looking sleepily at the pictures I took. Gabriella was right, but I can't make myself delete them. I know it's not because I want Jace back. I just don't want him with Elsie. A small part of me starts to hate this person I've become. I should want Jace to be happy. *What the hell is wrong with me?*

Unable to sleep, I decide that I need to talk to him.

Me: Are you awake?

He replies right away.

Jace: Yeah. I'm still at the music store. Getting ready to leave in about 15 minutes or so

I quickly sit up on my bed, anxious about all the things that could go wrong on his way home.

Me: You have to be careful

Jace: Hmmm. Okay. About what exactly?

Me: Just wait for me at the store. I'll come to you

He doesn't reply. I get up and start to get dressed.

Five minutes is all it takes to hear the engine of his Camaro in front of my house. Angry that he is such a careless fool, I rush downstairs and swing the door open.

"What the hell are you doing?" I ask.

"Well," he says, "I didn't want you to be roaming the streets this late at night, and you seemed off."

I shake my head, grab his wrist, and pull him upstairs and into my room. I close the door behind us, and he looks confused.

"I should probably not be here," he says.

"Because of Elsie?" I ask in a sarcastic tone, and he nods.

"I wanted to be the one who told you," he says. "I just didn't know how to."

"That doesn't matter," I tell him.

"Because you moved on?" he asks, and I scoff.

"What's going on with you, Heidi?"

"I remember what happened to me while I was missing," I say.

"You do?" he asks in shock, and I nod.

"Have you told anyone?" He closes the distance between us.

"No. And I'm not going to."

I start to pace back and forth. He takes a step closer and places his hands on my shoulders.

"What happened?" he asks.

He has to know. He deserves to know at least a variation of it.

"You can't tell anyone. I just want you to know so that you're more careful out there."

He gives me a puzzled look, but nods.

"This town, Jace . . . I was attacked by something supernatural that night. They're everywhere."

I can see the look of concern in his eyes before he pulls me into a hug. He runs his fingers through my hair. "You need to talk to someone, Heidi. I think whatever did happen, it was too much for you to handle, and your mind is just . . . playing tricks on you."

Of course he doesn't believe me. Angry tears fill my eyes. "I can show you. I can prove that I'm telling you the truth."

He pulls away. "Okay," he says. "But not tonight. Tonight, you're staying here, where you're safe, and as long as you are okay with it, I'm staying with you."

I nod, mostly because I'm not sending him off into that in the middle of the night.

He leads me toward the bed and lies down next to me.

I'm at the beach again. There is a guy standing by the ocean, his wings spread wide.

"Zane?" I say, recognizing his build and his clothes.

He doesn't respond. I start to walk toward him when I see a vision of a vampire drinking blood from my wrist. I freeze in place, looking confused. A voice comes through, but I can't make out the words. It's almost as if there is a lot of static muffling the words, then it clears.

"Help us understand. Help us correct your fate."

I make myself take another step forward toward the angel, but he disappears before my eyes.

I wake up feeling hazy. My head is pounding, but the first thing I notice is that Jace is gone. I try to remember what the voice sounded like, but my brain is a complete fog. I shrug it off. *Just a stupid dream.* Knowing that I can't be late to school again, I get up. I see a missed call and a message on my phone.

Jace: Can we talk after school?

I don't reply. I throw my phone on the bed and hop in the shower.

I put on a pair of ripped jeans, my favorite ankle boots, my new shirt, and I'm off to school. Today, I'm wearing my vampire slayer shirt. I figured I'd make this vampire week. Next week may be witches or shape-shifters.

Having a few extra minutes, I decide to stop and grab a hot chocolate on the way. I stand frozen steps away from Coffee Haven when I see Jace and Elsie sitting inside, having breakfast. He's holding his guitar, playing something, and she is smiling. I can't make myself move.

I feel Zane's presence before his hand slips into mine. I can feel tears run down my face, but I don't take my eyes off Jace and Elsie.

"I feel like I'm watching a scene of what my life should've been like right now. I don't think I remember the last time I was that happy."

"That could still be your life, Heidi. I know he was with you last night. He obviously hasn't gotten over you."

I look down at his hand in mine, and I quickly pull away. "I can't."

"Why? What changed, Heidi? Jace was the one thing you missed the most when I was helping you. I thought I'd bring you back and you'd pick up where you left off. That you'd be happy."

I chuckle. "You really don't know what changed, do you?"

He shakes his head.

"You happened, Zane."

He gives me a confused look.

"Last night wasn't what you think. I don't feel that way about Jace anymore. Besides, do you think I just go around kissing people like I kissed you that night?" I ask.

He stands there, frozen.

"But it doesn't matter," I tell him. "You are what you are. So please do what I asked and leave. That would make things easier on both of us."

I turn to the side and give him a kiss on the cheek, then walk away without looking back.

As I walk away from him, whatever I was feeling a moment ago is gone. I start to feel the same as I have every other day—anxious, angry. I pick up the pace, and once inside the school, I take off my sweater.

I don't get far before my vision is blocked as one of the seniors steps in front of me. I know he's a vampire, which makes this so much more interesting. I look up at him.

"Can I help you?" I ask.

"Nice shirt," he says with a smile. "Are you on a vamp kick or something like that?"

"Something like that," I say. "It's more of an all supernaturals kick."

"Interesting," he says as he rubs his chin.

I grin. "How so?"

"What brought that along?" he asks.

I shrug. Miranda swoops in.

"Do you not watch TV?" she asks him. "With all the supernatural shows on right now, how can anyone not be on a supernatural kick?" She giggles and rolls her eyes at him.

He shrugs and leaves.

"So what have you been watching lately?" she asks as we walk down the hall.

"Not much, really," I say, sidetracked by a group of students near us. She notices me looking at them.

"I think they're curious about how you're doing with Jace's situation and all," she says.

"Yeah, maybe."

"How are you?" she asks. "The two of you had been together for so long. This has to be hard."

"It is what it is," I tell her in a harsher tone than I meant to.

She gives me a sympathetic smile. Her memories right now are of me and Jace, together. She really does think I'm acting this way because of him.

It's a boring morning. When lunchtime comes around, I sit as far away from Jace and Elsie as possible and hide behind a book. I'm surprised when Ezra, the new student wearing jeans and a super tight black T-shirt, who also happens to be a vampire, comes in and slides down the seat next to me. The irony, considering the dream I had last night.

I stare into his gray-green eyes.

"Yes?" I ask, looking up from the book.

He grins. "Nice shirt," he says.

I catch glimpses of his memories of drinking blood from an animal in the woods. I try my best to mask my disgust—something that I feel I've been doing a lot of lately.

I roll my eyes at him. "Yeah, it seems to be a great conversation starter."

"Don't you ever wonder what it must feel like?" he whispers. Facing him, I catch him looking at my neck. For a moment, I can't even form an answer. He laughs and looks at my book. "What are you reading?"

"Is everything okay here?" I look over and see Jace standing next to the table. Glancing to where he usually sits with Elsie, I see her watching his every move.

"Yeah," I say. "Elsie seems worried about you, though. Maybe you should get back."

Ezra gives him a half smile, but Jace doesn't move right away. He stares at me as if he's searching for clues that I need to be rescued. I hold his gaze, hoping he will see that I'm okay and leave.

I was so frantic last night, I didn't even notice that I still can't pick up on his memories thanks to the deal I made with Ani, and by the sad look in his eyes, I am glad that is the case. He finally turns around and leaves.

"Ex-boyfriend?" Ezra asks.

"How did you know?"

He shrugs. "Gut feeling. And he isn't over you." He pauses. "And his girl is pissed. He can't seem to take his eyes off you." He chuckles. "This has got to be the most interesting lunch since my first day here last week."

"Look, I'm off the market, so—"

He puts his hands up. "You're direct. I like it!"

I roll my eyes at him.

"Relax. You're not my type."

"Really?"

He nods. I pick up on a memory of him kissing another guy. "Let's just say that your ex would be more my type than you are." He winks at me.

"Oh. Okay."

"Just looking to make some friends. As interesting as your shirt collection is, you don't seem to have many either."

I shrug.

"So, what are you into, besides vampires?" He laughs. If he only knew what I know . . .

"Not much lately. I used to be into ballet, but I haven't really gotten back into it since I— Well, it's been a while." I realize that talking to someone who doesn't know my past may not be that bad.

"Do you miss it?" he asks.

"Haven't really stopped to give it any thought. What about you?" I ask.

"I have a common interest in vampires." He chuckles.

"Of course you do," I say in a sarcastic tone.

He leans in my ear and whispers, "You know, don't you?"

For a split second, I freeze in place.

"Know what?" I ask.

He grins and winks at me. "Hey. What are you doing after school?" he asks.

"Going home and sulking."

He laughs. "I'm coming over. I need someone to show me what there is to do around here."

"What? Aurelia isn't showing you around?" I ask, knowing that he's staying with the Petran family, and that Aurelia, who is in a few of my classes, is by far one of the most bitter and bitchy girls in the school.

His expression goes serious for a minute. "You're kidding, right?" he asks, and I shrug.

"Yeah, she's been such a delight to be around," he says in a sarcastic tone.

I open my mouth to say something when he stops me. "I won't take no for an answer, and trust me—I can be very compelling." He winks again.

"I need to take care of some things, now that I think about it." He actually looks disappointed. *Ugh.* "I guess meet me in town square at five?"

CHAPTER 9

HEIDI

I fully intended to stand him up, but as five gets closer, I decide to take Gabriella's advice to make new friends. I remind myself that it will be nice to have someone around who doesn't know much about me.

I get to town square right at five and find him waiting for me. He is sitting on a bench, looking at his phone. He looks up as I get closer and grins. "I have to admit, I totally thought you were going to ditch me."

"I considered it," I say in a serious tone.

He chuckles. "I believe it. Why did you decide to come?" he asks as he nods toward the bench. I sit next to him.

"I don't know," I lie. A part of me has been craving a friend to talk to. Jace had always been that person. I'd been with him since middle school, and we always had our own thing going on. We had friends, but at the end of the day, we were each other's best friends.

He gives me a half smile.

"I told you I had a compelling personality," he says with a smirk.

Ezra catches me staring toward the music store where Jace works. We can see him inside, by the door.

"You know, I heard he was asking questions about me after lunch. He obviously still cares."

I give him a sad smile.

He bumps my shoulder with his. "Want me to help you get him back?"

I wish people would stop assuming that is the case. I shake my head. "No. He needs to move on. I just wish it was with someone other than his current girlfriend."

"Do you want to tell me why the two of you broke up?" he asks.

"We both needed space. Things weren't the same after I got back. We just grew apart."

"Got back from where?" he asks.

"Long story," I say in a cold tone.

"Is there someone else?" he asks, and I hesitate. "Someone from our school?" he asks with a smile.

"I wish. It's not that simple."

"Is anything ever simple?" he asks, laughing.

"Used to be," I say as I look down.

"So, what is the deal with the hair change?"

I look at him and raise an eyebrow. He just started school last week and we didn't even talk until today. I'm surprised he noticed.

"Just needed a change," I say. I start to feel like I'm under interrogation. "I know nothing about you. Start talking," I say, even though I know enough about him, but only through his memories.

Ezra tells me he was sent here to live with family after he got into some trouble at home in Romania. He won't talk about the reason, but from his memories, I know it was about his boyfriend and his dad not being so accepting of his lifestyle.

"We have an audience," he says. I look at him, and he nods toward the music store. Jace is standing at the door, looking over in our direction. I get a text.

Jace: Can I talk to you, please? Only 5 minutes.

I look up from my phone and see Jace watching me.

Me: Maybe another time.

He reads it, puts his phone away, and walks back into the store, looking upset.

"Let's get out of here," I tell Ezra.

"Where to?" he asks.

I shrug. "Somewhere away from people. I don't really feel like being around anyone right now."

He tilts his head to the side. "Thank you?" he says. "I guess I should feel honored."

I chuckle. "I hope your shoes are comfortable," I say, and he gives me a puzzled look.

I lead Ezra toward the Mills mansion.

"Good Lord, girl. You could have warned me we were going on a hike, ya know?"

I shrug. "You look like you're in good shape. Figured you could keep up."

We keep going until we reach the wooded area I'm always so drawn to.

Grateful that the ground is clear of snow, I sit down with my back against a tree, and he sits across from me.

"Interesting choice of place," he says as he looks around.

I get hit with a horrible headache again. I rub my temples. I see flashes of images of the beach and someone drinking from my wrist. They stop at the moment the pain goes away.

"You okay?" he asks.

I nod. "Yeah. Just a headache."

ZANE

Heidi walks toward a boy on a bench.

"Who is that?" I ask Gabriella as we watch Heidi from a distance.

She looks up from her freshly manicured nails. "Ezra Dimitrius.

He's Michaela Petran's cousin. He recently moved here from Romania."

"Okay? What's Heidi doing with him?" I ask.

She shrugs. "I did tell her she should make new friends. Maybe she finally listened to something." She pauses. "This is good, Zane."

"Not an ideal choice when his cousin is a member of the Court," I growl.

Heidi and Ezra stand up from the benches, and we follow from a distance.

"What is she doing?" I say out loud as they walk into the woods.

Gabriella looks as intrigued as I do. "Let's get closer," she says.

"We can't. She will see us—hear us."

"I took care of that," she says. I give her a puzzled look, but before I can ask anything, she's already next to them. I kneel down next to Heidi. I close my eyes for a split second realizing how much I missed this—the ability to be this close, to protect her.

"Can I ask you a question?" Heidi says, looking at Ezra.

"Sure. But only if I can ask you something first," he says as he plays with a piece of grass.

She shrugs. "Go for it."

"How do you know about—hmm—you know . . ." He lets his shoulders rise and fall. His lips part, and he runs his tongue over his teeth.

I freeze. "She just met him, and he already knows that she's aware of it all!" I growl.

But Heidi hesitates in answering.

"How did he find out?" I whisper.

"I won't tell anyone," he says.

She shrugs. "Let's say I'm psychic or something like that. I can pick up on things people have done."

I shake my head, fighting the urge to make myself visible right now and get her out of here.

"And that doesn't freak you out?" he asks.

She shakes her head.

"That is kind of neat," he says.

She scoffs. "It's hell, really."

"Does anyone know?" he asks.

"No," she lies.

"How does that work anyway?" he asks. "Do you pick and choose whenever you want it to work?"

"That is way more than one question," she says in a cold tone.

He nods. "You're right. Your turn."

She grabs a piece of paper from her pocket and leans forward to show it to him.

"What do these names have in common?" she asks. At first, even I don't make the connection. Ezra's eyes widen.

He stares at it for a while.

"I'm not answering that," he finally says in a tense tone. She gives him this wicked grin that is not quite like her.

Members of the Court of the Sun and the Moon, I think to myself. *The governing body of the supernaturals and the rest of the town.*

I look over at Heidi. I know every feature—every look—every single detail about her. So I instantly notice when her eyes darken. She looks distant. Her tone changes slightly—she almost sounds more . . . well, like she's reading off a script someone gave her.

"Have you ever bitten someone?"

"No," he says.

Her eyes go back to normal. She looks confused for a split second before they darken again. "Aren't you curious about what that would be like?" she asks.

He gives her a nervous smile. "That is more than one question."

She nods and looks away, but his gaze is on her. Studying her every movement.

"Sure, I'm curious, but I would never."

"How come?" she asks.

"Things would not end well. I could lose control and kill the person, for one thing."

"But you don't know that," she says with a grin. He stops to think about it but doesn't say a word. She goes on. "Okay, humor me for a minute. You feed from animals and bottles, right?"

He nods, looking confused.

"Okay. And when you are drinking you can stop when you want, right?"

"Yes," he says, with a puzzled expression.

"It can't be that different," she says.

"What is she doing?" I say out loud. Gabriella stands next to me. "Look at her eyes, Gabriella."

She does. "I told you something is off about her. It's not just about Jace, or about things changing."

"What are you getting at, Heidi?" Ezra asks.

"I want you to drink from me," she says. "I want to know what it would feel like."

I'm in complete shock at first, and that is what gives Gabriella time to stop me from making myself seen and throwing Heidi over my shoulders to get her out of here.

"Relax," says Gabriella. "He would never. There are consequences for both here. Just let this play out."

I glare at Gabriella.

"She will be okay," she says. "You're right here, after all. We both are."

Ezra laughs. "Not a chance."

"I wouldn't tell anyone."

He looks uncomfortable. "Why would you even want that?" he asks.

"I told you. Curiosity."

He shakes his head. "I can't, Heidi. There is no way."

She smiles at him, but even her smile is off. She lets it go, but I know the idea is planted in his head now.

CHAPTER 10

HEIDI

*M*y heart races as curiosity consumes me. Curiosity that goes far beyond what Ezra probably thinks. I wonder if he actually said yes, if I would heal as quickly as I did when I cut my finger. *Why am I not afraid?* Images from that dream invade my memory, almost as if it is a way to ensure me that this is what I should be doing.

The walk back is awkward. We both walk in silence, and I'm pretty sure I won't hear from him ever again. By the time I get home, it's already dark. Mom and Dad are watching TV, and I tell them I already ate. I go straight to my computer and open my blog. I grab the piece of paper from my pocket and open it, placing the paper in front of my screen. Through Ezra's memories, I have just what I needed. These are five of the people responsible for keeping the supernatural around here safe. If I expose them, it could be my chance to keep the humans safe. I open a new page and start typing.

A little over a year ago, my whole life changed when I realized that everything about the place where I grew up was a lie. My name is Heidi Bennett, and I grew up in Havenwood Falls. If you're reading this from somewhere outside of this town, it is pretty likely that you've never heard of Havenwood Falls. Even if you have been here before. Don't worry. I will explain the reason shortly. And if you live here, and you are like me

—someone who grew up in a lie—you won't believe me at first. But that's okay. If you just take the time to search for the truth, you'll see that I'm right.

As my eyes start to feel heavy, I decide to take a quick break. I close my eyes and start thinking about Ezra.

I fall asleep thinking about our conversation. What if he did lose control? Would that correct my fate? Why does this feel so right when it should be everything but?

Darkness.

I find myself at the beach again. The same angel stands by the water.

"Zane?" I ask.

The voice comes—still muffled. "He's coming for you. This is your purpose. Do not back out."

I jump awake, almost dropping the laptop. I look around my room. At first, I'm in a daze, wondering who will show up. My heart leaps at the thought that maybe it is Zane. I shake my head, knowing that I can't keep wishing for that. This is why I sent him away. We can't be near each other. As much as I wish otherwise, he is what he is, and the thought of him being punished even more because of me—

I hear something hit my window.

"What the hell?" I say. I go to the window and see Ezra on the street. I rush down the stairs and open the door.

He just stands there, looking nervous.

"Come in," I say. "Quietly. You don't want to wake up my parents."

He awkwardly comes in, and we go up to my room.

He keeps his distance, and he looks tense. I can't even pick up on any of his memories—it's as if he is too nervous to even think.

"You're staring at my neck," I tell him.

"Were you serious about your offer?" he asks, and I shrug.

"Sure."

"Why?" he asks. "The real reason."

"Let's say I have limits of my own to test."

He pulls something out of his pocket.

"What's that?" I ask.

"A taser," he says nervously. "I want you to use it on me if I don't stop—or if you feel weak, or weird about it all."

I take it from his hand. "Sure," I say, knowing that I don't even know how to use the thing.

"Are you ready?" he asks, and I nod.

He takes a step closer to me. I watch his every move, analyzing his body language, the way he looks at me. I'm almost disappointed that I'm not confronted with some sort of cold and predatory look. He looks terrified, really.

He stops. "I can't do this."

I roll my eyes at him, grab a pair of scissors from my desk, and put it against my wrist. "Do you need motivation?" I ask.

"Please, stop," he begs. "I don't know what I was thinking."

"Why are you so hesitant? Isn't that what your kind does? Drain humans of their blood?"

He shakes his head. "I don't know what's wrong with you right now, but you don't even know what you're talking about."

"Explain," I command, still holding the scissors to my wrist.

His hands are trembling. "Can you put the scissors away?" he asks nervously.

"Eventually," I say in a cold tone.

"I'm what you call a moroi. I don't feed from people. I'm sure you can do your psychic thing and confirm it. If I took one sip, I could lose control and turn into something I dread. I could lose my soul, and if caught, which in Havenwood Falls I'm certain I would be, I would be executed."

"How do you know?" I ask. "How do you know you would turn into something that you're not?" I ask.

He looks down. "Because that's what happened to my mom."

"But you came here tonight," I tell him. His eyes are now on the scissors as they make a dent in my skin.

∽

ZANE

I do a quick check-in on the poor soul I should be watching over. As always, he's sitting in his room, playing video games.

"Nothing is happening here," I tell myself before I rush back to Havenwood Falls. Gabriella is sitting on the roof, reading a magazine. I glance over at Heidi's, and her lights are on.

"What's going on?" I ask, as I see two shadows through the curtains.

She looks up from the magazine.

"Uh-oh. I thought she was sleeping. I got distracted."

I don't wait on her to say anything else. I make myself unseen and rush into Heidi's room. I find Ezra on one side of the room, looking terrified. Heidi is on the other side, holding a pair of scissors in her hand. Her eyes are even darker than earlier. She pierces her skin, and at the sight of blood, my gaze goes to Ezra. His body language shifts. He no longer looks terrified. He launches toward her. Making myself seen, I cut him off, grabbing his neck with my hand.

"Zane!" she says. I look at her while not letting go of him.

Her eyes are no longer dark. She looks like she's on the verge of tears. "I'm sorry. I'm so sorry. This wasn't his fault. I promise. Let him go. Please," she begs.

Ezra looks scared again.

I let go of his neck.

"Sit," I order him, and he does.

I rush toward Heidi and grab her hand. I watch her wrist heal right before me, then I look into her eyes.

"What's wrong with me?" she cries.

I pull her into a hug.

"Can someone tell me what's going on here?" Ezra asks, his voice shaking.

I run my hands through her hair as she sobs against my chest.

I tell him a very loose variation of the truth. "Heidi went

missing some time ago. She doesn't remember what happened to her, but she's not been quite herself lately."

Ezra nods.

I expect the boy to be eager to leave—to just run and do who knows what with that information—but I know I can trust him the moment he looks at me with a concerned expression and asks, "Is there something I can do to help?"

"Other than not sinking your fangs into the girl?" Gabriella asks as she shows up.

Ezra looks apologetic.

"Just don't talk about it with anyone," says Gabriella. Heidi's hold around me tightens.

Gabriella looks at me. She crosses her arms over her chest. She looks down at Heidi, and her gaze goes to my arms around her.

"You have a choice to make, angel," she says in a warning tone.

"I can't," I tell her.

"I have to report this, or it's my head."

Heidi sobs even more.

"I can't protect her if I'm not what I am," I growl.

She sighs. "Outside. Now."

I slowly pull away from Heidi.

I glare at Ezra, not too sure how I feel leaving her alone with him.

"I'm fine," he says. "I will stay with her until you get back."

I nod, then look at Heidi, but she avoids my gaze.

Gabriella and I go back to where we usually sit. She stands with her arms crossed, tapping her heels on the roof.

"You're forgetting that you have me to help you—the two of you. But you have to choose, Zane. You're at fault for all of this. We can't explain what happened, but there's one thing I'm certain of. She's more grounded when you're around." She pauses. "There are other ways to protect her. You being what you are is doing more damage than good. To everyone."

I nod, understanding that I put her in a bad position.

She sighs. "In a way, I'm a little jealous."

"Jealous?" I scoff. "I spend my existence in a constant battle between protecting her and trying to keep my distance from her so as not to break the rules that were imposed on me. Jealous of what, exactly?"

"I just wish I could remember what it feels like to be in love," she says. "But Zane—" She gives me a warning look. "You should've walked away from what you are when you first fell for her. Make your choice. I will help protect her—even if it comes to protecting her from our own kind. Although I don't think that will be necessary once you're around her in a way that both of you need."

I look toward Heidi's house.

"I choose her," I say, feeling the relief that these words bring me. "In a way, I always have."

CHAPTER 11

ZANE

I expected to feel different. I expected to feel shame for turning my back on everything I know. I expected to feel regret. But I don't feel any of that. I feel relief that I finally acted on what I knew a long time ago.

I know I won't be able to do so many things that I have always had the ability to do before, and my biggest concern is that those will become weaknesses when it comes to protecting Heidi.

The weirdest part of it all is probably seeing Gabriella's happiness over it. Her acceptance of my decision was a nice surprise, and her promise to help protect Heidi was a relief.

Gabriella takes me to the hallway that leads to Heidi's room. My invisibility is gone and so is my ability to get places like I used to.

The house is quiet. I know Heidi's parents are sleeping, but I can hear her and Ezra in her room.

"I'm sorry," she tells him.

"It's okay. I lost count of how many times you apologized, but I already told you countless times that I forgive you. Just don't do it again, okay?"

I walk in then. For a split second, she looks confused, then it hits her.

"Why?" she asks.

I ignore her question. "I need to ask you something," I tell her.

I look over at Ezra.

"Hmm. I guess I should go?" he says.

Heidi gives him a sad smile.

"I promise. It's fine," he says, knowing how bad she feels about what she did. "I'll see you later, okay?"

She nods, and he leaves.

"What's going to happen to you?" she asks as soon as the door closes.

I close the distance between us. "It's you that I'm worried about."

She chuckles. "I see that your inability to answer questions is still there."

My gaze goes to her lips. I wonder if it would feel any different to kiss her now—without all the guilt. But this is not something I'm going to find out tonight. When I do kiss her again, I want everything to be perfect.

"I know you weren't in control earlier," I tell her. "I could see it in your eyes." I pause. "That list of names you've been carrying around. How did you get it?" I ask.

"From Ani Rukska," she says.

Angry with myself for not realizing this before, I take a few steps away from Heidi. My tone grows colder. Angrier. "Gabriella mentioned that you made some kind of deal with a witch. Is that the one?" I ask, knowing that a spell is one possible cause for whatever is going on with Heidi.

She nods.

"What was the deal?" I ask.

She looks away. "To block people's memories from me, and—"

"And?" I ask.

She looks up at me, and she hesitates.

"To make me forget you." She looks away, avoiding my gaze.

It takes me a minute to process this. She continues, "In

exchange, I was supposed to check into certain people's memories for her."

"Okay, did she call off the deal? Obviously none of it worked."

Heidi shakes her head. "She tricked me. She blocked Jace's memories from me. That part worked. Forgetting you was impossible."

I grin at the way she says that last part.

"Don't let that go to your head," she says.

Focus, I tell myself. "What happened next?" I ask.

"I told her I wasn't going to do what she asked. She tricked me and the deal was off. I used the list of names she gave me as leverage."

My hands clench into fists.

"Where does she live?" I ask.

She pauses. "Do you think she has something to do with what's happening?"

"I don't know," I tell her. "But it's the only lead I have right now. Why on earth would you make a deal and then confront a witch, Heidi?"

"It didn't seem fair that she did that. If you're right, what can we do about it?" she asks.

"I'll fix the problem," I tell her, but truthfully, I have no idea what to do here. Every option leads to more people finding out about Heidi's abilities.

Heidi hesitantly gives me directions to where the witch lives, and I have to make her promise me to keep her distance, and not do anything stupid while I go search for answers. I decide not to tell Gabriella, knowing that there are certain things she would have to report—and this witch abusing her powers would be one of those things, which leads right back to more people, more angels, finding out about her.

It's two in the morning when Heidi walks me out.

"This is weird," she says. "You not just disappearing right in front of me."

"I know," I tell her.

"Are you coming back?" she asks.

I nod.

"Why did you do it, Zane? Why did you choose me? I'm not the same person I used to be."

I smile at her. "Yes, you are. Or you wouldn't have felt bad about Ezra. You wouldn't be asking me this question now, or be worried about what happens next. That night, you just got lost in more ways than you know. I'm going to help you get back to where you were before."

She closes her eyes for a split second and sighs. When she opens her eyes again, I'm closer. Reason tells me to turn around and leave, but I feel a pull toward her that can't be denied. As much as I want everything to be perfect—as much as I know I need to get it together and focus—deep down, I know I won't be able to do that until I kiss her. So I give in. I lean in and kiss her, and for the first time, without the world's weight on my shoulders.

I make my way to the witch's house without seeing a soul around, which I'm thankful for, considering that everyone can see me now. My plan is to wait until morning and catch her on the way out. I'll pretend that Heidi did the same to me as she did to her—getting a favor without fulfilling her side of the deal—and then, hopefully, she will share more information on what she has done out of revenge.

There are not many houses around hers, but I'm surprised to see that the lights are still on and music is blasting.

The music stops.

"Bring me another," I hear a male's voice I recognize all too well, as he yells his request. I clench my fists.

"No," I growl.

I walk slowly toward the house, wanting to confirm before I go get Gabriella to report his location. I move quietly to the window on the side of the house, and there he is. Bryson—the dominion angel behind Heidi's disappearance that night. He holds a beer in his hand, and his other hand is on the witch's lower back as she laughs hysterically. He drinks and jokes. He then takes a long swig of his drink and hands her the bottle.

"Get me another, will you?" he asks, and when she moves, unblocking my view, there is Gabriella, sitting on the recliner, sipping on a red drink while she comfortably looks through a fashion magazine.

CHAPTER 12

ZANE

I have to fight the urge to go in there, because right at this moment, there is nothing I can do. Not against all three of them, and not with my lack of powers.

I walk back to Heidi's house knowing that there is only one thing I can do. I will have to call on one of the elders, tell them everything, and hope they can help fix this and let Heidi be. That is the only way I know how to protect her. That is, if they even answer my call.

On the walk back to her, I keep wondering why Gabriella would do this. I decide not to confront her. Not yet, anyway.

I just want to spend one normal day with Heidi before this is all over.

The sun rises, and I wait until her parents leave for work before I go in. I sit on her bed and wake her up. Her eyes are dark once again.

She sits up, closes her eyes, leans her head down, and takes deep breaths.

"What's wrong?" I ask.

"Bad dream," she says.

"Do you want to talk about it?"

"No," she says, looking at me. Her eyes are back to normal. "I

167

don't remember most of it. It was dark. I remember seeing trees. There was a voice trying to say something, but his speech was slurred."

Of course. This must be how the witch and Bryson are getting to her, I think to myself.

"Did you find the answers you were looking for?" she asks.

I don't want to lie to her, so I ignore her question. "Why don't you get dressed? I want to take you somewhere today."

She gives me a confused look.

"It's a surprise. Come on." I smile. "I'll wait outside. Wear something comfortable."

"Hmm . . . okay," she says, looking even more confused.

Fifteen minutes later, she walks outside wearing yoga pants, tennis shoes, and a coat.

"Is this good?" she asks.

I nod. "Perfect."

"Where are we going?" she asks.

"First, breakfast."

As we walk down the street, I slip my hand into hers. She smiles up at me.

I lead her to Coffee Haven, knowing how much she likes going there. I realize that wasn't the best choice when she's ordering and Jace and Elsie come in, hand in hand.

"They are *together?*" I ask in a whisper.

"Ugh. Yes," says Heidi. "Unfortunately."

The barista gives us the total, and I feel bad when Heidi pulls out her wallet to pay for it. Not being used to being seen, I didn't even think about this.

Jace interrupts. "I'm paying for hers," he tells the barista.

Heidi and I look back at him.

"You don't have to," says Heidi.

"I want to," he says.

He looks over at me then.

"I remember you," he says, referring to the night at the library when he caught us kissing. "Just know that if you hurt her, you have me to deal with," he warns.

I nod, feeling awkward. Not just because he basically threatened me, but because for so long, he was my assignment.

"Can we just go?" says Elsie. "I'm not feeling well."

Elsie doesn't look sick. She looks mad. He pays for Heidi's order, then smiles at her, and they leave.

"How can I even compete with that," I say. Not meaning to say it out loud.

Heidi smiles. "It isn't a competition, Zane."

We eat, then we walk toward the dance studio. Heidi's eyes widen as soon as she realizes where we are going.

"I told you I was going to help you get back to where you were. You used to love this."

The disappointed look on her face throws me off. I stop walking.

"What is it?" I ask.

She sighs. "What happens when . . . if . . . I do get back to where I was? Will you leave again?"

"Never," I promise.

She goes from disappointed to shocked.

"What?" I ask.

She laughs. "I just can't believe you actually answered a question."

CHAPTER 13

ZANE

"*I* don't even have dance shoes," she says as we walk into the studio.

I look at her and smirk. "Just give me a few minutes."

I ask to talk to the owner, and I go into her office while Heidi waits. The owner tells me how much she missed having Heidi around and thanks me for bringing her in. She says classes are not until later in the day, so we're welcome to use the main room. When I ask if she happens to have extra ballet shoes around, she walks toward a cabinet in the corner of the room.

"Do you know her size?" she asks.

"Seven," I tell her, and she grabs a brand new pair.

"Come on," she says. "I want to welcome her back."

She smiles from ear to ear when she sees Heidi.

Heidi looks distant and maybe a little nervous. She pulls Heidi into a hug before giving her the ballet shoes.

"Please don't disappear on me again," she says. "We really missed having you here."

"You did?" Heidi asks.

"Of course!" she says. "I hope today means that you will be returning to classes soon?"

"I . . . hmm . . ." Heidi stutters. She looks at me, and I smile at her. "Yes, of course," she says.

"Well, I told your friend here that you can use the main room. Just yell if you need anything, okay?"

Heidi nods, holding tightly to the dance shoes.

I follow her as she walks to the middle of the main room. She looks at her reflection in the mirror before looking down at the shoes she is holding.

"Do you want me to leave you alone?" I ask, but she shakes her head.

She takes off her coat, throwing it to the side. She then sits on the floor, takes her shoes off, and puts on the ballet shoes. She stretches her legs out.

"How does it feel?" I ask her.

She smiles. "Like I never stopped. Thank you, Zane."

I give her a short nod and extend my hand to her. She slips her hand into mine, and the moment I pull her up, her arms instantly go around me. I hug her back, and we stay like this for a while.

"Are you ready to do this?" I ask.

She slowly pulls away and nods. She turns the music on, and I sit on the floor, against one of the mirrors. She twirls around as I watch her. At least an hour goes by without us even realizing. I could watch her all day. When she stops dancing, she looks back at the door. I follow her gaze and see the studio's owner watching her.

"Perfection," she says. "No rush. You can have the room for another thirty minutes, but make sure you stop by my office before you leave so we can get you registered for classes." She pauses. "I'm not taking no for answer."

Heidi looks so much lighter, happier.

She goes back to the middle of the room and lies down. I lie down next to her and slip my hand into hers.

"Why did you do it, Zane? Why did you give up everything?" she asks, looking over at me.

"I didn't give up everything, Heidi. I have you."

She blushes. "Wow. That was pretty smooth for an angel . . . or, well . . . that was smooth."

I chuckle. "You forget I read romance novels. I learned a thing or two."

She laughs.

I watch her. I missed that smile. I missed that laughter that comes from pure happiness.

"For so long I hated what I was—or at least the rules surrounding it all," I tell her. "From the day I first saw you, that part of me was already gone in a way. I hated feeling guilty for loving you."

I see that her eyes have widened.

I sit up. "I guess I just said one of those things that scare humans away, didn't I?" I pause. "I didn't mean to scare you, and I definitely don't expect you to feel the same about me."

She is sitting up now, too. She leans in and kisses me.

We spend the afternoon together. After sunset, I walk her home, and we stop by her front door, where we kiss again.

At the sound of someone clearing his throat, we pull away, and find Ezra staring at us.

"Am I interrupting?" he asks with a grin.

"Yes," Heidi and I both say at the same time.

"I don't understand why you are not running as far away as possible from me," says Heidi.

"Are you kidding me?" asks Ezra. "Aurelia was driving me insane. I needed normal people to hang out with."

"Normal?" Heidi asks while laughing.

Ezra shrugs. "You're not as bad as you think."

"Well, I guess, come on in," Heidi says, and we follow her to her room.

I sit on her bed, and Ezra sits by her desk.

"Hey, do you mind if I use your computer? Aurelia gets in a mood whenever I try to borrow hers."

"Is she ever not in a mood?" Heidi asks. "Go ahead," she says.

Heidi sits next to me. Ezra opens her laptop, then he goes quiet. When he finally turns around, he looks horrified.

"You haven't shared this anywhere, have you?" he asks. "You can't do that!"

Heidi tenses. I stand up and walk toward the laptop.

"I haven't," says Heidi. "Not yet."

Ezra moves from his seat and sits next to her, and I quickly click the delete button after scanning through it. When I turn around, she is staring down at the floor.

"I don't know just how much you are aware of, Heidi," says Ezra, "but the Court is there to *protect* the town. That includes humans."

She scoffs.

"My cousin, Michaela, told me about your disappearance when I asked her about you. Everyone was looking for you, Heidi—vampires, werewolves, shifters—everyone!" he says.

"They were?" Heidi asks with tears in her eyes.

"Whatever really happened, you can't blame everyone in town because of one bad apple, Heidi."

"But I don't remember ever picking up on memories of anyone searching, other than Jace and my parents. And the sheriff, but he is kind of obligated to do it."

Ezra puts his hand over hers. "I can promise you they were looking. My cousin would never lie about something like that. Not that cousin, anyway." He laughs. "Just let it all stay in the past. You got this cool ability. You got this hot guy," he says, making me uncomfortable. "Just forget the past."

She nods once.

Then she stands up, and I notice the shift.

"Heidi?"

"I have somewhere to be," she says. "I'll see you later, okay?"

"Where do you have to be? I'll go with you."

She rolls her eyes at me. "Come on, Zane. Don't be the clingy boyfriend. I just have somewhere to be. I will see you later," and she takes off. I'm left with no choice but to follow her.

"Stay here," I warn Ezra.

When she starts to go into the woods, I rush and get in front of her. "Where are you going, Heidi?"

She ignores me and keeps walking. I stop her. "I will throw you over my shoulders and carry you if I need to," I warn her.

She chuckles. I inch toward her with every intention to do as I said, but it's too late. Bryson, Ani, and Gabriella are standing behind her.

CHAPTER 14

ZANE

I quickly move and stand in front of Heidi, blocking her from their view. A part of me thinks that Heidi won't stay behind me, so I'm surprised when I feel her hold my hand. Her hand is ice cold, and I can feel her tremble.

My gaze narrows on Gabriella.

"Why?" I ask.

Her lips curl into a smile. "I'm merely doing what needs to be done, Zane."

"And that would be?" I growl.

"To correct her fate. She shouldn't be here."

"Actually, this is exactly where she should be. If anyone made her deviate from her fate, that was him," I say as I glare at Bryson.

Heidi's grip on my hand tightens.

"It's not just that. This connection that you have is an abomination. You should not have fallen for a human. And her—knowing what you are and still pursuing you—well, that is just as bad, if not worse."

"It's not up to you to judge," I tell her.

She looks over at the witch. "Now," she says.

The witch says a few words I can't understand, and next thing I know, my whole body starts to feel heavy. My hand involuntarily lets go of Heidi's, and I stand, frozen in place, held up by the witch's magic. Then my vision goes dark. I open my mouth to tell Heidi to at least try to run, but the words don't come out. I'm completely helpless.

"Bryson, get the girl," Gabriella says in a calm tone. I hear Heidi scream my name. I can feel her touch, but I can't do anything. I just keep thinking, *Run, please. Leave me and run!*

Everything goes quiet.

"I have her," Bryson whispers in my ear right before I hear Heidi cry in pain.

Stop! I growl, even though I know they can't hear me.

I hear Bryson's voice again. "How does it feel to know that I'm going to get rid of her again, and there is nothing you can do about it? You failed her once, and you're going to fail her again. Only this time, you are standing within inches of her."

I'm not losing her again. I can't lose her again. Please. I beg anyone who is listening. *Save her. I will go back. I will take whatever punishments you deem fit. Just save her.*

Silence. There is not one sound.

Then I hear Ezra yelling my name. "Zane! Zane!" He pauses. "Crap," he says.

Everything goes silent again, but not for long. The sound of Ezra talking to someone else warns me that it's all over. Everyone who shouldn't know about Heidi will know about her now.

"Michaela," he says in a desperate tone. "I need your help . . . Heidi is in trouble. Three people took her. Her boyfriend is here, but he's out of it. It's like he's frozen or something . . . No, not Jace. Zane . . . Come on, I'm new here, and *I* know that. Keep up, cousin . . . Where am I? Well, that is another problem. I have no clue. I followed them into the woods. I couldn't tell you how to get to where I am . . . uh huh . . . Yeah, I don't have a point of reference. All I see are trees and snow. Hey! I have an idea! I could use their prints on the snow to track them!" I can hear Michaela yell at him to stay where he is. "Yeah, I have the find my phone thingy on, but I'm in the middle of nowhere . . . Okay."

I can feel Ezra poking my arm, then pull on my jacket.

"Zane, if you can hear me, I'm following the footprints to try to find Heidi. Michaela is coming. I put my phone in your pocket so she can find you. Hopefully."

Part of me wants to yell at him to stay put. The other part is grateful he is going after Heidi. Either way, I can't do a thing about it.

Some time goes by—maybe minutes, but it feels like forever. As I begin to feel my body again, I drop to the ground on my knees. When I regain my vision, I see one of the elders, Zelia, in front of me. I frantically look around to find two other angels behind me. A young woman with brown hair comes running up behind them, her gray-green eyes searching all around me.

"Where's Ezra?" she asks.

"He went after Heidi." I slowly stand up.

"What happened?" Zelia asks.

I keep looking toward the footprints.

"We don't have time for this right now. Help me find Heidi first. Please," I beg. I look at Zelia. "Can you track Gabriella?"

The elder nods.

"Heidi was taken by Gabriella, Bryson, and a witch," I tell them.

I can see by their expressions that they all have questions, but they don't waste time asking. Michaela just watches our interaction curiously. Seconds later, the elder takes us to the back of the witch's house.

Looking through the window, we see Ezra and Heidi both tied up, with their backs to one another. Gabriella, Ani, and Bryson stand in front of them. Heidi shakes her head at something they tell her, and that's when Bryson grabs Ezra by his arm, pulling him up.

The angels, confused, look at one another. "We are not supposed to intervene," says one, and my mind goes right back to what Gabriella said about correcting Heidi's fate.

"We're not waiting," says Michaela.

I couldn't agree more.

"Take the front door," I tell her. "I'll take the back."

When I burst in through the door, I come face to face with the witch trying to run.

"You're not going anywhere," I warn her, closing the door behind me. I grab her by her arm and go toward the living room. When I step into the room, I see all three angels. Zelia stands in front of Gabriella and Bryson, who are kneeled down in front of her. One angel is tending to Heidi in one corner of the room as the other angel and Michaela tend to Ezra.

I let go of the witch's arm and rush toward Heidi when I see how hurt she is. I reach for her arm, where there is a large cut, which leads me to understand why they are keeping Ezra on the other side of the room. Michaela watches Heidi curiously, and her eyes widen as she sees Heidi heal right before her eyes.

I help Heidi up and put my arms around her.

"I'm sorry," she says.

"This isn't your fault," I assure her.

Zelia gives Heidi a sympathetic look before her gaze goes back to the other angels. "Take Bryson and Gabriella, please. I will deal with them later. Make sure they're supervised." She looks from them to Bryson and Gabriella. "At all times."

"Okay, who's going to tell me what's going on here?" Michaela asks, looking from Ezra to Heidi. "Ezra?" She lifts a brow in a warning look.

"He doesn't know," Heidi says. "I will tell you everything."

I nod over toward the back door—the witch shouldn't know more than she already does.

"Not here," I say. "Let's go outside."

Michaela glares at Ani, opening her mouth to speak.

"She will not be going anywhere," Zelia says.

Michaela looks from her to Ezra. "Stay here, please. Keep an eye on Ani."

Ezra nods.

When we step outside, Michaela crosses her arms over her chest. "What happened?" she asks, looking at Heidi.

Heidi gives me an apologetic look. This will change everything. I hold on to her hand.

"Go ahead," I tell her. There is no getting out of this now.

Heidi sighs. "That night I went missing, I was hurt by an angel. I died a few months later," she says.

Michaela keeps calm as she listens to everything. Heidi tells her about how she was stuck here as a ghost, and that after she moved on, I brought her back to life. Michaela looks at me then with such intensity, I almost want to run. Still, she doesn't say anything. She crosses her arms over her chest but keeps listening as Heidi tells her about her power to see people's memories. Michaela's eyes widen then, and she starts to put things together.

"And Ani knew about that?" she asks.

Heidi nods. "She gave me a list of names. She said she wanted me to find out what I could about them."

Heidi pulls the paper from her pocket and gives it to Michaela. Michaela stares at it.

"And you know what these names have in common?" she asks, and Heidi nods.

"Have you told Ani anything that you know?" Michaela asks.

Heidi shakes her head. "Nope. And that is how I ended up here tonight."

Michaela nods and looks down at the paper as if she is deep in thought—trying to figure out what to do.

"Why didn't you?" Michaela asks.

Heidi looks down. "I wish I could say it was because I wanted to do the right thing, but . . . it was out of revenge."

Michaela looks surprised.

"I asked her to erase my memory of Zane, and—" Heidi stops. "It didn't work," she says.

Michaela nods. "Do you know if she actually tried to erase your memory?"

Heidi gives her a puzzled look, and I take a step forward, standing in front of Heidi.

"You will not erase Heidi's memories," I warn Michaela. "Even if you try, it won't work. There is a lot that Heidi is immune to." I pause. "She will leave your secrets alone. She won't get involved with anything supernatural. She just wants to be left alone. We both do."

Michaela pulls her phone out of her pocket, and I tense. She dials a number, "Hi, Ric, It's Michaela. I need you to send one of your guys to pick up Ani Rukska from her house, and we need to have an emergency meeting."

She hangs up and looks at Heidi. "I want you to stay with Ezra until I can talk to the others. Can he stay at your house? Just give me a few hours, and we will call you."

Heidi nods.

Sheriff Ric Kasun is the one who comes to pick up the witch himself. Michaela goes with him, leaving Ezra with a list of instructions, which includes not letting Heidi out of his sight.

When they leave, Zelia walks toward us.

I let go of Heidi's hand and take a few steps away.

"I'm sorry," I say, looking down.

"Never apologize for how you feel." Zelia tilts her head to the side as she looks at me. She smiles. "Not when the feelings are so pure."

"But I shouldn't—"

She cuts me off. "Yet you do, son. I trust there is a reason for that. I'm not here to judge you, or to punish you."

She looks at Heidi then and reaches for her hand.

"May I?"

Heidi nods.

Zelia closes her eyes. When she opens her eyes again, she looks saddened.

"I'm so sorry that all of this happened to you. That night should never have happened." She pauses. "This gift that you see as a curse —I can't take it away from you, but I can help you control it."

"Thank you," Heidi says.

Zelia sighs. "I just wish that something could be done to make up for our errors."

Heidi looks down. Her tone lowers. "There is something," she says in almost a whisper.

Zelia tilts her head to the side. "Go on."

"Please let Zane stay," Heidi begs.

CHAPTER 15

ZANE

*T*hings start to change almost immediately. After arriving at Heidi's house, Heidi and I tell Ezra everything. Once he knows the whole story, Ezra calls his cousin and begs her to let him be at that emergency meeting and to vouch for Heidi not being a risk to anyone. Michaela makes him sit out for the first part of it, but once she allows him in, he tells them how Heidi just wanted a second chance at life, especially since she met me. It's enough to get Michaela on our side. Maybe some of the others too. And it doesn't hurt that the members of the Court have all known Heidi since she was little. Their only request is that Heidi attends Sun and Moon Academy to learn about the supernatural world and her abilities.

In Havenwood Falls, things couldn't be better. Now we wait to hear from the angels.

Several days after the Court meeting, Heidi shows up at her dad's store a few minutes before my shift is over. Yet another change since that night. Heidi introduced me to her parents as a friend who's new in town and in need of help. They know I'm not just a friend. I can sense that miles away, even without any abilities of my own. I think they're just glad she sounds more like herself and has someone in her life. Her parents gave me a job at their store and a room to stay in at their house.

"What are we doing tonight?" she asks, as I finish stocking one of the shelves.

"I thought I could take you out," I say. "Your dad gave me an advance on my first check."

"I love that you want to do that," she says, "but I don't feel like being around people." She lowers her tone. "I wish Zelia would just ask a witch to block everyone's memories from me, like Ani did with Jace."

"Well," I say, "that is unnatural, and unnatural usually means bad consequences."

She rolls her eyes at me. "Yeah, yeah . . ."

"Just keep practicing the exercises she gave you to control it. Between her help and the Academy, you'll get this. It just takes time." I finish up and look toward the back. "Mr. Bennett?"

"Yes?" her dad says.

"I'm done here. Is there anything else you need done?"

"That'd be it. Thank you, Zane. Go. Have fun."

We leave the store and head to Coffee Haven, where Ezra is meeting us.

On the way, Heidi stops me.

"Do you really think they will call on you or come for you, like Zelia said? She seems nice, but I don't get why they would do that. Can they make you leave?"

I move a lock of her hair behind her ear. "If that happens, just know that I will make my way back to you."

I can tell that doesn't make her feel any better, but she drops the subject. I just hope I can keep her mind off it.

Ezra is already waiting on us when we walk into Coffee Haven, and he has Heidi's favorites already ordered, waiting on her.

Heidi pulls her sweater over her head, and Ezra spits out his drink from laughing so hard. When she faces me, I just shake my head.

"Really?" says Ezra. "Did it have to be that one?" he asks,

referring to the *Vampires suck* shirt. She smiles, and suddenly, it's all worth it.

Her smile turns into a frown when a group of students I don't recognize walk in, talking about the Sweetheart Dance. I catch Heidi staring at them, looking distant.

I bump into her shoulder. "Do you want to go?" I ask.

Ezra kicks me under the table and shakes his head, and Heidi gives me a confused look.

"To the dance," I continue.

"Nah," she says. Then she excuses herself and goes toward the restrooms.

I look at Ezra, who is giving me an evil look. He looks down when I meet his gaze, but I get the feeling there is something he wants to say.

"Did I say something wrong?" I ask.

He nods slowly. "Just a little. Don't feel bad, though. Most guys would make the same mistake."

"What did I do?" I ask as I raise an eyebrow at him.

He puts the napkin down. "It was the way you asked her. Don't ask her to go just for the sake of asking. I know she was with Jace for quite some time, and from what I heard people say, he used to make a big deal out of everything. I mean—you were there for most of it, right? You gotta know you have big shoes to fill. Put some thought into it. Show her that you want to take her to the dance. That you can't imagine spending that night any other way than with her by your side."

Okay, maybe the kid has point.

"Do you have any ideas?" I ask.

He leans in and tells me what he has in mind.

I laugh. "There is absolutely no way I'm doing that. Why purple anyway?"

He shrugs. "It has something to do with a town legend I heard about—a witch who had two great loves. It actually reminds me of Heidi—with you and Jace. No offense."

I roll my eyes at him. "I never heard of it," I say as I look back, wondering why Heidi is taking so long.

"Well, I like my idea. You should go for it. I'll even take care of everything. You just have to stand there and look hot."

I shake my head, looking embarrassed. "Nope. And you're insane. This is the most ridiculous idea I've ever heard."

Ezra smirks and shrugs. "Worst case scenario, it would put a smile on that girl's face. I don't see how that can be a bad idea."

"What did I miss?" Heidi asks as she sits down.

"Nothing," we both say.

We finish our drinks, then Heidi has to get to dance class. Another thing her parents were so happy about, and so is she.

I offer to walk her to the studio, but she refuses, saying she could use some alone time to clear her head.

Ezra and I stay at Coffee Haven, and it's not until she leaves that I spot Jace sitting at a corner table, watching us. Once she's gone, he stands up and walks toward us.

"Hey, man, can I talk to you?" he asks.

"Sure," I agree, even though I'm certain he will punch me at any minute. "So . . . ?" I say.

Jace puts his hands in his pockets and shifts his weight from one foot to the other, looking uncomfortable. Finally, he says, "I just want to ask you to take care of her. No hard feelings. I want Heidi to be happy, and she's more like herself when she's around you."

I nod. I can see in his eyes that he means the Heidi that he fell in love with—that he's still in love with, even though he's with Elsie. I have a whole new level of respect for him for saying that.

When he walks away, I turn to Ezra.

"Swoon!" says Ezra. "Too bad he's straight."

I roll my eyes at him. "Fine. We'll do that stupid idea of yours."

He smiles from ear to ear. "I'll take care of everything. Just meet me outside the dance studio ten minutes before she gets out."

. . .

I pace in front of the studio. Five minutes before she gets out, Ezra shows up. I don't even know how he was able to find these, and in a way, I wish he hadn't. I heard some of the guys in town talking about their "man cards," and I'm pretty sure this leads to me losing mine.

And so here I stand, holding purple pig balloons and a poster that says, "When pigs fly, will you go to the Sweetheart Dance with me?"

Ezra grabs his phone. "Smile" he says. I don't, but he takes the picture anyway.

"I'm going to kill you," I say.

He laughs. "This is a little comical—a guy with your build, combat boots . . . holding that."

"Ha," I say in a sarcastic tone. I put the sign down. "Here," I try to hand him the balloons. "There is no way I'm doing this. It's ridiculous!"

"Too late. She's coming. Hold that sign up, boy." He laughs.

I think it takes her a minute to get it.

"RELEASE THE BALLOONS!" says Ezra.

I do, and she bursts out laughing, before she rushes in my direction and wraps her arms around me. She then looks at Ezra.

"Your idea?" she asks, and he admits to it proudly. "What's the deal with the pigs being purple?" she asks.

Ezra looks at me.

"Oh no," I say. "You tell her that one."

He laughs. "Fine. I heard this town legend about a witch and something to do with purple pigs. From what I heard, she had two loves, and it kinda made me think of you."

She raises an eyebrow at him. "First of all," she says in a playful tone, "the word *witch* traumatizes me a bit. And based on the legend, her two loves were her china and her pigs, and she went crazy at some point." She pauses. "What part exactly makes you think of me?"

"Oops." He laughs. "That's not what I heard."

She rolls her eyes at him, and I stand here watching how happy she looks. Finally, she meets my gaze.

"So, is that a yes?" I ask.

She nods with a huge grin on her face.

CHAPTER 16

HEIDI

*T*he night before the Sweetheart Dance, I head to my room right after dinner to do homework. I find a note on my bed.

Meet me at the library at 8?

I feel my stomach churn. Zane was supposed to stay late and help with inventory tonight, so this can't be good. I rush to the library. I get in and go to the second floor, where we used to spend so much time. I find Zane standing in the middle of a room full of books, wearing a suit. There is soft music playing. He turns on a lamp and stars dance around the room.

I look around, amazed. He walks toward me and extends a hand. I slip my hand into his, but as much as I want to be in the moment, I know something is off.

"What's this about?" I ask.

He looks intensely at me without saying a word. His hand goes to the small of my back, and he slowly pulls me closer, leans in, and kisses me.

When he pulls away, I look at him, waiting for him to say something . . . anything. When he doesn't, I know what this means.

"You're leaving again," I say. And I hate that it doesn't make me love him any less.

He nods. "I have to. They want to talk. But I promise you that I will be back."

"Let me go with you," I say.

He looks down, and I swallow the lump in my throat.

"You miss it, don't you? Having a purpose? I don't blame you. For a while, I missed that too."

"Heidi, you have a purpose. Your life shouldn't have been interrupted. You should be here now. You are here. Take advantage of that. And believe me. I'm not letting you go. I'll be back."

Out of desperation, I resort to a childish attempt to keep him here. "How do you know I'm not going to the dance tomorrow and will do something crazy? Maybe spread the truth about Elsie like I had planned before, and maybe others too—"

He cuts me off. "Because that wasn't all you, Heidi. That was Bryson and Ani and Gabriella messing with your head. Do you even still have those pictures you took at Elsie's house?"

I shake my head. "No. I deleted them all."

"I know you. You are good. You understand that none of that was Elsie's fault. Yes, she went a little psycho with the pictures on the wall, and I know you're worried about Jace, but—" He pauses. "Go to the dance tomorrow with Ezra, and have fun. For me. I'll be back as soon as I can."

"Why don't I believe you?" I ask.

"Because I don't have the best track record. But it's different now. I already walked away from it all, and I don't feel an ounce of regret. This is where I should be. With you."

ZANE

Before leaving, I make Ezra promise me to take her to the dance if I'm not back on time. I hate leaving her, even if temporarily, but I feel that I owe Zelia, and I want to make sure Heidi will be protected.

Zelia comes to get me. I fully expect to be taken in for a lecture and requests for my return, but instead, I find myself in a room full of angels. Bryson and Gabriella are kneeled down in the middle of the room.

"Come," Zelia tells me, and I follow her to the center. We stand in front of Bryson and Gabriella.

"Thank you all for being here today," Zelia says. "Yesterday, we went over everything that happened. Bryson and Gabriella have confessed to allying with a witch to control Heidi Bennett and to influence her through her dreams. Are there any objections to Zane weighing in on their punishment?"

My eyes widen. I don't know how to do this. I've never had such responsibilities. Yet no one objects.

"Zane?" she says. "What do you suggest?"

I stop to think about it. Still shocked that I'm face to face with the ones who put Heidi through so much, I'm inclined to show them some mercy.

I sigh. "I believe they shouldn't be allowed around humans again."

Zelia nods.

I think of Heidi's concern for Jace. "And I believe that my last assignment—Jace Edwards—would be better protected if away from Elsie Brooks," I say. At that, Bryson growls.

Zelia smiles. "I believe that is fair. Take him away," she tells one of the other angels.

"And Gabriella?" she asks.

I grin and tilt my head to the side. "I believe that Gabriella has become too infatuated with certain things from the human world. She should suffer enough if she's kept away from things like fashion, gossip magazines . . ."

Gabriella glares at me. I smile. Some of the angels chuckle.

"Very well," says Zelia. "We'll add that to her final sentencing, which we will discuss later. Now, about Heidi."

"What about Heidi?" I ask in an alarmed tone.

Zelia gives me a genuine smile. "I believe the girl means no harm to others. She was depressed and dealing with the shock of the tragedies she was put through. Bryson, Gabriella, and Ani's alliance only made things much worse. And due to our mistakes, she lost faith. We believe that you, Zane, healing and bringing her back has made her immortal, which will not be a problem—at least for a couple of years. Does anyone disagree that Heidi is not a threat and should be left in peace?"

Relief washes over me as no one speaks.

Then I ask the question about the one word that stuck in my mind. "Immortal? How?"

Zelia keeps her focus on me. "A lot about what happened to Heidi leaves us with questions. She died many months before you brought her back, Zane. You shouldn't have been able to revive her, unless you had special abilities of your own that affected her in unprecedented ways." She pauses. "Now let's talk about you, Zane," she says.

One of the angels speaks. "Will he finally be charged for bringing her back?"

The room falls silent again, and Zelia continues as if no one has spoken. "Zane has served his time. That is the end of that." She then looks at me. "Zane, it has come to my attention that you may have been coerced by Gabriella into making a choice. Was that what you truly wanted?"

HEIDI

Ezra makes sure I go to the dance. He insists and says that Zane made him promise a million times over.

I wear a black dress that Mom bought for me. Ezra picks me up, and Mom and Dad take a billion pictures. When they ask where Zane is, I say he had to take care of something personal.

"He will be back," I say, as if trying to convince myself that he is actually coming.

As soon as we walk into the open warehouse-style building, the Annex, I spot Jace by one of the food tables, alone. I wave a quick hello, and he walks up to me with a smile on his face.

"Uh-oh," says Ezra. "I'm not sure what to do here. Should I pretend to be your temporary boyfriend so he will back off?"

I laugh at him. "Relax."

Jace gets closer.

"Where is Elsie?" I ask.

He chuckles. "It seems that I have this horrible bad timing when it comes to dances and telling girls that I'm getting ready to move."

I raise an eyebrow at him.

"Dad just got a call about an hour ago. He's getting transferred to New York in a few months, and it makes sense that I live there. As a songwriter, there are just more opportunities."

"Wow. That's amazing, Jace."

"Where is Zane?" he asks.

"He's away for a while," I say.

"Oh."

"He'll be back," I say awkwardly. "Congrats on the move, though. I'm happy for you, Jace. I know you will do amazing things." I'm also happy he will be away from Elsie, but I don't tell him that.

"Well, do you want to dance?" he asks. I look from him to Ezra.

"Go for it," says Ezra. "Just don't forget who your real date is."

I roll my eyes at Ezra before Jace and I walk away.

We dance to a slow song.

"Hey, what is it that you wanted to talk to me about?" I ask.

"Nothing," he says. "It doesn't matter anymore."

I hear him chuckle.

"What?" I ask as I stop dancing and look at him.

He nods his head toward the entrance. "I guess he couldn't stay away from you too long."

He gives me a sad smile. I stand here, staring at Zane at the door as he stares back at me. I look from Zane to Jace, not knowing what to say.

"Go," he says. "You deserve to be happy, Heidi. Always did. It just sucks I'm not part of the picture."

Tears well up in my eyes.

He gives me a half smile. "Go!" he says.

I pull him into a quick hug before I walk toward Zane. I stop about two feet away from him. He closes the distance between us.

I shake my head. "You have this horrible habit of leaving, and every time you come back, I feel like I've fallen for you even more," I say.

He grins. "Should I leave again?" he asks.

I laugh. He takes a step closer, wraps his arms around me, and whispers in my ear, "I'm here to stay. I choose you, Heidi. I always have."

ABOUT THE AUTHOR

Daniele Lanzarotta is the author of young adult and new adult paranormal, fantasy, and contemporary novels, including the Academy of the Fallen Series, the Sudden Hope novels, and A Mermaid's Curse Trilogy.

Daniele is also a filmmaker and CEO & Founder of Elysian Nightfall Studios—a brand development, audio & video production, and film company. She has recently worked on Virginia-based short films as the Second Assistant Director and Still Photographer. Daniele is currently working on the development stage for the adaptation of her novel, *Sudden Hope*, which she also plans to film in Virginia. She is also working on other film and writing projects.

She enjoys watching hockey, playing Rock Band and Guitar Hero, and spending time with her husband, two daughters, and the family dog.

For more about Daniele and her novels, please visit www.danilanzarotta.com

ACKNOWLEDGMENTS

It takes a village.

Thank you, Kristie, for allowing me the opportunity to be a part of this world. I fell in love with Zane and Heidi when I wrote *Avenoir*, and I'm thankful for the opportunity to share more of their lives.

Thank you to all the Havenwood Falls authors for the amazing communication and collaboration.

I can't wait to see what the future holds for Havenwood Falls!

ASCENDING DARKNESS

J.L. WEIL

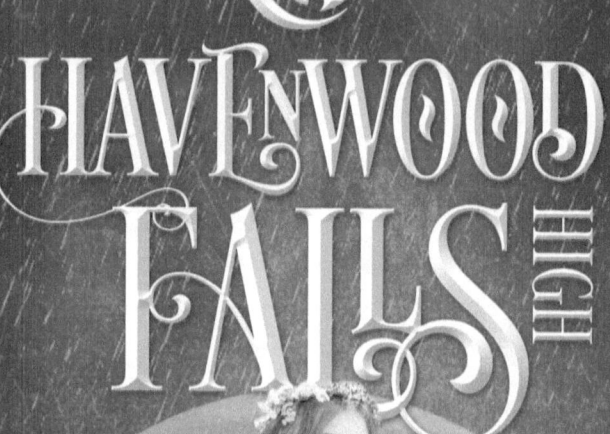

HAVENWOOD FALLS HIGH

Ascending Darkness

USA Today Bestselling Author

J.L. WEIL

~ A Havenwood Falls Young Adult Novella ~

ALSO BY J.L. WEIL

DRAGON DESCENDENT SERIES

Stealing Tranquility

Absorbing Poison

Taming Fire

Thawing Frost

THE DIVISA SERIES

Losing Emma: A Divisa novella

Saving Angel

Hunting Angel

Breaking Emma: A Divisa novella

Chasing Angel

Loving Angel

Redeeming Angel

LUMINESCENCE TRILOGY

Luminescence

Amethyst Tears

Moondust

Darkmist – A Luminescence novella

RAVEN SERIES

White Raven

Black Crow

Soul Symmetry

BEAUTY NEVER DIES CHRONICLES

Slumber

Entangled

Forsaken

NINE TAILS SERIES

First Shift

Storm Shift

Flame Shift

Time Shift

HAVENWOOD FALLS HIGH SERIES

Falling Deep

Ascending Darkness

SINGLE NOVELS

Starbound

Casting Dreams

Ancient Tides

For all those who encouraged and supported my dreams.

CHAPTER 1

The window in my bedroom was closed and yet, for an instant, I smelled the sea, heard the call of the water, felt its coolness wash over my face. Here and then gone. The longing to be in the water swelled in my heart, like an endless love.

Not that I knew a lot about love.

Why Torent Stark's face instantly flashed in my head at the mention of love was something I'd rather not dwell on. In fact, I'd rather not think of him at all. Too bad my mind didn't feel the same way.

Torent was a boy.

Okay, he wasn't just any boy. First, he was a half-demon. That right there was a giant red flag waving in my face and should have been enough to tell me he was bad news. Then there was the crazy ex-girlfriend drama. Torent's ex-girlfriend had made me her archenemy. Sometimes too much baggage was not worth the risk, but my heart didn't seem to care about his past relationships or the dark streak inside him he worked so hard to hide and control. I gave him mad props. He had so much more control over his abilities than I did.

My magnetic energy was still unstable, causing inconvenient outbursts, like the time a box of staples almost embedded itself into one of my instructors at Sun and Moon Academy during one of my night classes.

What I was going to do about Torent was another one of those mysteries of life, and damn if my life hadn't become a long Nancy Drew novel. So much secrecy shrouded my past, and I was only recently unearthing the answers, but I had more questions.

Before moving to Havenwood Falls, my life was normal. I'd lived in Wisconsin, gone to an average high school, watched my mother end yet another marriage. And in a way, things had returned to that habitual norm. Mom got a job, which Gigi was thrilled about. I had settled in at school and was coming to terms with being a water nymph.

Okay, so not your typical normal, but my life was average by Havenwood Falls standards.

However, some things never change.

Take Brooklyn Kendall, for instance. She still hated my guts. Turns out she didn't need a magical object to feel such strong enmity for me.

Torent was still trying to get me to go out with him. He was persistent—I'd give him that. And cute. And charming. And . . .

A bird squawked outside my window, interrupting my internal list of all of Torent's redeeming qualities. At this time of the year, the local birds had already migrated south, but a few stragglers had taken up residence in the tree outside my window. They had spent the last week waking me up before my alarm, and that put them on my shit list. I was not a morning person, not before at least two cups of coffee. I hadn't thought much about it, but this morning, something about the sound gave me the heebie-jeebies.

My eyes narrowed, and I went to the window to push aside the curtain and peer out into the yard. The sun was just peeking over the mountains and, it being late November, the air would be brisk. A light sheet of snow carpeted the grass.

Perched on an icy branch, the black bird gave another warning screech. His midnight feathers were in stark contrast against the barren tree. Beady eyes of charcoal watched cautiously through the glass. Strange. His feathers ruffled as he stretched out his wings, and I smiled, tapping lightly on the window.

"Where are all your little friends?" I asked, not really thinking about the fact I was talking to a bird.

He cocked his head to the left and right, eyeing me. Then he kicked off the little branch and flew straight into the window. *Thwack.* I jumped back, unable to believe what had happened.

The bird had just committed suicide.

A blotch of blood smeared down the glass, and my stomach turned. I backed away, feeling uneasy about what I'd seen. It wasn't every day I witnessed a bird snapping its own neck.

So much for that *normal* life.

My cell phone buzzed on the bed, and I turned my back to the massacre streaming down my window to pick up my phone.

"Crap," I grumbled, staring at the time on my phone. My third alarm had gone off, and if I didn't move my ass, I would be late for school.

I tossed on a pair of jeans, a white tank top, and a flannel, only to stop in front of the mirror. *Dear God, is that me?*

My hair looked like one of those black birds had made a nest in it, blond curls messily framing my face. The mascara I was too lazy to remove last night was smeared over my eyes, giving me a Goth look. I was going to have to roll with it. On my way out the door, I snatched a tube of lip gloss and applied it hastily to my lips, then sprayed two squirts of perfume over my clothes, unsure if they were clean or not. I grabbed a brush, my car keys, and my book bag before dashing down the stairs into the kitchen.

Gigi was sipping a mug of hot coffee.

"Morning." She grinned cheerily.

I grumbled an inaudible response and plucked her cup of coffee from her hands, downing half of it. "Thanks. I needed that."

"I guess so," she replied, taking back the nearly empty cup. Her blue eyes were shining. For a woman in her sixties, Gigi was sharp as a whip.

Mom came around the corner and stopped halfway to the coffeepot, eyeing me. "What happened to your hair?"

She was dressed in black slacks and a white button-down shirt, one button too many undone at the top. No one was more shocked Mom had gotten a job as a file clerk at Bishop Enterprises than Gigi.

The two of them constantly harped at one another. It was as routine as taking the garbage to the curb on Wednesdays.

"Don't ask," I mumbled, moving through the kitchen. I threw a hand in the air, waving bye, and stepped out the front door.

Icy breezes wrapped around me, and a blast of wind blew through my flannel. I cursed myself for not grabbing a to-go mug of coffee. It would be a long-ass day. Not to mention what this wind was doing to my already disastrous hair.

Jogging down the stone path to my old and semi-reliable car, I twisted my head toward the tree outside my bedroom window, my thoughts returning to the bird. I didn't have to time check on his little corpse, and yet I found myself moving off the path and onto the lawn. The frozen grass crunched under my weight. I grew closer, and eventually my Converses skidded as my steps faltered.

What the—

There wasn't just one poor dead bird under the aspen tree. There were at least half a dozen strewn over the cold ground, their small necks angled oddly off to the side. My heart knocked in my chest.

My hand flew to my mouth, and I took a step backward. A trickle of unease ribboned down my spine as I tried but failed to make sense of the scene in front of me. What had happened here? I wanted to believe it was a natural event, not something supernatural, but I couldn't shake the sneaky suspicion it wasn't Mother Nature at play.

God, it would be just like Brooklyn Kendall to arrange a bird graveyard to freak me out. Things between my fellow water nymph and me were anything but smooth sailing. She still wanted to make my life miserable and blamed me for pretty much everything wrong in her seemingly perfect life. Misery loves company, as the saying went.

I suppressed a shiver and got into my car, backing out of the driveway with enough speed to kick up gravel.

I whipped my car into the parking lot of Havenwood Falls High. The three-story red brick building was bustling with students rushing to get to class. Throwing my car into park, I sat staring at the arched front doors and considered skipping the entire day. The whole dead-bird thing had gotten to me, more than I realized.

But ditching classes would earn me a Saturday detention and would tarnish my pristine college resume. I had a plan. That plan didn't involve me being stuck in Havenwood Falls for the rest of my life.

A world existed behind these mountains and waterfalls, and I was going to see it all. I *was* going to get that college scholarship. No deranged pranks or cute boys were going to stop me from pursuing my dreams.

I dashed through the front doors as the bell for first period rang. Son of a bitch. I was late. Again. My feet flew over the brown marble floor toward my first class. No time to stop at my locker.

"I hope this isn't going to become a weekly occurrence, Ms. Dorian," Mr. Zander, my AP English Lit teacher, scolded while I was sneaking not so stealthily into class.

I slumped into my seat, a tight smile pasted on my lips. "I wouldn't dream of it."

He went back to waving the black marker in the air, telling the class to open their textbooks to page seventy-three.

What a way to start the day.

I managed to get through my morning classes. Silver and blue snowflake decorations lined the cream hallways for the upcoming holidays. There always seemed to be some school event going on. HFH's mascot was a dragon. How fitting. The fierce-looking dragon was plastered everywhere—floors, walls, banners, flyers—you name it and he was there.

I slid my butt into the seat across from Beck, who was picking at something under his nails. Someone had given his hair color a boost last night. The blue was extra bright today.

"You know I'd dye your hair for you," I said, grabbing one of his hands and surveying the damage to his fingers. The skin was tinged blue, along with the tips of his nails.

He pulled his hand back to his side of the cafeteria table. "It looks so damn easy in the commercials."

I rolled my eyes. "You're supposed to wear gloves."

His nose wrinkled in disdain. "They make my hands sweat."

My brows rose in question. What was the big deal with a little hand sweat? It beat having blue fingers for a week.

"Wolf thing," he stated. "I was thinking of painting my nails black anyway."

Beck Winslow was the first real friend I'd made in Havenwood Falls. He was also a wolf shifter. Not a big deal in a town full of supernaturals.

I pushed aside some of my wayward second-day hair. "You're not going to believe the morning I've had."

"Hello, blue fingers," he replied, waving his hand in the air. "There is definitely something funky in the atmosphere. I'd say we're in for a snowstorm. I can smell it." His eyes shifted to the large square window that overlooked the parking lot.

That wasn't quite what I had in mind, and despite the sun beaming this morning, an incoming storm would explain the hint of water I sensed in the air. My eyes followed his, seeing the beginnings of gray clouds rolling in. "Is weather predicting a wolf thing?"

He grinned, and it lit up his face. "Intense senses."

My fingers drummed on the tabletop beside my untouched salad. What had possessed me to get rabbit food when what I really wanted was an entire pizza from Napoli's?

"I might need to borrow your intense senses," I said, half joking.

Beck plucked a cherry tomato from the top of my lunch and popped it into his mouth as he leaned over the table. "What's up?"

I nibbled on my lower lip instead of my salad. "This morning, a bird flew into my bedroom window, but that wasn't the strangest part. When I left for school, there were half a dozen dead birds scattered outside my bedroom. Tell me that is normal?"

"*That* is a bad omen, chica."

"Peachy," I said dryly. "Just what I need. So you're saying I should be worried?"

He shrugged. "It's hard to say. This time of year the animals get a little restless. It could be nothing. Oooor," he dragged out, "you might be cursed. Piss someone off lately?"

I sighed and leaned my head into my hands. "That narrows it down."

His eyes spanned the lunchroom, landing on a trio of girls giggling annoyingly. "I can think of one particular popular girl who would love to throw a flock of dead birds at your house."

In sauntered the bitch of the hour.

Brooklyn Kendall.

Would she really do that? Yes, although it didn't explain the bird flying into my window. But the other birds dead on the ground? I wasn't sure. The whole thing smacked of some devious plot Brooklyn would concoct.

The devil herself was giving me a mad case of the stink eye as she crossed the cafeteria with Leena and Cora in tow.

"Is this feud between us ever going to end?" I muttered.

Beck's sparkling gray eyes trailed the nymph squad. "I hope not."

I playfully smacked him on the arm. "Dude, that's not funny."

He rubbed at the spot on his bicep, grinning. "I can't help it. Things have been so much more . . . colorful since you moved in."

My head tilted to the side while I regarded him. "What's the name of your therapist again? I think it might be time to switch your meds."

He laughed, throwing back his blue head and gaining the attention of a few tables surrounding us. "See, this is what I'm talking about. This school needed you, Mal."

I wasn't so sure about that. Brooklyn blamed me for ruining her life. Her ex-boyfriend was derailing me from my life plan. Mom put on a brave face, but I could tell something had her worried. And I had unruly magnetic powers. None of these were things I construed as good.

CHAPTER 2

*S*torms never really bothered me. Maybe it was my connection to water that offered calm during the howling of the winds, the crash of thunder, and the spears of lightning slashing across the black sky. Beck had been right. Havenwood Falls was in for a helluva storm, and for the end of November, ice was definitely in the forecast. For now, the sky was putting on quite the show.

I raced across the parking lot to my car, my bag jostling behind me. The last place I wanted to be caught was on the road when the mixture of rain and ice decided to fall. My steps faltered at the sight of Torent leaning against my Chevy Malibu, and dammit if the car never looked so good. He had a way of making everything around him hotter.

Sighing, I walked around him and opened the backseat door, tossing in my bag.

"What are you doing?" I asked, spinning to face him.

He boxed me in with his body, pressing his palms on either side of the car. My breath hitched at his sudden nearness. *Don't think about how close he is or how wonderfully intoxicating he smells.*

I sank into the cold metal of my car, but it didn't help. My senses went into overdrive. I hadn't been exactly avoiding him, but more or less evading temptation. Damn him and his sexy demon dimples.

"I missed you," he replied in a deep and rich voice that melted over me.

Be strong. You can resist that smirk.

"Torent," I groaned, making the mistake of putting my hands on his chest. They were supposed to push him away, yet ignoring the command my brain sent to my hands, they rested over his beating heart. When was I going to accept that I didn't want to avoid Torent or only be his friend?

He grinned, tugging on the end of a frazzled curl. "I love it when you say my name."

I leveled him with a stare that did absolutely nothing to wipe the wickedness from his violet eyes. Tiny flecks of gold were sprinkled in those irises—his demon. I'd only seen Torent lose control once, and although it had been scary, I hadn't been frightened of the darkness that lived within him.

"You're never going to give up the chase, are you?"

"Not when I want something," he crooned.

It was a thrill to hear he wanted me. I couldn't deny the rush his silky words gave me, but I wasn't impulsive or reckless. I'd thought of little else the last few weeks than what my life would be like if I dated a demon.

"What happens when you get bored?" I challenged, although this wasn't the first time we'd had this conversation. It seemed we were doomed to spin circles around each other.

His nose brushed over the tip of mine, bringing our lips too close for comfort. I only had to tilt my head an inch up and I'd be doing the very thing I longed for—kissing the shit out of Torent Stark. One of his hands lifted off the car and trailed down my arm to lace our fingers together. I shocked myself by letting him. In fact, I wasn't sure I could let go.

"Never going to happen, crash car. There's something between us not even I can explain."

"That doesn't make it right."

A gust of wind blew in from the south, and thunder struck over our heads.

"How do you know unless you give us a chance?" His other hand tucked a wayward strand of hair behind my ear, and I shuddered. His body pressed into mine. "I don't know why you insist on resisting this."

This being the irrational feelings between us. He was wearing me down. I no longer seemed to remember why I was fighting so hard against what he made me feel. It was exhausting working each day to stay away from him, to not give in to the urge to wrap my arms around him or kiss him brainless in the middle of math class.

He was a distraction.

And there it was. The reason Torent was bad for my health. If I spent all day staring at his gorgeous face, I'd fail all my classes. I'd be stuck in Havenwood Falls with Brooklyn breathing fire down my neck. I'd probably run off and marry him straight out of high school and end up with a dozen equally gorgeous little demon babies.

Sparks lingered at the places his fingers had touched my cheek. Torent, being part demon, could produce a light he called hellfire. I hadn't seen its full potential, but the bits I'd been exposed to were mesmerizing.

"You make me lose myself," I admitted softly.

His focus was completely on me, which was more than a little unnerving. "Why do you see that as a negative thing?"

I angled my face closer to his as if compelled. "I have dreams, plans for my future."

"It doesn't have to be one or the other," he said softly.

Maybe not, but I was afraid of how much I would be willing to give up for him if I let myself, because I knew with certainty that I would fall head over heels in love with him.

This conversation was getting too deep. It was time to divert. "Don't tell me you need a ride. Again."

Torent had used every creative excuse and then some to find

time alone with me. It was impossible to not be flattered by his ingenuity . . . or his lingering looks and charming smile.

He gave me a lopsided grin. "The Jeep is in the shop."

"Uh-huh. You need to come up with new material."

His shoulders lifted in a shrug. "Why? This one works so well."

"Get in," I grumbled. I was going to regret this.

He lingered, keeping me pinned to the car with his body. "We're not done talking about you and me. Not by a long shot."

Strolling to the other side of the car, he opened the passenger door.

I exhaled the breath I'd been holding and slid into the driver's seat as he folded himself into my compact vehicle. He made it seem tiny.

Lifting his glorious tush up to one side, he pulled out my brush. "Is this yours?"

I winced, taking the hairbrush he dangled in the air. "Sorry. It was a hectic morning."

Torent relaxed back into the seat. "I heard you were late again."

I tossed the brush into the back of the car and stuck the keys into the ignition, waiting for it to kick over. "Are you keeping tabs on me, Stark?"

His lips twitched as he buckled his seatbelt. "I wouldn't dream of it."

I shifted the car into reverse. "Liar."

He leaned over the center console, fumbling with the radio as I pulled out of the parking spot.

"Are you going to tell me what has you on edge today?" He sounded like he was asking about the weather. "Or am I going to have to seduce it out of you?"

I smacked at the hand that had landed on my thigh. "Don't you dare. I'm driving. Do you really want me to get into an accident?"

He looked so adorable with his jet-black hair disheveled from the wind. "What I want is for you to admit you're enamored by me."

My mouth dropped open. The gall of him! Snapping my mouth shut, I put the Malibu into drive.

"Or . . . you can tell me what's going on," he prodded, as he was so good at doing.

I maneuvered my car in line behind the mass of vehicles trying to exit the parking lot, the weather delaying traffic more than usual. Someone's ball cap flew over the hood of my car and out to the field. I sighed, biting on my lower lip. What could it hurt to tell him the crazy conspiracy theories? It was likely I was worried for nothing. And the worst that would happen was Torent would laugh or tell me I was being silly. I could handle both.

"Beck is convinced I'm cursed. I think Brooklyn is still trying to get revenge on me."

Torent waved at Seth Cooper crossing the parking lot before his eyes ran over me. "Why would you think that? Has something happened?" When I didn't immediately respond, a glint of ominous suspicion sprang into his eyes. "Mallory," he growled so low it caused goose bumps on my arms.

"Geez. Don't get all demon on me. I'm sure it was nothing. I found a bunch of dead birds outside my window this morning."

His fingers brushed at the tiny stubbles under his chin that I found so appealing. The shadow of hair gave him an air of darkness I was clearly attracted to. "Why didn't you tell me?"

Shrugging, I flipped the wheel hand over hand, moving with traffic onto the main road. "I didn't think it was a big deal, but you and Beck are starting to freak me out over it."

Not entirely true. I had already been upset by it this morning, but for some reason, I didn't want to appear weak or superstitious. I didn't want to be that girl who ran to a guy every time she had a problem. I wasn't a damsel in distress who needed to be saved. I had every intention of saving myself.

"Birds often don't die in mass suicides, not in Havenwood Falls."

"I'm learning nothing happens in this town without a reason. I swear, if Brooklyn is still tormenting me because she blames me for taking her powers, I'm going to staple her ass to a chair." The thing was, with my abilities, I could very well carry out the threat.

The muscle along his jaw worked. "Let me talk to her."

"No!" I shouted, nearly swerving off the road. "Don't do that. It would only make things worse. I can deal with her on my own terms."

Torent scowled, either at my driving or at my refusal of his help. "Do you remember what happened the last time you faced off with Brooklyn?"

Did I ever. She nearly killed me. "How could I forget?"

"All the more reason you need to let me find out if she is behind this," he insisted.

"Do you think that's a good idea? You know how touchy she is about us. I don't want to push her and have crap escalating."

"So you're saying there is an *us*?" Torent's eyes twinkled.

How did our conversations always derail so quickly? It was an impressive skill. My lips formed a straight line. "Focus. We were talking about Brooklyn."

Some of the humor dried up, and he got serious. "Go out with me on Saturday."

Oh, my God. I give up. I was done fighting him. "Why would I do that?"

He leaned closer, and his fingers twirled a strand of my hair. "Because it would be fun. You remember fun, don't you, Mal?"

Okay, so Torent wasn't the only one with creative excuses. Mine just happened to always revolve around me studying or doing homework. But he had a point. I hadn't gone out in weeks, not even for coffee, and that was just a sin in my book. Locking myself up in the house was not me—it wasn't how I wanted to live. "If I say yes, will you stop asking? One date and that's it."

His lips twitched into a half smile. "One is all it will take."

I shook my head, trying to keep my eyes on the road.

"You really need to work on your confidence," I said dryly. The sky chose that moment to open up, letting the icy rain pour. It plummeted from the black clouds, hitting my windshield with a pattering force that made visibility dodgy. "What is this, the apocalypse?" I'd lived in Wisconsin. I was no stranger to winter, but this was nasty to the tenth degree.

"Maybe we should pull over until the storm passes?" Torent suggested, his eyes narrowing at the ominous clouds above us.

My fingers clenched on the steering wheel. "If I didn't know better, I'd swear you planned this."

He chuckled. "Controlling the weather is unfortunately not one of my skill sets."

I was slowly inching the car along the road and was seriously considering pulling over as Torent had advised. "But you have friends—"

What the hell?

A dark shadow was sailing straight at me, and I had no time to react, only brace myself for impact.

Whack!

I gave a yelp, my heart roaring in my ears. Something had hit the windshield. I stomped on my brakes, hitting a patch of black ice, and my car spun in a circle. Talk about déjà-freaking-vu.

CHAPTER 3

I don't know how he did it, but Torent took control of the wheel as it spun. It felt as if the car would never stop. A scream lodged in my throat just as he was able to straighten out the wheels and land us in the ditch, narrowly avoiding a massive pine tree.

Torent quickly turned to me, his fingers sliding under my chin to glance over my face. "Are you okay?"

My hands were attached to the steering wheel in a death grip. "I will be as soon as I swallow my heart back down to my chest."

"You're not hurt?" he asked again.

"I-I don't think so . . . but my car," I groaned, staring at the massive spider crack that fissured over the entire windshield in a jagged pattern.

"It's nothing that can't be fixed," he said, trying to downplay the situation.

I failed to mention I had no money, and I hated to ask my Mom. She just started a new job, and there were bills that had to be paid, thanks to her latest divorce. I killed the engine, needing a few moments to collect myself and figure out what I was going to do next. The icy rain was still coming down in buckets.

He surveyed the damage.

"There's a reason I call you crash car," he said, sounding amused. My head hit the back of the seat.

"Not funny. Did you see what it was?" I asked, unclear what I'd hit or what had hit me. The details were fuzzy.

Dark brows furrowed together. "It looked like a small dog."

"What? I hit someone's *dog*?" I shrieked, my heart dropping into my chest. Had I killed a family's dog? I couldn't live with that. This was turning out to be the day from hell.

"It could have been a fox," he added, changing his initial guess, probably to make me feel better. It wasn't working.

"You've got to be shitting me." Unease spread through me like a weed choking the life out of me.

Torent lifted up in his seat, scouring the area surrounding us. "Whatever it was, it's gone."

But was it hurt? Bleeding? Dying alone in the woods?

"You're shaking," he said, gruffness moving into his voice.

I hadn't even realized it until Torent brought it to my attention. Light tremors racked through me. He took my fingers in between his, and a yellow-orange light emitted from his palms, warming up my skin.

"Twice in one day is not a coincidence," I muttered.

"No, it's not."

"What's happening?"

"I wish I knew, but we're going to find out. I'm not going to let anything happen to you."

And I believed him. No one made me feel as safe as Torent did, and that spoke more about my feelings than I was ready to admit. Leaning on him would mean he had the power to hurt me . . . to leave. But facing this problem alone would be stupid. I knew so little about the supernatural world. This was *his* world.

"I'm glad you needed a ride."

The smirk I anticipated spread over his lips. "Good, because I'm picking you up tomorrow."

"I can drive myself to school," I insisted. The aftereffects of shock were slowly starting to wear off.

He glanced at the shattered windshield. "Not in this, you can't."

My head angled left and right, trying to see around the spider crack that splintered over most of the driver's side window. He had a point. It was definitely not safe to drive.

He held out his palm. "Hand me the keys. We'll drop it off at the shop, and I'll grab the Jeep."

What would I do without him? The question scared me.

"Thanks," I said, putting the pink puffball attached to my car key in his hand.

He glanced down at the soft poof and then met my eyes with a raised brow of cynicism.

The corner of my lips lifted. "Pink suits you."

"You suit me."

I swallowed. He had to stop saying things like that. "What am I going to do with you?"

"I could think of a few things." The pitter-patter of rain hitting the roof of the car became the only sound as we shared one of those long heated glances that were becoming far too frequent lately.

I could feel myself getting sucked in. It was a spear of lightning that jolted me from the spell of Torent. "All right, Romeo, let's go before a deer or a bear decides to have a wrestling match with the rest of my car."

"I'd pay to see that."

"You'd pay with your life," I countered, reaching for the door handle.

His raspy chuckle was the last thing I heard as I stepped out of the car to switch places with Torent. I squealed at the first drop of freezing rain on my face. Laughing, we passed each other at the front of the car, headlights beaming over the gravel, and made a mad dash to get back inside the comfort of my Malibu.

Inside the car, Torent cranked the heat so we didn't freeze to death.

"I can't believe there are people who actually love winter," I chattered, shaking out my wet hair.

"Are you telling me you're not a snow bunny?" he asked, adjusting the seat to fit his long frame.

It was weird being on the other side of the car, and I hated to admit it, but I liked the look of Torent behind the wheel. He seemed to be able to fit into every part of my life without trying.

Rubbing my hands together in front of the heater, I snorted. "Hardly."

Easing back onto the road, he asked the question rolling around my own head. "Still think it's Brooklyn screwing with you?"

"I honestly don't know. She does have friends in low places. I'm not ruling anything out at this point." I was more afraid of it not being Brooklyn. I had dealt with her animosity before. A new enemy was the last thing I needed.

"You're just making friends all over the place."

I frowned. "I'm a bucket of rainbows and unicorns."

The drive to Havenwood Falls Garage should have only taken a few minutes, but the storm hampered our time. It was a silent drive, with Torent concentrating on the slick road and me stuck in my head. I had a million questions. Mysteries weren't something I enjoyed, not even in my movies or books. I liked to have all the answers and absolutely hated open endings.

Why would a writer do that? Just why?

I exhaled in relief when the garage came into view, and Torent eased my car into the parking lot. Joshua, the owner, was in the garage, and Torent waved at him as we switched vehicles and jumped into Torent's black Jeep. He had the kind of car that would be able to handle any weather Colorado unleashed. I felt ten times safer.

Snapping my seatbelt together, I glanced over my car one last time. We'd been lucky. The accident could have resulted in more than a broken windshield and shaken nerves. My mind relived those terrifying seconds over and over again. I chewed on my nails as the Jeep began to move.

What if the animal I hit was a shifter? It was possible. I didn't know what was going on, but I was officially on the verge of an emotional meltdown, which would undoubtedly send Torent running for the hills.

"Hey, are you going to be okay?" he asked, and I blinked.

The Jeep was rolling into my driveway. I had spaced the entire ride home. I turned to him and gave him a weak smile. "Yeah. I will be."

What a strange day.

"You're going out with me on Saturday," Torent reminded me, reaching out to tuck a piece of damp hair behind my ear.

I flushed. "I haven't forgotten."

His hands returned to the steering wheel, and I instantly missed his touch. "Good. I'll pick you up in the morning."

"Thanks for the ride." His eyes caught mine in a trance that warmed my blood. I sat unmoving. *Get out of the car, Mallory.* Maybe it was because he looked mouthwatering soaking wet. Maybe it was the brush with disaster. Maybe it was because I hadn't kissed him since Halloween night. Or maybe it was because he wasn't expecting it, but before I changed my mind, I leaned over in my seat, invading Torent's space and pressing my lips to his.

At the brush of my mouth against his, something akin to magic rippled along my skin. Waves of it rose inside me until I could hear the crashing of water. A dizzying excitement fluttered within my chest.

Slowly, watching his stunned eyes, I pulled back to whisper in his ear. "See you tomorrow."

His fingers curled into my wet hair. "We're not finished yet." He reclaimed my lips.

Hunger swept through me as I tasted his breath and the cool metal of his tongue ring. My body ached to press against his, and it took every ounce of my willpower to not climb across the seat into his lap.

God, it was so, so much better than I remembered.

When the kiss ended, he left my lips trembling for more, unfulfilled. Unable to believe I had broken my no-kissing-demons rule, I gathered up my stuff and shifted to open the door, only to quickly spin back to face Torent.

"Wait. I just remembered I have class tomorrow night at the Academy."

Torent cocked his head to the side. "Thursday Awakening class. Not a problem. I can swing by and give you a ride. It will give me an excuse to see you."

"Don't get used to it." I exited his Jeep and ran through the frigid rain into the house, feeling as if my feet never touched the ground and wanting more than life itself to be back inside the warmth of his arms.

Dropping my wet book bag in the front entrance, I ditched my shoes and hoodie before heading toward the kitchen. Gigi had something simmering on the stove that made the house smell like cinnamon and chocolate.

"Was that the Stark boy who dropped you off?" she asked, giving me one of her famous knowing smiles. Her long silver hair was braided to one side.

I nodded, my cheeks flaming with color. Had she seen me kiss him? Or more like devour him?

She opened one of the drawers and withdrew a ladle. "What happened to your car?"

I sank into one of the kitchen chairs, watching her pop around the kitchen, her flowing skirt swishing as it stirred with her movements. It was comforting and homey.

"I got into a little accident."

She flipped her eyes in my direction, suddenly alarmed. "Oh, dear. Are you okay?"

"I'm fine," I quickly assured. "It was a freak accident." Or so I desperately wanted to believe. I didn't want to worry Gigi.

"Another wolf dart into the road?" She was teasing me now.

"No," I said slowly. "I think it was a fox this time. Something sprang into my windshield and cracked it to smithereens. Torent took my car to the shop and gave me a ride home."

Lucky for me, she didn't ask for details. Clucking her tongue, she turned back to the stove. "And in such weather. He seems to always be around when you need him."

Wasn't that the truth, but it was the implication in Gigi's voice that gave me pause. If I didn't know better, I'd think she was encouraging a relationship with a demon. "I guess."

"You like him," she said, not beating around the bush. Her forthrightness was one of the reasons we always got along so well, unlike me and Mom. Gigi joined me at the table with two mugs of hot chocolate topped with whipped cream and peppermint shavings.

My hand wrapped around the Santa mug, letting its warmth seep into my still-cold fingers. There was something to be said for living with Gigi. Mom might not have liked it, but I had never felt more at home or happy. Gigi seemed to always know what I needed.

"The jury's still out." I swiped my finger over the mound of whipped cream and licked it off, doing everything in my power to not think about the kiss Torent and I had shared.

"Hmm." Gigi pursed her lips. "You can't always control your heart."

Sipping on the hot cocoa, I folded my right leg underneath my left. "Boys are complicated. Demons are out of my realm."

She threw her head back and laughed. "Don't let your mother's past dictate your future. You deserve to be happy and have fun, Mal. Enjoy every second of your youth."

How did she know I'd been thinking about my mom and her past relationships? It was uncanny. "I know."

We talked about school, how my night classes at the Academy were going, and my powers. But not once did I mention the dead birds that had been sprawled outside my window this morning. I didn't want to worry her more than I already had with the car incident.

When the hot cocoa was gone, I went to my room feeling better about my crazy day. How foolish would I feel if I was wrong or jumping to crazy conclusions? My life had been anything but simple since I'd come to Havenwood Falls. Was I looking for trouble when there was none?

CHAPTER 4

*T*ucked away near the main waterfalls in town sat Sun and Moon Academy. It was at this exclusive and hidden academy that students with supernatural abilities like me attended classes. Some went full time during the day, but for students who attended the public schools, the Academy provided night classes during the week.

Torent steered his Jeep through the guarded gates and drove up the long stone road flanked by trees on either side. The perfectly manicured yard was blanketed with white snow that twinkled under the numerous stars and the lanterns placed along the driveway.

"How are classes going? Have you accidentally almost killed anyone else?" Torent asked.

He was referring to my first week in class, when I had nearly embedded a pair of scissors into Otis's chest. Thank Goddess for inhuman reflexes. Word spread quickly about the girl with unpredictable affinity to magnetic energy. I had made quite the name for myself, and not in a good way. Making friends after that had been difficult, to say the least.

"Ha. Ha. Ha. Not yet, but you might be my next victim."

"Being your victim doesn't sound that bad." Torent guided the Jeep around the circular driveway used for drop-offs. When the car halted, he angled toward me and brushed a lock of hair off my cheek. "Try not to stab anyone in the eye tonight."

I couldn't help but notice how frequently he found little ways to touch me. It happened more and more as of late. I gathered my books and notebooks into my arms before we had a repeat of the other night and ended up making out in front of the Academy.

"Is that why they lock up the weapons before I get there?" I quipped.

He chuckled, and I shut the door on the deep sound, but it had a way of staying with me, even as I walked away.

Stone pathways led up to the main entrance, and the heels of my boots clattered on the cold rock. My fingers pinched the lapels of my coat together. *Don't look back. Don't you dare look back at him*, I chanted in my head, and I made it all the way to the door before I gave in, glancing over my shoulder.

His Jeep was idling, and through the passenger window, he winked at me. I didn't bother to see if anyone was around when I flipped him an obscene gesture and turned around smiling.

Strolling through the arched doors and into the interior courtyard, I headed for the Falls Campus. It was the wing closest to the gushing waterfalls. Christmas was only weeks away, and the town had begun displaying its festive décor. That included the Academy, but the means of decorating was a bit different here than in the town square. Leave it to a magical school to use a holiday as a training session. Magic trembled in the halls as I walked by a group of witches who were streaming strands of garland with fairy lights along the archways, no electricity needed—not when you had magic.

Thursday night at Sun and Moon Academy was Awakening Lab, my favorite class. It was there I got to work on honing my magnetic powers.

Monday nights I had basic supe 101 class. The things I learned in there blew my mind. I never imagined so many different kinds of supernaturals were running around in the world. How had I never noticed before? You'd think I would have seen something, just once, but then maybe I had. The mind conjured justifications for the impossible.

Vampires, fae, werewolves, witches, and many, many other types of teens with mystic abilities moseyed down the halls to class and to the library, or hung out in the halls. I came to the Falls Campus wing, where classrooms spanned off the corridor. I hung a right into one of the rooms. Gianna, the instructor's daughter, smiled at me as I took my seat in the third row beside a fae with blond hair and pretty blue eyes.

There were about twenty other students besides me. I had a few minutes to kill, so I flipped through the supernatural bible, as I referred to the thick textbook. It was a guidebook to the different species. I'd already combed the sections about nymphs and demons.

Because so many of us had different skills, we often split up into groups. I pitied the ones that got stuck with me, but I wasn't the most dangerous. Far from it.

Mrs. Augustine glided into the room as if her feet never touched the ground, her black tunic flowing behind her. Dark curls swept off her neck into a waterfall up-do today.

"Good evening." Her voice was radiant with infectious enthusiasm as she dropped off some papers at her desk. Instead of sitting in the chair, she breezed to the front of her desk and sat on top, letting her feet dangle just above the floor. "As many of you are discovering, your abilities can be linked to your emotions. We'll be exploring some ways to control your powers when your feelings get the best of you." She dove into her lecture.

Mallory, a deep voice murmured, interrupting my note-taking. It sounded as if he was sitting directly behind me, but that was impossible, considering a pretty girl with bright red hair was in the desk at my back.

I lifted my pen from the notebook as my eyes darted over the room. Was one of the guys playing a trick on me? Telepathy was possible. I just hadn't met anyone who could project thoughts into my head. Concluding I was losing my mind, I tuned back in to the lecture, but it was harder to concentrate. I kept waiting for the voice again.

Eventually, we were divided into pairs to work on our individual powers. My partner was a witch with an affinity to earth. Elise was a little taller than me with beautiful rich sienna hair that reached the middle of her back. She gave me a polite smile, but I could see in her soft brown eyes she would rather be partnered with someone else.

"Hey." I smiled back, hoping it would put her at ease. "I promise not to use you as a pin cushion." I cringed inside. I had wanted to make a joke, but sometimes they sounded funnier in my head.

Lucky for me, Elise giggled and didn't immediately demand a new partner. "You have an extraordinary gift. Is it true you're dating Torent Stark?"

I choked. Were people really talking about us? "Um, it's complicated."

She let out a dreamy sigh. "Half the girls here would like to be complicated with Torent."

Good to know . . . Actually, I didn't want to know. It caused a hot fire to lick inside my belly. I was jealous. The idea of other girls lusting over my demon caused irrational feelings, a dangerous cocktail for a newbie nymph with strong emotional ties to her powers. Bad things happened if I lost my shit.

The pen on the table beside me trembled. I slapped my hand over it.

Hold on. Did I really think of Torent as my *demon?*

God, I'd fallen for him. *It's just a high school crush*, I told myself, not feeling better at the idea.

Something in my expression must have given away what was going on inside my head. "You have it bad, huh? Not that I blame you. I'd take any of the Stark brothers."

So not helping.

Before I started to become a possessive maybe girlfriend, I suggested Elise start her portion of the lab first. She nodded and went to gather some materials. All around the room my peers practiced honing their skills. Elise came back with a pot of dirt and a package of orchid seeds. Tearing open the paper packet, she put a single seed into a small pot. Then with a wave of her fingers and a few soft spoken words, she lifted her hand, encouraging the plant to grow. And grow it did. No water. No sun. Just magic.

"That is amazing," I commented in awe. The ability to inspire and nurture life seemed so much more important than my gift. My hand reached out to touch the velvety pink petal, but the moment my fingers grazed the plant, the petals turned a nasty shade of black and withered to dust.

Uh. Holy crap. Please tell me that did not just happen.

I jerked my hand away, mortified. Half the class gasped.

Elise took a step away from me, staring at me in horror. "You've been touched by death."

I glanced around the room, seeing so many eyes on me, and panicked. "I-I don't know what that means."

Everything metal in the classroom began to wobble. Chairs. Staplers. Screws. If it was metal, it was vibrating. I had begun to grasp the inner workings of my abilities, but tonight all the training of the last few weeks came undone. And I was horrified by my lack of control. Everyone in the room was now staring at me.

"Mallory," Mrs. Augustine softly spoke my name. "Take a deep breath like we practiced."

Deep breaths, my ass. I was past breathing exercises. Hell, I was struggling to get air into my lungs at all. Mrs. Augustine guided me into a chair and gently eased my head forward so the blood rushed downward.

Oh, God. I was having a legit panic attack in class, and the only person I wanted to see was Torent.

After a few minutes, the air going in and out of my lungs returned to normal, as did the surge of my powers. The trembling of metal objects ceased.

I didn't believe it was death that had touched me, but a vengeful nymph who would do just about anything to gain her powers back.

Damn you, Brooklyn.

∼

"You're not going to believe what I did in my class last night." It was Friday. Beck and I were in study hall.

He scooted his chair closer to me, getting comfortable, the textbooks beside us forgotten. "Oh, do tell. I hope it's juicy."

"Not exactly. Try humiliating."

He rubbed his hands together. "Even better. Dish."

I relayed the events of my incident with the plant. He already knew about my car and Torent coming to my rescue. Beck approved wholeheartedly, declaring Torent my knight in shining armor. Gah. Beck was such a hopeless romantic and soaked up every nice thing Torent did or said.

Sympathy shone on Beck's face. "Between the dead birds, your car, and the death omen from Elise, I'd say you've gotten yourself into a witchy mess."

"So Brooklyn had me hexed?" I concluded, trying to make sense of what was happening to me.

"It's possible," Beck said, tapping his black-painted fingernail against the table, thinking. "But she is going to great lengths for revenge. Brooklyn doesn't like other people to do her dirty work. It wouldn't give her the satisfaction or attention she craves. This feels like something more."

Ugh. I hated to agree. This didn't feel like jealousy or vengeance. It was subtle. Dark. And personal. Had I made another enemy without even realizing it? "So how do I find out for sure?"

"You need a witch or . . ."

"Or what?" I prompted, a weird feeling of dread opening up in my chest.

"Or an immortal," he murmured.

I sunk back, exhaling loudly. "And where would I find one of those?"

I knew a few witches—Elise was one of them, but I wasn't sure I could convince her to help me, especially if it meant breaking the rules.

Beck lifted a single brow. "Actually, you already know one, sort of. It's possible you might be able to summon her."

I edged forward, leaning in close to Beck. "Who?"

"Styx."

"The goddess?" I mulled the idea around in my head, remembering when I had gone into Peacock Lake and awakened the nymph inside me. Beck's idea might be crazy enough to work. Who better to tell me what was happening to me than the goddess who was my ancestor? I knew next to nothing about the scope of her powers or if she would even answer my call, but it was worth a shot. The alternative of doing nothing and letting the stench of death follow me caused a dry lump to form in my throat. "You're a genius, Beck."

He ran his hands through his vibrant blue hair, his chest filled with cockiness. "Hell yes, I am. So when are we going?"

My shoulders dropped as I remembered my promise to Torent. "I have a date tomorrow."

A grin split over Beck's face. "About damn time. The smoldering glances between you were burning everyone within ten feet."

I said nothing to that and steered the conversation back to my dilemma. "You think Torent would be up for a picnic at Peacock Lake?"

Beck angled his head to the side. "For you, doll, he'd drain the lake if it was what you wanted."

Dramatic much? I rubbed at the back of my neck, trying to release the tension that had been mounting there the last week. The motion didn't go unnoticed by Beck.

"You know what would alleviate some of your stress?" he asked, stretching out his long legs under the table.

I was going to regret asking.

"A massage at the spa?" I suggested, because my muscles could use the relief. Tension had its claws in me.

"Sex with Torent," he said matter-of-factly.

I coughed. "How is that going to uncomplicate my life?"

He shrugged. "Beats me, but it would feel damn good."

"And how would you know?" I retorted, squinting my eyes.

The corner of his lips quirked. "Intuition . . . plus, just look at the guy. He screams amazing in bed."

He had me there. For a few moments, I entertained the idea of getting sweaty in between the sheets with Torent. God knew every fiber in my body wanted to do the nasty with the demon.

CHAPTER 5

*I*t had been snowing on and off all day—just a light dusting, but enough to make Havenwood Falls look like an idyllic shaken snow globe. Torent would be here in thirty minutes for our date, and I was still strutting around my room in nothing but a T-shirt, trying to decide what to wear.

The problem was, Torent and I had very different plans for tonight. How did one dress to summon a goddess? I settled on jeans and a warm knitted sweater in soft teal that brought out the color of my eyes. The doorbell rang as I finished defining my eyes with black liner.

With a long exhale, I left my room and walked down the hall. I heard Torent's deep voice greet Gigi and Mom. When I came down the stairs, the two of them were drilling Torent with questions, but the demon didn't seem to mind. If I didn't know better, I would have said he was enjoying himself, having the attention of Mom and Gigi.

"Am I interrupting?" I asked, standing on the bottom step with my arms crossed.

Mom gave me a crooked smile. "We were just occupying Torent while you finished getting ready."

Her platinum blond hair hung down the center of her back. She wore a dark blue gypsy skirt that fell almost to her bare feet, where a gold chain glittered on her ankle.

I pursed my lips, eyeing the two of them because if I glanced at Torent, they would see just how bad I had it for the demon. "Hmm. I'm sure that's what you were doing."

"I'll make sure to have her home before curfew," he told Mom and Gigi, like he was a saint. He had to be the most polite demon on the planet.

"Be safe. Don't do anything I would do," Mom warned.

I rolled my eyes and mouthed goodbye, closing the door before I sustained further embarrassment. "I'm sorry about that. I had no clue how interested they would be in my dating life."

He opened the passenger door to his Jeep. "At least you finally admit we're dating."

I spun around as I was about to hop into his car. Torent sent me a characteristic look, those direct violet eyes boring into mine. This was that moment I had wanted to avoid inside. That second where our eyes connected and nothing else in the world mattered but him. My heart and stomach turned in twirls. I wanted him to kiss me so badly, I could barely stand it. We hadn't even gotten into the car yet, and I was already melting at his feet.

I swallowed the rapid beating of my heart. "Let me rephrase."

His finger pressed to my lips. "There is no way I'm letting you take it back, crash car."

His smile nearly killed me. If he was going to play wicked, so could I. Licking my lips, my tongue flicked over his finger, and I watched as his eyes darkened, glimmering with flecks of gold.

Making out in my driveway was not what I had in mind for this date. We had to at least get into the car, but if he kept looking at me like that . . .

Flashes of blue, purple, and pink streamed over our heads, drawing my attention. I realized I'd intertwined my fingers with his other hand. The streaks of Northern Lights were a product of our combined powers.

"We should probably go," I whispered. "Before we end up with an audience."

His husky chuckle drifted over me. "Not until I hear you say it."

"That I'm not dating a demon," I retorted, and slipped into the Jeep before he could argue.

Shaking his head, Torent closed the door and made his way around the car.

I settled into the seat, shifting my body so I was turned toward Torent, and fumbled with a piece of yarn from my sweater. "I need to ask a favor."

Torent tensed, the lines on his face deepening. "Normally, I wouldn't hesitate, but there is something in your voice that is giving me pause."

He wasn't the only one, but I pushed forward, trying to make light of what I was going to ask of him. "Don't go all holy on me now."

He ran a hand through his hair. "What kind of favor are you asking for?"

Here goes nothing. I didn't know exactly how Torent would react to my request. "I need to go to Peacock Lake."

"Why, exactly?" His chest rumbled. "You know it's freezing out, right?"

The weather wasn't my concern. The dead things that kept happening to me definitely were. "Answers. I need answers, and the only way I can think to get them is to ask the goddess who gave me these blasted powers. Maybe something went awry."

"I'm not sure that's how it works," he declared, sounding more confident than I felt. "The likelihood of a goddess screwing up seems highly doubtful."

I jerked my chin up and attempted to keep the snap out of my voice, but I failed. "Look, I need your help. Are you in or not?"

Couldn't he see how vital this was to me? I had promised him a date, and I refused to go back on my word, but at the same time, this wasn't something I could shrug off. The importance of it stained the air like a dark shadow looming over me.

"If I say no, you're just going to go out on your own." It wasn't a question, but more of him thinking out loud.

I didn't lie. Not to him. "Yes," I agreed.

His dark eyes flicked to mine. "Is it dangerous?"

"Probably," I replied with equal coolness, then jumped to plead my case. "I know this wasn't what you had planned for tonight, but I think it is important I go. I'll make it up to you." I was so going to regret that promise, but every bone in my body was telling me I needed to go to the lake. It was there I would get the answers I sought . . . I prayed.

His grin was slow and daring. "How can I say no to a little danger? And if it gets me another date with you, I'm in."

The air was chilly on my nose and cheeks as I pulled my coat closer in around me. *Why hadn't I thought to bring a hat or gloves?* With the sun gone, the temperatures had plummeted.

My boots crunched through the frozen grass. I matched my strides with Torent's, having to take twice as many steps to keep up with him. Trees surrounded us from all sides, their branches and leaves glistening under the moon and canopy of stars.

Noticing I was lagging behind, he slowed down and reached for my hand, interlacing our fingers. A flare of light burst from the center of his palm, sending a stream of warmth into our joined fingers.

"Are you sure this is a good idea?" he asked for the third time.

I nearly sighed at the heat of his hellfire. A hug would be amazing. "No, but I don't see what other choice I have."

The closer we got to the lake, the faster my heart raged in my chest, in my throat. We were getting close. A tingle of both excitement and terror tiptoed down my—

A wolf howled through the trees. I automatically moved closer to Torent.

"Maybe we should have brought Beck," I murmured. These woods were filled with all types of shifters, among other things.

His arms tightened around me, and he tipped his nose to look down at me with a raised brow. "You don't think I can protect you?"

"I didn't say—"

A blur of color sped past us, kicking up grass and dirt. I stiffened in his arms, my heart racing like a gazelle.

"Did you see that?" I asked in a whispered hiss. A brush of ice slunk across the nape of my neck, but Torent didn't seem as concerned.

His body stayed warm and relaxed against mine. "It was just a vamp out hunting."

My mouth dropped open. "Just a vamp?" I shrilled, my voice echoing over the treetops. "And a hungry one at that."

"Relax. We're not going to be dinner. Demon blood is not very appetizing."

"What about nymph blood?"

The curve of his lips was immoral. "Oh yeah, you're a delectable five-course meal."

"Torent," I hissed, frustration coating my voice.

His hands landed on my shoulders as he leaned down to gaze directly into my eyes. "This was your idea, but you have nothing to fear. I won't let anything happen to you. I promise."

Ensnared by the mixture of violet and gold in his eyes, I exhaled. Why did he have to say things like that? I nodded, afraid my voice would give away the plethora of feelings he sent off inside me.

In the distance, my ears picked up a gentle hum of music, like a lullaby beckoning me.

"We're almost there," I murmured, stepping away from Torent toward the sound.

I barely knew these woods, had only been here once, but I knew if I closed my eyes, I would be able to find Peacock Lake without even trying. We had a connection, the lake and I.

It was only a few more minutes of trekking through the woods before we came upon Peacock Lake. A fine mist swirled over the slightly frozen pond. A thin layer of ice blanketed the surface, shining like glass. The small waterfall trickled over stone and a hum of lovely voices called me to the water.

Entranced, I slowly walked toward the edge of the lake. Torent stopped me, encircling his hands around my waist. "Whoa. You can't go in there, Mal. The water is ice."

"It's okay. I won't feel the coldness of the water. Nymph thing," I assured, going with my gut. When my hand grazed the surface, I felt nothing but welcome.

His voice grew tight, and I sensed his eyes on me. "I guess we all have our thing, but I would feel better if you let me help, just to be sure."

I couldn't mistake the concern I heard. He was worried, and I couldn't blame him.

It was a struggle to pull my gaze from the water and look at Torent. The pull to submerge myself in the lake was strong. I didn't know how long I could hold off. "Suit yourself."

I slipped off my boots. Torent came to the edge beside me and crouched down. He dipped his hand into the frigid water, and I watched in fascination as his eyes turned the color of melted gold and his fingers glowed with hellfire. The light spread through the depths of the glassy lake, from one side to the other, encompassing it completely. White steam billowed higher, lowering visibility. He leaned forward, the gold in his irises brightening.

My eyes narrowed as something in the water captured them. A dark phantom shadow rose from the bottom straight for Torent. Panic clawed in my chest for a split second. I grabbed his arm and yanked him back. "Not so close."

Something about the lake wanted Torent, sort of in the same way I did . . . but more—to possess him. I had sensed its desire in my soul. There were things that lurked in the small lake, things I didn't understand and wasn't sure I wanted to.

If he thought my attitude suddenly strange, he didn't let on. Perhaps he had sensed the power of this place as I did.

"That should keep you from freezing to death," he said quietly.

Because I had forgotten to bring a change of clothes, I slipped out of my jeans and sweater, leaving me in a tank top and my undergarments. My teeth chattered as I stepped one foot and then the other into the shallow part of the lake. I spun around to look back at Torent. "Don't go far."

His eyes blazed, the muscle at his jaw tightening. It was clear from his expression he wished I would come back to shore. This was possibly one place Torent couldn't save me. "I'm not going anywhere without you, crash car."

I gave him an encouraging smile for both our sakes and made an impulsive decision I hoped would ease some of his tension. I blew him a kiss and went under.

Water caressed my face like silk. I was calmer than I imagined. It was the lake. The idea of summoning a goddess underwater should have caused considerable anxiety.

I swam sure and strong, going deeper into the dark blue lake. And like the first time, it called to me, a gentle song I had to answer with my own.

When the light in the water began to change, I hovered, the song growing louder around me. My lungs worked effortlessly underwater as if I'd grown gills, a freaky thought. I wasn't sure what to do next or what to say, so I opened my mouth and called her name.

"Styx. I need your help."

The water surrounding me was mesmerizing—the lethal, gentle beauty of such power. I waited. And waited. I listened to the serene quiet, but no divine response came. Instead, a bead of light formed below my dangling feet. It soared toward me, enhancing until I was nearly blinded by its brightness. It encased me from all sides.

Then I heard her voice, clear and powerful. "I know why you've come, daughter, and this is what I can offer you."

The light swirled, and from the ribbons of water and magic, images formed. My hand reached out and went through the projection, rippling the vision. Within seconds, I was sucked into the past.

CHAPTER 6

A man with sand-colored hair crept through the trees like a
lurker. Beyond the thick woods in front of him was a clearing
where a group gathered, one of them being my mother. She looked so
young and yet so much the same. A shadow of sorrow and fear cloaked
her eyes as the four of them formed a circle, two other women and a
young man. None of them looked much older than me.

My eyes volleyed between the tree line and the clearing. I couldn't
shake the feeling that something bad was about to happen. The air
seemed to tremble with fear and anger.

The four joined hands, and a woman with dark hair began to
chant. Her voice didn't carry as I had hoped. I had to stretch to try to
understand her words, picking up only bits and pieces of what I
believed was a spell.

My education on witchcraft was measly, so even what I heard didn't
make sense. I couldn't decipher what sort of spell she was performing,
but I got the feeling it was important.

The witch lifted her face to the stars, color spilling over her
porcelain cheeks. "Watchers and guardians of the elements, I ask for a
shard of your powers—"

Her voice was carried away by a gust of wind, leaving me on the *cusp of the clearing still clueless as to what was happening, but one thing was certain—the lurker was about to make a move.*

I opened my mouth to warn my mother, but a flash of silvery moonlight hit the man's face, and I gasped. Recognition speared through me. I knew that face. Not from a single memory, but from a photograph.

He was my father.

What was he doing here?

Maybe I had it wrong? Perhaps he was here to help my mother.

But a few moments later that theory was blasted out of the water.

My father struck out with a spell of his own, his voice bellowing over the glade. The circle disbanded, and pleas were exchanged, but my mother wasn't able to dissuade my father. His eyes hardened, filling with such rage, it caused the hairs on my arms to stand up.

A flash of light hurled from the brown-haired witch, and the air filled with screams. My father, a mage or sorcerer with superior skills, reacted with magic of his own. My vision was impaired by the brightness of the magic. I couldn't see what was happening, only hear the horrible cries and the dead silence that followed. When my eyes adjusted, the body of the young man who had been part of the circle lay awkwardly on the ground, his blood seeping into the earth and my father towering over him.

The vision dispelled, leaving only the murky depths of the blue waters. Styx appeared, her hair floating around her like a halo of darkness. "You, my daughter, will suffer the sins of your blood."

Well, shit. That sounded dreadful.

"What sins? What had my father done?" I asked, feeling like I had more questions than answers.

Her cloak of pure white gleamed in the water like a ray of hope. "There is some magic that binds to your bloodline, including the hex bestowed upon your father. When you awakened, you also activated that blood hex within yourself, as his only living heir."

Fucking fabulous. I'd never met the man who helped create me, yet it was his past that haunted me. Sometimes parents sucked.

"How do I break it?" I asked, doing my best to keep calm and not let the surge of panic draw me under.

Her white eyes dimmed, growing sad. She didn't have to tell me what I already knew. Not even a goddess had all the answers. "That is your burden to bear, for blood magic is not of my realm, but you *must* stop death from consuming you."

"I don't know how," I said softly.

"I'm sorry, daughter. You must go." Her arms swept through the water, not giving me the chance to drill her with the millions of questions jumbled inside my head. She created a wave of water that lifted me upward.

I broke through the surface, sucking in a sharp bite of air that scored my throat, and stared into Torent's dark eyes.

"Christ, Mallory," he swore, dragging me against him. "I swear to God, you ever do that to me again and I'll drown you myself."

Shivering against his chest, I threw my arms around him and clung to his neck. "I'm sorry," I shuddered.

Fear and something close to anger smoldered in his gaze. "I thought you drowned."

We were wading in the edge of the lake, the moon shining high over our heads.

"I'm okay." *As long as you keep holding me,* I said to myself. But we both must have wanted the same thing, because his arms never let go as he led us out of the water to the rocky shore. "I saw my father," I said after a few heartbeats.

"In the lake? You had a vision?"

I nodded. "Styx gave it to me."

His hand reached out for me, and I shivered as he brushed cool wet fingers along my cheek. "Did she give you the answers you were searching for?"

Tears welled up in my eyes. I was on the verge of losing it. My bottom lip trembled.

"Shit. I got you," he murmured, engulfing me in his arms a

second time. His hellfire flared to life, keeping me warm from the night's chill.

An onslaught of emotions came barreling at me, and I could no longer fight them off. Leaning into Torent, I let him be the strong one, dropping the walls around me and letting the tears come. They racked through my body, shaking my shoulders. It suddenly felt like I had lost control of my life. Just like that. Nothing made sense. Not who I was. Not who my parents were. And at the same time, it all made sense. Why Mom had left. Why we had never come back. What she had been running from—protecting me from.

It was only a few minutes that I allowed myself to wallow in self-pity. Drying up the tears, I pulled back and glanced up into Torent's face. I bit my lip. "I didn't mean for that to happen."

The hand he had moved into my hair came to settle on my cheek, brushing at the dampness. "Come on, let's get you home. You can tell me what happened on the way."

Did I have the strength to tell him what I had seen without the waterworks boiling up a second time? Torent squeezed my hand, and I realized with him at my side, I had more strength then I'd ever had in my life. He gave me courage and fortitude.

We hiked back through the woods fairly quickly. I had finished relaying all that I had seen and heard while I'd been in Peacock Lake as we emerged from a cluster of pine trees.

"My girlfriend is hexed. We make quite the pair, you and I," he said, grabbing my hand to cross the road to his car.

My lips turned down, and I tried to wiggle my fingers out from his, but he wasn't letting go. "I'm not your girlfriend."

"It's only a matter of time," he added with a shit-eating grin.

Leave it to Torent to make me forget about the blood hex for even the briefest amount of time. He would know exactly what to say to get under my skin.

We approached his Jeep, and I was more than ready to go home, but before I could reach for the door handle, I found myself pressed up against the cool metal of the car, Torent's firm body capturing me there. My heart raced at blinding speed, and I cursed him for making me feel like this.

"Don't you ever scare me like that again." His fingers were on my wrists, thumb pressed against the inside of my pulsing vein.

"It was never my intention. I just wanted answers." Answers I still didn't have, but Styx had given me something to start with, and it was more than I had an hour ago.

He idly traced circles up my forearm. I breathed in the scent of him, earthy and crisp. The combination of his touch and smell caused my stomach to flip.

"I make you nervous," he murmured, his lips hovering so close to my cheek his hot breath rushed over my skin. "This thing between us scares you."

Lifting my lashes, I met his smoldering eyes. "And it doesn't you?"

"You should be a little afraid. You bring out the darkness inside me." Gold flecks brightened in the center of his irises, and I saw he was on the verge of losing control, but the problem was, I was right there with him.

His lips came down on mine, not soft or gentle, but with a passion that made my heart burst. Did I feel this connection to Torent because we both had something dark and evil in our souls? If that was so, should we be embracing or running from each other? I didn't know, didn't have the answers. All I had was this moment and how he made me feel. Beautiful. Powerful. Desired. Loved.

He broke off the kiss as swiftly as he took my lips, leaving me gasping and aching for more. My hands struggled against the hold he still had on my wrists, dying to dive into his hair and pull him back for more. He was taunting me. His tongue traced my lips, and I shivered, feeling the cool metal of his piercing against my mouth. He took a lazy journey along the column of my throat, sparking electricity wherever he kissed.

I sighed when he released one of my hands to trace the pad of his thumb over my bottom lip.

"Open for me," he whispered, reclaiming my mouth, but this time, his tongue swooped in.

My entire world fell off balance, and I was spinning wildly out of control. His fingers intertwined with both my hands, and I squeezed, holding onto him for dear life.

Ending the kiss, he murmured thickly, "I want to be anywhere right now other than here." A pause lingered in the air between us. "Get in the car. I need to take you home."

It was probably a good thing we weren't somewhere else. With my emotions all mixed up, I didn't have the energy to refuse what my body and heart clearly wanted. One thing was certain. I wanted Torent. That hadn't changed.

CHAPTER 7

The house was dark and silent when I got home. Nothing stirred. Feeling like an emotional basket case, I tiptoed to my room, looking for solitude to sort out what I'd learned, besides the fact that I was falling wholeheartedly in love with a demon.

That was a problem for another night.

After stripping out of my grimy clothes, I flopped down on my bed, telling myself I wasn't going to have another pitiful-me moment. For so long, mystery swirled around the man who was my father, but tonight I discovered he was a mage, a detail no one had bothered to share. His aspiration for power had led him down a dark path—the darkest.

Although I hadn't inherited his power, I had inherited his blood hex.

I needed more information about that night. Who was the man my father had murdered with his spell? I had a hunch, but I needed facts. Mom would have been the most accurate source, but she had gone to great lengths to keep this from me. Something told me she wasn't going to be extremely forthcoming with the details.

Did she know about the repercussions of that night? About the blood curse? I didn't know if I was more afraid to find out she did or didn't. Either way, she had hidden this from me, had lied to me.

Thinking about the man I never got the chance to understand and only dreamt about caused my heart to tighten. Abandonment was a strange thing, inducing emotions that appeared in sporadic patterns. At this point in my life, I rarely thought about the man who fathered me. He had become only a tiny piece of my past that was better left in the past. I did have those few days a year I wallowed, becoming a little girl who wanted nothing more than to see her father . . . just once. Then I'd stepped foot into Havenwood Falls, and it seemed the past was determined to taint my future.

I had so many questions, most of them not good.

As a child, I learned to stop seeking those answers from Mom. Seeing how upset they made her was enough to have me biting my tongue. I hated to cause her sadness, and it was evident my father was the source of deep scars that had never healed.

Rolling over, I swung my feet off the bed to grab my laptop. Time to slap on my cryptic detector. If there was one thing my generation had skills at, it was the Internet.

I slunk behind my desk and opened my computer. It was amazing what you could find on the web—and truly frightening at the same time. When the Google homepage came up, I took a deep breath and typed in his name.

Roth Dorian.

How many times had I searched his name over the Internet? A hundred at least, but not once did I get a hit on a Roth Dorian from Havenwood Falls. Why would this time be any different?

Except . . . it was.

My heart beat triple time in my chest at the results scrolling down the screen. Headlines from the Sun & Moon Tribune popped out at me, causing a sick twist in my stomach. A part of me wanted to believe the vision had been false—a lie. My father couldn't possibly be a murderer, because if he was, what would that mean for me? Did that mean I was truly doomed?

I mulled over the words on the screen:

Breaking news. Family seeks answers after the mysterious death of their son.

One dead in an apparent murder, rocking the small town of Havenwood Falls.

Roth Dorian convicted of murdering his best friend.

Local news had chronologically documented the events. Something or someone in Havenwood Falls had kept it from leaking out. It was the only explanation, which meant it was definitely supernatural causes that had killed . . .

What had been his name—the poor guy my father had chosen to play God with?

I clicked on one of the headlines, skimming through the text. It was dated six months from the month and year I was born. His name jumped off the screen, and my temples started throbbing. It couldn't be.

Ryle Kendall.

Suddenly pieces of the puzzle were fitting together. I'd stake my nymph powers on Ryle being related to Brooklyn and the root of the rift between our families. Who could blame them? My father had murdered someone they loved, but just who had Ryle Kendall been?

Scrolling further down, a picture caught my eye. I gaped at my father's image from over eighteen years ago. Seeing the man who was responsible for my creation made my belly tangle in knots. He had changed from the single picture Mom had tucked away in a keepsake box. I used to sneak into her room and climb into the back of the closet, playing with the trinkets and staring at the smiling man with his arm around Mom. They had seemed so young and happy in that second captured by film.

But in his mug shot from that horrific day, he appeared older, harder, and cynical. His auburn hair was disheveled. Long lashes surrounded vibrant green eyes, no longer twinkling with lightheartedness. I had his slim nose and almond-shaped eyes. It was weird staring at him and seeing parts of myself.

Murderer. Murderer. Murderer.

The word stared back at me as if it was flashing in neon lights, bold and bright on every screen.

With an exasperated oath, I snapped my laptop closed and faced the view outside my window—tall oak and aspen trees towered toward the sky, glittering with a dusting of white snow.

I toyed with the end of my braid. My father had killed Brooklyn's relative. No wonder her family hated mine. I couldn't believe Mom had any involvement. She wouldn't have.

This had to be the reason she had run from Havenwood Falls.

I spent the rest of the weekend stressing over what I was going to do with the information I'd learned. Torent texted me a few times to check on me. I was grateful for his support. Dealing with this on my own would have sucked.

Multiple times on Sunday I tried to work up the nerve to talk with Mom, ask her what had happened that night, but the right time never came up. Or maybe it was me. Maybe I wasn't ready.

Monday came before I knew it, and I realized who I needed to talk to. It wouldn't be easy, but she could fill in some of the remaining holes.

I was dreading lunch, knowing it was the only time to corner Brooklyn. My stomach twisted like a pretzel, and I was positive I wouldn't be able to eat without hurling.

Taking a seat at my usual table, my knee whacked into the edge, and I swore. My nails scraped against my teeth as I chewed on them, watching Brooklyn strut into the cafeteria like she was queen. She liked to make an entrance and was often the last to arrive, which only prolonged the nerves scrambling inside me.

Beck snuck up behind me. "Why do you look like the green hot dogs they serve on Wednesday?" He slid into the chair next to mine.

I gritted my teeth. "Because I feel like one."

He raised a brow.

"I have to talk to Brooklyn," I explained with anguish.

A grim expression crawled onto his face. "Do you have a death wish?" he hissed.

"Today, I do." Staring at the table where Brooklyn and her sidekicks, Leena and Cora, were sitting, I drew in a breath. Stalling was my specialty. Instead of stalking straight up to her and unleashing what I had on my chest, I quickly gave Beck a rundown of my date with Torent.

"That is some serious family baggage." He ran a hand through his blueberry-colored hair. "Do you really think you're hexed?"

"I don't want to believe it, but there is definitely something happening to me."

"God, this is so messed up. You're too nice of a person to be cursed by something your father did."

I rubbed my eyes, suddenly bone tired. "Thanks."

Beck glanced over at Brooklyn's table with wary eyes. "Good luck," he whispered and patted me between my shoulder blades. "I got your back if shit goes south."

I hoped it didn't come to that. The last thing I wanted was another confrontation with Brooklyn in front of the school. Forgoing food, I grabbed a vanilla shake and weaved my way through the cluster of tables toward the center of the cafeteria. Brooklyn and her friends always sat in the same spot, the table directly in front of the large window.

Brooklyn saw me immediately. She was chatting with Leena and Cora, twisting her midnight hair around her finger. Cora laughed at something Brooklyn said, but Brooklyn's lips puckered when I stopped at their table. She narrowed her dark blue eyes. Everything about Brooklyn reminded me of an untamed tsunami, and for a second, I thought about turning around and leaving.

No.

I would solve nothing by chickening out and hiding in my room, pretending the problem didn't exist. Things would only get worse. The only way to break this blood hex was to find out more about its origin, and I needed Brooklyn to do that.

My nails tapped on the table. "Mind if I join you?"

"Yes, I do mind," Brooklyn snapped. "We don't associate with trash."

I had expected nothing less than a cold welcome from my fellow nymph. Ignoring her ill behavior, I plopped my ass into the seat beside Leena, not caring if I pissed her off. She was already always angry with me. The entire room went on edge, wondering what would happen next. Our complicated relationship was no secret at school, so the stares and whispers were expected. I glanced at Brooklyn, Cora, and Leena. The four of us were nymphs. We should have been friends, but circumstances made that impossible.

And that was why I was here.

I wanted to know what information Brooklyn had. She might be able to fill in all the holes about that night, and with any luck, she would know something about the blood hex, but I needed to be careful. The last thing I wanted was for Brooklyn to use it against me somehow.

"I need your help," I stated, meeting her directly in the eyes.

Brooklyn threw her head back and laughed. "That's rich. Why would I ever help you?" Her voice had grown louder.

My stomach clenched, but I forced my lips into a half smile. "You're going to make a scene, huh?"

Leena and Cora had become very interested in their salads. I couldn't blame them. Brooklyn had a way of drawing attention, even negative attention.

She flipped her hand over, examining her hot-pink-painted nails. "Is there a time I don't?"

My chest heaved. "Fine. Let me get to the point. We've already established you hate me. I'm not looking to be BFFs. I have some questions."

Her eyes hardened. "You've got five minutes before I give you the shock of your life."

She wasn't kidding. Brooklyn would be the kind of supe who wouldn't care about rules. No magic in front of humans, so it would be wise to heed her warning.

"You said my father was evil. I know he was convicted of

murdering someone in your family," I said, getting straight to the point. I didn't have time to beat around the bush.

Leena and Cora both let out audible gasps, hands flying to their mouths. I took it Brooklyn hadn't told her besties about the strife between our families.

The expression on her pretty face could have been construed as impressed—or maybe it was haughtiness. It was hard to tell. "I can't believe it has taken you so long to figure out. He was my uncle, my father's brother. I was deprived of knowing him, thanks to *your* father."

I didn't think this would be easy, but Brooklyn was going to make it worse than swallowing a mouthful of bile. "Looks like we have more in common than either of us would like."

She scoffed. "I'm nothing like you."

"Whatever. I didn't have time to make you a list, and I don't want to argue. What I want to know is if you have any information on what happened that night."

Her dainty shoulders shrugged. Brooklyn loved nothing more than having the knowledge I wanted. It gave her an edge. But she surprised me by divulging information. "Only what I've been told, that your father was a power-hungry warlock who turned to the dark side. His dabbling in black magic corrupted his heart and soul. My mom and my uncle, who was a year younger, had been friends with your mother. When your mom noticed things had changed inside your father, she wanted to leave him and turned to my mom for help. Your mother knew your father wouldn't let her go easily, especially if he found out she was pregnant, which he had. The three of them sought the help of a witch to perform a spell that would sever any ties with your father, including memories of your mom being pregnant."

A nasty sinking feeling settled in my stomach. What Brooklyn was saying coincided with the vision. My heart hurt for my mother and what she must have been going through. But my heart broke for the boy who lost his life that night.

Everyone around the table was on the edge of their seats,

including me, waiting to hear what happened next. Brooklyn might be a raging lunatic, but she wasn't a half bad storyteller. Who would have thought?

"The night they gathered with the witch to perform the spell, your father showed up. He broke their circle. My uncle lunged, and his heroic actions to protect *your* mother cost him his life. Your father hit him with a death spell," she spat, her voice growing in anger.

Maybe this wasn't such a good idea. She seemed to be getting heated over the retelling. "I'm sorry, Brooklyn, but you have to know that has nothing to do with me."

"You're wrong. It has everything to do with you. It was because of you," she barked in a thin voice.

If I snapped back, I wouldn't get any more details from Brooklyn. I had to rein the growl back and remain calm.

"What happened . . . after?" I asked as smoothly as I could manage.

Crossing her arms over her chest, Brooklyn glared at me. "They locked your father up."

My life had become something out of a paranormal novel. Hell, my life was a paranormal murder mystery.

Her head tilted to the side as she continued to glower at me. "They said he went mad in prison. You're going to end up just like him," she hurled with venom strong enough to poison me.

Did she—? Had she—? I couldn't even grasp the implication behind her words. I got it. She hated me and had more reason to hate me than anyone else. But me? Murder someone? Was that the curse? Was I doomed to kill someone? Torent? Beck? Brooklyn? Okay, the last idea I could entertain for a hot minute, but no matter how ugly Brooklyn could be, I would never have the heart to end her life.

But throw a milkshake at her?

Hell yes.

Something inside me snapped. It happened so fast, a gut reaction. Before I got the chance to process what my hand was doing, the vanilla shake clutched in my fingers was sailing across the table. The semiliquid ice cream splattered down the front of Brooklyn's shirt. Poor Cora, who was sitting next to Brooklyn, caught some of the stray drops.

I had assaulted the mean girls with a milkshake.

"You basic bitch," Brooklyn seethed, jumping to her feet. Flames radiated in her eyes.

"Oops," I said with a sly smile, a hand flying to my lips. Things just got a little messy. This wasn't going to bode well for my social status.

"You'll pay for this." Brooklyn's voice had gone so low, prickles formed at the back of my neck.

Wasn't I already?

CHAPTER 8

I ran from the lunchroom. Someone called my name over the cafeteria chatter. I thought it was Beck, but I kept going, quickly turned the corner, and smacked into Torent. I swear the demon had ESP when it came to me. He had a way of always being in the right place at the right time. The universe was telling me something, and I was being too stubborn to listen.

His hands landed on my shoulders, preventing me from bolting. "Hey, what's wrong? You look like you've seen a ghost."

"I need to go home," I rushed out, trying to maneuver around him a second time, but he wasn't having it.

His fingers stayed firm on my shoulders. "Fine, I'll drive you."

"There's no point in us both getting detention for skipping class." I could sense the metal around me—the lockers, the screws in the walls, and the supports under the floor—but the school's wards kept me from going full metal freak-out. Otherwise, I might have very well brought the school walls down around me.

The idea was terrifying, but the dark shadow of thoughts in my head petrified me more.

What if Brooklyn was right? What if I was as dark as my father? What if the combination of being the daughter of the goddess of night and a warlock doomed me to an ill-omened fate?

His hands trailed down my arms, and he interlaced our fingers, giving them a squeeze. "You're worth giving up a Saturday for."

I nodded. No arguments this time. I needed to get out of here.

Torent drove us out of the school parking lot toward my house in silence. I stared out the window at the snow-covered mountains rolling by. The view was always beautiful in Havenwood Falls and with Christmas just a few weeks away, the town looked like something out of a painting with its colored lights, bright red bows, and handcrafted pine wreaths, but today I barely noticed. My mind glazed over the landscape, stuck in my own thoughts.

"Are you going to tell me what happened?" Torent asked, breaking me out of my trance.

I pulled my gaze from the side window to look at him. He had the kind of dark beauty a girl could easily get hung up on. "Only if you promise not to laugh."

He took a hand off the steering wheel for a second and held it up in a salute. "Demon's honor."

I snorted. A demon's honor meant crap, but this was Torent, and I had come to trust him as much as I did Beck. "I threw a milkshake at your ex-girlfriend."

His lips twitched. "I would have paid to see that. Any chance I could get you to do it again?"

Crossing my arms, I sank down in the seat. "I'm sure it's already up on YouTube."

"What did she say to piss you off?"

He knew Brooklyn well and how she loved to push my buttons. Being short-tempered and on edge didn't help the situation. I was angry, along with a shit ton of other emotions. "She can be such a heinous bitch."

"Very true," he agreed, keeping his focus on the road.

"She isn't entirely to blame," I admitted, even though the admission left a bad taste in my mouth. "I don't know what I was thinking, going to her for information, but she did fill in some missing gaps about my father and what happened that night."

His lips turned down into a frown. "And that's what has you running?"

I wasn't running, was I?

Maybe a little, but more than anything I wanted my mom.

It was time she and I had a little chat. No more secrets. No more lies. I deserved the truth. I wasn't a child to be protected any longer.

I walked through the front door and was overwhelmed with a sense of nostalgia. I hadn't grown up in this house, but over the month it had become my home and represented everything I had ever longed for. Stability. Love. Roots.

My boots shuffled over the hardwood floors into the family room, where I found my mom curled up on the couch with a book. The fireplace was roaring, wood popping and crackling in the stone hearth. She looked so beautiful with the glow of amber highlighting her golden skin and hair. Today was her day off from work.

"Mom?" My voice was soft but carried over the room.

She jumped, the trashy romance book she had been engrossed in falling into her lap. "Mallory, you scared me." Her eyes glanced over the clock on the wall before her brows furrowed together in confusion. "What are you doing home? Shouldn't you be in school?"

I tried to keep the tears at bay as I walked to the couch. She pulled her feet in closer so I could sit.

"Honey, what's got you so upset?" she asked, placing the book from her lap onto the coffee table.

The words came pouring out. "Why did you never tell me my father was a murderer?"

She wasn't shocked by what I said, not like I imagined she would have been. The only reaction on her face was a slight lift of her eyes, but the few moments of silence spoke volumes. "I'll make us some coffee. We could both use it. And then we'll talk."

I was grateful for a minute or two to collect myself. She came from the kitchen with two mugs, offering me one before sitting back down beside me on the couch.

Lifting her feet up on the rectangular table, she stared into the fireplace. "I've dreaded this moment since the day you were born. It was foolish of me to have taken you from Havenwood Falls. I see that now, but back then, I was scared and desperate to save you from a fate not of your making. I wanted more than anything to give you the life of your choosing, but some things can't be undone. If I'd had the power to give you a different father, I wouldn't hesitate. You deserve so much more."

I pulled my legs up onto the couch, tucking them to the side. "I know why you did what you did. I just don't know why you never told me."

Her fingers tapped lightly against the Christmas mug Gigi was so fond of. "At first you were too young and as time went by . . ." She shook her head. "I didn't want to blow up your world. As you grew older, I noticed little things that only another supernatural might see. Your powers were manifesting, and there was nothing I could do to stop them, no place I could hide you from who you are. I struggled for months over telling you, and it was Gigi who convinced me we needed to come home. I had every intention of telling you after you'd settled in, but you came into your powers quicker than I anticipated, and you adjusted so well. We made the right choice coming back here. In truth, I was scared. I didn't want you to hate me."

"I could never hate you, Mom. We're a team, you and I. Always have been. Always will be," I said, offering her a soft smile of encouragement. It was hard to see the female figure in my life vulnerable.

"He wasn't always so . . . ambitious," she finally decided, choosing her words carefully. "We started dating freshman year in high school, and it was a whirlwind romance. We were so in love and had dreams. Big dreams, but in hindsight, I should have seen it. He changed right before my eyes, but I was too blinded by my love for him. And then it was too late. I couldn't save him." Her eyes turned misty. "But maybe I could save you. So I ran. And kept running."

I was thankful for the warmth of the fire to relieve the chill that had settled into my veins. "What happened to him?" I asked.

She seemed to lose herself in the past before responding, her voice sad. "The temptation of darkness can be seductive, like a drug. Once you've had a taste, you crave more until it is all you can think about. It poisons the mind. Roth had a curious mind, like you, but he didn't have your strength. He would sneak across the borders of Havenwood Falls to experiment with his powers, which led him to some potent spells—dark magic. On more than one occasion, I followed him, fearful the Blackstone witch hunters would uncover his secret. He was a skilled warlock and learned quickly. By the time I realized he was no longer the boy I fell in love with, I was already pregnant with you, just a few months after graduation."

I sipped on my coffee as I listened. It was hard to believe this was a true story and not fantasy, but that could apply to most of my life. I'd heard of the Blackstone witch hunters from Beck, but only in passing.

"I desperately wanted that boy back and begged him to stop practicing," she continued. "He refused, breaking my heart, but I didn't have just myself to think about, so I ended things. I told Roth it was over. It was naive to think he would let me walk away. I was a possession to him. And I kept my pregnancy a secret; not even Gigi knew. The only people I confided in had been Mira and Ryle. The biggest mistake of my life."

Her coffee was forgotten, cold in her hand. I couldn't help but admire her poise and courage as she recounted what was the worst night of her life.

The sadness in her expression faded into worry. "Roth found out about you. I was only nine weeks pregnant and barely had time to contemplate the fact that I was going to be a mom. I don't know how your father discovered my secret, but if I had to guess, it was dark magic. He knew I was hiding something. Roth wasn't just curious; he was also extremely perceptive, especially when it came to me."

"You went to Mira and Ryle for help," I supplied.

She nodded, her finger circling around the rim of her cup. "I didn't know what else to do, who else to turn to, but I wish more than anything I had never sought their help. It seemed the only way, a simple spell to make Roth forget me. I refused to let him take you from me, which was exactly what he threatened."

God, my father sounded like such an asshat.

"I didn't know what he had planned that night. If I had, I would have tried to stop him. I would have warned Ryle and Mira. They were my best friends. I never would have let him hurt them."

It was clear Mom still tormented herself with the guilt of Ryle's death and her lost friendship with Mira. My heart squeezed for her.

"Styx gave me a vision of that night," I said softly.

Her eyes widened a fraction. "That doesn't surprise me. I haven't been back to the lake yet. I can't bring myself to go." She set aside the coffee and folded her hands in her lap. "He came upon us near Peacock Lake with a witch, Lyra Beaumont. She was in the middle of her spell, which had drained some of her energy, but even at full power, I don't think she would have been a match for Roth. He had grown stronger each day, and that night I feared him more than death itself." A shudder rolled through her petite frame as she relived that horrible event. "He struck with dark violence before we had a chance to defend ourselves. His target had been Lyra, to stop her from finishing the spell. Ryle threw himself in front of her. The spear of darkness hit him in the center of his chest. I'll never forget the look in his eyes, full of shock and pain."

A lump of emotion lodged itself in my throat.

"He killed him and just took off," I said, unable to disguise the repulsion in my voice.

Mom's voice faltered for an instant. "No. He might have done more harm, but that kind of magic doesn't go unnoticed in Havenwood Falls. It was a matter of minutes before Roth was surrounded. That night was the last time I saw him."

"He was sentenced to jail."

She nodded. "He was. Life without parole."

"Even with him locked away, you still decided to leave?"

"I didn't trust a supernatural prison would hold him, not even one bound by fae magic. Fear drove me from Havenwood Falls. I didn't want him anywhere near you. Gigi agreed. She helped me leave and find a safe place to stay until you were born. I made Gigi swear to never tell you. She gave me her word, but she didn't agree. I don't think his parents ever knew about you, but his family left Havenwood Falls shortly after his sentencing."

I couldn't imagine how alone she had felt. The picture was clearer but didn't make the burden I now faced any lighter. Did Mom know about the blood hex that had been passed down to me? If not, could I burden her with more guilt? I couldn't.

Maybe it was my turn to protect her.

CHAPTER 9

$\mathcal{T}$he wind was howling and whipping outside the Academy building, the classroom of my Awakening Lab unusually cold. More than a week had passed since I'd found out about my father. I tucked my chin inside my hoodie and let the sleeves drape over my fingers. A shiver curled down my neck.

I glanced around the room. No one's teeth were chattering. No one else had goosebumps covering their skin. I seemed to be the only one freezing half to death.

My arms folded over my chest to keep the warmth close. Too bad Torent wasn't taking classes at the Academy. I could use a dose of his hellfire. The thought no sooner crossed my mind than I did feel something . . . something weird and unfamiliar. I glimpsed over my shoulder, my eyes darting over the class.

Again, I was alone in my suffering.

Not a single soul flinched as I did. Otis chewed on the end of his pen. He was a shifter with an infatuation for putting things in his mouth. Gianna continued to twirl her glossy hair around her finger, listening to her mom talk. The girl beside me snapped her gum.

But the eerie feeling continued shimmying up my spine until an odd tremor spread over my shoulders, down my arms, and into my fingertips. The first tendrils of unease bloomed in the pit of my belly like a vine of ivy twisting around my insides.

Returning my focus to Mrs. Augustine's lecture, I did my best to ignore the chill of concern that had taken up residence inside me. I couldn't shake the distinct feeling something was about to happen —something dark and unnatural. It was driving me crazy that no one else could sense it. Was I losing my mind?

It's the fingers of death—my legacy.

Unless Mrs. Augustine had suddenly become a dude with a deep voice, that had not been her speaking.

"I'm sorry. What did you say?" I blurted out before my brain caught up to my mouth.

Utter silence followed. Mrs. Augustine paused in her speech to address me. "Do you have a question, Mallory?"

I had a million questions, but I doubted everyone else in the class wanted to sit there as I peppered Mrs. Augustine with my inquiries about hexes, dead birds, and apparently now mysterious voices in my head. I shook my head. If I could have crawled under my desk and disappeared, I would have.

A few of the people around me shifted in their seats or chuckled. Amusing the class had not been my objective. My heart picked up its pace, and I could feel sweat dotting my palms. Any more outbursts like this, and I'd get kicked out of class.

Mrs. Augustine cleared her throat.

"Sorry, I, uh, didn't mean to interrupt." Maybe I was getting sick, not that I'd ever heard of the flu causing voices, but it could very well be a supernatural side effect. That was it. I had a supernatural flu bug. Gigi would definitely have a remedy for that.

You're not sick, Mallory.

Holy crap on a cracker. The voice burst my bubble.

Because there were still a few sets of eyes on me, I refrained from sticking my fingers in my ears to drown out the voice. I doubted it would help. Forcing myself to draw in several deep breaths, I attempted to curb the panic attack rising in my chest.

If I wasn't sick then it had to be stress. I needed sleep. Lots and lots of hard Z's.

Nothing you do will stop death.

Enough. My palms slammed on the desk, and I once again found the class staring at me. Heat painted my cheeks. "Sorry," I mouthed and returned to stare at the blank page of notebook paper in front of me.

Death becomes you, the voice hissed, causing a shiver to ripple through me.

That wasn't ominous.

Who was the voice? And what did they want with me? Did it have anything to do with the dead birds?

I didn't want death to become me. I didn't want this at all. None of it.

Gigi was out for the night, and Mom was watching TV on the couch when I got home after night class. Still shaken from what happened in Awakening Lab, I popped my head in to let her know I was home and headed upstairs to my room. Tonight was a bubble bath and a pound of chocolate kind of night.

My mind was already on the tub and the bath bomb I'd splurged on a few weeks ago as I walked through my bedroom door. I slipped my fingers under my hoodie and whipped it off. Tossing it aside, I unbuttoned my jeans and found a pair of sparkling eyes staring at me from the corner of my room.

I yelped, equal parts fear and shock coursing through me.

Holy fuck.

Someone was sitting in my room—in the dark—like a total serial killer. My powers instinctually activated, going into defense mode. I didn't know what this dark figure wanted, but if he had come to kill me, he was going to have a fight on his hands. My brain automatically assumed it was a guy, but my stalker could very well have been female. It was hard to tell in the dark.

No way that's Brooklyn. Is it?

If anyone suffered from an obsession with me, my money was on my nymph nemesis. I'd hate to say that ten times fast.

Throwing out my hand, I summoned the closest metal object I could find in my room—a nail file from my desk—and sent it sailing toward the mysterious perp with glowing violet eyes.

Wait.

Is that flecks of gold I see in them?

There was only one person with eyes like that.

"Torent?" my voice squeaked in the dark. At the last second, I stopped the nail file flying across my room just short of gouging Torent's eyeball.

"Do you think you can drop the pointy object before you accidentally scar my handsome face?" The texture of his voice was silky as night and wicked.

A whoosh of air left my lungs, and I set the nail file on the dresser. "It would serve you right for scaring the shit out of me. How did you get in here?"

He stood up, and a beam of moonlight streaked over the left side of his cheek. I caught a hint of a smirk on his lips. "Haven't you learned? Locks can't keep me out."

Shutting the door to the hallway, I pressed my back into it.

"Okay. That still doesn't explain why you snuck into my bedroom," I hissed, attempting to keep my voice low so as not to alert Mom anything was amiss. I had a boy in my room. Not just any boy. A hot demon I couldn't seem to keep my hands off.

This was bad. Like epically bad.

A muscle feathered in his cheek. "You didn't answer my text, and I got worried, so I came to check on you."

Damn demon. "You almost lost an eyeball."

He lifted a brow, eyeing the nail file on the dresser. "I noticed."

"As you can see, I'm fine. You should leave." *Quick, before I do something reckless like kiss you.*

His long legs easily crossed the room, and the smell that was uniquely Torent reached my nose. *Why does he have to smell so good?*

"Do you have a problem with being in the same room as me?" he asked.

Uh, I could barely breathe the same air as him without wanting to tackle him and kiss him to death.

"Torent, you shouldn't be here. It's dangerous to be near me. If anything happened to you . . ." My voice trailed off, emotion clogging my throat.

I blinked, and he was suddenly in front of me. "I might not be immortal, but demons don't die easily."

Now that he was here, I wanted him to stay more than I wanted that bubble bath. I chewed on the inside of my lip, wrestling with myself. What happened in class tonight came back to haunt me. Death. The stench of it lingered on me like cigarette smoke. One of the reasons I had craved a bath. I wanted to rid myself of the dirty feeling it left stained on my skin.

Torent's finger slipped under my chin, and he peered into my eyes. It was as if he could reach my soul. "What happened?" he demanded.

A smart guy would have already run far away from me, but not Torent. He headed straight for the heart of danger and would face the greatest of evils to protect those he cared about. I was one of those people. My whole body radiated like the center of a star, casting points of light to every finger and toe.

Overwhelmed with an outpouring of emotion that strongly resembled love, I opened my mouth to tell him—

Then my bedroom window shattered.

Glass sprayed all over the room, and a streak of black sliced through the air. Torent's reflexes kicked in, tucking me against his body as he dropped down to the ground, shielding me from the raining glass. The sound was ear piercing, causing my whole body to wince. When the dust settled, a large mangled crow lay on my floor, covered in a pool of glass fragments.

God damn. How many birds was this curse going to kill before I figured out how to break it? There was no way I was going to let what my father did take me down too. I would find a way to end this torment.

"Mallory!" My name belted from downstairs, followed by rapid footsteps. My mom was coming, and we were less than a minute away from being busted.

Lifting my head, I met Torent's luminous gaze. "Hide," I ordered him, pushing at his chest.

He didn't immediately move, to my frustration. "You owe me a thanks, crash car."

"I'll give you a million thanks, just get in the closet." His grin was going to make me regret those words, but he disappeared into the shadows just as my bedroom door whipped open.

I carefully got to my feet and brushed the glass off me. Argh. It was in my hair. Torent was sliding the closet door softly closed.

Mom stood in the threshold, her eyes sweeping over the disarray of my room with horror before finding me. "What happened? Oh, my God. Are you hurt?"

She rushed over, running her fingers over my face looking for cuts.

"I'm fine," I assured softly.

Her eyes once again roamed over the catastrophe that was my room, landing on the dead bird. It was simple math to put two and two together.

"Did he fly through your window?" she asked, incredulity lacing her tone.

"I was about to take a bath, and he came crashing through the window. I didn't know birds had that kind of strength."

Her lips pinched together. "They don't normally." Relaxing her features, she rubbed her hands up and down my arms to comfort me . . . or herself. I wasn't sure which. "The important thing is you're okay. I'll help you clean up the glass and secure the window until we can call someone tomorrow to fix it."

I nodded, feeling numb. The curse was progressing, and I didn't know what to do about it.

"Are you sure you're okay?" she asked, noticing the odd expression that had crept onto my face.

I couldn't very well tell her Torent had shielded me. Doing everything in my power to not look at the closet, I replied, "I'm still a bit shaken up."

She nodded and left to grab supplies. A cold gust of wind hurtled through what was left of the jagged window. I turned to the closet, spotting the glowing violet eyes.

"Don't move," I told him. "And don't think about going through my stuff."

A husky chuckle came through the crack as if he had been caught red-handed. I should have shoved him out the broken window before Mom came back, but I didn't want him to leave, so in the closet he stayed.

I swept up the pieces of glass. Mom disposed of the bird, wrinkling her nose in the process and both of us trying to not squeal like little girls. Knowing Torent, it was either torture or entertaining watching Mom and me handle the cleanup. It was probably grating on his hero soul to be unable to swoop in and save the day. That was what he was good at.

Together we covered the window with plastic and sealed it up with tape. It wasn't pretty but would do for the night. Mom brought up a space heater from the basement to make sure I didn't freeze to death. I was grateful Gigi was out tonight with her "bridge club"—a cover for the little old ladies of Havenwood Falls to get together and gossip.

The door clicked shut behind Mom twenty minutes later, and I spun around. Torent emerged from the closet dressed in all black. He had ditched his hoodie, leaving the cotton T-shirt stretching across his chest. I was relieved he hadn't come out with a thong on his head. It was mortifying enough knowing he had been eavesdropping on Mom and me.

My eyes darted over his face like a mermaid yearning for the sea, but it was the sight of something red on the side of his neck that had me crossing to him.

"You're bleeding," I whispered, lifting to inspect the damage. It was only a nick, most of the blood dried.

He hissed through his teeth, reaching for my hand. "Don't poke at it."

My lips twitched, and I tried to hide my amusement. "Sorry."

Encircling my wrist, he brought my hand to his chest, covering it with one of his own. "The curse is escalating."

Tell me something I don't know. My grin slipped off my face. "All the more reason for you to not be here. You should keep your distance."

He walked over to my bed and fluffed a pillow, then dropped down on top of it, making himself comfortable. The mattress bounced under his weight. "Not going to happen. I plan on sticking close just in case anything else weird happens."

"By close, you mean you're planning on spending the night? In my room? With me?" *Way to not sound lame, Mallory.*

He grinned and patted the bed.

This was insane, and yet I was calmer. I should be freaking the eff out, but having Torent near made me worry a little less.

"What are you doing?" I inquired, though it was crystal clear what he was up to.

Sprawled on his back, he laced his fingers under his head in a sign he had no intention of leaving. "What does it look like?"

I stood in the center of the room like a lost puppy. "Like you're taking up more than half of my bed."

What did he expect? For me to climb in beside him?

Those lips formed a grin. "Isn't it past your bedtime? You've had kind of a rough day."

"Is that so?" How could any single guy look so good lying in a soft pink bed?

Long lashes framed his eyes, drawing my attention to his face. "Mallory, come here."

A shiver skipped over my skin.

"I need to use the bathroom," I announced, feeling my cheeks brighten in color. *Smooth, Mal.* I turned and hightailed it to the safety of my adjoining bathroom to shower, change, and brush my teeth. Close quarters with Torent called for fresh breath, and I doubted he would appreciate the glass in my hair. Not that I was anticipating anything to happen between us, but I was a girl who liked to be prepared for all possibilities.

Again I found myself fidgeting and staring at the floor. What was wrong with me? I stood in the doorway, telling myself I had nothing to be nervous about. This was just Torent.

His eyes glided over me in an unhurried perusal. "I'm not going to attack you like an animal."

My heart tripped up in my chest as my feet padded slowly over the floor. Was I seriously getting in bed with a demon? I climbed in, keeping my gaze glued to his, and rested my cheek on the pillow. I turned on my side.

"You don't need to stay. I'm fine," I insisted, but I really did want him to stay for purely selfish reasons.

"I'm staying. I don't want any more surprises."

That made two of us. I'd met my quota for the day. My heart couldn't take more. Then again, I wasn't sure my heart could take sleeping alongside Torent Stark. Sex and all things naughty should have been the furthest thing from my mind, but he smelled so good.

Torent mistook my nervousness. "We're going to figure out how to defeat this curse."

"I don't know where to start. What if I end up like him?" I glanced away, staring at where our feet lay at the end of the bed.

His knuckles brushed along my cheek, drawing my eyes back to him. "Our parents don't define us, crash car. We make our own fate. We're all capable of darkness, but that doesn't mean we're evil. You're many things, but malicious is not one of them. Don't doubt who you are."

That was the thing. I didn't know who I was anymore.

CHAPTER 10

"I don't want to talk about the curse anymore. Tell me about your family. I want to know more about what it's like being a demon." A distraction was what I needed, and Torent provided the perfect outlet to get my mind off the curse.

He opened an arm. "Get comfortable, crash car. This is going to take all night."

"Perfect," I replied dryly, but curled up against him, laying my damp head in the nook of his arm. Sleep was out of reach for me tonight. The splintering of glass still echoed in my ears.

His fingers slipped over my hand relaxing on his chest. "If you want a distraction . . ." The suggestion in his voice made my belly flutter. It was as if he could read my mind.

I lifted my head slightly to peer down at him with a ghost of a smile on my lips. "As tempting as it is, and believe me I'm seriously tempted, it's not a good idea. I don't trust myself."

Shifting his head on the pillow, he kept our fingers laced together. Seconds later, my ceiling was painted with pink, purple, and teal sparkling lights dancing. "I'm here to protect you, not the other way around."

"And why can't I be the hero for once?" I asked blandly.

"Because I'm not the one with a death curse."

I nudged him in the side. "Hey. I thought we weren't going to talk about the curse."

"Right," he agreed, turning his gaze upward to watch the colors frolic and twinkle. "Well, my family is insane, volatile, treacherous, and amazing," he added, grinning. I could hear how much he cared for them. "And those are just my brothers."

"What about your parents?" I inquired, curious about the people who had created such a perfect male. I pressed my chin on his chest so I could stare at his face. Splashes of colored light reflected over his skin.

"My father is larger than life with a laugh that booms across a crowded room. And my mom is petite, but don't let her size fool you. She isn't a woman to mess with."

"I can't wait to meet your family," I said, sort of kidding.

He laughed. "They are going to love you."

A pack of menacing demons . . . I wondered what they would think of their youngest son dating a nymph.

"Do you always pursue girls this hard?" I asked the question that had been on my mind for weeks.

His eyes deepened in color. "Never."

I believed him. "Then why me?"

"Does there need to be a reason?" he countered.

He wasn't getting out of it that easily. I sincerely wanted to know what it was that made me different from every other girl. I wasn't special or prettier. I was just me, and I was curious how *he* saw me. I gave him a pointed look, the lines in my face set.

His leaned forward so our noses were only inches apart. "You're more beautiful than any enchanted meadow. You're stubborn but filled with goodness. You care more about other people than yourself. And no one has ever made me feel the way I do when we're together."

Sweet hell. His words caused a chain reaction to go off inside me as if my veins were filled with millions of starlights. How did I respond to an admission like that? Thank you didn't seem to cut it.

"You're nothing like I first thought." He was so much more.

"And what exactly was your first impression of me, other than I was extraordinarily good looking?"

I snorted. "You just proved my initial thought—that you were arrogant." But I had been wrong.

We talked for hours until I was barely able to keep my eyes open and the day was finally catching up to me. I dozed off. It was a miracle, considering I'd spent a creepy amount of time staring at Torent while he slept. He looked nothing like a demon and everything like an angel.

I was on the edge of consciousness, but not fully ready to give up sleep. My body was burning like the sun, and I couldn't figure out why. Did I have a fever? Had someone cranked the heat? No. It wasn't that kind of heat, not the sweat-drenching-over-my-skin-heat.

This was internal and made me tremble. With shallow, uneven breaths, my eyes fluttered open, and I tilted my head to the side, leaning into the dreamy sensation. It was only then I realized it was Torent's lips causing my hormones to go haywire.

His mouth was restless, rushing down my neck and over a bare shoulder. The T-shirt I had worn to bed had slipped off to the side, giving him all the access he desired. It was as if it was vital for him to taste all of me. My brain foggy from the sudden onslaught of sensations rocking through my body, I couldn't tell if this was a dream or very real.

I wanted it to be real.

"Mallory," my name tumbled from his lips, low and vibrant like an enchanting prayer. I felt worshiped. "Mallory?" he whispered again, but this time in question—he was asking permission.

I didn't know whose mouth found whose, but our lips met. The kiss started out sweet and exploratory, but it didn't stay that way for long. As he took my mouth deeper, our tongues twined, the cool metal of his piercing teasing me. It only took that one kiss for me to make a decision. I wanted this. I wanted Torent. *What about the hex?* a voice echoed in my head. The blood hex would continue weaving itself in my veins, growing stronger, to the point it might progress from plants and birds to those I cared about.

For the briefest of moments, I pulled away. Was I making a mistake?

Every pore in my body was aware of Torent. His mouth reclaimed mine, and I was no longer thinking at all. Power soared inside me, the fire spreading fast and wildly.

His hands dove into my hair, fingers raking desperately to pull me closer.

"Tell me this is okay?" he murmured gruffly. "I'll stop if this isn't what you want." The idea sounded as if it pained him, but I knew from the bottom of my heart it would only take one word from me and he would stop.

I swallowed, letting my hands frame either side of his face. "I want this. I want you," I whispered, brushing my lips across his.

His entire body relaxed into mine, and I paused to shed my shirt. He watched my every move, hardly breathing. A ravenous, primal hunger darkened his eyes that were more gold than violet. I should have been afraid or at the very least cautious, but I felt neither.

Gentle hands explored my body, and I tried not to let my insecurities get in the way.

"You're so beautiful," he said, tracing lazy patterns over my belly.

I trembled at his touch.

"Are you scared?" he asked, gazing into my eyes.

I'd never seen such a color before, the way his human and demon eyes blended together. I was awestruck by him. "No. I'm not afraid. Not of you. Maybe a little of how you make me feel."

His head angled to the side, regarding me with a devastating smile. "How do I make you feel?"

Every fiber in my body was screaming for me to tell him that I loved him. Instead, I showed him. Fisting my fingers into his silky hair, I ground my lips to his, yielding completely to the storm swirling inside me. Everything beyond this room, beyond Torent, became a void of darkness.

My bare legs hooked behind his, and I ran my ankle down his muscular calf. He breathed my name over and over again. I couldn't tell where I ended and he began. He was mine, and I was his. Our bodies were meant to be together; I didn't know how else to describe it. The connection between us was like fire, burning and intense. We clung to one another, body to body, as the shimmer of pleasure glistened over our skin. The only sound in the room was the beating of our hearts in perfect wild harmony.

Afterward, I lay in his arms, our legs intertwined, and I told him I loved him . . . in my head.

The next time I woke up, beams of warm sunlight were taking their first peek over the horizon as the last dusting of stars winked out of the sky. Utter calmness seemed to settle over the world.

I stretched out in bed, my heart bursting with happiness and so many other emotions. Why did it feel like this demon belonged in my bed—at my side?

I didn't want to start the day. In fact, I wanted to stay here with Torent, but I doubted Mom or Gigi would agree. They would be getting up soon, and it would be wise if Torent was gone before then, but looking at him sleeping peacefully beside me, I didn't have the heart to disturb him. Plus, he was mesmerizing to stare at.

I should really stop, but I couldn't help myself.

Lifting a hand, I brushed a stray strand of hair off the side of his face and watched his lips slowly begin to curve.

"Good morning," he said huskily, his eyes still closed.

My mouth echoed his grin. "Hey."

This didn't need to be awkward, so I told myself to be cool, and *hey* was what I'd come up with. Real cool.

Those long legs stretched like a predator cat's after a long night's nap. "How did you sleep?"

My cheek pressed into the top of my hands as I turned on my side. "I survived the night, and my window's still broken."

His lips curled. "My job here is done."

And I didn't kill him while he slept—that was something. Perhaps the hex was only effective on animals and plants?

I loved my wishful thinking, but it gave me something to cling to—hope.

"Mallory!" Mom shouted my name from down the hall. "You're going to be late for school."

Shit. I'd completely forgotten it was a weekday. There would be no lazy morning snuggles.

I bolted upright on the bed, my sudden wide eyes bouncing from the closed door to Torent. His dark messy hair was spread out over the white pillow. He didn't so much as flinch at the sound of my Mom's voice.

"What are you doing?" I shrieked in a hushed whisper. "You've got to go. Now!" I said, pushing at his heavy body.

Why did he have so many muscles? It made shoving him off the bed nearly impossible.

Sitting up, he ran his hand through his hair. "You look cute frazzled."

Oh, my God. He was still naked. I was naked! I jumped out of bed, throwing on a shirt and locating his discarded shirt and jeans.

"Quick, get dressed," I ordered, throwing the clothes at him. The shirt landed on his face. I wasted no time crossing back to the bed. My fingers latched on to his arm, and I yanked.

With an oomph, Torent tumbled to the floor.

"Mallory, are you okay?" Mom's voice carried through from the other side of the door.

"Yes, just getting dressed," I hollered back, buying myself a few minutes.

Torent looked up at me from the floor. "You're lucky I don't pull you down here with me."

I blew at the disarray of hair that had fallen into my face. "Now is not the time for games, Stark. And why aren't your clothes on yet?"

His smile was troublesome. "Is my nakedness bothering you?"

"Yes! And unless you want my mom to string you up by your balls, you need to move your fine ass."

The grin on his lips did not waver. He was not in the least intimidated by my threat. "It is a pretty spectacular ass."

"Torent," I groaned, and it was enough to get him moving. As he finally dressed, I scanned the room and realized I had a problem. Panic tore inside me. "How the hell did you get in here?" I asked, realizing I needed a way to get him out of my room undetected.

"Through the window," he answered, blasé.

Both our heads whipped toward the broken and taped up glass.

"Shit," I mumbled under my breath. "That isn't going to work now." My fingers dashed through my hair as I racked my brain for a plan.

His pants were on now but unbuttoned as he slipped his T-shirt over his head. "Don't panic. We'll figure something out."

Too late.

My pulse had already quickened, my chest tightening. "You'd better hurry and come up with a stellar idea, because I've got nothing."

A light rap of knuckles sounded on my door. "Honey? Gigi wants to know if Torent wants breakfast."

My face fell. *Damn. Damn. Damn.* Living with a bunch of magical nymphs was going to be hell on my dating life . . . now that I had one. There was no going back after last night.

The notorious demon's lips twitched. "I would love breakfast," he mouthed.

I elbowed him in the gut and went to the door, throwing it open. I tried to angle my body in such a way that Torent's form was obscured.

"I can explain." The words popped out of my mouth.

Mom stood on the other side of the door attempting to school her expression, but I caught the sparkle of amusement in her eyes. Her perfect daughter getting caught with a boy in her room. I wouldn't be surprised if she was a bit proud too.

"You think you're the first person to sneak a boy into this house? I've got a tip for you. Nothing gets past Gigi's eyes. I learned that the hard way." She tweaked the end of my nose. "Morning, Torent," she said, her gaze going past me into my bedroom, where Torent was standing with his hands shoved into his jeans.

Those vibrant violet eyes glinted with humor. "Good morning, Ms. Whitt."

"Didn't I tell you to call me Wendy?" She wrinkled her nose. "Ms. Whitt makes me sound old." And Mom definitely didn't want to be that.

"He was just leaving," I interjected before things could possibly get any weirder.

"Uh-huh," Mom said, pursing her lips. "Just don't be late for school again, okay?" She turned and strutted down the hall, her hips swinging from side to side.

I shut the door and leaned my back against it. *Why does this stuff happen to me?* I wanted nothing more than to climb under my bed and never leave my room again, let alone have to face Gigi.

Torent, seeing the distraught expression on my face, laughed. "This has been the most fun I've had in a while. You're something else."

The features on my face remained impassive. "Not funny."

"It kind of is."

"Oh, yeah?" I grabbed the closest thing I could find and chucked it at his head. He caught the fuzzy slipper midair, laughing harder. "You're the one who is going to be doing the walk of shame into class this morning," I snapped, thinking stupidly that would wipe the smirk off his lips.

The joke was on me.

"It was worth it," he said, his deep tone sexy as sin.

My heart cartwheeled.

CHAPTER 11

*T*orent had returned my car last week good as new. You'd never be able to tell the windshield had been shattered. We drove separately to school, and I told myself some space was a good thing, especially after the embarrassing morning. My cheeks had never been so red when I shuffled downstairs, ushering Torent out. Gigi didn't say a word, but I didn't doubt I would get one of her talks after school.

Not that I minded them. Truthfully, most of Gigi's advice was spot on. My family might be eccentric, but living with all women had taught me how to be strong and independent.

At lunch, Beck and I drove over to Sakura Buffet to grab something to eat. It was close to school, and the service was quick. We didn't always leave campus for lunch, but today I needed to get out of the stuffy classrooms for a bit, and my sudden craving for Chinese food was too mighty to ignore.

A little bell rang over the door as we walked over the threshold and into the dining room. We went up to the buffet bar. The cashier rang up our orders and handed us two plates. Beck and I moseyed down the line, filling our plates with sweet and sour chicken, rice, noodles, egg rolls, and some kind of beef.

Spotting an empty booth that overlooked the parking lot, we slid in and set our plates down.

"God, I'm starving," I said, picking up my fork.

"Maybe it might have something to do with your late nights with Torent?" Beck prodded. "Have you taken my advice?"

He was convinced having sex with Torent would loosen me up. I hated to admit he might have been right.

Something in my expression must have triggered his internal sex alarm. "Oh. My. God. You did it, didn't you? You actually took my advice."

Twirling my fork in the soft noodles, I did everything I could to keep a straight face, including shoving the fork into my mouth.

"I don't know what you're talking about," I mumbled, in what sounded like one long word.

He picked up his egg roll and dunked it into some sweet and sour sauce.

"Then why am I still detecting tension in your aura?" he countered, calling my bullshit.

Damn wolf senses. Time for a quick topic change before half the restaurant got intimate details about my love life.

"We have important things to discuss," I said, leaning over the table and dropping my voice.

He waved his egg roll in the air. "What could possibly be more important than what Torent can do in the bedroom?"

I rolled my eyes, but a hint of a smile curved my lips. The memories were too incredible to suppress. I shook my head. *Focus, Mal. And not on Torent's body.* "I need to break a hex. What do you got?"

A scoop of rice that was halfway to his mouth fell off his fork. "You figured out it's a hex?"

The door jingled behind us, and a group of kids from our school sauntered in, including Brooklyn and her nymph cronies.

"Shhh. I'd rather not have the whole school talking about me . . . more than they already are," I added at the lift of Beck's brow.

He stabbed a piece of chicken with the end of his fork. "We need code words for this shit, considering it keeps coming up."

Talking about the supernatural world out in the open was forbidden. Humans might overhear.

"I'm open to suggestions, but I really need your help."

"Beck to the rescue. What kind of . . . uh, cake are we talking about?"

"Cake?" I echoed. "That's the word you chose?"

His shoulders lifted up in a lazy shrug. "I'm eating. What did you expect? It was the first thing that popped into my head."

"It's the kind of cake that kills animals and plants. A death cake," I whispered.

His silver eyes went wide. "Jesus, Mal. You sleep with a demon, and he serves you cake afterward? I never would have pegged Torent as that kind of guy."

I rolled my eyes. "He isn't. The cake has nothing to do with him. It's my father who baked the cake and burned it."

This whole food analogy was absurd. Next time I had something secret and important to discuss with Beck, it was not going to be in a public place. Some lessons about being a supernatural were harder to implement into my daily life.

He swallowed, trying to control the shock on his face and not choke at the same time. "Your father?"

I nodded. "I dug up some dirt on him after I went to Peacock Lake with Torent. Remember the whole milkshake incident?"

"How could I forget? It's going to go down in HFH history as one of the greatest moments ever."

Suppressing another series of eye rolls, I continued to tell him what I'd learned about my father and Brooklyn's family without actually referring to anything supernatural. I then told him about the window last night and why Torent had spent the night but left out the *other* details. The last thing I needed was Beck to go off on another sex tangent.

"So I need to figure out how to throw out the cake before it poisons someone I love." Or destroys me.

"Got it. When it comes to investigation, I'm your guy." I could already see the wheels spinning in his head. Research and snooping were Beck's specialty. He was the nerdy king, in a really cool way.

"That's what I was counting on." If anyone could find something about a death curse, it was Beck.

"How much time do we have before things go boom?" he inquired.

Boom? I sure as hell hoped things didn't explode. "I'm not sure. It seems to be progressing though."

"Let's rendezvous after school. I know someone who might be able to help. Have you mentioned anything to your mom?"

I crossed my legs under the table. "Not about the cake. We talked about my father and what happened that night, but she's already carrying so much guilt. I'd rather not involve her unless I have to."

Beck raised his brows. "And Torent?"

Shoving the rice around on my plate, dread wormed its way into the bottom of my belly, making the food I'd eaten roll. "He's already involved."

Beck gave me one of his shithead grins. "I knew it. You loooove him."

I flung a pea at him. "Say that again and I'll bend that fork around your neck."

His grin only grew.

What the hell were friends for if not to help you when shit was about to hit the fan? Having a shifter nerd for a best friend was handy. It was as if the universe knew I would need someone like him when I moved to Havenwood Falls to keep me out of danger.

"I want to hear more about what happened last night, and not the window thing—the stuff after that." Beck waggled his brows.

School had ended, and the two of us were in my car, driving to someone's house. He had given me directions and instructed me to drive. Like the good little sheep I was, I followed. I didn't have any other options. If I didn't need to keep both hands on the wheel or risk going off the road, I would have whacked him on the back of the head.

"I'm a walking death time bomb, and you want to talk about my sex life?"

He looked at me without blinking. "Duh. How else am I going to live vicariously through you?"

"Where are we going?" I asked again, attempting to divert the conversation for the fifth time since school ended.

He glanced sideways at me. "I know what you're doing."

I smiled at him and batted my eyes. Of course he did. I'd been avoiding his attempts all day to get me to dish the deets on my night with Torent. Some things were meant to stay private.

"She's a witch." That was all the information he revealed. Just who was this mysterious witch?

It made sense to seek out another witch's help to break a hex. "And you think she can break the curse?"

"That's the thing about curses. They're tricky. It depends on the type of curse and the magic the witch used to cast it. If she can't break it, then maybe she can at least help us search for a way."

It was hard to not get my hopes up, but if this didn't shed some light on my situation, I was going to have to involve my mom, and that was the last thing I wanted to do.

We pulled up to a gated community, and my car idled in the cold, the exhaust billowing white smoke behind us as we waited to be let through. Iron fences bordered the upscale neighborhood of Havenwood Heights. My fingers tapped on the steering wheel with nerves and impatience.

"Does she know we're coming?"

"She knows," Beck assured with a ghost of a smirk on his lips. "Just wait for it."

What for what?

And then it happened. There was no gate keeper, no one to

wave us through, but the beautifully designed gate suddenly, slowly swung open like magic.

It wasn't *like* magic. It was magic. The tang of it scented the air.

"She knows we're here," Beck announced, looking smug.

"Wonderful," I mumbled, wondering what kind of witch we were seeing—light or dark? I probably should have asked Beck before I agreed to go up here, but I trusted him. If he believed she could help, then what was the harm in talking to her, regardless of which side of the field she waved her wand for?

Your father chose dark magic and look where that got him, a little voice in my head reminded me.

In prison.

I made a decision right there. If breaking the hex required the use of dark magic, then I had to find another way. My soul was a sacrifice I wasn't willing to make. No one I cared about would be hurt by this darkness. It stopped with me.

I guided my car through the gates as my eyes absorbed the enormous old houses. Aspens and evergreen trees separated each estate. Many of the homes had a Gothic style I found interesting. Any other time, I would have loved to drive around and gawk at the craftsmanship.

"The founding families of the town live here," Beck told me, seeing my eyes linger over the houses as we passed by. "Lots of old money."

I blinked. "Old or new, I'd take any money. I'm not picky."

"Same," Beck agreed, smiling. The road wound as we drove deeper into the community of Havenwood Heights. "Turn left here," he advised when I came up to a fork in the road.

"It's so quiet here. I can't decide if it's eerie or peaceful."

Beck's eyes sharpened. "I'd say it's both. A lot of power and magic dwell here."

A shudder rolled through me. "I'll say so."

"That's her house there." He pointed to the right side of the street where it curved into a cul-de-sac.

I pulled my car up to the side of the road outside a three-story mansion. The exterior was a deep brownish-red brick with white trim that popped against the dark walls. Ivy clung and climbed over the arched windows. Two round towers flanked the house on both sides. A set of double doors greeted us as we strutted up the stone pathway from the driveway.

"How do you know her again?"

"School, but we don't talk much outside of class. Different social circles."

"Can we trust her not to blab to the entire school?" I inquired.

"She's trustworthy," he assured.

I exhaled and extended my hand to press the doorbell, but my finger never reached the glowing button. One of the massive doors swung open, and a woman in her forties with long dark curly hair swept into a messy bun stood in the doorway.

"Hello, Mallory. Beck." She nodded at my best friend beside me.

My mouth dropped open as I continued to stare at Ronya Augustine, my Awakening Lab teacher.

"You're the witch?" I blurted.

CHAPTER 12

She winked, her eyes sparkling. "Life is just full of surprises, isn't it?"

I'll freakin' say.

Gesturing with a sweeping motion of her hand, she stepped to the side. "Come in. Beck mentioned you might be in need of some help."

I cleared my throat. "Yes, thank you," I replied, hoping the stunned expression would soon leave my face. As we followed Mrs. Augustine down her hallway, I nudged Beck in the side. "Why didn't you tell me your witch was a teacher?" I whispered between my teeth.

"You know the rules," he gritted back.

Humans couldn't know we existed, and talking about supernaturals in public was highly frowned upon due to rule number one.

Beck and I sat on a plush cranberry-colored couch decorated in a paisley pattern. It was one of the softest pieces of furniture I'd ever sat on. A fire was burning low embers in the hearth, filling the expansive ceilings with the sounds of crackling wood. The room oozed warmth.

In my head, I pictured a black cauldron with murky green goop bubbling over a fire and a broomstick leaning against the wall. Nothing could have been further from the reality of Mrs. Augustine's home. It was absolutely lovely.

"Tell me why you think you need my talents?" she asked, getting straight to the point. I appreciated her directness.

"Mallory is hexed," Beck proclaimed candidly.

Mrs. Augustine's eyes bounced between us, brows lifting ever so slightly. "I see. Tell me why you think you're cursed, Mallory," she directed at me.

Under these conditions, I figured it was best to hold nothing back. "Goddess Styx told me that a blood hex was inflicted on my father, and I inherited his blood debt when I came into my gifts, being his only child."

Her expression remained unmoved, and I took that as a good sign. "Do you know what kind of blood hex we're dealing with?"

I paused, unable to answer immediately. It was difficult to admit what I was afflicted with. "Death," I said flatly.

The room went utterly silent. I swear even the fire in the hearth stopped breathing for a moment. Mrs. Augustine took a deep sigh. "A blood spell is serious magic. Do you know who cast the spell?"

I shook my head. "No, not exactly."

Her lips pursed together. "Well, it would be helpful if we knew more about the curse and its origin, but considering who your father was, we'll have to work with what we got."

"You can help me?" I tried to keep the desperate hope at bay, but this was my only hope.

"I'm going to do my best. This is a kind of curse that doesn't have room for error, or you can accelerate its potency."

"We definitely don't want to do that," Beck said, echoing my thoughts.

Mrs. Augustine uncrossed her legs and stood up before going to a bookshelf on the same wall as the fireplace. Her fingers ran along the spines, searching for a specific book. They all looked old and dusty to me.

"Here it is," she said, tapping her finger on the spine before removing it from the shelf. She didn't immediately come back to the chair but stroked her hand down the front of the cover as if she was paying homage to the words that lay between the pages. "This has been in the Vanden family—my family—for generations." Her feet sank into the plush carpet as she came to sit back down with the book resting in her lap.

I got my first look at the spellbook I prayed would rid me of this hex. The leather bounds were weathered and frayed slightly, as if the book had been quite loved. The cover had an emblem on it, possibly the Vanden Coven's crest. It was a piece of history, and I wanted to touch it, was drawn to it. The book itself seemed to pulse with energy that woke up the nymph inside me.

I wasn't the only one who felt it.

"Holy shit," Beck exhaled, drawing my gaze to the shifter at my left. His eyes were burning like hot molten silver, hands clenching the end of the couch cushion.

I wanted to ask him if he was okay but thought it might be better not to draw attention to the pull of what we all felt, so I refocused my attention onto the book.

Mrs. Augustine had opened it up and was flipping through the pages until she came about midway through. Her finger skimmed over the text. "Hmm. That's what I thought." She adjusted her glasses and glanced upward at Beck and me. "A blood spell requires blood to break it."

"I hope you're not squeamish," Beck commented.

I shot him a droll look, because I was exactly that when it came to blood . . . and needles . . . and sacred knives used in magic.

"What does that mean? I need to sacrifice some of my own blood?" I asked.

"Or get a vampire to siphon it," Beck mumbled. He was so not helping.

A light shone in Mrs. Augustine's eyes. "You'll need more than your blood. This kind of spell is created with darkness. It must be broken with both light and dark. The blood of a goddess is as pure as it comes."

It was the dark that had me worried. That was exactly what had started this mess.

"And the dark?" I inquired.

"Demon blood," Beck piped in.

I turned to Mrs. Augustine for confirmation. She mulled it over for a hot minute. "Yes. A demon would do."

"But not all demons are bad," I opposed, making sure I had all my supernatural facts correct.

"No, but the root of their heritage is, just as the origin of yours is good," she explained.

Beck crossed his legs and leaned back into the feather soft cushions. "How lucky for you that you're dating a demon. Makes things less complicated."

I frowned at Beck. "How so?"

"You don't have to go hunting one down now," Beck said.

"Torent is only half demon," I pointed out.

Mrs. Augustine took the floor again. "Many of us have blood that's been diluted down through the ages, but the essence of where we come from is still there. I don't think the spell requires purity. A demon's blood, combined with yours, should be strong enough to weaken the touch of death."

I pushed against the unease that had slithered inside me. This was what I had asked for—a way to rid myself of the death following me. "Great. Now I have to convince him to give me his blood."

Beck's lip gave a one-sided shrug. "Shouldn't be hard. He's in love with you, after all."

I elbowed Beck in the side.

"What do I do with the blood?" I inquired to Mrs. Augustine. Details were important when dealing with magic. "Spread on the ground in a star or something during a full moon?"

Mrs. Augustine continued to read through the old text. When she lifted her gaze, unease skittered through me. Something in her eyes alarmed me. "You drink it."

That's what I was afraid of. "Wonderful. I'm a bloodsucker now. I can't drink his blood."

"You will if you want to stop randomly killing things," Beck snapped.

He had a point. I did want the curse to stop. "Am I supposed to walk up to him and ask to suck his blood? That's not creepy or anything."

Beck rubbed the tip of his nose. "Like you said. Vamps do it all the time. Not a big deal. Put it in a milkshake."

I wrinkled my nose. "Except I'm not a vamp. I'm a water nymph. No blood."

Beck brushed off my abhorrence to blood with a noise in the back of his throat. "He'll probably be all into it. Make it sexy or something. Suck on his neck," he offered.

"You're so not helping," I groaned, dropping my face into my hands.

"Hey, I did find someone to help you break the curse, didn't I?" he reminded me. What a good friend he was.

I lifted my chin. "Yes, and I love you for it. I seriously don't know what I would do without you."

Beck's eyes twinkled. "I could only imagine the walking hot mess you'd be."

"Before anyone goes drinking someone's blood," Mrs. Augustine interrupted. She had the patience of a saint, listening to Beck and I ramble without telling either of us to chill out. One of the reasons she was a great teacher. "You need to bring me the blood so I can enchant it first, and it can't be done just anywhere. We'll need to return to the spot where your father last cast his magic."

There was always a catch.

I swallowed. The idea of returning to the place where a boy had been killed and my life had been altered before I was born gave me chills. "And this will end the hex?"

"Yes, I believe so," Mrs. Augustine said, giving me a soft smile. "A full moon would give the spell its most potency."

In theory, it sounded too simple. I found that the simplest

things were often those hardest to achieve, so I was under no delusion that ridding myself of death would be easy.

Beck and I left Mrs. Augustine with a solution, but I didn't feel relief as I expected. What I did feel was as if something dark was on the horizon, just waiting to crush my hopes. A shudder rolled through me like a spider walking down my spine. This hex wouldn't give in without a fight. The shadow of death on my soul was growing. I could sense it, whether I wanted to admit it or not. Perhaps it was aware of my plans to destroy it. Perhaps that was part of its defense. I only knew that the urge to hurry was racing through my veins.

"How are you going to ask him? Maybe we could make a sign or litter the ground with roses, make it romantic." Beck had been chattering nonstop since we got in the car. I only actually absorbed bits and pieces of what he was saying, but I got the gist of his question.

I shook my head. "I'm not asking him to the freaking prom, Beck."

His lips curved as the golden ball of sun began to dip over the horizon, streaming rays of orange onto his blue hair. "This is way more intimate."

A weird phantom of cold traveled in my chest, causing my breath to catch. And then it was gone.

"It blows my mind you think that," I managed to respond, rubbing a hand over the spot between my breasts.

He shrugged. "You'd be surprised the power blood can have on us."

I didn't want to know, and yet, I didn't have a choice in the matter. I was going to find out how important blood could be. Ironic, since it was why I was in this mess to begin with.

But seriously, how was I going to ask Torent for his blood? I don't know why I was suddenly stressing about it. He would gladly give me a gallon of his blood if it meant saving me. Why was I having such a hard time digesting the way he felt about me?

I should be rejoicing or some shit.

~

I took the weekend to marinate on the whole I-need-your-demon-blood thing and decided I would ask Torent face to face on Monday. It was the kind of request that required a personal touch, no hiding behind a text.

Odd thing was, Torent seemed to be avoiding me. I didn't want to come across as the clingy girlfriend, but it was unusual for him to flat-out ignore my texts.

My whole weekend was blah. I felt out of touch and disoriented, and I didn't know if that was because of the situation or if the hex was affecting me. But by Monday, I was going stir-crazy and dying to get out of the house.

I was eager for the week to start. Said no teenager ever. Case in point. Something was truly wrong with me.

Mine was one of the first cars to swing into the parking lot, which meant I had time to kill. Time was not my friend. My knee bounced while I let the car idle, keeping the heat on low so my bones didn't freeze.

When most of the lot was filled, I took another sweeping glance for Torent's Jeep. Had I missed him somehow? Digging out my phone, I sent him another text to join the twenty other unanswered ones I'd typed since Friday after leaving Mrs. Augustine.

My insecurities were rearing their ugly heads. *This was one of the reasons you hadn't wanted to date,* I reminded myself. *Your heart gets crushed when he inevitably disappoints you.*

But I'd thought Torent was different. He had me convinced he was not just any other guy. Then why was he giving me the cold shoulder? Why had he suddenly dropped off the face of the earth? Had he finally given up on me? Or maybe all he had ever wanted was sex. Well, he had gotten it and now was no longer interested.

The game of chase was over.

And I was the one left to pick up the pieces.

I exhaled sharply, leaning my cheek against the chilled window.

Calm down. You're jumping to conclusions. You don't know what's happening. Maybe he lost his phone.

That was it. He must have lost his phone.

Exiting the car, I joined the masses herding into the building, all the while keeping my eyes peeled for Torent and his Jeep. The sinking feeling in my stomach was becoming heavier. Skipping my locker, I headed down the hall toward his, hoping to catch him before the bell rang. I continued to watch my peers rush down the halls and tried to muster up courage. *You can do this, Mal. There is no way Torent would refuse. No. Way.*

The problem was, he was nowhere to be found.

The bell rang, and a hole formed in my chest. It wasn't like Torent to run off to class without seeing me first. Had I become dependent on him always being there without even knowing it? I put on this I-don't-need-a-guy front, but deep down I relied on him.

My internal alarm was telling me something was wrong, but my brain was telling me not to be a clingy girlfriend, so I brushed it off, consoling myself it wasn't a big deal. I'd catch up with him in class or at lunch.

Wrong.

By the end of the day, I realized Torent hadn't shown up to school today. He was taking a mental health day. Nothing unusual about that, but I felt as if I was scrabbling at excuses for what my gut was warning me.

Two more days went by with no word from Torent. He wasn't at school. He didn't answer my calls. Or respond to my texts. All of which caused my worry to quadruple.

Something was wrong. Torent only had a week of school before finals, and then he would have the credits to graduate. He wouldn't jeopardize that unless something was seriously wrong.

Beck came up behind me and draped an arm around my shoulders. "This has gone on for long enough. You've been moping around all week. Have you forgotten about the cake?"

I cringed at our secret word for the blood hex. My feet kept slowly walking down the hall toward my locker. "How am I supposed to ask for his help if he is ignoring me?"

"It doesn't make any sense. Why would Torent be avoiding you? He loooooves you." If hearts could shine in someone's eyes, they would be glimmering in Beck's as he drew out the word love. He was such a sucker for romance.

A frown pulled at my lips. "How should I know? He won't take my calls."

Beck squeezed my shoulder. "I guess then we make him talk to you."

"Just how do you propose we do that? And before you suggest kidnapping, the answer is no. That's off the table, not even a suggestion," I said, already anticipating where his thoughts would go.

An ironic twist appeared on his lips. "God, your mind is dark."

I angled my head to the side. "Are you telling me that wasn't what you were thinking?"

Removing his arm on my shoulders, he adjusted the bag on his back, lifting the strap up higher. "I plead the fifth."

"I'm not looking to join my father in jail."

"Good point," he conceded, after rolling the idea around for a few breaths.

I grabbed Beck's hand and pulled him faster through the hallway, heading away from the lockers. Twinkles of Christmas stars glittered over our heads, the school in full holiday spirit. "Come on."

His footsteps were quick to match my strides. "I take it we're no longer going to get tacos?"

How could he think of food at a time like this?

"We're going to his house," I declared, feeling alive for the first time in days. It was time I acted. My brooding days were over. No more feeling sorry for myself. "He can't avoid me forever. If I did something to upset him, then he can be man enough to tell me to my face." We raced out of the doors and into the parking lot.

"Damn straight. Get it, girl," Beck cheered.

I rolled my eyes. "Just get in the car."

"Are we going to make it back before lunch ends?"

"Probably not."

Beck thought over what I was requesting of him, skipping classes and who knows what else. "Let's do this," he finally said with purpose. "I'm your emotional support. Detention can suck it. My friend's sanity is on the line. That trumps perfect attendance."

I don't know what I would do without a friend like Beck.

CHAPTER 13

Skipping my afternoon classes was becoming a bad pattern I was going to need to break . . . once I rid myself of death.

"We can always grab tacos after," Beck offered, a compromise on getting food.

My appetite might be shot, but Beck was a bottomless taco pit. The shifter could eat every day, all day, and I wasn't about to stand in between him and tacos.

"Sure. We'll confront Torent and then bury my problems with Mexican food."

"Drama queen much?" Beck murmured, making himself comfortable in the passenger seat.

I shot him a glare as my car stopped at the main road. "I think I'm entitled to a moment of self-pity."

Looking left and right, I bit my lower lip. Some impatient junior with road rage honked at me.

"Why aren't we moving?" Beck asked, staring at me.

I glanced in my rearview mirror to see a line of cars starting to pile up behind me.

"I don't know where he lives," I admitted, realizing I'd never been to Torent's house before. If I was going to be his girlfriend, I needed to step up my game.

His nose wrinkled in his disbelief face. "How is that possible?" He shook his head. "Never mind. Make a left and hit the gas before the angry mob behind us decides to get hostile."

Punching the gas, I whipped the car to the left. I was a bundle of nerves when we pulled up to the Starks' house. And what a freaking house. Torent seemed to have failed to mention his family was loaded, not that it mattered to me.

A combination of burnt bricks and mahogany wood covered the exterior of the house. Bright windows lined the two stories. A three-car garage curved around the side of the house. I parked my car behind a Jeep similar to Torent's but was a cherry red with plates that read FLAMIN.

Cute.

"Do you want me to come in with you?" Beck asked, breaking the silence that had descended.

My eyes swung from the house to Beck. "I can't go into the demon's den alone."

I was pretty sure the Starks were mostly civilized, but it couldn't hurt to bring a wolf just in case.

He let out a squeal of delight. "I've been dying to get inside Torent's bedroom since the fifth grade."

Together we walked up to the front door. I wiped my sweaty palms on my jeans, telling myself I had nothing to be nervous about. There would be a reasonable explanation for Torent ghosting me. I really wanted there to be a reasonable explanation, one that wasn't him breaking up with me.

My lungs tightened. Holy crap. I was petrified he didn't care about me anymore. I had let myself fall hopelessly in love with him. If he rejected me, it would do more than sting. It would crush my heart into a million tiny pieces.

A part of me wanted to dash back to my car and run home. If I didn't confront him, I could avoid the rejection, but it wouldn't change the torment of not knowing. That would continue to plague me.

So here I was. Still in the same predicament, and I couldn't forget I needed Torent's blood.

"Have you changed your mind?"

Beck's voice jerked me out of my head. It was a dark and dangerous place to be at the moment. No more overthinking or overanalyzing. It was time for action.

Schooling my face into a neutral expression, I extended my arm and pressed the fancy iron doorbell. What would I find behind the door of a demon's house? Dungeons? Black candles? Shag carpet? Chains? To be fair, his mom was human. It had to take a brave and confident woman to marry and make a life with a demon.

I steeled my chin. It wouldn't matter what I found behind this door, only that I saw Torent.

I might be scared shitless to meet his father, but nothing about Torent frightened me, other than losing him. Still, I really, really didn't want his father to answer the door. Mr. Stark was a different level of supe.

Relax. He's probably at work.

Footsteps sounded from the other side, followed by a deep voice that was muffled by the thick wood between us.

What kind of job did a demon have? Lawyer? Drug lord? Executioner?

Judging by the looks of their house, papa demon made good money doing whatever unethical thing it was he did with his days . . . or nights.

I was being stereotypical, but it was because I was nervous as hell.

The door opened, and I held my breath, waiting to see whose face would appear. Torent? His father? Or . . .

My mouth went dry.

Or neither.

A young guy answered the door. He was shirtless, his jogger pants hugging low at his hips. A fine sheet of gleaming sweat glistened on his skin, as if I'd interrupted his workout. My eyes ran up the bare chest to a face that was equally as impressive as the flat abs. He leaned a lazy hand on the doorway, regarding me with a lopsided grin and a twinkle of wickedness in his violet eyes. They looked so much like Torent's that my heart cartwheeled. Those eyes collided with mine.

"Please tell me you're too old to be selling cookies," he said in a deep, hypnotic voice that made my cheeks flush.

"Hey, Zaren," Beck purred as he stepped out from behind me.

Zaren lifted a brow.

"Beck," he greeted. His eyes were quick to flicker back to me.

Zaren was one of Torent's roguish older brothers. Where Torent's hair was dark as sin, this Stark had streaks of auburn woven into his locks.

I cleared my throat. "Is Torent here?"

Zaren folded his arms like he had all the time in the world. "You must be the girl. My little bro always did have good taste."

"In girls or cookies?" I chided.

Those full lips spread into a smile that would make girls everywhere tremble. And he had the Stark dimples. Damn them.

"Both," he replied, those dimples flashing on either side of his cheeks.

Beck might swoon next to me. His hand landed on my shoulder to steady himself.

"Dear God," he whispered under his breath.

I shook off the dazzling effect from Zaren's grin and blinked. "So, is he here or not?"

"Sadly, he is not, but I am sure he is going to be disappointed he missed you."

My heart sank. If he wasn't here, then where the hell was he?

"Do you know when he'll be back?" I asked, doing my best to not sound desperate . . . and probably failing miserably.

Zaren's sparkling eyes dulled. "He's been avoiding you, hasn't he?"

I nodded.

"My brother is an idiot." Zaren opened the door wider and gestured Beck and me to come in. Together we stepped over the threshold. "I don't entirely know what my baby brother is up to, other than it was important. He left Friday in a hurry and gave us few details."

Why would he leave without saying goodbye? It didn't make sense. This sucked.

"If you talk to him, could you tell him I stopped by?"

"Sure, love."

"You have no idea where he went?" Beck inquired.

Zaren shook his head. "I wish I could help."

"He isn't in danger, is he?" The question sprang from my lips.

"With Torent, it's hard to say, but if he was in any real danger, I would know. My brother might be reckless at times, but he is smart. He would reach out to one of us for help." Zaren seemed so confident in the fact that Torent was alive and safe that he left little room for argument.

The problem was, I wanted to argue, to demand he call Torent and let me speak to him, but I refused to succumb to the title of desperate girlfriend.

"Thank you," I said to Zaren. "Will you tell him I came by?"

Zaren grinned. "Of course."

Leaving the Starks' house with virtually nothing, I felt worse. I turned in the car, angling my body inward and blurted out to Beck, "Now what? Got any brilliant ideas?"

My best friend looked at me, his brows creasing together. "Road trip?"

"We don't have the faintest idea where to begin looking."

"Shit." Beck cursed. "We could ask Zaren for his blood. He's not his brother, but he's mostly a decent guy and half demon. Ticks off all the qualifications."

Very true. And I should have probably marched back up to the house and asked him to come into the woods with me so I could use his blood to break a hex. I wouldn't sound crazy at all. At the moment, I didn't care about my mental state. But asking Zaren would mean explaining why I needed his blood, and I didn't want to have to go into the long-winded story of my family's history.

So that left me at a crossroads.

My foot tapped on the floor of my car. Without demon blood, I was screwed. If word got out about my hex to the Court of the Sun and the Moon, the rulers over the supernaturals . . . I shuddered to think what would happen.

CHAPTER 14

I stayed in bed through dinner that night, unable to muster an appetite. Mom and Gigi didn't pester me about my sullen mood, and I was relieved. I wouldn't be able to get the words out without losing my shit.

With Torent gone, I had to devise a backup plan. Soon. A shadow of darkness swirling inside me was growing stronger, digging its phantom claws into my soul. I was spiraling down a dark hole.

Near bedtime, a soft knock sounded on my door.

"Mal? Honey? Are you okay?" It was Mom.

I rolled over in my bed and closed my eyes, evening out my breathing. The door creaked open, and I continued to pretend I was asleep, saying nothing. After a few moments, she shut the door and padded quietly down the hall to her own room.

I lay awake until past midnight, contemplating my options and trying not to let my emotions get the best of me. Round and round I went—an endless circle. I had to undo the hex. To do that, I needed demon blood. The only viable option was to ask a complete stranger. Zaren was my best shot.

Shit. Shit. Shit.

Frustration stung at my eyes, a film of tears blocking my vision as my fist hit the pillow, taking out all my aggression and misery. When I'd exerted myself and felt no better, I pressed my face into the pillow, a bone-deep sadness coming over me.

The dried tears were replaced by a dull ache behind my eyes. Then came the anger. It was so intense my body was vibrating. This was my father's fault. If I hadn't hated him before, I did so now with a fervent loathing.

Morning stirred before I got the chance to sleep, and getting out of bed was a chore—one I didn't want to do. To rise would mean I had to deal with the fact it was time I told Mom what was wrong. She and Gigi were already suspicious and knew something was bothering me. They were watching me.

Mom came into the room, and I was still in bed with the covers pulled over my head, shutting out the sunshine. Who needed light when I was filled with nothing but darkness?

She sat on the edge of the bed, and the mattress dipped under her weight. With gentle hands, she peeled back a corner of the blanket.

I squinted and groaned. My body sunk into the bed like it was a tanker truck loaded with iron. Everything hurt. My head. My bones. My muscles. My heart. I had no energy to move and barely enough to open my eyes, but I forced them to part.

Concern flickered in her thickly lashed eyes. "Rough couple of days, huh?"

My gaze took her in. She looked good, the best I'd ever seen her. Her skin was creamy, soft, and flawless. The dark circles and light wrinkles were missing from around her eyes, and there was even a rosy flush to her cheeks. I nodded, my throat closing up. She was happy, and I wasn't ready to be the one who put the shadow of gloom into her eyes. She had enough of it in her life.

"You want to talk about it yet?"

Yes. Yes. Yes.

My emotions screamed.

I shook my head. "It's just cramps and a headache."

We both knew it was bullshit. She kissed my forehead, tucking my hair behind my ear as she studied my face. "Take a mental health day. Work through what is bothering you, and if you want to talk tonight, I'll listen. You never know, I might even have some solid advice for the first time ever in your life."

I forced what could pass for a smile. "Thanks, Mom."

Giving my hand a squeeze, she eased to her feet, but paused in the archway leading into the hall and glanced over her shoulder. "Things are turning around for us. I never thought that Havenwood Falls would be home again, but it always was."

Mom needed me to be happy, so I gave her the best encouraging smile I could, not wanting her to spend her day worrying about me when she needed to be concentrating on her job. She was content. For the first time in her life, it wasn't because of a guy. How could I burst her bubble?

I made the decision to keep my secret a little bit longer. I'd take the day to nurse my broken heart, then the time to feel sorry for myself came to end.

Curled up on the couch with one of Gigi's knitted blankets in the colors of the sea, I sat in front of the TV, watching reality trash. It made me feel slightly better about my own life . . . just a smidge.

Gigi was out doing volunteer work at the local animal shelter. Once a month she dedicated her day to helping Isa Hilton, the local vet and owner of the shelter, with the stray and abandoned animals of Havenwood Falls. I was grateful to have the house to myself.

An hour went by, and I hadn't budged from my spot on the couch, not even an inch, and I was satisfied to stay here for the rest of the day, doing nothing but watching mindless entertainment. I must have dozed off for a little bit, the lack of sleep finally catching up to me.

I dreamed.

I dreamed I was walking through my house, down the carpeted hallway into the kitchen. Something was off about the way I moved. It was me but it wasn't me. I didn't know how else to explain the feeling of knowing your body moved but you weren't controlling its movements.

Stopping in the middle of the kitchen, I twisted my wrist in the air, and a knife from the butcher block wiggled before unsheathing itself completely. The blade hung in the air level with my nose.

So simple. It had been like snapping my fingers, summoning the knife to do as I bid. The power I wielded often frightened me. In my dreams, none of that fear lived, only a desire for more. My power filled me with the strength and roaring of the sea.

I smiled, twirling the blade in circles.

Knock. Knock.

My eyes glanced at the hallway that led to the front door. Someone was there. Who could it be? This was a dream, after all. The grin on my lips widened.

Knock. Knock. Knock.

Knuckles rapped against the front door in a more persistent rhythm.

I glided down the hallway with the floating blade in tow. This version of me had a thing for knives. I didn't like how I was feeling inside, the strange elation swimming in my veins. Something wasn't right about it. Something foul was at play. Something dark loomed inside of me.

I closed my fingers over the doorknob without looking outside, but when my hand touched the metal, a surge of heat pulsed from the other side of the door. I hesitated, my hand paused on the knob. The glint of the silver blade at the corner of my eyes reminded me I had nothing to fear. I wasn't powerless or defenseless.

I brought the hovering knife forward, so it would stand between whoever was behind the door and me. One hell of a warm greeting.

My fingers fumbled with the locks, and I whipped open the door, expecting to see the face of my father or someone equally menacing. Instead, a white light burned around the figure, making it impossible for me to see their face.

What the hell? What was this?

Rotating my fingers in the air, I commanded the knife to move forward, closer to the flickering form radiating heat in waves.

"Show yourself," I demanded.

"Mallory," the light spoke my name.

I cocked my head to the side, regarding the figure. Was it dangerous?

Yes, a dark voice in my head replied. *Eliminate.*

The blade was still in the air, just waiting for me to give the order. One quick twitch and it would be over. Blood would spill.

"Mallory," the voice behind the blinding light shouted.

It was so familiar . . . yet, I couldn't recall the face the voice belonged to, or a name.

My shoulders shook. I looked away as the light grew brighter, blinking. Color swirled behind my eyelids. Then it burst, leaving me shrouded in darkness. My breath came out in short pants, the sound echoing in my ears.

"Mallory?" a gentle voice whispered.

I blinked, realizing my eyes had been shut, hence the darkness. My hand gripped onto the doorframe as I steadied myself, trying to make sense of what was happening. The sun warmed my face from the open door, and a cool breeze blew over my cheeks.

I went rigid when I noticed the blade hovering a few feet in front of me, and I paled seeing who it was pointed at. Torent. He glowered, staring at me with an odd expression. My mind blanked, then I was assaulted with an onslaught of emotions.

"Torent," I sighed, staring at the half demon.

The blade clattered to the floor as my power whooshed out of me. What had I done? What happened to me? I hadn't been dreaming, I'd been sleepwalking, and what I could have done . . . It scared the crap out of me.

"Hey, it's okay. You're safe." His hands framed my face. I hadn't noticed until then that I was trembling.

I cast my eyes downward to where the knife lay on the ground. "I could have killed you. Oh, my God. I almost killed you."

The voice. It had coaxed me, wanted me to hurt him.

His thumb brushed over my cheek. "But you didn't."

My gaze lifted, colliding with his. He was here. I launched myself into his arms.

His arms swooped around me, and the tension in his muscles relaxed against my body. A long whoosh of breath left his chest, and he clung to me for minutes, as if he was never going to let me go.

I had so much to say to him, but I held Torent, allowing myself the immense pleasure of being in his arms. He smelled as I remembered, woodsy with a hint of mint.

After some time, he pulled back to look down at my face, and the first thing I noticed was his eyes. They were more violet than gold, but the flecks of his powers lingered.

"Where the hell have you been?" The high of seeing him alive and in the flesh faded, leaving me with a million questions. "Do you have any idea what you put me through this week?"

His face nuzzled the side of my cheek. "I'm sorry," he murmured.

Lacing our fingers together, I tugged him inside. "Why didn't you call me?"

His eyes shifted to our joined hands before looking back up. "Where I went, cell phones don't exist. I never would have gotten a signal. It wasn't until I returned to Havenwood Falls that my phone sent through all the messages."

"You left Havenwood Falls? Why?"

"For you. I had to do something to help."

My lips pressed into a thin line. "And you didn't think you should have told me before you left?"

"But then you would have talked me out of it," he explained casually. "I would have stayed if you asked, and I needed to at least try to find a way to break the hex."

I crossed my arms, about to tell him I'd already figured out a way to break the curse, but I angled my head to the side. "Where did you go?"

"It isn't important. I got nothing useful, just the ramblings of a trapped man."

"You went to see my father?" I guessed, knowing it was like Torent to go directly to the source, screw all the red tape.

He didn't deny or confirm, but said, "I'd do anything for you . . . even risk death itself."

Dammit. Why did he have to go and do that, get all mushy on me? I wanted to stay annoyed at him, but how could I?

"What did he say?" I hated myself for even asking. Did I really care what my father had said?

"Most of it didn't make sense, but he did say something about a mark of death. How your mother wanted to take you from him, and he found a way to ensure that never happened. With this mark, he'd always have a connection to you."

I gulped. My father had done this to me—he had cursed me. I'd had my suspicions, but to hear it confirmed . . . It made me sick to my stomach. Sympathy shone in his eyes as I met his gaze. He hated being the bearer of such devastating news, but sometimes the truth hurt, and to be honest, my father had been dead to me most of my life. I wasn't going to let him win.

"I appreciate you wanting to help me, but Beck and I found a spell that might break the hex. At least, Mrs. Augustine thinks so."

His brows arched. "Mrs. Augustine, the teacher?"

I nodded. "She's a witch."

Leaning a shoulder against the wall, the corner of his lip tipped up. "I know. I'm just surprised you sought her help. Smart."

"It was Beck's idea," I supplied, giving credit where credit was due.

Torent shoved his hands into his front pockets. "I have to give it to the shifter. He's handy to have around."

"There's just one thing," I added, biting my lip. "I need your blood."

"My blood?" he echoed, a hint of incredulity glinting in his violet eyes.

I gave him the rundown of the spell Mrs. Augustine believed would free me of the darkness, of what I needed to do and where.

The light shifted in his eyes. "Magic always finds a way to

balance the light with the dark. If it is my blood you need, I will gladly give you a pint, but . . . I want something in return."

I was taken a little aback by his request for something in return, and my expression slackened. "What did you have in mind?"

He twirled a strand of my hair around his finger. "Go with me to the winter dance."

A dance? Why was he talking about a dance? It took me a few breaths to catch up. "The Cold Moon Ball? Do you really think that is a good idea right now? My life is complicated. I don't see how going to a dance is going to fix what is happening to me. The hex won't give me a night off. In fact, it's probably a bad idea. What if something happens?"

"It's my last one before I graduate, and I want to spend it with you, if only for a few hours. You deserve to have fun, Mal." He put his finger to my lips before I could protest again. "And it falls on the full moon."

That got my attention. The full moon was when Mrs. Augustine would perform the spell, the lunar phase of the moon being at its height of energy.

"I'll go with you, but I'm warning you. You might not leave with all your toes." I was a swimmer, not a dancer.

His response was a dimpled grin, full of wickedness.

CHAPTER 15

$\mathcal{T}$he night of the Cold Moon Ball also happened to be the winter solstice. It was convenient—the perfect cover. While the town celebrated the winter solstice, Beck, Torent, and I would be sneaking off to meet Mrs. Augustine in the woods near Peacock Lake. I promised Torent a dance, but then the *fun* really began.

The day. The time. The place. It was all set into motion. We were to meet Mrs. Augustine around eight o'clock to get everything we needed in order. When the moon was at its highest point, she would cast her spell, and I'd drink the magical concoction.

And it wasn't a moment too soon.

From the time I'd woken up this morning, my world felt off-kilter. Although I couldn't pinpoint what was making me feel so foreign in my own body, I told myself to get through the night. As long as I didn't have another sleepwalking episode, it would be all over by tomorrow, and I could go back to living my life, concentrating on things like graduating, swimming, and Torent.

To have a normal life with a hot guy—such an alien concept, especially since he was anything but average.

Beck had dragged me to every shop in Havenwood Falls the weekend before the big town celebration, something I dreaded as much as what would happen during the dance. Some girls loved makeup, hair, and frilly dresses. Then there were girls like me.

"Why did I let him talk me into this?" I mumbled to myself. I was alone in my room, trying to wiggle into an organza gown of baby blue and white. "What was wrong with yoga pants and a sports bra?" Talking to myself was my way of dealing with crap I didn't want to face. And tonight was a double whammy.

Dancing and a hex.

Go me.

The last thing I wanted to do was get ready for a party. My palms were sweaty. My stomach was close to heaving with nerves. And my hair wouldn't cooperate to save my life.

The silver-blue sparkly and sheer material looked itchy, but I was surprised to find it didn't irritate my skin. Slipping my arms into the straps, I found the bodice was slimming and silky with teal jewels that resembled flurries of snowflakes. Mom had managed to salvage my hair, sweeping it up onto the crown of my head, a tiny braid curving around the base of the hair tie. Blond curls cascaded over my shoulders. When she brought out the sparkle hairspray, I nearly chucked it into the garbage, but Mom was in her element, having the time of her life dolling me up. Since we were both feeling emotional and sentimental for two entirely different reasons, I only sighed, crossed my arms, and let her work her magic.

"There, all done," she said, smiling pleasantly at me in the vanity mirror. Putting the cap back onto the soft pink lipstick she had applied to my lips, Mom stood up. "Go have a look," she encouraged, gesturing to the full-length mirror in the corner of my room.

I stepped in front of my reflection, taking in the glittering material like woven snowy stars as it draped to the floor. My gaze connected to the aqua eyes in the mirror, framed with thick black lashes and shimmering eye shadow of smoke with hints of teal. A silver snowflake charm hung from a ribbon choker around my slender neck. I didn't have words for the woman who stared back at me. She was a dream. I was afraid to look too deeply, for, behind the awe, darkness ascended.

"You've never looked more beautiful, Mallory." Mom swept a curl off my shoulder, a mist of tears in her eyes.

Something was in the air, other than perfume, hairspray, and glitter. Perhaps it was the reenactment I had looming in front of me, the worst night in Mom's life and the moment that shaped mine. We were both sappy. I hugged her.

"I don't know what I would do without you," I admitted.

She flicked the end of my nose. "Right back at you, kid."

Growing up, I never felt like I was Mom's top priority. It always seemed as if she was chasing some kind of happiness that didn't really involve me, but I understood now. She had been trying to forget the past, not forget me. I knew she loved me, but now I felt loved.

The ball was a blur of people in fancy attire, twinkling lights, strumming music, and delicate cuisine. Not even the numerous weddings I'd attended, mostly Mom's, held a candle to the Cold Moon Ball. I lingered at Torent's side, my hand looped through his arm. I tried to smile, to have a good time for Torent's sake, but what we were going to do later in the night plagued my thoughts.

I only had to survive another hour. In my current state of mind, it felt like a lifetime.

"Relax," Torent whispered in my ear.

The skirt of my dress floated lightly around me as Torent and I strolled through the grounds.

"This is me relaxed," I said through my teeth.

His soft chuckle warmed against my neck. "Have I told you how breathtaking you look?"

Only a dozen times, but I didn't mind. Torent looked equally impressive in all black. He forwent the traditional tux for jeans, a button-down shirt, and a vest. I still had a hard time comprehending that this dashing male was my boyfriend.

"How about we skip the dance and go straight to making out in your car?" I proposed.

"Don't tempt me." The huskiness of his voice curled around me like a magnetic hug, pulling me closer to him.

That was the thing. I wanted to tempt him. And I wanted to stop my brain from hashing over what was still to come. My eyes connected with his, and a craving unfurled inside me. It was moments like this when it became so clear that we belonged together. My soul knew it.

"What can I do to change your mind?"

His hands slipped to my waist, and he leaned toward me, his jaw grazing my cheek. Tingles radiated from my heart, and my pulse quickened. His breath was warm and intoxicating. I arched up on my toes to press—

"What up, lovebirds?" Beck sauntered up to us with a stupid grin on his face. His wolfish silver eyes were beaming under the moonlight—the cold moon. It was fitting for my best friend. He never looked more alive, more in his element. The lapels of his navy velvet blazer were accentuated by the hues of his hair.

I found it difficult to be miffed at him for interrupting what could have been a blissful moment of peace only found in Torent's arms.

"Look at you," I said, my eyes taking him in fully from head to toe. Unraveling myself from Torent's hold, I went and gave Beck a hug. "You look amazing."

"Likewise, chica. We're all set for tonight," he murmured near my ear before pulling away.

I nodded, feeling that pesky lump return in my chest. It would follow me until this night was over and the hex banished.

Beck's eyes scanned the bash. "Have you eaten?" he asked.

I shook my head. "I don't think I can."

Beck clucked his tongue, his eyes sharpening. "Mal, you need your strength."

"He's right," Torent added, the two of them ganging up on me. "Come on, let's get some food."

Torent met Beck's gaze, and a silent exchange passed between them. My guess was they had made a pact to look out for me or some other macho promise.

How could I be annoyed? They cared about me, and I would have done the same for both of them.

I let them lead me to a table for four, where we were served an elaborate feast of turkey, potatoes, salad, and more food than I could possibly eat. For their sake, I made myself pick at my plate, forcing down the tasteless food. It wasn't that the appetizers, salads, and meats weren't delicious. They were probably some of the best food I'd ever had, but I couldn't enjoy the flavors.

As the ball shifted to the Mills Mansion and the crowds began to move out, Torent, Beck, and I took off in his Jeep, going the opposite direction. I glanced over my shoulder out the back window, watching the horse-drawn carriages fade in the distance.

My hands were shaking as I changed out of my fancy dress and traded my heels for boots. My attire was not fit for traipsing around the woods. Beck may have killed me if I'd gotten blood on the dress he claimed brought joy to his life.

He was such a weirdo sometimes. I couldn't help but love him.

"You ready to make magic, crash car?" Torent stated in an attempt to quiet my nerves.

Lifting my boot up on the seat, I tied the laces. "After tonight, I'm taking a break from this supernatural stuff."

"I'd say you earned it."

Our drive toward Peacock Lake was short from the center of town. Torent got as close as we could get by car; the rest of the way we would be trekking through the woods.

The three of us slunk off into the snow-dusted trees. The land itself seemed empty, as if the plants and animals sensed what was about to transpire and bowed to the laws of magic. Peeking through the dense branches, moonlight danced over the shadows. As we passed a small frozen stream made by the occasional melting snow during the day, Torent came to an abrupt halt. His head swung over his shoulder, and those violet eyes were tinged with glowing gold flecks.

"What is it?" I asked when he didn't say anything but continued to stare into the dark trees behind us, searching for something.

"I'm not sure. I can't shake the feeling we're being followed." His body was tight.

"Who would be that dumb?" Beck pointed out, but he turned in the same direction and let his inner wolf peek out, eyes glowing silver. "The wind would be stagnant tonight of all nights," he grumbled. "I can't pick up a scent."

"It could be nothing. Let's keep moving. We're not far."

My boots snapped and crunched twigs and frosty blades of grass. As we drew closer to Peacock Lake, I became alive. I had no other way to describe the sudden tingles in my blood, the splash of waves in my ears, or the pull deep in the marrow of my bones. I inhaled, letting the crisp air burn my lungs. Being here, close to the lake, had somehow eased the dread that pitted in my gut.

We came to a fork in the path. One led to Peacock Lake, the other toward the greater falls. The vision Styx had given me was of a clearing hedged with various conifers and wild shrubs.

"Which way?" Beck asked as our eyes bounced between the two paths.

The trees to my right seemed to bend outward, forming an arch into an invisible path I couldn't see. I blinked, and it was gone.

"This way," I said, not waiting for either of them to object, and I took neither path, but veered into a section of the woods intertwined in a thick weave of untamed pines and snow-covered oaks and elm trees. Snow crunched under my feet as I pushed forward until the thicket gave way to the cultivated glade.

A flock of black birds soared out of the tree canopy.

"That wasn't ominous in the slightest," Beck said dryly, breaking the silence.

Magic seemed to tremble in the air, and the clearing felt ancient, a place of great natural power that existed long before humans walked the earth. Moonlight shone over the ice-tipped grass, making the glade appear like glass, enchanting and fragile. The three of us stood on the edge, taking in the wonder of this place. It was impossible not to feel it, human or supe.

Beck checked the time and his phone, after scanning the towering and thick trees for Mrs. Augustine. "She should be here already," he muttered.

Puffs of cold air exhaled from my lungs, and I wrapped my arms around myself. *Please don't let anything go wrong.*

"You're cold," Torent stated. "Beck, be a gentleman and give her your jacket.

"I'm fine," I chattered, convincing no one.

Beck came up beside me and draped the warm, velvety coat over my shoulders. "That's better," he said, rubbing his hands over my arms to encourage blood flow.

"You're late," a woman's voice sounded from the shadows. Mrs. Augustine emerged, the frost-tipped grass crunching under her feet. She too had been at the Cold Moon Ball but had slipped away a half hour before us. Her dress was a deep red, popping against the white-dusted trees and ground.

"Is everything in place?" Torent asked, forgoing pleasantries and taking charge. Crispness had entered his tone, making his words sound clipped. He wanted to get this over with. We had that in common.

"I just need the blood." Her voice was different from what she used in the classroom. Gone was the teacher. The woman who stood in front of us was every inch the witch. Energy tingled in the air around her.

At the sudden reminder of what was going to transpire here, I felt the blood drain from my face, and my stomach twisted.

Torent joined our hands. "Let's get the show on the road."

CHAPTER 16

$\mathcal{M}$rs. Augustine stood inside a charred circle as if she had burned it into the ground. Since she made no move to leave the ring, the three of us joined her in the middle. My eyes immediately went to the sacred blade in her hand.

Son of a bitch.

I gulped, and Torent's hand tightened in mine.

"It's going to be okay," he murmured.

Mrs. Augustine handed the blade to Torent first. "Remember, I must do the spell when the moon is at its highest, giving us just under an hour. We don't have time to waste."

Torent released my hand and took the offered dagger without blinking. He flipped it over his hand, making a smooth slit across his palm as if he'd done it a million times before. Not even a flicker of pain shone in his expression. As he clenched his fist, the blood flowed, dripping into an iron goblet Mrs. Augustine had brought with her. The drip, drip, drip of Torent's blood hitting metal had my stomach pitching.

I closed my eyes and took a deep breath.

"You'd make the worst vamp," Beck joked. He was standing on the other side of me, assuming a supportive stance identical to Torent's.

"I'm still not convinced you're an actual wolf," Torent said, before turning to me. "Your turn, love." The encouraging smile on his lips warmed my cold blood slightly, and the endearment helped.

I nodded, my eyes shifting to the knife he held out. My fingers trembled as I wrapped them around the cool and smooth hilt. The wood was heavier than I'd expected. The dagger shook as I clenched it tighter, bringing it to lie over the inside of my palm. My fingers curled over the blade, and all I had to do was pull it out. I inhaled, my lips trembling, and the world seemed to hold its breath with me, going still.

"I-I can't do it. Here," I quailed, unfurling my hand and outstretching the dagger to Torent. "You do it."

"Are you sure?"

I shoved out my hand. "Yes," I whispered, squeezing my eyes shut while I waited for the pain.

It was quick, a surprise sting that startled me more than hurt, and was followed by a gentle squeezing of my hand. I didn't open my eyes until Torent pressed a kiss to the center of my palm.

"All done," he murmured.

My lashes fluttered, and I found myself captured in a sea of violet starlight. His eyes held mine and steadied my pulse.

"Thank you," I mouthed.

He only gave a slight incline of his head before turning toward Mrs. Augustine, who was waiting at the heart of her spellbound circle. Taking the goblet with both hands, she tilted her head to the moon and the stars.

"To the winds of change, I call thee tonight.
To the spirits from the other side, I summon thee to me.
Shift the source of illness borne.
Unleash the power hidden from day, in the night so deep.
Blood to blood, as I will so mote it be."

Her words were harmonious, ringing over the glade with conviction, and the wind picked up, howling like a banshee as it blew at my back, sending my hair flying in a cluster of chaos.

Torent's hand was my anchor. I held onto him tight, praying.

And then silence descended. Nothing moved or stirred, as if the elements surrounding us respected what had been summoned.

"It's done," she said, offering me the cup.

I dared to look inside, unsure what I would find. The dark liquid swirled like sparkling cranberry juice. *Not so bad*, I told myself, lifting the glass.

"Bottoms up," I mumbled. The cool metal of the rim pressed to my lips, and I tipped my head back, ready to—

A rustling of leaves and branches sounded from the edge of the tree line, and both Beck and Torent went on alert, their bodies hardening. I licked my lips, lowering the goblet.

"Did you come alone?" Mrs. Augustine demanded, her eyes narrowing.

Torent's body had gone tight beside me, and a low snarl erupted from Beck's throat like an animal.

"Yes. We told no one," Beck assured, but Torent and him sharing a look, and I wondered if they too were remembering that feeling of being watched in the woods.

"And you weren't followed?" our teacher reiterated.

Torent's eyes were glowing as he scanned through the shadows and thicket. "Not that we know of."

"I wouldn't be so sure about that," Mrs. Augustine warned, a hawk-like expression hardening her face.

"Beck." Torent gave a slight tilt of his head, giving a command.

A complete shocker to me, my best friend obeyed, and before I comprehended what was happening, Beck had undressed and shifted into a beast. Gray fur replaced his creamy skin. Silver eyes sparkled under moonlight. I'd never seen Beck in his other form. He was majestic, his lean body stronger as a wolf.

Keeping low to the ground, Beck padded over to the trees where we had emerged not long ago, using his keen senses to sniff out any unwelcome visitors. Paw prints stamped the frosty ground. His ears went back, a low growl rumbling deep in his throat.

Then he lunged, disappearing into the darkness of the woods.

Twigs snapped and crispy leaves crunched, but I could see nothing. The wrestling was shortly followed by a female squeal.

I knew that voice.

Beck was dragging out the intruder by the hem of a beautiful red satin dress, snarling through his clenched jaws.

Oh, for the love of everything holy!

"Brooklyn?" Torent's voice echoed over the clearing.

My fellow nymph was playing tug-of-war with Beck, fighting to get the wolf to release her dress. "Bite me, mongrel, and I'll make a fur coat out of you," Brooklyn threatened, glaring at Beck.

"What the hell are you doing here?" Torent demanded, shoving a hand into his hair.

She gave one hard yank, and Beck chose that moment to release his locked grip, letting gravity take over. Brooklyn's arms went flailing in the air as she fell backward on her ass with an audible oomph. Red-faced with rage, Brooklyn clenched her fists in the ground. If it was possible, steam would have expelled from her ears, she was that spitting mad.

Shit.

Before Beck had the chance to put some distance between Brooklyn and himself, she shot out her hand, zapping him with a bolt of electricity.

Beck yelped, scampering backward as fast as his four legs would allow, and followed up with a growl of warning.

It was my turn to get pissed. I stepped forward in between them, forcing Brooklyn to look at me. "Try that shit again, Brooklyn, and I'll chain you to a tree."

Torent was instantly at my side. "What are you doing here?" he asked again with no less patience than the first time.

Shoving to her feet with her chin jerked upward, she brushed off the dusting of snow and dirt from her soiled dress.

"I saw the three of you leave." Her words were short and clipped.

"And you took it upon yourself to follow us. Why?" He was relentless in his tone.

Her dark blue eyes pinned me, pretty lips curling in disgust. "She's up to something, and I want to know what."

"It's none of your business. Now go, Brooklyn, before someone notices you're not at the ball," I spat.

"If it's all the same, I'd rather stay and watch the show." She threw Beck's words back at us, the little schemer.

"We don't have time to argue." Mrs. Augustine stepped forward, her voice carrying over the clearing. "Mallory, you must drink before it's too late."

I'd forgotten about the goblet clutched in my hands. Brooklyn sneered, but I ignored her. I had far more important things to deal with than her meddling in my life. In one quick motion, I threw back the contents of the cup, not allowing myself to think about the cocktail of blood and magic I was putting into my body.

"Why are you drinking spelled blood?" Brooklyn interrupted, watching me with scrutiny.

I turned to Mrs. Augustine. "How long before we know if it works?"

"The spell should banish the hex immediately."

I probably should have asked if this was going to hurt. So I waited. And waited. Four sets of eyes stared at me expectantly.

"Nothing's happening."

Beck had shifted back into his human self and was buttoning up his shirt when he asked, "Did we do something wrong?"

"There's no reason it shouldn't have worked. Mixing your blood with a demon's should have been enough to counteract the hex," Mrs. Augustine confirmed.

My chest hollowed out. "So why didn't it work?"

"You're too corrupt," Brooklyn snarled in an almost laugh.

"Why are you still here?" I snapped back, ready to slam her head into the frozen ground.

"To watch you fall on your face." Her lips grew into a pleased grin. "So you're hexed? I'd love to kiss the witch who spelled you."

The urge to cause Brooklyn bodily harm tripled, but what she had said sparked an idea. "Wait. Maybe she's onto something. Give me your blood," I ordered.

"As if I would ever stoop so low," Brooklyn squeaked. "Absolutely not. I wouldn't give you my blood even if the world depended—"

Beck tackled her to the ground. "Quick, cut the bitch."

Oh. My. God. What was even happening? This couldn't be my life.

And yet, it was.

Unlike me, Torent didn't hesitate. He snatched the dagger and pricked the tip of Brooklyn's finger.

"Ouch!" Something violent and predatory crept into her dark blue eyes. "Release me, mutt," she barked at Beck. A second later his hands jerked back in swift movements. "I'm going to dismantle you, Torent Stark!"

"She shocked me. Again," Beck proclaimed, staring at his now hairless arms. She had singed them clean off.

"You'll pay for this," Brooklyn hissed at me with hate as I crouched down to catch the blood now dripping into the goblet.

"I'm sure I will," I replied. "But if this works, I'll be in your debt."

Beck helped Brooklyn to her feet as Torent sliced his other hand, adding his blood to Brooklyn's. My fellow nymph might not be a saint, but her bloodline was as pure and good as they came. I don't know how the hell the goddess Aphrodite ever blessed someone like Brooklyn.

She fought against Beck's grip, jerking her arms with revulsion. "Let me go," she seethed.

He waited until Torent had handed the goblet over to Mrs. Augustine before releasing her.

"Behave," Beck warned.

Brooklyn's chin jutted out, her eyes blazing in the night.

Mrs. Augustine's lips formed a thin line, watching us with disapproval. "I might not agree with your methods, but you better hope this works. The spell might not be as strong as the first. All we can do is pray it's enough."

Making haste with her magic, she spoke the words, and once again I drank from the goblet, downing every last drop of the enchanted mixture.

It was warm and thicker than I remembered as I forced the blood down my throat, my nose wrinkling. I shuddered at the bitter taste. A minute went by. Then another.

Mrs. Augustine let loose a disheartened sigh.

Brooklyn laughed haughtily.

Beck swore under his breath.

And Torent and I just stared at each other.

I was about to say screw it when my breath began to come fast and hard. I panted through my teeth in what I was sure was a panic attack.

A small noise came out of Brooklyn's mouth.

"Quiet," snapped Mrs. Augustine. "Open yourself up, Mallory. Don't fight it."

Something thrummed and pulsed, rising and lashing through my blood. Something not of this world. Something old and very, very dark. The thing inside me was roiling, desperate to keep its claws gripped to my soul. It shook my body with a building force as the magic, combined with Torent and Brooklyn's blood, hunted for a way to rip off the very essence of who I was.

A rumble thundered under my feet, followed by a whoosh and a bloodcurdling scream that resonated to the stars.

My scream.

"Mallory!" My name bellowed from Torent's lips, but it was too late.

Images slammed into me, breaking the void of blackness, but as I saw them, I wished for the darkness. One after one, they rolled through my mind.

My father looming over Ryle's dead body, grinning. The pleasure killing gave him, the power he desired, expelled in the air like a toxic poison.

I saw my mother sprawled out on the forest floor, blood pooling around her, eyes vacant and gone. Gigi was beside her in a similar fashion, her long silver hair glowing under the moonlight, streaked with red.

And then there was me, standing proudly beside my father, thriving on the power he had bestowed upon me. In my right hand was the ceremonial knife, dripping with blood—my family's blood.

I shook my head.

No. I don't want it. I don't want to be like you.

He didn't seem to hear me, didn't so much as flinch.

Help me! Help me, help me, I silently begged. *Torent. Beck. Anyone.* I pounded against the darkness, tears streaming down my face. *Get me out. Please,* I pleaded.

But no one heard. No one saw the fear, the panic, the desperation swallowing me, and it became clear. I was going to have to claw my way out of the darkness, but I was frozen in place, undiluted terror keeping me prisoner.

"Mallory," a voice of silk and shadows crooned.

"What do you want from me?" I screamed.

"Accept who you are," it seemed to coo without actually speaking. *"My daughter."*

Rippling terror buried deep inside me, rooted my feet in place, but I refused to give in. *No,* my mind softly rejected the temptation. *I'm not just your daughter. I'm also the daughter of a goddess.*

I held on to that thought as if my life depended on it, and it a way, it did. I had no idea how long it had been since I'd drunk the potion, but for me, time seemed to have dragged, ensnaring me in my own personal hell with darkness. Each passing heartbeat, my resolve weakened, until something brushed against my hand, a touch.

I recognized that light caress.

Torent's fingers closed around my mine, joining our hands and with it, our powers. The pad of his thumb stroked over the back of my hand. It was the encouragement I needed, grounding me. I unleashed my power—the power I'd almost forgotten I possessed.

Torent and the feelings he elicited reminded me what I was capable of.

A flash of pure white light exploded behind my eyes, banishing the darkness that held me.

The light faded and I blinked, surprised to find myself on the ground, curled into Torent's arms.

He glanced down into my face, relief in his violet eyes. "Hey," he said.

"I'm going to be sick." Turning my head to the side, I vomited, but not my dinner.

A smog of black expelled out of my mouth. Blackness swirled from the night, curling around me like a mist of death, cold and evil. It poked at every inch of me with little phantom talons of smoke, looking for—no, demanding—a way back in.

"What the hell is that?" Brooklyn shrieked.

"We need to trap it before it can find another host," Mrs. Augustine informed.

Torent scooped his hands under my elbows, lifting me to my feet. He shoved me behind him, trying to stay between the shadow mist and me. "And just how do we do that?" he hissed.

"With this," Mrs. Augustine said. I took my eyes off the cloud of blackness just long enough to see her holding up an elongated glass bottle tinged in seafoam green.

"A bottle?" Torent said with incredulity. He took the bottle from Mrs. Augustine and cracked his neck. "This should be fun."

The shadow sprang from nightmares. It crawled and slunk over the ground, with no real shape or form, searching for its next victim or for me. The five of us backed away, each contemplating how the hell we were going to coax it inside the bottle in Torent's hands.

Why did it have to be him?

I should have been the one trying to capture the darkness. This was my fault, my problem.

"Anyone have a plan?" Beck mumbled. He and I were shoulder to shoulder with Torent on the other side of me.

"If I die, I swear I will haunt you," Brooklyn said to me, not taking her gaze off the shadow.

"Zap it or something," Beck snarled at Brooklyn.

"Me?" she squealed. "This is not my problem."

I refrained from rolling my eyes, afraid to take my attention off the shadow stalking us.

Torent stepped forward, putting himself in harm's way.

"What are you doing?" I pleaded.

"Taking this thing down." His voice was low and gritty. He didn't give me the chance to argue, throwing out his arms. Hellfire erupted over his body, casting an aura of amber around him. The fire crackled and popped along his skin.

Anticipating the threat, the shadow hissed right before it morphed a small section of its form into a black, gleaming talon. Torent stepped closer, and it hissed in a noise that sounded like a thousand children screaming.

It slashed out with its talon, striking Torent in the face. His head whipped to the side, the fire along his fingers and arms sputtering.

"Torent!" I cried out, my heart knocking in my chest.

He raised his head, irises glowing nearly gold. Blood oozed from under his right eye. "That wasn't very nice."

I reacted without thinking, unaware of what I was doing until a surge of power trembled out of me. No one was more surprised than me when the shadow froze under my command.

Someone gasped.

Holy crap. It had magnetic properties.

"Gotcha," I muttered.

Beck, Torent, and Brooklyn all pinned me with equal gazes of shock. "Are you doing this?" Torent asked, the flames of hellfire extinguished.

I nodded. "It must have particles of metal inside the shadows."

The mist shrieked, bucking against my restraint, but I held on.

"Think you can get it inside this?" Torent held up the bottle.

"Only one way to find out," I ground out, keeping my concentration wholly on the shadow.

Using my power for something good, I steered the perilous smoke straight for the bottle outstretched in Torent's hand. If I slipped up . . . If it broke free . . . I refused to think like that.

The smoke of shadows thrashed and struggled against me as I slowly began to force it to move toward us. I reinforced the power flowing through me, putting all the energy I had left in my body into trapping the curse.

"This is not how I thought my night was going to go," Brooklyn grumbled, but even when complaining, her voice had a silky threat to it.

Beads of sweat gathered at my brow, but I almost had it to the opening of the bottle. Getting it inside would be another obstacle, one I was determined to see through.

"You're almost there," Beck coaxed.

Brooklyn snorted next to him, and from the corner of my eye, I caught my best friend jabbing her in the ribs with an elbow.

I blocked out the two of them and shoved the smoke and darkness into the bottle. My eyes met Torent's. Mrs. Augustine was there, slamming a metal stopper onto the bottle, which she promptly spelled, trapping the shadow inside.

All five of us stared at the swirling mist as it clawed and curled around the glass.

"I'll turn it over to the Court. They'll want to keep it secure until it can be destroyed," Mrs. Augustine said, breaking the stunned silence that had followed.

It was done. I was safe. The curse was gone. I loosed a breath of steam that swirled in the cool air as my shoulders slumped in exhaustion. "What was that?"

The wind whipped at Mrs. Augustine's long hair, but her expression remained fixed on the glass bottle. "Darkness ascended," she declared, her gaze lifting to mine. "The blood hex is gone, Mallory. It stops with you."

My throat was too tight to respond. I only nodded, falling into Torent's waiting arms.

CHAPTER 17

I frowned, staring at the scar just under Torent's eye. It had been a week since the Cold Moon Ball—since I rid myself of the blood hex. The jagged cut Torent had received from the smoke of darkness was mostly healed, leaving behind a pink mark over his golden skin. Every time I looked at it, I was consumed with guilt.

His pretty face was marred because of me.

He gave me a lopsided grin, noticing where my attention had wandered. "Chicks dig scars, you know."

To be frank, he really didn't seem to mind the permanent reminder of what went down that night.

We were on Main Street in front of Shelf Indulgence bookstore on our way to Coffee Haven.

"Is that so?" I smiled back, looping my arms around his neck, and lifted up on my toes to softly press a kiss to the mark. "I think you might be right."

His fingers laced around my waist, keeping me snug against his body and moving us to the side of the path. "Are you ever going to tell me?"

I tilted my head to the side, gazing into his sparkling violet eyes.

"Tell you what?" I asked, batting my eyes.

That glimmer in his eyes grew wicked. "That you're madly and deeply in love with me."

My heart began to beat wildly in my chest, and I shook my head. "God, you really don't lack confidence, do you?"

"I want to hear you say it," he murmured, his voice dropping as he leaned in.

How could I possibly resist? Why shouldn't I tell him how I felt? If there was one thing being cursed taught me, it was that life was too short. I needed to live each moment as if it were my last. Torent became the light at the end of the tunnel—a demon. How ironic.

I had planned on telling him how I felt and had been waiting for the right moment. Now was as good as any, although I should have made him suffer for being so arrogant. My fingers played with the hair at the nape of his neck, my gaze locked on his.

"I love you, Torent Stark. Demon and all. Are you happy now?"

"Almost." He took my mouth, fast and hard, trapping me with the hardness of his body. The kiss stole the air from my lungs. "It just so happens that I'm in love with you. You're stuck with me. I'll never love anyone the way I love you, crash car. You're magnetic."

A laugh fluttered up from my heart. "Cute."

Above our heads, pink, blue, and teal lights danced in the skies. Love like I never felt bloomed inside of me. Not an ounce of darkness.

Thank you so much for reading! I hope you enjoyed Torent and Mallory's journey. I'm grateful and honored you chose to read their story.

xoxo

Jennifer

We hope you enjoyed this story in the Havenwood Falls High series of novellas featuring a variety of supernatural creatures. The series is a collaborative effort by multiple authors.

Stay up to date at www.HavenwoodFalls.com

ABOUT THE AUTHOR

J.L. Weil is a *USA Today* bestselling author of teen and new adult paranormal romance, fantasy, and urban fantasy books about spunky, smart-mouthed girls who always wind up in dire situations. For every sassy girl, there is an equally mouthwatering, overprotective guy. She lives in Illinois with her family who puts up with her *Supernatural* and *Harry Potter* fanatics. It's a problem.

You can visit her online at: www.jlweil.com or come hang out with her at J.L. Weil's Dark Divas on Facebook.

ACKNOWLEDGMENTS

This book would not exist without Kristie Cook. Thank you so much for inviting and letting me be a part of this wonderful and magical world. I enjoyed the challenge!

To the Havenwood Falls team and authors, it has been an absolute joy to take this journey with all of you.

To the readers who continue to show my books so much love, words can't express my gratitude. You continue to uplift me and support me in ways I never thought possible. I am truly lucky.

And to my family, thank you for putting up with all my "just one more sentence" promises, and reminding me to step away from the laptop and enjoy life.

AN EXCERPT

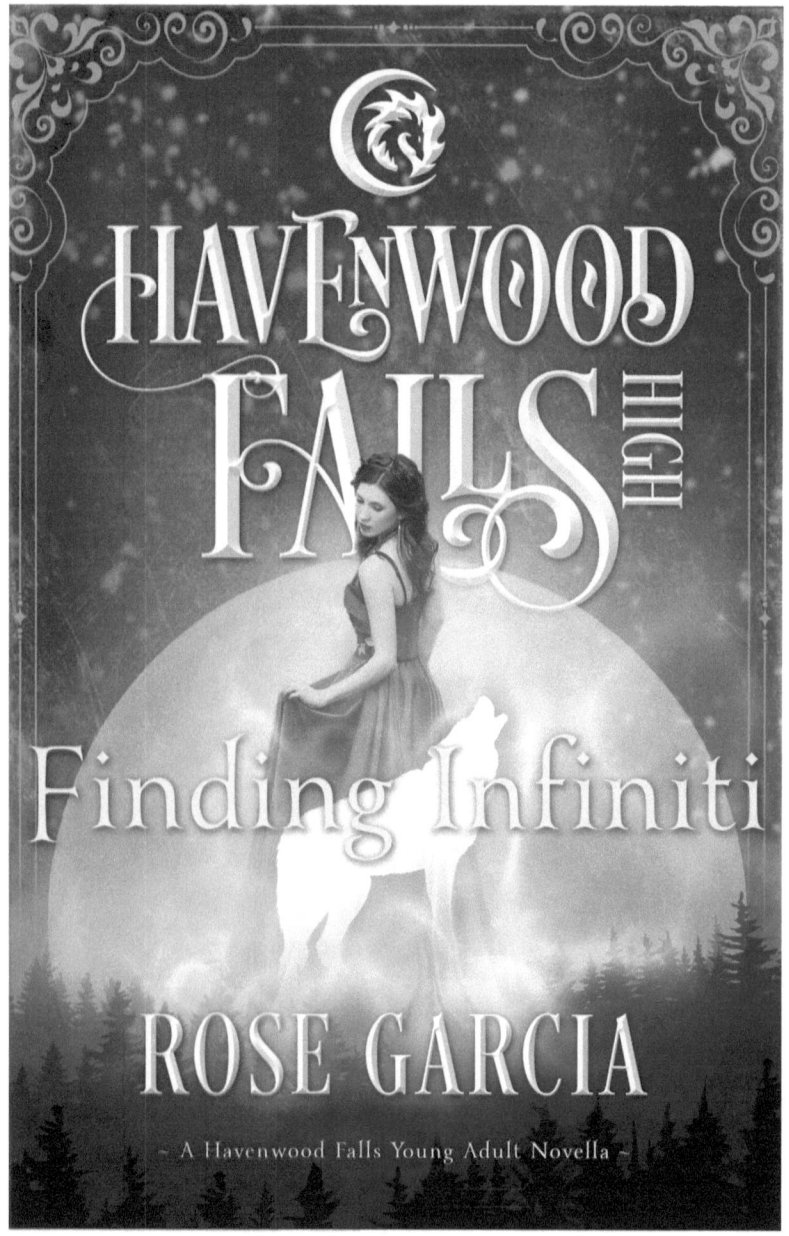

HAVENWOOD FALLS HIGH

Finding Infiniti

ROSE GARCIA

~ A Havenwood Falls Young Adult Novella ~

Finding Infiniti (A Havenwood Falls High Novella) by Rose Garcia

The highly anticipated sequel to *Saving Infiniti*—can Joe find Infiniti again or is she lost to him forever?

Joe Greg has reunited with his soul mate Infiniti Clausman only to lose her in a cruel twist of fate. Separated by time and space—and a memory ward that has wiped him from her mind—he vows to do whatever he can to find her, but so far nothing has worked. Believing he'll never be able to see her again, he starts losing all sense of himself. Worse than that, he can't shake the growing feeling that Infiniti's life is in danger . . . again.

Infiniti Clausman is trying to make the most of summer, but something isn't quite right. She feels like she's stuck, as if she can't move on, as if she's missing something or someone. She dismisses the sensation, calling it a case of the graduation blues, but when her psychic neighbor tells her about a quantum event that's been happening since the Cold Moon last December, Infiniti can't ignore the feelings any longer.

Soul mates separated. Memories forgotten. Time slipping. Joe must find Infiniti before it's too late—or he might lose her again, this time for good.

FINDING INFINITI

BY ROSE GARCIA

Joe Greg studied every detail of Infiniti Clausman, desperate to sear her image in his brain because he didn't know if he'd be able to find her once she left Havenwood Falls. Long dark hair, ivory skin, the most gorgeous face he'd ever seen. She had time traveled with a Transhuman guy named Fleet from Houston to Havenwood Falls so she could find a protection spell. With their mission complete, they were about to return to their proper place and time, and Joe could hardly bear it. Her magnetic beauty had sparked a connection deep within him, so deep that he was called to her and would be bound to her forever—a wolf shifter and a human. Together against all odds, yet about to be separated in a cruel twist of fate. He knew he'd never be the same without her.

Her lips parted, as if she wanted to say something, just before she vanished from view.

"Infiniti!"

Joe dashed to the spot where she had been standing. Dust particles from Fleet's supernatural energy stream floated in the air. A warm electrical charge filled the cool space. Joe glanced around, as if they'd reappear, but they didn't.

They were gone. She was gone.

Heartbreaking silence filled the room.

"I'm very sorry, Joe," Ms. Howe said in a low voice, still clutching the book she had used to cast her protection spell on Infiniti.

Joe nodded, his heart crumbling. A lump the size of a football lodged in his throat. He felt as if a piece of him had been ripped away. And he didn't know if he'd ever get it back.

"I'll let you have a minute," Ms. Howe added, leaving the room.

Joe couldn't remember the last time he had cried, but watching Infiniti disappear brought hot tears to his eyes. He rubbed them away with the back of his hands, forcing himself not to lose it.

Not here anyway.

He tucked his crutch under his arm, his body throbbing with pain from the wild wolf attack at the Mills Mansion during the Cold Moon Ball earlier. He drew in a deep breath, then hobbled out of Ms. Howe's office and to the front of the herbal shop. He needed to get out of there. He kept his gaze down, avoiding eye contact.

"Thanks for everything, Ms. Howe."

"Sure thing, Joe."

He fumbled with the keys in his pocket as he painstakingly made it out of the shop and into his car. He sat there for a minute, letting the frigid air wrap around his body as the smell of the shop's herbs left his lungs, replaced by the scent of his newly washed car.

Twinkling white, red, and green holiday lights were strung up and down the street. Yet their cheerful and festive message fell flat on Joe. Despair had taken him over. Hours earlier, Infiniti was sitting next to him, dressed like a princess for the ball, and now she was gone. He leaned his head back against the headrest, thinking of their amazing kiss and the promise he had made to find her.

Could he really do it?

He started his car and headed home. Driving through the quiet streets of the town, a slew of memories exploded in his brain. A few months after Infiniti had vanished back in December 2012, he had a series of dreams of horrible things happening to her, incidents that all resulted in her death. Another car accident, being swept away by a tornado, drowning in the ocean, even catching on fire. He shuddered as dread worked its way through him.

He thought of that damn reaper, Shade StormIron, and his words: "The doll's soul still wants me. I can feel it. I'll be back in due time."

A blast of icy fear invaded his senses. Had they sent Infiniti back to 2012 only to die?

He slammed on his brakes and screeched to a halt. He made a U-turn in the middle of the road and sped back to the herbal shop. He parked the car, hopped out, and rushed over to Ms. Howe as she emerged from the door.

"It didn't work!"

She huddled into her long dark coat and wrapped her arms around herself. "What do you mean, it didn't work?"

"We sent Infiniti back to 2012, and she's going to die there! I know it!"

Ms. Howe looked away for a second, as if contemplating the possibility.

"Listen, Joe. I don't know if you're right or if you're wrong, but I do know a thing or two about destiny, and I can tell you that destiny cannot be changed. Not ever." She stared up at the night sky. "It's like telling the moon not to be bright. It simply can't be done." She flashed him a look of concerned sympathy. "So whatever will be, will be."

He looked down at the sidewalk, wracking his brain for a response, when an idea came to him.

"Okay, fine, I get that about destiny, I really do. But what if her coming here was another type of destiny? A way for the right destiny to counter the wrong destiny?" He stopped, thinking his words weren't making any sense, but went on anyway. "I mean, we didn't bring her here, yet she showed up needing our help. Maybe she needs our help again."

He hobbled forward, waiting for the red-haired witch to give him some sign of hope that she understood what he was saying and would help him.

She nodded but held a pensive look on her face. "Maybe she does, Joe. Maybe she does. But let's get through the holidays first, okay? We can take up this conversation later."

"Okay," Joe said, trying to calm his excitement. "That sounds great. I'll come by after the new year. Thank you, Ms. Howe."

Joe felt better, but there was no way he could wait until after the holiday break to do something about finding Infiniti. He got back in his car and drove home, his mind searching for his next move. Once home and in his room, he texted Kase, knowing he'd still be up.

Me: Dude
Kase: Sup
Me: Need your help
Kase: About the girl? Did it work? My dad told me

Joe wasn't surprised that Sheriff Ric had said something to Kase about what had happened to Infiniti, and he didn't mind. Kase was his best friend. He would've told him everything anyway.

Me: Yeah, I think. And now she's gone
Kase: Sorry
Me: It's ok. But I have an idea. Come over tmr. I'll fill you in
Kase: Ok

Joe set his phone down and lay on his bed, exhausted and feeling like crap. But more than anything, he was determined to find Infiniti Clausman. And no one could stop him.

He turned off his bedside lamp and eyed the streaks of moonlight that poured through the blinds of his window. His mind swirled with different ideas of how he could find her when a soft knock sounded on his door.

"Joe, it's Mom. Can I come in?"

"Yeah, sure."

He sat up and switched his lamp back on. The soft light illuminated his blue-and-gray-hued room. His mom sat on the edge of his bed. Her long blond hair was wet from a recent shower.

"I heard you come in and wanted to check on you." She patted his leg and gave him a reassuring smile. "You okay?"

His fight with the wild wolf pack back at the Mills Mansion had left his body cut and bruised, but nothing could compare to the pain crushing his heart. He rubbed his head, masking his emotions, and focused instead on his physical pain.

"I'm fine. Just a little sore."

She gave him the all-knowing mom look. "I wasn't talking about your wounds, son."

"Oh," he murmured, not wanting to go there with his mom. "You mean Infiniti?"

"Yes, I mean Infiniti."

He thought of telling her his fears about Infiniti returning home only to die, but decided against it. She'd never let him try to find her. Neither would his dad. And really, he couldn't blame them. Try to find a time-traveling human girl he was called to? It was a crazy idea. Besides, they didn't even know he'd been called to her.

Joe shrugged. "She came here to do what she needed to do, and she's gone now."

His mom gave a slight nod. She patted his leg one more time and stood up to leave. "I'm very sorry, Joseph."

"Me too."

Alone again, Joe eased himself back into bed. He stared at the ceiling until the night crawled by and transformed to day. And when Kase finally showed up at his house later that morning, he hadn't slept a wink. He also hadn't formulated a plan for how he was going to find Infiniti.

"Dude," Kase said, looking his friend over. "You look like hell."

"You don't even know the half of it."

Joe limped his way down the hall, leading Kase to his room. He locked the door so they wouldn't be disturbed by his little brother, Boris.

Kase kept staring at Joe's bruised face. "My dad told me you were in a fight, but he didn't mention you got your butt kicked."

"I was swarmed. If that Transhuman guy Fleet hadn't shown up when he did, I don't know what would've happened."

Kase shook his head. "I wish I could've been there for you on that back patio instead of inside the Mills Mansion with Elle. I guess I was so wrapped up with her, I didn't even catch on that you needed help."

"Well, you can still help. That's why I texted you to come over."

Kase sat on the chair at Joe's desk. His leg bounced. He rubbed his hands together, ready for action. "Sure. Whatever you need."

Joe waited a few seconds before he continued.

"I need you to help me get to 2012."

Kase's eyes widened. He eyed Joe for a minute before laughing. "Uh, what?"

"Infiniti is in trouble. I felt it back in 2012 when she disappeared from the medical clinic, and I feel it again now. So I need to go to her. Right away. Before it's too late and something happens to her."

Joe kept a steady gaze on Kase, letting him know he wasn't kidding. The message finally sank in.

"You're serious?"

"Yeah, I am."

Joe moved across the room. He peered out the window and eyed the wintry landscape, wondering if Infiniti was still alive, when an idea came to him.

"I'm so stupid!" he called out. He snatched his laptop from his backpack and opened it on his bed. He ran a search for Infiniti Clausman Houston.

"Good idea!" Kase said, looking over his shoulder. "We can find her and help her from here. Time travel not required."

Joe's search turned up zero results. "Crap," he mumbled. "Nothing."

"Gimme that." Kase turned the laptop toward him. He typed Infiniti Clausman Texas. He clicked the search button. Still no results.

"Boys!" Joe's mom called from the other side of the door. "I've got some snacks if you're interested."

Joe's fingers hovered over the keys as his mind raced. There had to be a way to find Infiniti online. There just had to be. Or maybe there was no information on her because he was too late and she was dead.

His gut clenched tight. A knot formed in his throat.

"Be right there, Mrs. Greg!" Kase answered. He rested his hand on the laptop screen before closing it shut. He eyed his friend. "Joe, dude. She's back where she belongs, six years in the past. You need to let her go."

Joe knew right then and there that he couldn't involve Kase any further in his search. It'd be too dangerous, too risky. Plus, Kase didn't understand what it was like to be called to someone and have them ripped away. He'd have to go it alone. He forced a smile and put his hand on Kase's shoulder.

"You're right," he blew out, faking defeat. "I need to let her go."

"Exactly," Kase said with an encouraging smile. "Now, let's go eat."

Kase and Joe's little brother Boris dove into a mound of fritule pastries as if they hadn't eaten in days. Joe's mom made the donut-like fried Croatian delicacies every holiday. It was her most prized recipe that had been handed down from generation to generation. Joe usually had no problem matching their enthusiasm for food, especially for fritule, but this time he could barely finish a few bites. His stomach had twisted into a permanent knot, and he couldn't get his mind off Infiniti. Plus, exhaustion was beginning to set in after a night of life-altering events and no sleep.

Joe's mom caught on right away. She started clearing the kitchen table.

"Maybe you should rest, Joe. Take a nap or something. You did have quite the eventful evening."

"Yeah," Joe said, his eyelids so heavy he struggled to keep them open. "I could use a nap."

Kase got up and stretched. "Yep, I could use a nap, too. Thank you, Mrs. Greg." He patted Joe on the back. "See you later, dude."

Joe rubbed his throbbing shoulder, wincing a little from the sting of Kase's pat. He wondered when his wolf-shifter healing abilities would kick in as he retreated to his room. He eased himself onto his bed, his bones so sore he could hardly move. But as tired as he was, his mind was too busy to sleep just yet. Instead, he started formulating his plan. Go to Ms. Howe after the holiday and see if she'd help him. If she couldn't or wouldn't, then he'd have to find someone else to help him time travel to Infiniti. Question was, who could do it? And would they? He wasn't sure, but he was determined to find someone.

With a long yawn, he draped a blanket over himself. His body melded into the soft cotton while exhaustion took over and his brain finally shut off.

Early the next morning, Joe was back at it. He scoured the internet for any mention of a death of a Houston teen girl in 2012 but found nothing that matched Infiniti's description. He took that as a good sign and decided to go with the theory that she was still alive.

With his online search pretty much exhausted, he started looking into time travel. He spent days at the Sun and Moon Academy library reading every book on magic and time travel he could find, but couldn't make any of the spells work for him. He thought of talking to Gallad Augustine or even Addie Beaumont to see if they'd help him, but their connections to the Court of the Sun and the Moon would be too risky. The last thing he needed was to cross the leaders of the town. His dad would be furious.

With the holiday break finally over, Joe went to see Ms. Howe at her herbal shop. She ended up giving him a long explanation for why he shouldn't meddle with fate and destiny. When school started, he subtly brought up the topic of time travel with some of his teachers, but nothing they mentioned helped him.

Days turned into weeks. Weeks morphed into months. Joe was beginning to think he'd never find Infiniti. Desperate and fresh out of ideas, he decided to change his tactic. Instead of searching for Infiniti in the past, he'd search for her in the present. He'd go up and down every single street in Houston if he had to. He didn't care if there was a six-year difference between them. Couples had age differences all the time. And in the larger scheme of things, six years was nothing. But what if he found her and she thought he was crazy? Or what if she was married? Or maybe she really was dead. He forced himself not to think of worst case scenarios. He had to keep trying until he found her.

But still, deep down, he couldn't shake the overriding feeling that he wouldn't be able to find her in the present because something horrible had happened to her in the past.

"Hang on, babe," he said as he started a fresh search on his laptop. "I'm coming."

This time he searched for flights to Houston for after graduation. He scribbled the prices on a piece of paper. Factoring in food and thinking he could sleep on park benches, he'd need at least eight hundred dollars. With the graduation money he thought he'd be getting, plus the money he'd be making over the summer, he'd have more than enough. As for his parents, he knew they'd be pissed, but he didn't care. He had to go.

The seasons changed from freezing to mild to sunny, and before Joe knew it, the end of the school year had arrived. Graduation had come and gone. His friends were either making plans to go away for college or stay nearby and attend the new Sun and Moon Academy College of Supernatural Guardians. He had been invited to be a member of the inaugural class of the college, but had turned it down. He needed to focus on finding Infiniti. Nothing else mattered, and his flight to Houston couldn't come fast enough.

Purchase *Finding Infiniti* where books are sold.

www.ingramcontent.com/pod-product-compliance
Lightning Source LLC
Chambersburg PA
CBHW031316280626
47169CB00019B/1636